TRISTANO
THE SYNDICATE

CALA RILEY

Copyright @ 2023 by Cala Riley

All rights reserved. No part of this publication may be reproduced, distributed, or transmitted in any form or by any means without the prior written consent of the publisher, except for brief quotes used for reviews and certain other non-commercial uses, as per copyright laws. This is a work of fiction. Names, characters, businesses, places, events, and incidents are either the products of the author's imagination or used in a fictitious manner. Any resemblance to actual persons, living or dead, or actual events is purely coincidental.

Cover Design: Books and Moods

Editor: My Brother's Editor

Formatting: Dark Ink Designs

If he won't unal*ve for you, is he even the one?

Mia,

If he doesn't kill for you, he isn't the one.

love

Ceela + Riley

PROLOGUE

Serena

Looking up at the house from the car, my body shivers.

I don't want to go in there. How can I?

"It's time for you to go now," his angelic voice murmurs.

He's been patient with me. Letting me sit here watching as the rain pours down. Letting me lose myself in my thoughts.

"How do I move on from this?" I whisper.

He scoots a little closer, opening his arm so that I can slide against him on the bench seat. I cuddle further into the hoodie he gave me. It smells like him. Cedarwood and a hint of mint. It's calming.

"That's up to you. You can take this experience and let it break you. Let it own every part of your life until you are a shell of the girl you once were. Or you can learn from it. Take steps to ensure it will never happen to you again. Self-defense classes are a good start. No matter what you decide, I'll be here for you."

"Aren't you afraid I'll break down and tell them everything? That you'll get in trouble for what you did?"

He gives me a sad smile. "If telling on me helps you heal, then do it. Don't worry about me or the consequences I'll face. All you need to focus on is getting yourself to a better place."

"I'll never forget this, will I?" I can feel the tears welling up again.

"No. You won't. As much as you will want to pretend this never happened, it will still linger in the back of your mind. Even sixty years from now, you will remember what you have gone through. The question is, how will you react to those memories? It's your choice, but if I were you, I would get a therapist. Talk to someone about what happened."

"What do I tell my uncle? He will want to know where I've been the past couple days. He probably has half the force out there looking for me."

"You make the decision. Tell him whatever you want. This is about you, Serena. No one else. In this situation, nothing else matters."

I squeeze against him, hugging him closer to me. "I don't want to go in there. I feel like we are in a bubble."

"We are in a bubble, but living here isn't realistic. You need to go now."

Pulling back, I look up at him. "Will I ever see you again?"

The thought of never seeing my hero again causes my chest to tighten. I don't like the thought of that at all. I only just met him, and already I feel like I need him.

He brushes a piece of hair from my face. "I'll stay in touch. I promise."

"Good." I breathe out, making him laugh.

"Time to go now before we get caught."

I look back out at the sun kissing the horizon.

"Okay."

Sliding out the door, I turn one last time to look at the man who changed everything.

"Thank you, Tristano."

Then I close the door and head toward the shitstorm I know is coming my way.

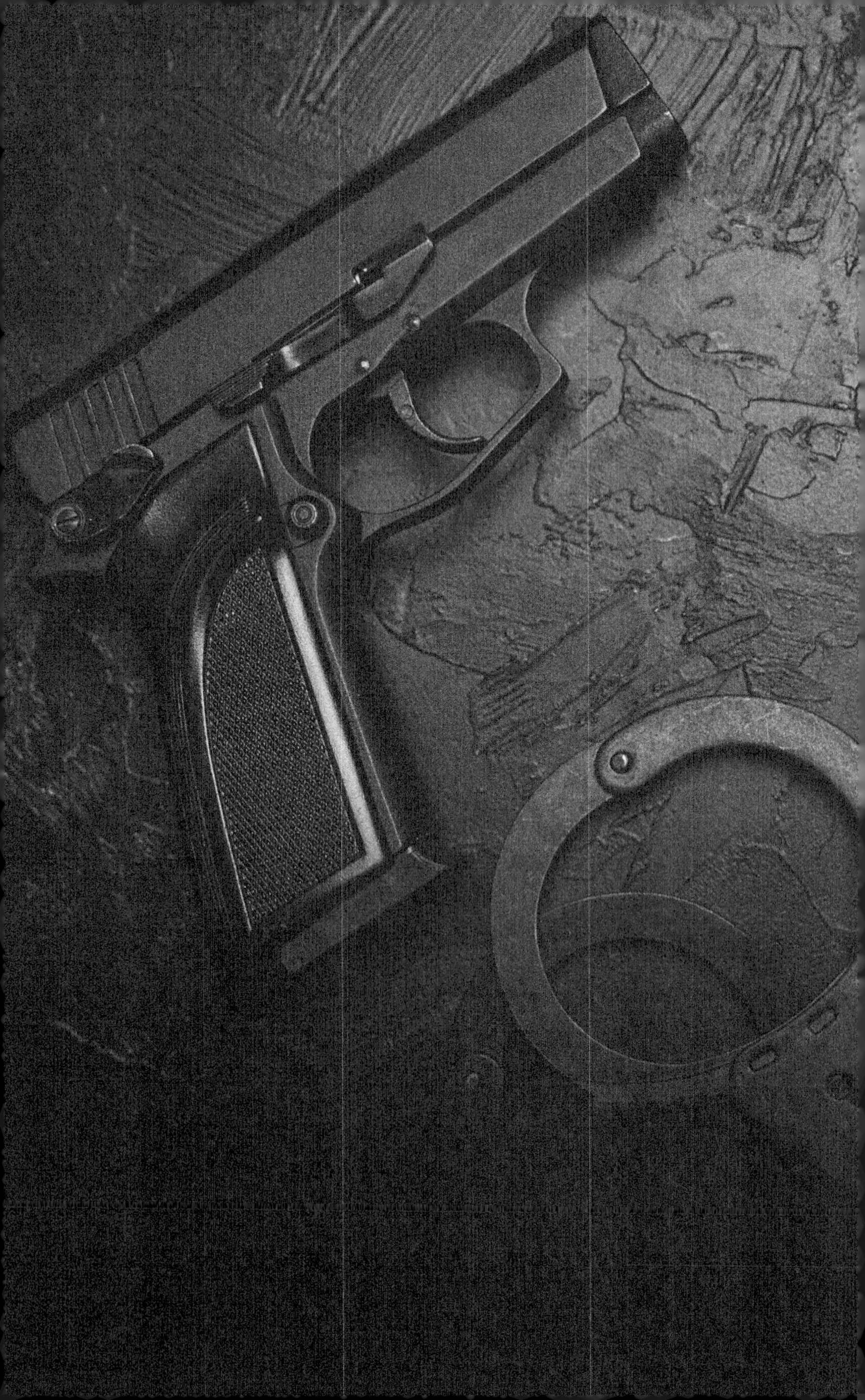

CHAPTER ONE

Serena

FIVE YEARS LATER

Dirty bars gross me out. It could be the way my feet stick to the floor as I walk through the room, or maybe the smell of stale beer and body odor. Then again, it could be the way the men eye my body like I'll be their next conquest.

In their dreams. Tonight, I'm only here for one man.

Seeing the man in question, I make my way through the smoky room toward the booth. I cough a bit, hating that they break the law so blatantly, but with a shithole like this, no one really cares. So much for the New Jersey Smoke-Free Act.

Sliding into the booth, I look up at the older man. He gives me a small smile, which I return.

"Nice to see you, Sabrina. You look good. I wasn't sure you would show."

Licking my lips, I cross my legs as I lean forward to give him the money shot down my shirt.

"You asked me here, silly. Of course I would come. Did you bring that fancy car you told me about last time?" I bat my eyes at him.

He lets out a small laugh. "I almost didn't, but the thought of disappointing a beauty like you wouldn't let me do it."

I let out a childlike giggle, making his eyes light up.

I want to throw up in my mouth. I hate what I have to do, but someone needs to get these guys. Knowing Edgar likes little girls, specifically teenagers, and that he believes I am a seventeen-year-old high school student looking to escape my family helps keep things in perspective. He has kindly offered to help me in exchange for something, but he hasn't named his price yet. I'm hoping tonight is the night. Edgar is also the mayor of Newark, our neighboring city. Mayor Edgar Johnson. Real scumbag. Getting him off the streets is a priority.

"I'd love to take a ride." I reach over, rubbing my hand on his.

He turns his to catch mine until he is holding my hand.

"Let's get out of here then."

I nod, letting him pull me from the booth. I hate the way he preens as the men watch him lead me out, envy all over their faces. His hand slides lower and lower on my back as he guides me out of the bar until it's on my ass. I want to smack him, but I have a part to play, so I bite down the urge.

When we finally reach the car, he squeezes my ass before opening the door. It's a sleek Mercedes Maybach, much more expensive than a man with his salary should be able to afford. That is, if he wasn't accepting kickbacks from corrupt corporations.

After he shuts my door, I watch as he walks to the back of the car. He pauses, taking something out of his pocket before popping it in his mouth. I have a few guesses as to what that might be. Then he continues around the car until he's at the driver's door.

Once he slides in, he turns on the car, turning to me.

"What time do you have to be home by?" he asks.

"They think I'm staying at Katie's house tonight, so no curfew. If you would do what you said and get me emancipated, I wouldn't ever have a curfew. I could live with you." I lean closer to him.

He hums thoughtfully. "Soon, my dear. How about we go to my penthouse in New York?" he asks.

That's not a good thing. I need him to stay in Jersey City where we can arrest him. So instead, I reach over, rubbing his leg.

"It takes forever to get there. Can we at least have a little treat before we go? If you pull around back, no one would even notice."

The bulge in his pants grows larger at my words, making me want to gag. I don't let it show, though. I need him here with me in this moment.

"I guess we could have a little taste before the main course." He puts the car in drive, going around to the alley before parking.

Once parked, he pushes his seat back as far as it will go before he unzips his pants, pulling out his dick.

"Is this what you wanted, little girl? You want a taste of your daddy's big cock?" he asks, rubbing himself.

"Mhmm. That's a big cock, daddy. You want your little under-aged seventeen-year-old slut to suck it?" I hum out, still petting his leg.

"Oh god, yes!" he moans out.

"Does it turn you on that I'm only seventeen years old? That I'm not legal, but you can have me anyway?" I continue.

"Yes. I love it."

"Do you love fucking underage girls in general, or is it just me?" I guide him, my fingers moving to his chest to keep him engaged.

"You, baby. Just you," he promises, his hand still stroking his dick.

"Don't lie to me. I think it's hot that you like taboo girls. Tell me the truth. Am I the only one?"

He shakes his head no. I smack him a little, making him jump.

"Verbal responses, daddy. I like hearing your voice," I coo at him.

"No. You're not the only one."

"How old was the youngest?" I murmur, moving in to kiss his cheek.

"Fourteen," he pants.

"Tell me about her. What was her name? How did she look?"

He grunts as he picks up the pace of his jerking. "Adalyn. She was a gorgeous blonde-haired girl. She was like you. She had issues with her parents and rebelled a lot. She liked spending my money almost as much as she liked swallowing my cock."

"What happened to her, daddy?"

He groans, "She turned eighteen."

That's the kicker, isn't it? He only likes them until they are legal. Adalyn wasn't his first victim. She was a bright young girl who did like to rebel, but she didn't know that accepting money from the mayor would lead to her nightmare. She never wanted a sexual relationship with him. He made her feel like she had no choice. With his position and power, her family was too afraid to go against him when she finally admitted it after he stopped messing with her.

Men like him are despicable.

Before I can say another word, there's a knock at the window.

"Go away!" Edgar calls out, continuing to stroke himself.

Then the red and blue lights turn on, making him freeze.

I play my part well.

"Edgar? Oh god. I can't be caught with you like this. They will kill me. Edgar, what do we do?" I ask frantically.

He pushes me back, pulling at his pants. "Sit in your seat and keep quiet. I'll handle this."

I have to bite my lip to keep from laughing. Of course he thinks he can control this. He's the mayor of his city. Only we aren't in Newark, and his corruption has been well-documented. Fucker is about to be in jail for the foreseeable future.

I keep quiet as he manages to zip his pants before opening his window.

"What seems to be the problem, officer?" Edgar asks, his voice hinting at none of the anger he had prior to opening the window.

"License and registration," my handler, Ricky, demands.

Edgar hands over the information as Ricky plays his own role, calling in the license with dispatch.

After several minutes of uncomfortable silence, Edgar finally breaks.

"Did you see the name? Do you know who I am? This is ridiculous. You need to give me my shit back and go back to doing actual police work."

"Excuse me, sir?" Ricky asks, seemingly surprised.

He's not. We planned this. I learned from my time with Edgar that he hates being looked over. He thrives on the attention his position gives him. So having someone ignore him is burning his ass.

"You heard me. I'm the mayor of Newark. I could have your job for this, son."

"Sir, I'm going to need you to get out of the vehicle."

Edgar is turning red now. "What? Why?"

"Sir, please do as I say."

"No."

"Sir, if you do not exit the vehicle, I will forcibly remove you. Do you understand?" Ricky tells him.

I withhold my smile as I see several other officers begin to arrive.

Edgar sees it too. He relents, huffing as he gets out of the car.

As soon as he is, Ricky turns him, pinning him to the vehicle.

"You are under arrest for the solicitation of underage prostitution," Ricky informs him as he begins to read him his Miranda rights.

Edgar is cussing as another officer comes to my side of the vehicle. I roll my eyes at Nigel. He's a rookie on the force but knows me very well, seeing as he is the son of my mentor and pseudo-uncle.

"Excuse me, miss, I need you to exit the vehicle," he tells me.

I do as he asks, conjuring tears as I turn to face Edgar. His eyes are wide as he looks at me.

"Daddy, don't let them do this to me. Don't let them take me. Please. You promised."

"Shut up, girl. I don't know why she's calling me daddy. She's a disturbed child," Edgar calls out.

Nigel frisks me quickly before cuffing me and leading me to the back of Ricky's patrol car.

Then I wait. For at least twenty minutes. The entire time I go through all of the emotions. Exhilaration for another one being caught, yet apprehension. Will the charges stick, or will he talk his way out of it?

Once he's booked into the station, it's out of our hands.

Finally, Ricky slides into the driver's seat.

"What took you so long? I almost thought I was going to have to touch that fucker somewhere I didn't want to."

He snorts. "Had to take a phone call."

"Really? Right then?"

He looks at me in the rearview mirror.

"Boss wants a word with you."

I swallow hard. "Oh."

"Yeah, oh. What trouble did you get into this time?"

I shake my head. "Nothing. Is that where we are going?"

Usually after they take me away from the scene, they drop me off in a nondescript area outside the city. Anything to keep my cover.

"Yep. You're getting booked this time."

I snort, but don't say anything else.

Seems like the boss may have found out about my side project.

I'm in deep shit.

Tristano

I LOVE MY JOB. I really do, but sometimes it can be so boring. Especially when the boss lady has control issues.

"Are you ever going to let me do any work, or do you plan to do it all yourself?" I ask as I lean back in my chair, throwing a ball into the air.

"Seems you don't mind letting me do all the work. You get to fuck off," Greer huffs at me, not taking her eyes off the computer.

"Only because you came in here just to grab some papers and overtook my entire computer. Seriously, Greer, you need to go home. Go work on your own shit."

"Tristano, do not push me. I'm hormonal as fuck right now," she warns.

I hear Enzo snort from the other room. He's been hovering more than normal with her being pregnant. He has more than one precious life to care for. Still, he knows when to give her space. Like now. I saw it in his eyes the moment they walked through the door. We have snarky Greer in our presence today.

"Greer, I will call your husband. Don't think I won't."

Her ice-cold eyes meet mine over the computer screen. I almost shudder but hold my composure.

"I dare you to call him. When he shows up, I'll kick his ass, then I'll kick yours."

"Seriously? Come on, Greer. You wouldn't hurt me. You love me."

"I love Killian more, and I almost shot him," she deadpans before moving her eyes back to the screen.

"Cold." I rub my chest over my heart. "I really do want to work. Can you please go work from home?"

She growls, but I add, "Pretty please with a cherry on top" with my best innocent smile.

She pushes her chair back, standing up.

"Fine. You're beginning to annoy me anyway. I fixed the bug in your algorithm, by the way. Hopefully this runs better. You need to pay closer attention to detail. You're good, but you still make stupid mistakes."

I clear my throat, all joking leaving me. "Yes, ma'am. I'll be better."

"Good. Back to work, you go."

I watch as she leaves before moving back to my computer. I see that she did fix the code I was having issues with. Truth is, I didn't miss the issues. I was too proud to ask for help. It's an issue I've always had. Ever since I was little, I never liked asking others for help. Instead, I'd rather be the one they come to for help. It's a flaw I'm working on.

Focusing back on work, I look over all the data collected. I know there is a connection here, but we haven't found it yet. It's driving me absolutely bonkers.

There's no rhyme or reason to the kidnappings. Sometimes they take well-off college students and never ransom them. Other times they take high school students who have no money. Then there are the women who I know are never reported. If it weren't for Declan and Yamato's connection to the working girls in their area, those missing girls would have fallen through the cracks.

The only similarity I have been able to connect is that they don't kidnap anyone over the age of twenty-five. What are they doing with them, though?

We have been tracking the meat markets and taking them down slowly and quietly. None of the girls coming up missing have shown up there.

So what could it be? What am I missing?

"Why is it so quiet in here?" Enzo's voice jolts me from my little world.

"Wear a fucking bell, man. You almost got shot." My hand is on my chest, covering my fast-beating heart.

"Eh, I like my chances. Your hand didn't even reach for it." He shrugs as he makes his way to his desk across the room from me.

"What are you even doing here? Don't you have a home to go to?" I snip at him, frustrated at myself more than him.

He rolls his eyes at me. "After I took Greer home, I decided to come back. The girls are having a mommy-daughter date. Daddy is not allowed apparently."

"Hearing you call yourself 'daddy' is the highlight of my life. Can I call you daddy, daddy?" I give him my signature smile.

Fake it til you make it, right?

"I will shoot off your left nut. Tempt me," he says, his face dead serious.

"Oh, come on. You are a daddy, though," I tease.

"Not yours."

"Ouch. Testy tonight, huh? Blue balls? Is Danica not giving it to you enough?"

He takes a deep breath. "You test my patience more than my child does."

"Aww, I knew you loved me."

"That is absolutely the opposite of what I feel for you," he grumbles.

"Oh, admit it, Enzo. You could have chosen anyone to hang out with tonight, yet you came here to be with me."

"I came to work."

My smile grows wider. "You can lie to yourself all you want. You knew I would be here. You wanted to hang out with me. It's okay. You don't have to admit it. I know in my heart that we are besties."

"Insufferable." He focuses on his screen, squinting.

"You know, you really should get some reading glasses with a blue light filter like me. You are straining your eyes too much." I pull off my glasses to prove a point.

When you work on the computer as much as I do, it's smart to protect your eyes. Of course mine are just blue light. I don't need reading glasses yet, but old man Enzo seems to.

"Fuck off," he says without looking up at me.

Before I can respond, a message pops up on my computer. My eyes widen as I read it.

"Holy fuck."

"What is it?" Enzo asks.

"It's the piece of the puzzle I think we have been missing."

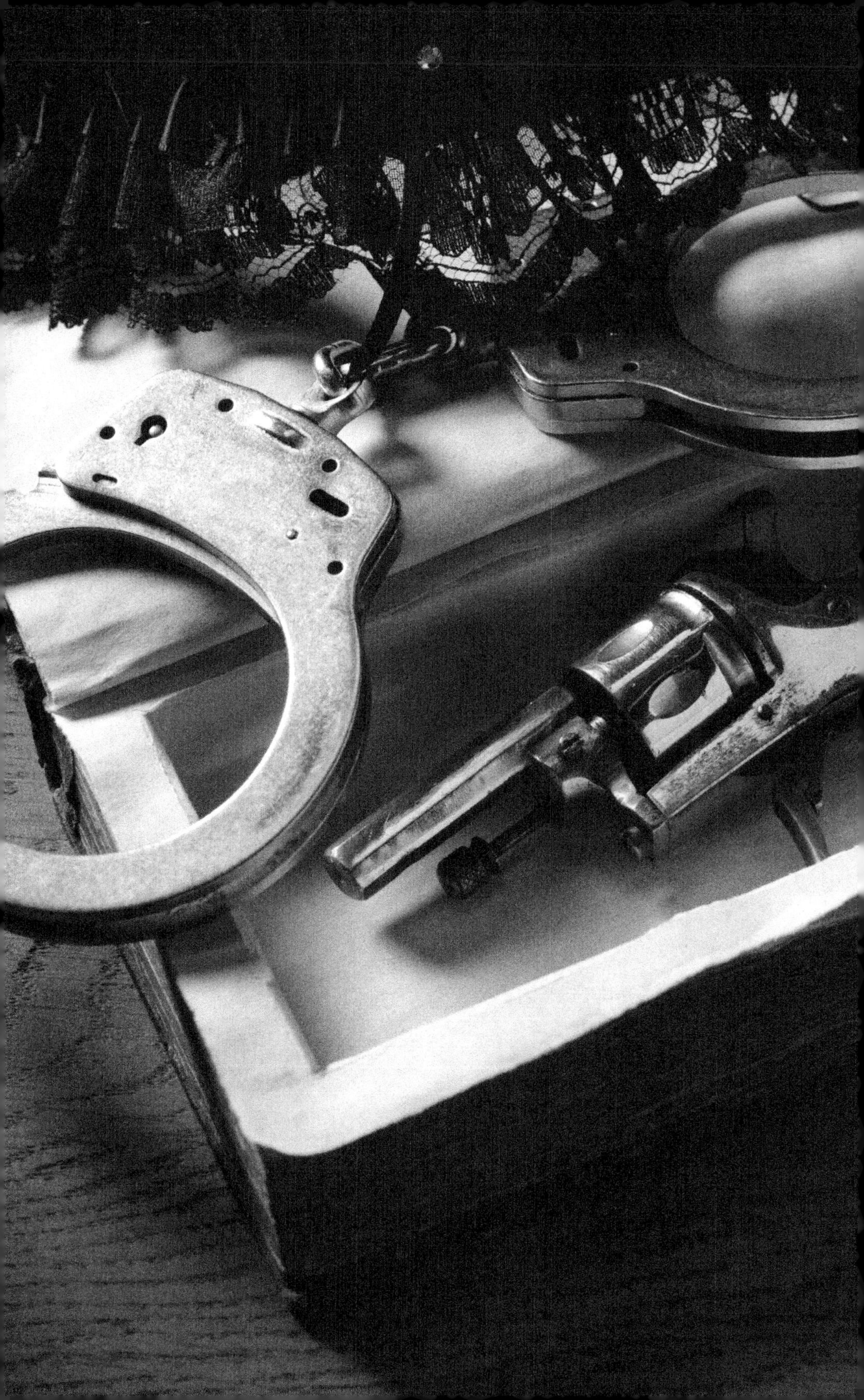

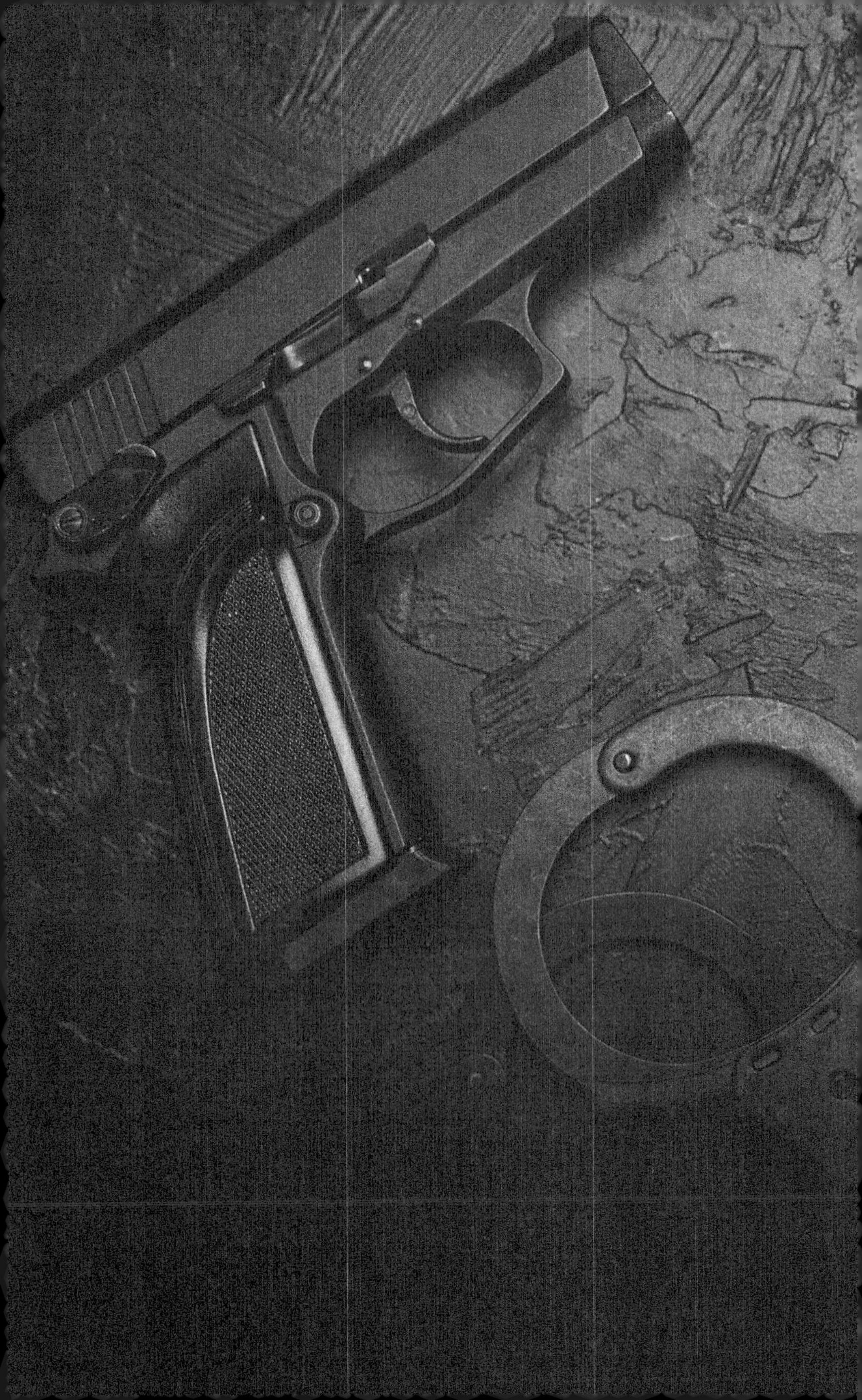

CHAPTER TWO

Serena

The trip is rather quick, the booking even quicker. Finally, I'm being led to a cell, only for my boss to intercept us.

"I'll take this one. I have some questions for her," he tells the booking officer.

"Of course, Chief."

Then it's a short walk down to his office where he closes the door before finally taking the cuffs off.

"Have a seat, Serena."

I wince at the use of my real name. Usually it's Selbear. The nickname he gave me as a child. When he uses my real name, I know I'm in trouble.

He takes his time, making himself a cup of coffee as I sit here and look around his office.

I smile at the photo of me, him, and my grandfather on one of his shelves. I was only six then, but I wanted to be like my grandpa, so they took me fishing with them. Only to find out that I didn't like touching the fish. That's how we got that picture. Someone at the dock took it for us. Uncle Ben is holding up the line with the fish in front of me, with my grandpa holding my shoulders as I try to smile, but my eyes never leave that fish.

It's a funny picture. A memory from the good old days. Too bad they came to an end. My grandfather passed away, leaving me to Uncle Ben, who I found out was never really my uncle.

"What were you thinking?" he finally asks as he settles behind his desk.

"I don't know what you're talking about. Can you be more specific?"

"Don't get smart with me, little girl. You might be an adult now, but that doesn't mean that I can't still dish out your punishments. You've been investigating missing persons cases. Some of the detectives have started asking questions about you, or rather, Sabrina. You are going to blow your cover," he reminds me.

As if I didn't know that already. Some of the other girls have told me some detectives have been snooping around about me. I've just been quicker to stay away from them. No one but our small team knows I'm undercover. As far as they are concerned, I'm a teenage hooker. Anyone who asks about sweet Serena, who Uncle Ben raised, gets told the same story. I'm doing well in another state, living my life. I don't get back to visit much, but Uncle Ben prefers it that way because it means I'm healing.

No one knows the truth.

When I announced that I wanted to go to the academy, Uncle Ben hated the idea. He finally caved and agreed to let me go if I went out of state. When I came back, the precinct had a complete overhaul and almost an entire new staff.

"I'm not trying to blow my cover, but there is a connection here. These girls are being snatched from the streets. Not just working girls. Last week, a college girl came up missing. Maddie Smith. She's twenty-two years old and an aspiring actress. She went for a casting call and was never seen again. What are we doing about this? This is an epidemic in our city."

"It's not your job to worry about. When I hired you on and put you through the academy, I went against every single nerve in my body to do so. When you begged me to go undercover, I almost said no, but you assured me you could handle it. You said that you were in a unique position due to your age to catch predators that would normally not fall for our operations. You wanted to go after the pedophiles. So why now are you switching the script? Missing girls is not your issue."

"Maybe it should be." I raised my voice. "Maybe I have an opportunity to get close to these girls and find out how they are being targeted. Maybe I could even go undercover with a tracker and try to get them to take me. Then we could save lives and shut down the operation."

"Absolutely not. Do you hear yourself? You haven't even been on the force but a year and a half, and now you want me to let them take you? Do you know how dangerous that is, not to mention against agency policy? You have lost it. You need to go home for the weekend and rest. Come back Monday, and then we will discuss your future with this department."

I gasp, "What does that even mean?"

"It means that you are tying my hands. I may be the chief of this department, but I have people I answer to, and they are not as understanding as I am. You are making waves when you should be flying under the radar."

I swallow hard. "So you're saying I'm done?"

He rubs his face. "Selbear, you are running yourself ragged. You never take breaks between busts. Enough is enough. You need to take a break. If you show me you truly took a break this weekend and come back refreshed Monday, we will discuss getting you another case."

"What about the missing girls?"

He sighs. "Let the detectives handle it. Stay out of it."

"They aren't doing enough."

"Sometimes there isn't much they can do. You need to understand that not everything is going to be tidied up in a little bow like what you do. Sometimes the best we can do isn't enough."

He looks so worn down and tired. I almost feel bad for stressing him out. Almost, but not quite. If I don't advocate for those girls, no one will.

"Fine. I'll go home," I lie to him.

He gives me a look like he can tell I'm lying, but he doesn't call me out on it. Instead, he gives me a quick nod.

"Alright, I'll drive you home."

I shouldn't be here. I know I shouldn't, but I couldn't leave it alone. Thursday night, after Uncle Ben dropped me off, I did what he asked and went to bed. Then Friday, I tried to watch some murder documentaries to keep my mind off it. It didn't work.

That's how I found myself here. Dressed in my Sabrina clothes on a corner with another hooker. One who has become a sort of friend to me.

"How's business tonight?" I ask her as I move to stand near her.

It feels eerie being out here by myself. Normally my team is close by, ready to have my back. Tonight, I'm all alone. No one to rescue me if something goes wrong. Then again, nothing has ever gone wrong before, so why would it tonight? I won't actually be looking for any johns.

"Shady as always, girl. I thought I wouldn't see you for a while. Heard you got popped with that sugar daddy you had been playing with." She takes a drag from her cigarette.

"Yeah. Fucker left me in jail too. I had some money saved up, though, and bonded myself out. I think I'm done with the wannabe sugar daddies," I tell her.

"Sure you are, and I'm the Queen of England. We both know that if they flash the dough, we are there. It's the way of life."

"The way of our lives at least," I grumble. "Anyone come up missing?"

"Not that I've heard. You're really worried about getting kidnapped, aren't you?"

I grimace at the insinuation. It's one I've allowed her to believe. She thinks I'm some paranoid seventeen-year-old afraid of my own shadow. It's why she's so nice to me when usually these girls tend to get mad at you for trying to share their corner. Not Meredith. She's taken me under her wing.

"They take girls within my age range. Don't tell me you haven't seen them all over the news."

"News? That would mean having a television. Where do you get to watch television?"

I shrug. "The shelter sometimes has one on. So does the diner when I stop in there."

She nods, accepting my lie.

"Don't watch that shit. It's all fabricated anyway."

I'm about to ask another question when a car slowly rolls toward us.

"You want this one, honey?" she asks softly.

I shake my head. "You go ahead."

I watch as she saunters over to the window. After a brief conversation, she crosses the front of the car as she waves at me.

I take note of the make and model as she drives off. I shake my head, hoping I don't need to remember it.

As I turn to head back toward the bus station, I get the feeling someone is watching me. Being as inconspicuous as possible, I take in my surroundings, but nothing's there.

Then, all of a sudden, I hear tires squeal. Looking over, I see a van screeching to a halt in front of me. Before I can blink, the doors are open, and a sharp pain hits my neck.

I try to take in the men before me, but my eyes grow dim, and before I can even scream, blackness overtakes me.

Tristano

T<small>HIS MIGHT HELP</small> *in your search.*

That one sentence, along with data from Veles, California, has changed my entire picture. Before, we figured they were only hitting big cities because it was easier to hide the missing girls. The data from Alexei and the Bratva changes this entirely.

We aren't looking for any run-of-the-mill kidnappers.

No, this is a cell of people targeting the outlying areas of cities with organized crime. Veles isn't as big as Chicago or New York. In fact, I would place a bet that most people have never even heard of it. The population is a fraction of the size of the bigger cities. So why take women from there?

I think I've figured it out. The people who live in those areas are hesitant to contact the police. Due to the illegal activities commonly occurring in their neighborhoods, most people adopt a "look away and pretend you saw nothing" approach to life.

So even if we have witnesses who see these women getting abducted, they won't say anything. Why? Because they are afraid of what might happen to them if they get involved. If it's mob related, it could be them next. They take the "see nothing, say nothing" to heart.

It's our own fucking fault. We have ingrained this into them so deeply that they aren't even coming to us to report it. Which makes me wonder what type of men are taking them. If they looked out of place, then people would say something.

What if they are dressing like us? Acting like us?

They are using our own organizations as a cover.

"You are furiously typing now. Are you ever going to spill the beans? It's been hours since you said you needed to double-check the information. Share your theory now." Enzo demands.

I huff, taking off my glasses to rub my eyes. "Okay. Fine. I am still researching some other areas, but I believe that these people are using our organizations as a cover. They have to have extensive knowledge of who runs which area and their characteristics. Alexei sent me their new data now that they have weeded out their organ harvesting cell, and it's become clear. They aren't targeting big cities. They are targeting cities run by organized crime. Now, I have no proof yet, but I think they have studied us and learned how we do things like dress and act. I think that's how they are getting access to these people. They never come directly into our territory, but they still dress and act like us so the people in those areas don't question them. I mean, look at this. Girls keep going missing in Jersey City and Newark. That's just across the bridge from us. It's considered unclaimed territory, but the people who live there know who we are and what we do. They would never wonder why a man in a suit is forcing a woman into their car. They would assume she made some slight against the Mafia and is going to get whacked. Rather than help, they would look the other way so they don't get involved. It's a perfect plan, really. Most organizations would never notice."

"Most organizations don't have Greer. She's what changed this up. If it wasn't for her starting to look into these missing cases, they would never be caught," Enzo admits.

"No, they still might not. Sure, now we know how they are getting them, but we still don't know what they are for. I have been monitoring the organ-selling sites on the dark web, but none of our girls have been on there. If we can figure out why they are being taken, we can get these fuckers." I throw a pen across the room, needing to let some anger out.

Enzo doesn't even blink an eye. "You need to rest. It's past midnight. Go home and sleep."

"How can I sleep knowing there are women and children out there who need our help? What if my couple hours of sleep are the difference between them living or dying?" I cry out.

"You are no good to them dead, and that's what is going to happen if you don't take care of yourself. You can't help others if you aren't helping yourself."

He's right. I know he's right, but every time I hear about another girl being taken, all I can think about is her.

My angel of a girl who was taken from her home and plunged into hell. My girl who didn't let her circumstances pull her down. Instead, she's used them to prosper. To be a better person for it.

She had that opportunity because I was there to help her. What if I'm too late for these other women? What if I don't save them?

"Okay. Fine. I'll rest." I start setting up my code to keep collecting data while I take a nap.

"Not in the bunkroom. I want you to go home, eat, shower, then go to sleep. If you are here when I get here at six in the morning, I will be pulling your ass down to the gym to spar for two hours without mitts. Got it?"

I rub my shoulder as the phantom pain from the last time I sparred with Enzo triggers. He's no joke in the ring. He can beat the best of them.

"Fine. I'll go home and go to bed like a good boy, daddy."

"I swear to Jesus," he mutters as he collects his things.

He waits for me to finish up before walking out with him. We separate on the street, him going home to his family while I go to my empty home.

I know I'm trying my best, but going home seems like a cop-out.

All I can keep thinking is what if my best isn't good enough?

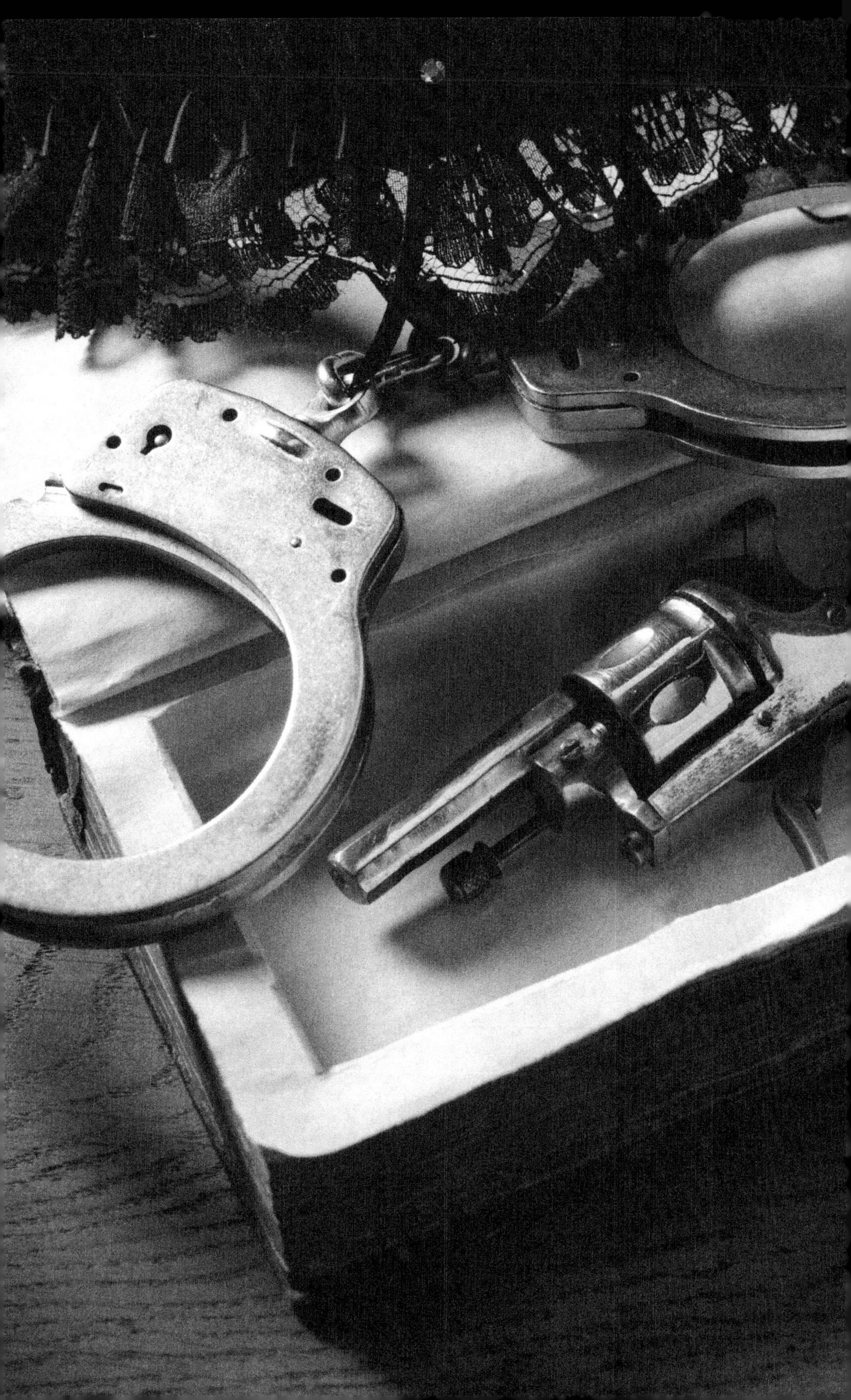

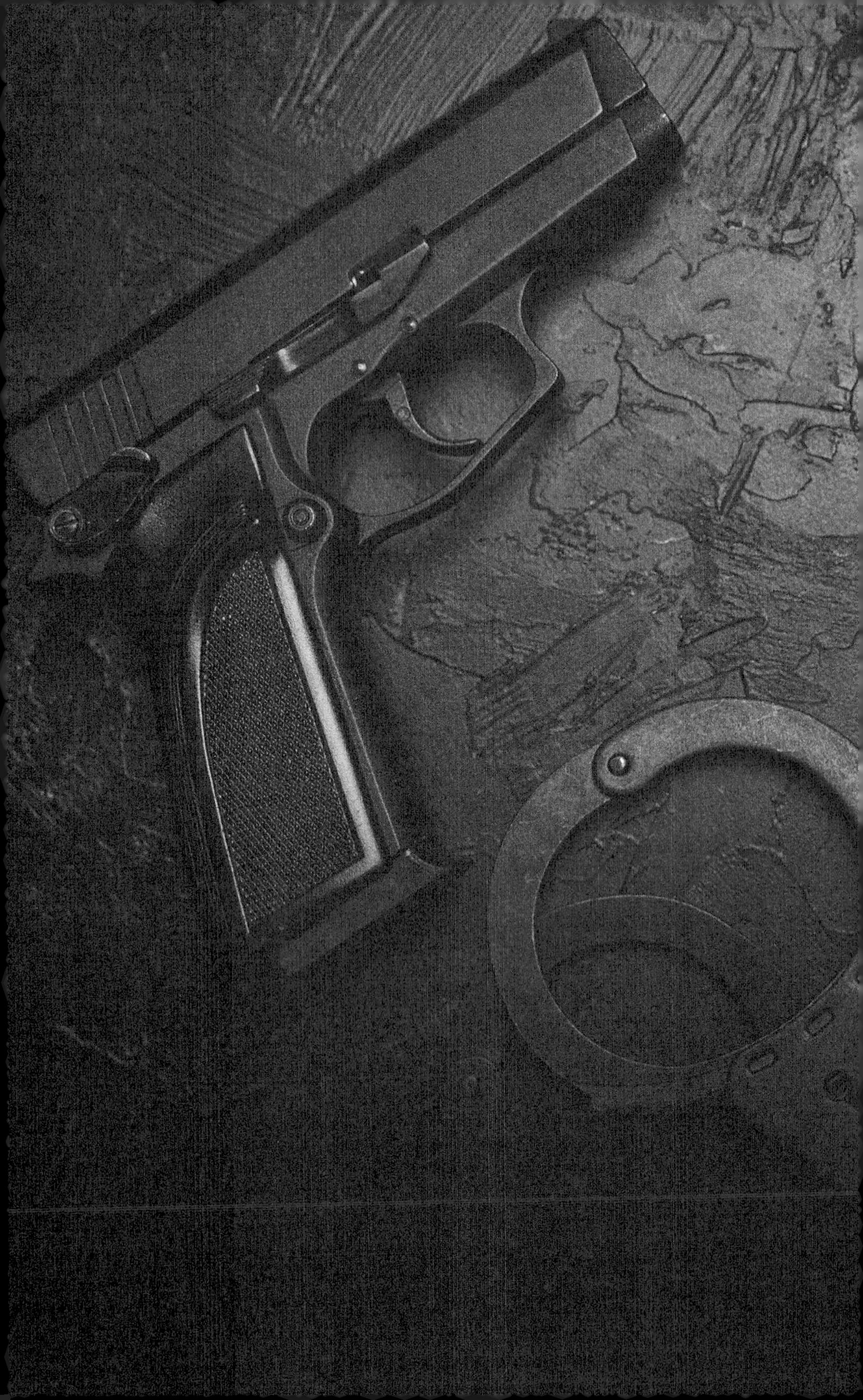

CHAPTER THREE

Serena

The first thing I notice as I start to come to is the crying.

My brain is foggy trying to catch up with reality.

Who's crying? Did something happen to me while I was undercover?

The next thing I notice is that I'm freezing, and I can feel the cold concrete underneath me. I keep my breathing even as I take stock of everything else. I feel something attached to my wrists. My head pounds and everything is distorted.

How long have I been out?

The sobs get louder, and ever so slowly, I peel my eyes open far enough to see out but closed enough to still appear asleep.

I push down the fear as I take in the cement room with women chained to the walls.

Not all are women.

Some are much younger.

Oh fuck me running.

Some of my cellmates look strung out, some are awake while others are sleeping.

I pray they are fucking sleeping.

Even the ones not moving are chained to the walls. None of us have very many clothes on. Actually, it seems like we are all wearing hospital gowns.

What's the last thing you remember, Serena? Think.

I remember finishing up an undercover case. Then I was booked, but only so that I could talk to Uncle Ben. I remember him telling me to leave it alone. I was planning to do as he asked, but I couldn't.

So, like the idiot I am, I went on my own.

"W-why a-are her lips blue?" a young voice stutters.

Internally, I groan. That's what I was afraid of. There are dead bodies in here with us.

Slowly, I push myself up and lean against the wall.

"Welcome to the land of the living," a girl with brown hair rasps.

"How long have I been out?"

"About a day."

My heart skips a beat. I figured at most a couple of hours, but an entire day?

I start to mildly panic. Leftover feelings from the first time I was kidnapped come roaring back.

It's okay. You're not that girl anymore. When you don't show up to work in the morning, someone will come looking.

I repeat the words, trying to calm myself, as the girl continues to talk. "Yeah, they drug you when you're taken, then drug you again once they drop you off here, and usually anytime they move us."

"Sounds like you've been here for a while. What else have you figured out?" I ask, focusing on the girl and being in the present instead of being thrust into the past.

The girl scoffs, shaking her head. "I was the first. Every night they bring another girl and repeat it over and over. So far, they haven't come back to take anyone out though. I haven't worked up the nerve to try and ask questions."

I take a quick headcount. There's five of us, counting the dead child. If this is the same group I've been tracking, we have a few more days. This is good. That means Ricky and Uncle Ben have a little time to find me.

"That's smart. Don't draw any attention to yourself. What's your name?"

"Mandy."

"Nice to meet you, Mandy. I'm Sabrina." I tell her my fake name. "Can you tell me anything about the people who drop off everyone?" I nodded at the women around the room.

She narrows her eyes. "Are you planning to do something stupid? I don't want you to get us all killed."

"No. Nothing like that. Knowledge is power, though. It gives us something to focus on so we don't lose our sanity. Besides, what if someone rescues us? Don't you want to be able to tell them everything you know?"

"I guess you're right," she relents. "I can't tell you anything, really. Every time they come in, we all pretend to be asleep. It's men for sure. They have deep voices with a slight accent and don't speak English unless they are speaking directly to us. They wear all black, gloves, and have masks covering their faces." She swallows hard. "One of them smokes cigars."

"That's good." I nod. "Do they bring food or anything in?"

"With every new girl, we get something small to eat. Nothing much though and never anything to drink." She pauses. "What do you think they want with us?"

"I don't know, but whatever it is, it can't be good." I look down at my wrists and eye the cuffs.

These are nothing like the cuffs Tristano gifted me when I graduated from the police academy a year ago. The last time I saw him in person.

"What are these for?"

"These are for you to practice picking," he says as if it's obvious.

"Why would I need to know how to pick a lock? I plan on putting them on criminals, Ferrari, not wearing them myself," I tease.

He raises a brow and smirks. "Never say never, anima gemella."

I look away as my cheeks heat.

"No," he says, bringing my attention back to him. "If you continue on the road you're on and pursue going undercover, I need to know that you can get yourself out of any situation you find yourself in."

"That seems to be a little on the wrong side of the law," I tease.

"Tomato, tomahto." He moves his head from side to side.

I look down at the cuffs and smile. It's an oddly thoughtful gift. One that only someone on the other side of the law would think of. I hate what Tristano does, and I know I should stay away, but I can't. Because if he's bad, then I am too after what we did together.

"Thank you."

"Good luck getting out of those. I've been trying for days. They're solid metal," Mandy says, pulling me out of the past. "Whoever these guys are, they're smart too. I had some bobby pins in my hair when I was taken, and when I woke up, they were gone."

"Lovely." I sigh.

I had noticed that I had been stripped of my weapons but didn't even think about what might be in my hair.

A young girl next to me starts to wake up.

"Daddy..." she cries out softly.

"I'm sorry, sweetheart," I say as I reach out to touch her back.

The girl flinches away from me, and I have to fight back the urge to scream.

"My name is Sabrina, what's yours?"

"A-addie."

I take in her dirty, tear-streaked face as my heart breaks. This isn't fucking right. Nothing about this is okay.

"We'll get out of here soon, okay? As soon as we do, we'll find your daddy," I say softly.

"Y-you mean that?"

"I do."

The lie feels heavy on my tongue.

I just hope that my team doesn't make a liar out of me.

Tristano

Leaning back in my chair, I look around the conference room.

If you would have told me two years ago that I would be in this room waiting for the Don of the Catalini crime family and the head of the Westies to show up, I for sure would have thought you were lying. I don't know what Don Bastiano Catalini saw in me when I was doing lower-level shit for him, but when he offered me the job to shadow his sister, I couldn't pass it up. I mean, who wouldn't want to work with a beautiful woman? There was always a chance she might give a wise guy like me a shot.

Quickly, it became apparent she had eyes for the leader of the Westies, Killian O'Reilly, which crushed those dreams. Really, who would blame the woman, though? I'm straighter than a nail, and even I'd fuck him. If he wasn't happily married to my boss, of course.

It must be the Irish blood in him. Somehow it makes him seem majestic. Otherworldly even. I wonder if...

"Are you here?" Enzo snaps his fingers in front of my face.

"I'm sitting right next to you," I deadpan.

"Yet you are spacing out like a cadet. Focus. They will be here any minute. Do you have everything ready?"

"Of course." I scoff. "What do you take me for? Some kind of rookie?"

Enzo shoots me a knowing look as he sits.

So I may have fucked shit up a time or two. I've learned. I think.

I mentally check off the list of things I need to do as I change the subject.

"How are V and Danica doing?" I ask, diverting the conversation to his wife and child.

"Fantastic, as always." He smiles.

It's still surreal to see him smile. Back when I first met him, the only person he smiled around was Greer. He's been her bodyguard for over a decade. Because of their fifteen-year age gap, they banter like only siblings normally do. Hell, I think Greer's closer to him than she is her own brother.

Then he found out about his daughter and met Danica around the same time. They changed his life for the better. Happiness looks good on him.

"I'm here, sorry I'm late." Greer rushes in, almost losing her balance.

Enzo shoots up and grabs her arm. "I thought we talked about giving up heels when you're this far along," he lightly scolds.

She rolls her eyes and sets her tablet and drink on the conference table.

"Funny, I thought we had that same conversation, *a ghrá*," Killian says as he trails behind her with Conor, his second, by his side.

"Are you two teaming up on me now?" she demands.

"Yes," Killian and Enzo say in unison.

I chuckle under my breath. When Greer walked into our office eight months ago and announced she was pregnant, I didn't know what to expect. I had never been around a pregnant woman before until her. You never know what will set her off any day. I find it hilarious.

"What are you complaining about now?" a new voice calls out.

I sit up a bit straighter. Don Bastiano Catalini is an intimidating man. One not to be messed with. Unless he considers you part of his circle, you better watch yourself.

Being newly added to said circle still has me on nerves. I still even call him Bastiano from time to time, even though he has told me countless times to call him Bash. It's unnerving.

As he clears the door, I see his second and third commands behind him, Lorenzo and Giovanni. I nod my head in greeting and remind myself not to shit my pants.

"I need all you men to stop being so overbearing. I'm pregnant, not an invalid. Stop treating me like I might break." Greer huffs.

"*Uccellino*, you look beautiful as always, but shouldn't you get off your feet in your condition?" Giovanni asks as he leans over, kissing her cheek.

"Men," she mumbles as she sits.

"Any contractions yet?" Lorenzo asks.

"Not yet, but who knows, that could change any minute." Killian rubs his hands together. "I can't fucking wait."

"Thank you, love, for telling the family about my bodily functions. Now let's get started," Greer snarks.

Everyone moves to sit down. A clear divide in the room, with Greer sitting between the two families. Irish on one side, Italian on the other. It's an odd setup. One you would rarely see, but it seems to work for us. At least for now.

"So, what's going on?" Bash asks from his seat, with his hands steepled in front of him.

Greer picks up the remote from the middle of the table, and the screen across from us lights up. Maps of New York and Chicago pop up, along with one of California.

"Don't tell me those red dots are all missing girls," Giovanni moans as he stares at the screen.

"All those red dots are *clusters* of missing girls," Greer confirms.

"Hot spots, if you will," I chime in.

"I wish they represented only one girl, but try more than twenty," Enzo mutters.

"How do you even let the girls out of your sight?" Lorenzo questions Enzo.

Enzo shoots him a dirty look. "Trust me, it's taking everything in me not to lock them in our home and throw away the key."

"While it's concerning, thankfully whoever's behind this isn't hitting our neighborhoods." Greer soothes before cringing. "Only the edges."

"Tell me more," Bash demands with a frown on his face.

Greer sighs as she clicks on the New York map. Instantly hundreds of dots fill the screen. Some colored blue while others are colored green, identifying each family's respective area. "If you look at the dates, they hop back and forth. They grab a girl from next to La Cosa Nostra territory one night and then hop over next to the Westies. After about ten days, they basically come to a halt."

"None of the girls look alike. We can't profile their types," I say, rubbing a hand over my jaw. "They don't discriminate when it comes to ethnicities, body types, lifestyles, or ages."

Enzo picks up where I left off. "The only thing we can say for sure is the girls range in age from about fourteen to twenty-five."

"That's one hell of a gap," Conor, Killian's right-hand says.

"What about that downtime?" Giovanni asks.

"That's when they hop to a new city," Greer says as she brings up another map. "They hit all over again in the same pattern in Chicago and then in California."

"We have suspicions that they hit other areas too. I have found some connections to some of the areas managed by other organizations, but without reaching out to them directly, we can't be one hundred percent sure they're connected. We get a few weeks of reprieve, and then it happens all over again. The worst of it is they never hit at the same time during the month. We can't tell women and girls to stay home and keep the doors locked during the second week of every month because it's always changing," I add.

"It's a shitshow," Greer says as she rubs her stomach.

"Thank God we're having a boy," Killian mutters under his breath.

Out of the corner of my eye, I watch Greer reach out and smack her husband in the stomach, making him grunt.

"Not the time," she hisses.

"Forgive me for being blunt, but you guys have been working on this for over a year, and this is all you got?" Conor says.

"Do you have any idea how many people go missing every day in this city?" Greer demands. When he stays quiet, she continues. "There are over forty reports a day made over a missing loved one."

Enzo cuts her off. "While not all of them are legitimate reports, we still have to look into them all. Where this person doesn't have a type, it makes it hard to narrow down. Everyone is a victim. These are just the girls we know about too. So many of the lower-income or working girls won't ever get reported. So the numbers could be significantly higher."

"Add in the fact we're weeding through not only our city, but Chicago and Veles, and we're in over our heads. Even with Declan, Yamato, and Alexei's help. Nikolai has his men out on his streets working hard on shutting it down as does Callum and Haruaki, but it's not enough. Just two months ago, Nikolai shut down a Ukrainian organization stealing women from his territory to harvest their organs. That adds a whole other layer. Now we know there is more than one group kidnapping girls for different reasons."

Greer hits another button, and a collage of missing women come up.

"Look at those faces," she demands, pointing at the screen. "None of those women deserve this, especially those kids."

Conor looks properly scolded and holds up his hands in surrender. "Sorry."

I look at the screen and something catches my attention. Pushing back my chair, I walk closer to get a better look.

"Motherfucker," I mutter under my breath.

"What is it?" Enzo asks.

I look down at my watch and see the date. Sure enough,

tomorrow would be the day we normally check in with each other. Looking back at the screen, I swallow hard.

"Greer, can you pull up this girl's information?" I ask, pointing at a photo.

Without asking a question, Greer does what I ask, and what I see takes my breath away. I hear everyone talking behind me, but I can't make out the words.

It can't be.

Not her.

Not again.

Beautiful brown eyes stared up at me from her prone position in the road. The rain pours on her face as she looks up at me with fear.

"It's okay. I won't hurt you."

"Help me," the girl sobs out before screaming.

Her strangled cries still haunt me to this day.

"Tristano, what is it? What's wrong?" Greer asks as she sets her hand on my arm, pulling me into the present.

"I'm fine. Sit back down." I force a smile.

She frowns as she walks back to her seat, and I stare at the photo.

"This one's wrong," I tell them.

"What do you mean it's wrong? Is she no longer missing? Her uncle made the report two weeks ago," Enzo says.

I turn and face everyone as I wipe my hand over my mouth, trying to find the words.

"It's wrong because that's not her name, and she's sure as hell not seventeen."

"And how do you know?" Killian asks slowly.

"Her name is Serena Taylor, not Sabrina Tyler like that says," I say, pointing at the screen. "She's barely twenty-two. I know that for a fact because five years ago I met this woman in a less-than-fortunate situation and helped her out."

"Keep going." Greer presses.

"She had a problem that needed to be taken care of and I took care of it for her. That's all I'm willing to say on the subject."

"You took care of it for her? What does that mean?" Lorenzo asks, his voice chillingly cold.

"It means I took care of it. That's all." I cross my arms, leaning back in my chair.

"You work for me which means you do not keep secrets," Bash reminds me, the tone a telling one.

If I don't tell him, he might decide to end me. For her, it's worth it.

"I respect your position, but this was not something I did for the family. This was a personal decision that has no ties back to us or what we do. This is her story." I point to her picture on the wall. "I will not betray her trust to satisfy your curiosity. All you need to know is that I took care of it, and it will never come back on us."

Bash is about to speak up again, but Greer cuts him off. "We can respect that. So she's been kidnapped under a different name then. Why would her uncle file a missing persons report under the wrong name?"

"Well..." I hesitate, rubbing the back of my neck. "I might have forgotten to mention an important detail."

Greer looks at me suspiciously. I think she already knows and is just waiting for me to admit it.

"I'm afraid to ask," Giovanni mutters.

"She kind of, sort of, works for the Jersey City Police Department."

"WHAT!" everyone yells in unison.

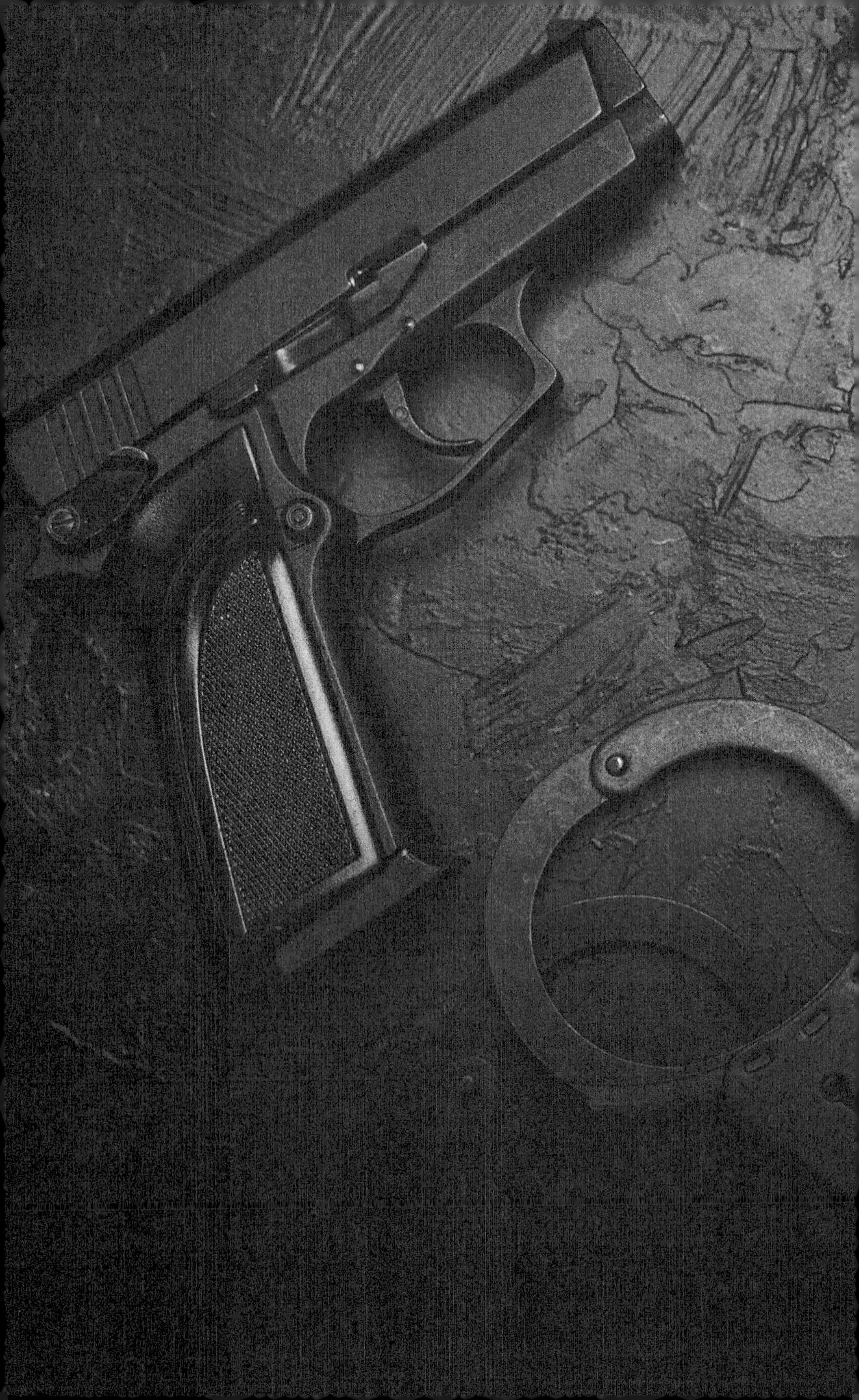

CHAPTER
FOUR

Serena

"So Tristano, can I call you Tris?" I whisper in the quiet truck cab. Logically, my brain tells me I shouldn't have gotten in, but my gut says I can trust this man.

"You can call me whatever you want, principessa." He smirks, winking at me.

How he can still flirt at a time like this is beyond me. I bury myself deeper into his sweatshirt and stare down at the sweatpants that he gave me to wear.

At first, I was hesitant to accept them, but when he pointed out that I was naked, I rushed to grab them from him. It's weird how living without them for days had changed my need for them.

Instead of reacting to his flirty tone, I ask the question that's been weighing on me.

"You did that so easily." I nod toward the pigpen. "Does it not bother you?"

His face loses all humor as he looks at me seriously.

"He hurt you, right?" he asks, his tone low.

"Yes," I respond, my voice barely breathing out the words.

I bury my face into his hoodie. I need to find out what kind of cologne he wears because it smells fantastic. It's calming. Cedarwood and mint, I think. Something for me to focus on instead of the trauma I know I will need to process.

"Did you notice the scratch marks on the wood next to where you were tied up?" he murmurs, looking out over the pigpen.

"Yeah..." I admit.

I was too scared to think about what it meant. Tris isn't going to give me that out though.

"That tells me you weren't the first. If I wouldn't have killed him, he would have done it again."

His blunt way of looking at the situation is jarring. He is so sure of his actions. I wish I could feel the same.

I think what scares me the most is that I'm not sorry that he's dead. I feel some sick joy watching the man be eaten alive by pigs.

"We could have called the cops," I mutter, needing to hold on to some thread of my moral compass.

Tristano scoffs before I even finish the sentence.

"Yeah, and cross our fingers that they are actually competent and could do their job. No.," He shakes his head. "I handled it. He will never hurt another woman again. It's better this way. You know he is gone. He can never come back again."

"Not all cops are bad." I sigh, pushing some hair out of my eyes. "Trust me, I know. My dad was a cop, and his father before him, and I plan on following in their footsteps. My uncle is even going to help get me into the academy this fall."

Tristano tenses next to me.

"Is he now..."

"Yes."

"And what about tonight? Are you going to turn me in, *principessa*?"

I turn away and bite my lip. That part of me needing to hang onto that innocence I once held wants to say yes. She wants to do what her father and grandfather would have told her is the right thing to do. That we should have let the law handle this and not resorted to vigilante justice. Then there's that other part. The one who remembers the way this man held me down while I screamed. The way he did horrific things to my body against my will. That part thinks that even this punishment is far too easy for him. Even with his screams as he was eaten alive.

"No," I whisper after a few moments of silence. "But I hate keeping secrets."

Tristano shrugs. "If you have to tell on me to make yourself feel better, then do it. I don't want you to feel bad about what I did for even a second. I would rather spend the rest of my life in jail than let a single ounce of guilt hit that pretty mind of yours."

He pulls me back so we're leaning against the windshield of his car, our feet lying on the hood.

I look over at him and study his profile. His dark hair is going every which way from him running his hands through it. His jaw is sharp. He's too handsome for his own good. Hell, I bet with a five o'clock shadow, he would be even more attractive.

He's right. Part of me feels guilty. Hearing him tell me that I have nothing to feel guilty for helps relieve that pressure on my chest.

"Thank you."

"You're welcome." He smirks. "Just think, one good thing came out of all of this."

"What's that?"

"You met me."

"You say that like it's a good thing."

"It is. Because now, whenever you need a dark knight to save you, you know I'll be there."

"Promise?" I ask as my heart beats wildly.

"Promise, *principessa*."

Slowly I wake up and realized we were moving.

I can still smell the cedarwood and mint that has always brought me comfort. I wish he was here with me.

Opening my eyes, I see that there is one dim light swaying from the metal roof. Looking around, I see the other girls, some passed out and others wide awake. I groan, rubbing my head.

We are on the move. I think it's been about five or six days since I've been taken. What I think was last night they finally brought us water with our food. After drinking it, I realized the mistake I made. They drugged it.

The screeching of brakes makes me cover my ears. We must be on a train. I wonder where they are taking us now. I guess wherever they plan to sell us or whatever it is that they do.

The sound of retching makes me sit up. Mandy is in the corner with her back to us as she dry heaves.

"That's fucking gross," some girl who can't be a day over sixteen sneers.

"Yeah, well, it's not like she can help it if she gets motion sickness when they have us locked up now, can she?" another snaps.

The longer we are captive, the more irritable we all get. I haven't lashed out, but I've wanted to. Some of these girls aren't old enough to have better control over their emotions. Add in the high-intensity high-stakes situation and it's assumed at least one of us will lose it at some point.

Leaning against the wall, I shut my eyes and go over everything I know. When I was taken, I was the sixth girl. They didn't take anyone the day after me, but then the four days after that they did. I think it was yesterday I drank the water, but I can't be sure.

"Does anyone know what day it is?" I say loudly over the train.

"I'm not sure, but when I was taken it was April first," the girl next to me says.

Looking over at her, I remember she was the eighth girl taken. So it has to be either the fourth or fifth of the month.

Hope blossoms in my chest.

Maybe that's why I dreamed of him. I was supposed to check in with him via phone on the first. It's our routine. I have never missed even when undercover.

He has to be looking for me, right?

I wish I had made a different decision back then. The one and only time outside of the day we met that he came to see me was when I graduated from the police academy when I was nineteen years old. I still remember the way it felt to be with him again.

"You came." *I rush over to hug him.*

He picks me up, spinning me around before setting me back down.

"Of course I did. These are for you." *He hands me a bouquet of flowers and a gift bag.*

"What's in the bag?" *I ask.*

He smirks. "I'll show you, but only if you come with me."

He looks around at all the cops hanging around my backyard.

I nod knowingly. This has to be weird for him. It's why I didn't think he would come. I should not be seen with him, but I so wanted him to be here. More than anything really.

"Let me go make an excuse to my uncle. I'll meet you down the street."

It didn't take me long to convince my uncle to let me walk to the store for some ice. He was deep in discussion with another officer so I know he won't miss me when I'm gone longer than I should be.

Tris is waiting where I told him. I take a moment to take him in. He's even more gorgeous than I remember. I wish I had a picture to look at while I pine away for him. He doesn't know it, but I live for our monthly calls. I was surprised when the burner phone showed up that first month. Then it became the highlight of my life.

Taking a deep breath, I make a choice. I stride up to Tris, wrapping my arms around his neck until my fingers dig into his hair. Then I press my lips to his. He freezes a moment before kissing me back. It's so deep and needy that I feel myself getting lost in it.

When he finally pulls away, my lips are still tingling. He lets his forehead fall to mine.

"We can't do this," he whispers, pressing a kiss to my forehead.

"I'm not a kid anymore. I'm legal. Why can't we?" I demand, trying to *pull out of his arms.*

He shakes his head. "Trust me, I know you're not a kid. I've noticed. That's not why this is a bad idea."

"Then why?" I feel the tears welling up.

"Don't cry, anima gemella. It breaks my heart. We can't do this because you are on the right side of the law and I'm not. If you ever want to have a career, you cannot be connected to me. Someone will find out one day and it will ruin everything. As much as I want to be your everything, I can't be in order for you to have your dream."

"I don't care about that. I want you."

He sighs. "You worked so hard to get to where you are. You have goals of saving the world. Go out and achieve those goals. I'll be here in the shadows cheering you on."

"This isn't fair," I whisper into his chest.

"Life isn't fair."

Isn't that the truth? If life were fair, I wouldn't have been abducted not once, but twice. None of these women would be getting taken for the sick joys of other human beings. I would be with Tristano without worrying about how it would affect other areas of my life.

Over the years, there have been times that I wished I could see Tristano, but I knew why I couldn't. We're both on different sides of the law, and it wouldn't be fair to either one of us to choose. He loves his life with La Cosa Nostra, and I would never ask him to walk away from them, no matter how much I wish I could. I thought I loved my life in law enforcement, but what difference am I really making? Catching one or two men here and there?

That day was the first time I really hated the decision I made. He had stopped calling me *principessa* and started calling me *anima gemella*. I had to look it up later, but when I found out it meant "soul mate" it made it even harder to stick with my decision. I did though. Now, I wonder what it was all for.

"I wonder where we're going now," one of the girls asks, drawing my attention back to the present.

TRISTANO

"Right before they gave us our last meal, I heard them talking outside. Someone mentioned Chicago," Mandy tells the room.

Her eyes are on me though. We have been discussing it in whispers. What we will need to do to get out of here. One of which is getting any information we can from our captors. So far it's been a bunch of gibberish in another language, but what I did learn is that not all of our captors are the same. The men in New Jersey were speaking Russian, while some of the others they had there were speaking another language. One I don't recognize.

Chicago, I mouth to her.

She nods.

Chicago is good. It's a big city, but it's also a city well known. Hopefully Tris can track me down to here.

Taking a deep breath, I try to evaluate what I'm feeling. Part of me is hopeful that maybe, just maybe, Chicago will be where this ends and we're all rescued. On the other hand though, a small part of me wants to see this through to the very end. If we're rescued now, that won't bring an end to this trafficker's reign. We won't have all the information we need to close a case.

As another round of crying starts up, I do the only thing I can do. I shut my eyes and try to listen to every detail I can.

Anything that can save our lives.

Tristano

"BABY SMOKES CRACK!" I sing at the top of my lungs as I drive through the night.

I snort at my new variation of the classic Sir Mix-A-Lot song.

It's about three in the morning, and there's not a soul in sight. The stars peek through the trees as I speed down the deserted road. Reaching over, I grab a bag of Sour Patch Kids and dump them into my mouth. The loose powder hits the back of my throat just right, making me cough so hard my eyes water.

I drop the bag into my lap and wipe my eyes. "Fuck me," I mutter to myself as the song rolls onto the next.

Something up ahead catches my eye in the ditch.

I watch as a woman crawls onto the road in nothing but her birthday suit.

"What the hell," I yell as I slam on the brakes.

The girl doesn't even attempt to get out of the road. She just brings her hand up to her eyes to prevent my headlights from blinding her.

Coming to a stop, I throw the car in park and get out.

"Are you okay?"

The girl jerks away from me until she's lying prone on her back, shivering as the rain pours down.

Beautiful brown eyes stared up at me from her prone position in the road. The rain pours on her face as she looks up at me with fear.

"It's okay. I won't hurt you."

"Help me," the girl sobs out before screaming.

"Shhh. It's okay. No one is going to hurt you. I've got you. You can trust me."

I don't know if it's the sound of my voice or what, but she calms down, staring up at me now like I might be God himself.

Turning from the girl, I head back to the truck. Digging around, I find the blanket my nonna insisted I start carrying when I started driving. Slowly I approach the woman.

My breath catches when I see she's probably my age, if not a little younger. I hadn't noticed that before. I lean down to lay the blanket on her but stop when she flinches.

Idiot. She's clearly been through hell.

"I'm just going to cover you up, okay? I promise not to touch you without your permission."

The girl nods.

"Can I help you get out of the middle of the road? Give you a ride somewhere?"

She gives me another small nod, not meeting my eyes.

Cautiously, I help her stand as she clutches the blanket around her body. "Thank you."

"Can I ask what happened?" I ask as we walk toward my truck.

"I don't know how it happened." She shakes her head. "I was coming out of work the other night and someone hit me in the head from behind. When I came to, I was here."

The words leave her in a rush, her body shaking violently against me. All I want to do is pull her in close and keep her warm and safe.

"Where is here?" I say as I look around.

With a shaky hand, she points over my shoulder toward the tree line. "There's a farmhouse back there. He kept me locked up in the barn."

"For how long?" I ask through clenched teeth as I help her into the passenger seat of my truck.

She frowns. "Three, maybe four days. He kept me tied up with a rope." She holds up her battered wrists. "But tonight, after he r-raped me, he forgot to tighten my wrists back up and didn't tie my feet together at all. I waited until he fell asleep and then ran."

"Good job, principessa. Off we go," I say as I shut the door.

As I round the back of the truck, my hands shake. The girl has clearly gone through a hell no one should ever have to live through. Taking a deep breath, I get into the truck and turn it on. "Where are you from?"

"Jersey City."

"Lucky for you, that's where I'm going," I lie.

I'm going to New York City, though, so close enough.

She's quiet for a moment as I drive down the road.

Out of the corner of my eye, I see her shake her head.

"What's wrong?"

"This isn't me. I don't catch rides with strangers. I pay attention to my surroundings, but it wasn't enough," she says as a tear tracks down her face.

"I'm sorry." My hand flexes on the gearshift to keep from reaching over to her.

She jerks her chin toward the road. "I think that's the driveway."

Without a second thought, I slow down and pull off the road.

"Where are we going?" she pants, clenching the blanket.

"Don't worry, you aren't going to get out of the car, but I have something I need to take care of before we head home."

"W-what are you going to do?"

"I'm going to right a wrong," I tell her as I slow down. "Tell me, what's your name?"

"Serena."

"Well, Serena, my name's Tristano. Just think of me as your personal devil."

I shut off my lights and drive by moonlight farther down the driveway.

"That man will never hurt you again. No one will. I'll make sure of it."

My head jerks, causing me to almost fall out of my chair, startling me awake.

"Motherfucker." I groan and rub my face.

It was just a dream. No, not a dream. A memory. One that's haunting me.

I made a promise that no one would ever hurt her again, but here we are. She's been snatched again. As far as I can tell, she wasn't undercover. I hacked into her uncle's computer. The last assignment she was on ended the Thursday before she was taken.

The only reason he listed her as missing under her undercover name is because he lied to his superiors. He's covering for her while trying to find her himself.

He's doing a shitty job of it, which is why I hate the local police. They have too much red tape to cut through. She's already out of the city by my calculations, which means he will never find her.

I will though.

I look around the quiet office and see Greer sitting at her desk, staring at me.

"Can I help you?"

"You said her name in your sleep," she says softly, making me tense.

"What time is it?" I ask, changing the subject.

I know she wants to press me on Serena, but she also is aware that I'm being cagey for a reason.

The reason being Serena has slowly become the most important person in my life. It doesn't matter that I can never have her. I couldn't care any less that she is law enforcement and may turn me in one day.

She's also a beautiful, intelligent, funny young woman who stole my heart. At first, I just wanted to stay in touch to make sure she was receiving the care she needed. Then I showed up when she graduated from the police academy.

Big mistake or best decision of my life depending on how you look at it.

No more was she the victim I had stored in my mind. Instead, she was this woman who was gorgeous and who smiled at me like I hung the moon. She hugged me, and I swear my body reacted, wanting to absorb her into my being until we were one.

It was the weirdest feeling in the world. I had never once been so attracted to or fixated on a woman before. Yet there she was.

Then she kissed me, and fuck if I didn't kiss her back. I gave her everything for a solid minute before I finally pulled back. It took all my self-control not to claim the girl as mine right then and there. I wanted to so bad, but it wasn't what was best for her.

She was starting her life as a police officer, and I'm the man she's supposed to hunt. It was never going to be able to work. Still, I gave that to her because selfishly I needed it myself.

Then we agreed to be friends, shattering my heart in the process. It was the right decision though. She's killing it as an undercover cop. At least she was.

What happened to get her kidnapped?

"It's six thirty in the morning," Greer tells me after a moment. "Are you okay?"

I raise a brow. "Came in a little early, huh? I don't know how Killian would feel about you sneaking out of bed before the sun. Especially to come to see me. We all know he's jealous of my good looks."

Greer rolls her eyes as she rubs her stomach. "I know what you are doing, and I'm going to allow it for now, but eventually you will have to tell me about her." She sighs. "If Killian's son let me sleep, I would still be in bed. He knows damn well that my eyes are solely on him, so no need for jealousy." She eyes me cautiously. "Find anything?"

Back to the task at hand.

"Honestly, I'm so tired right now I can't even remember." I rub my face, yawning.

"I hate saying this, but Tris, you won't save her if you aren't taking care of yourself. You need sleep." Her nose wrinkles. "And a shower."

I barely raise my arm and put it down. Already smelling myself. Fuck, that's disgusting.

Ever since I saw her name on that board, all I have been able to do is work on this. It's all that matters.

"I can sleep when I'm dead... but a shower would be nice."

"Why don't you go down to the bunkroom and take a shower? Maybe catch a real nap and I'll watch what you have running."

I pop my knuckles. "Yeah, okay, but you'll wake me if anything goes off."

Greer smiles. "Of course. Now go."

I get up and make my way to the door but pause.

"Hey, Greer," I say over my shoulder.

"Yeah, Tris?"

"You're a pretty awesome boss. You know that, right?"

"Thanks. Now let's hope you still feel that way in a few weeks when we're trying to get some work done while passing around a baby."

I chuckle. "Touché."

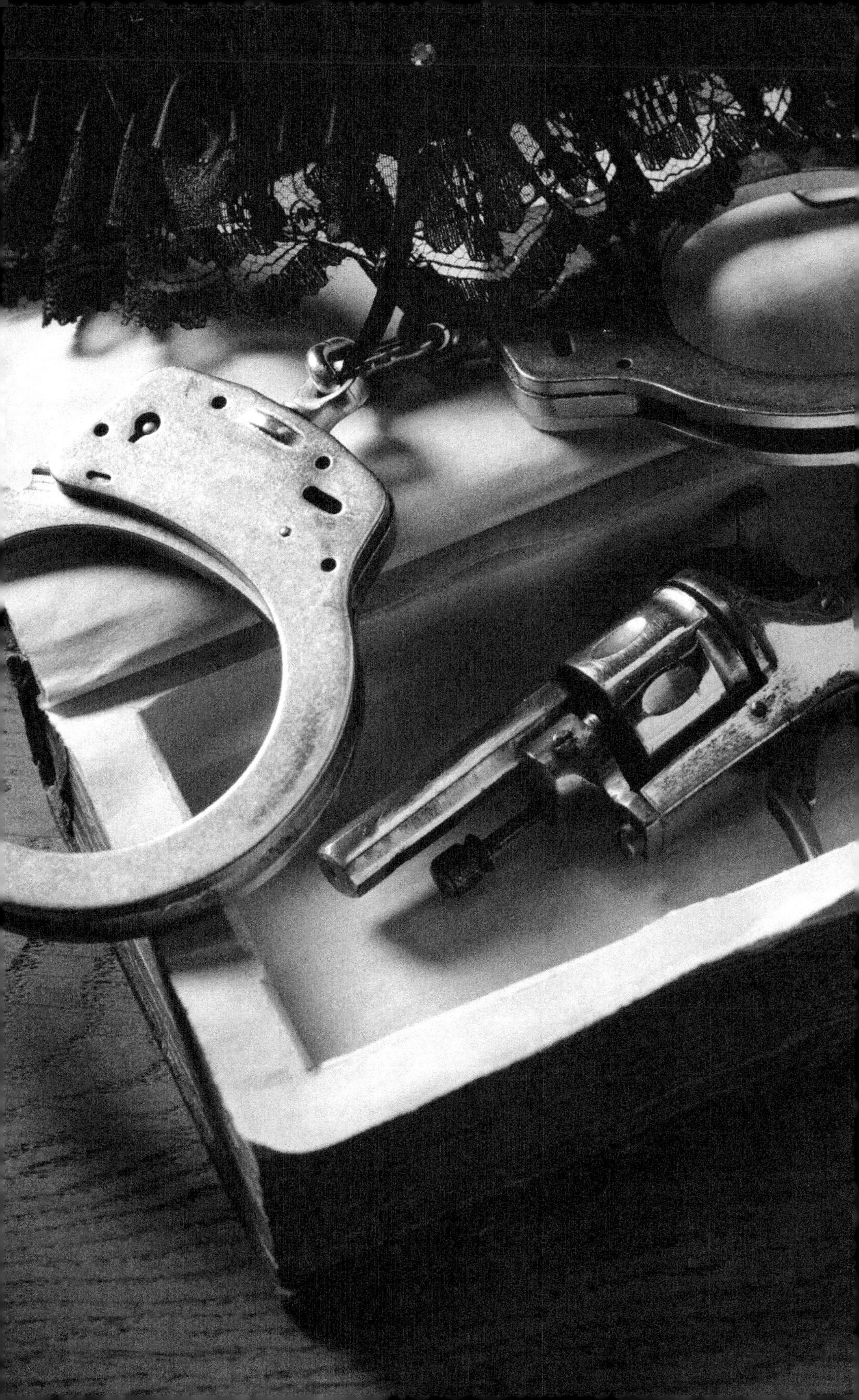

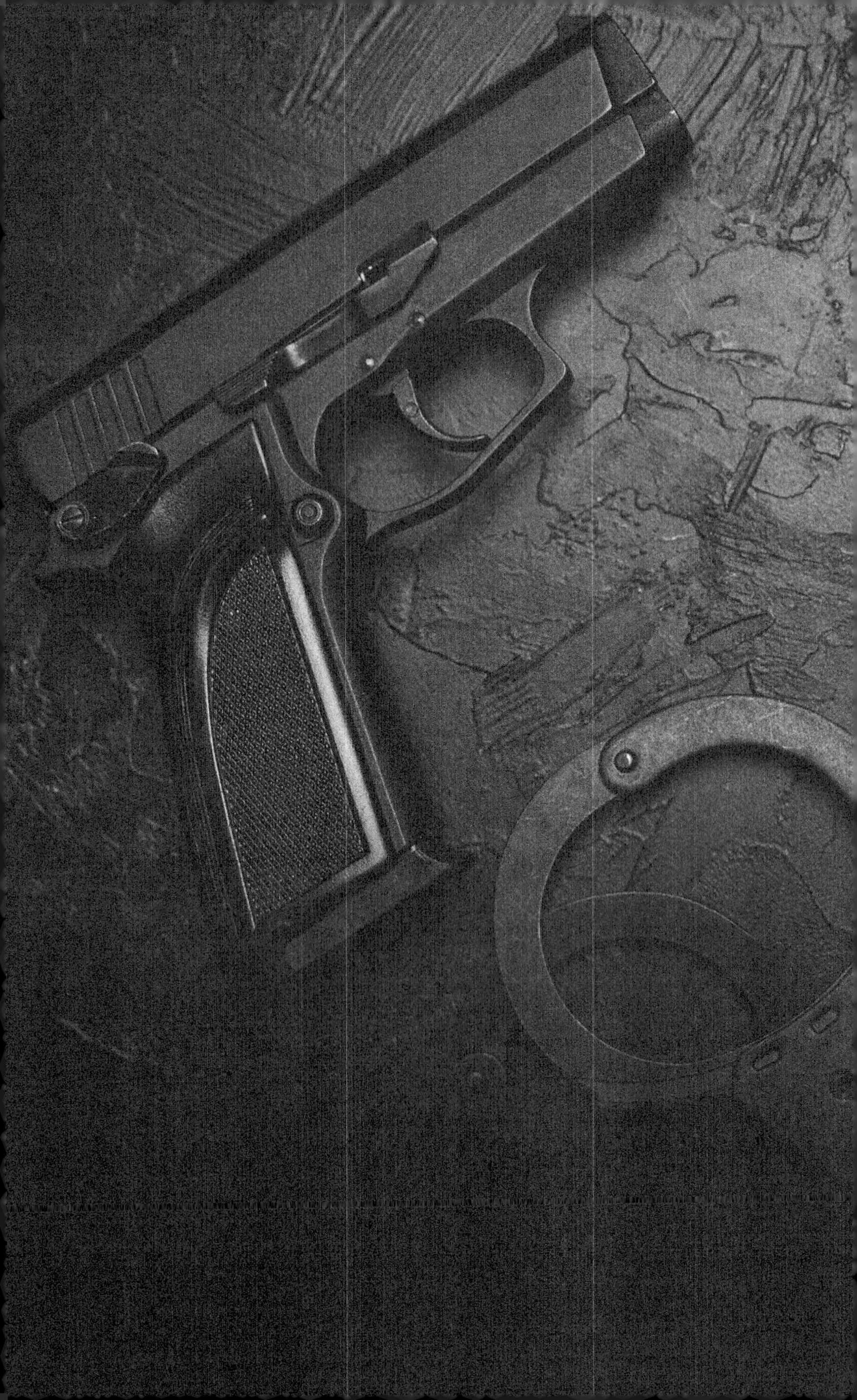

CHAPTER
FIVE

Serena

Three days. We have been in Chicago for three days.

I overheard one of the men speaking in English with someone about taking photos of us. Whatever they are planning to do with us, it's going to happen soon. We need to be thinking of what is going to happen once we get to that point. Many of the girls are so weak, I don't think there will be much of a fight on our hands.

They moved us again. This time I didn't drink the water and only pretended to be knocked out. It was hard to resist the urge to gag when the men touched me, but I kept it together. I had no other choice.

When the choice is between dignity and survival, survival wins out every time.

Thankfully none of them raped me. Nor did they even get close to my vagina. They mostly groped my breasts a bit as they moved me from the train to a box truck. Then they moved us into a warehouse an hour later. I only know the time it took because I counted. It was hard with my pounding head, but I had to do it.

The men haven't been back in here since they dropped us here. I don't know if that's a blessing or not. I wish I had sipped at least a little of that water. It might have made me drowsy, but my mouth is drier than a cotton swab. They haven't fed us either. Another one of the girls died yesterday. Her body is still lying in the corner where they had her handcuffed.

"They haven't brought any new girls. Do you think this is our final place?" Mandy whispers, her eyes still closed, almost as if it hurts to open them.

"Maybe," I choke out. "I haven't seen or heard anyone in three days. I've been keeping count."

"What if they are leaving us here to die?" another girl wails.

"Stop," I hiss at her. "If they are outside guarding us, you'll only draw attention. Trust me, their attention is not the kind you want to get."

"We are going to die here aren't we?" one of the younger girls asks.

I shake my head. "I don't know."

Then I hear it. The footsteps.

I shush the girls as they all go limp.

I should too, but I can't help it. I need more information. This passiveness isn't helping.

The man walks in, setting trays down at each girls' feet.

"We need water," I tell him.

He jolts, looking over to me.

"Oh, we have a brave one," he says, his voice heavily accented. "You need more water? How about I fill up a bowl and you can lap it up like a little dog?"

I shrug. "If that's a choice, I accept. Whatever you plan to do to us, you need us alive. You left food at that girl's feet over there, but do you see her? She's dead. That's two girls gone. Can't be good for business."

He curses in another language before getting in my face. Spit flies from his mouth.

"I can't wait to get you up on the website. Pretty little thing like you would already get a pretty penny. Add in your mouth, and men will pay to break that spirit of yours."

Ding. Ding. Ding.

They are going to sell us on the dark web.

I don't know how that really helps since I'm here, but maybe, just maybe, someone will catch these men in time. I wish I had telepathy. I could send the information back home.

Instead, the triumph of my win slowly fades as the man storms from the room.

I sigh, hating that I angered them. Hopefully this doesn't speed anything up.

I would hate if my actions got any of the others harmed or punished. God forbid they cut the already small rations we get. I mean, it's not like we are getting five-star meals, but even the bread with peanut butter on it is better than nothing. I don't even care that half the time the bread is dirty and moldy. I'd eat a rat at this point if I had to.

When you are forced into such a dire situation like we are, you do whatever you need to in order to keep breathing. Maybe that's why I lashed out. I can't see an ending to this where we all don't die of dehydration or starvation.

You'd think since they took us, that they would at least want to keep us in good condition, but it seems they don't care. That only makes me worry more about what they are planning to do to us. Maybe they don't need us alive for what comes next.

The girls begin to move before the door bangs open again, causing them all to jolt. Then the same man is back, throwing water bottles at everyone. When he gets to me, he opens the bottle before spitting in it. Then he throws it at me with a smirk on his face.

I don't know why he seems so proud of himself. I'm dying. Literally, I feel my body trying to shut down.

I have no dignity left. No reason to turn down or sneer at this bottle of water.

Hell, it could be brown and contain E. coli and I would probably still drink it.

It's what you do to survive.

So instead of focusing on him, I open the bottle, chugging down several swallows before putting the lid back on.

He grunts, leaving the room.

"Why did you do that?" Mandy asks.

I look over to her, my mind weary. "If we don't get water every three days, we will eventually die. I bought us a chance to survive. I don't know if it was a good decision or not. Based on what he said, we might be better off dead."

I hear a few of the girls whimper at my words. They are bleak, but the truth is all we have.

We can't live on false hope anymore.

All we can do is try our best to survive.

Tristano

"T*ris*..."

It's her voice I hear. Her voice calling out to me.

Grunting I wave my hand in front of my face, refusing to open my eyes.

"Tris...I need you."

"Serena," I mumble.

Something hits me in the face, jolting me awake.

I peel my eyes open and find Greer squatting in front of me.

"I need you," Greer hisses at me.

"Why does your face look like that?" I ask as I take in her contorted face.

She reaches forward and slams her fist into my chest. "Because I'm having a fucking contraction, you asshole."

"What!" I yell as I shoot up, making Greer sway back. As I stand, I grab her arms. "Are you okay? What do I need to do?"

She makes that ugly face again as she digs her nails into my forearms.

"Breathe..."

Once the contraction passes, she pants, "I need you to help me downstairs. Enzo ran across the street to grab me one of those fruit smoothies."

"Talk about shit timing," I mumble under my breath as I usher Greer toward the door. "How far along are they?"

"Close enough." She cringes.

"You were already having them when you sent Enzo on the drink run, weren't you?" I smirk as we step into the elevator.

Greer ignores my question. "I booked you a ticket to Chicago."

I feel myself tense when what she says registers. "Why..."

Greer grunts and holds onto me with one hand and her stomach with the other.

These are too fucking close. If this elevator doesn't hurry the fuck up, I'm going to end up seeing what's between her legs, and not in the fun way.

"Because right before I woke you up, another girl was reported missing in Chicago. Two days in a row. I called Declan. He will be waiting for you at the airport."

The elevator comes to a stop and we step out.

"Hey, what's going on?" Enzo asks, frowning as he approaches.

"She's in full-blown labor. If we don't get her to the hospital,, we will be playing rock paper scissors who gets to catch the little prince," I say, pointing at her stomach.

Enzo tosses the drinks in the trash next to him and rushes forward.

Greer whimpers. "I really wanted that."

"Did you call Killian?" Enzo asks as he grabs onto her arm.

"He will meet us there." Before she can say anything else, she cries out and comes to a stop.

I hear something hit the tile floor and look down.

"Uh, Greer…" I say hesitantly. "Did you just pee your pants?"

Enzo reaches over and hits the back of my head. "Her water broke, you idiot."

"Dammit, I really loved these shoes, and now they're ruined!" she cries out.

"It's okay, I'll have Danica go out and get you another pair. Now let's hurry," he says softly as he pushes her forward.

"Do you promise?"

"I do," he says as we step outside.

We walk her forward and help her into the car.

I move to get in, only for Greer to block me. "Airport, remember?"

"Right." I shake my head. "What time's my flight?"

"In an hour and a half. If you leave now, you might be able to make it in time." She cringes.

"Okay," I say as I look up and down the street for a cab. "Keep me updated on all of that," I say, waving my finger toward her stomach.

"Will do," Enzo says as he gets into the car.

He slams the door shut, and the car pulls out.

I run my hands through my hair and look up at the sky. Holy shit, talk about a way to wake up.

A car comes to a stop next to me with the window down.

"Hey, are you Tristano?" the driver asks.

"Yeah…"

"A dude named Greer scheduled a ride to the airport for you."

TRISTANO

"Woman," I correct him as I reach for the door and get in.

"Huh, weird name for a girl," he mumbles under his breath.

As he drives, the reality sets in.

Greer is in labor. She's going to have a baby.

Not only that, but girls are being taken in Chicago. That means that Serena might be there.

Laying my head back on the seat, I pray like hell to God that we find her.

I can't live without her.

"Hey, you made it," Declan says as I get into the car.

"Barely."

He raises a brow as he pulls into traffic. "No bags?"

"I didn't have any time," I tell him as I turn on my phone. "What did I miss?"

I send off a text to Enzo.

Me: Anything?

While I wait for him to respond, I check my notifications and see nothing of importance and darken the screen.

"So far, two girls have been taken, fifteen and twenty-three."

"Fucking kids, man." I shake my head in disgust.

Out of the corner of my eye, I watch Declan's hands flex on the steering wheel. "We're meeting up with Kenji. He's going to introduce us to a hooker who can hopefully give us an in on the working girls."

Kenji is the right-hand man to the Yakuza's leader, Haruaki. Last I heard, he was newly taken. My face must give away my line of thinking because Declan shakes his head.

"Nah, not what you're thinking. Jada used to work at The Currency but did him dirty. She stays in touch, sends them girls from time to time who she thinks would be better off working as escorts instead of on the street. She's the one who has been reporting girls going missing."

"Makes sense." I nod.

My phone vibrates, and I look down.

Enzo: *Picture.* Kieran, Mama, and Papa are doing well.

I stare at the baby in the photo and shake my head. It's crazy that just a few hours ago he was safely tucked away in Greer's stomach.

"Greer had her baby," I say, flashing the screen toward Declan.

"That's awesome. Cleo will be excited," he says, referring to Killian's niece, Haruaki's wife.

"Oh, for sure. Hey, do we have time to stop and get me a change of clothes?" I ask.

"Easy enough. Do you need suits or something a little more casual?"

I eye my friend and his clothes. "Is that what you usually wear?"

He's wearing a pair of jeans and a T-shirt.

He points over his shoulder. "Callum is a little more lax on what we wear here. I still have a suit when needed, but it's the Wild West out here. We can wear what we want. I can have a tailored suit sent to The Currency for you if you'd like."

"Nah. I want to blend in, not stand out. Let's just stop for some basics."

"Sounds good. We have a little time before we meet with Kenji and Jada. I figured you would be more comfortable staying at The Currency." He cringes. "My place isn't exactly set up for company."

"That works for me."

After making a quick stop, I have everything I need. As we get out of the car outside of the hotel and casino, I slip on the hoodie I picked up.

"I don't think I've ever seen you dressed that casual," Declan says as we walk toward the building.

"I usually don't."

"Hmm..." Declan hums.

I had no intentions of buying the sweatshirt, but when I walked by it, I remembered back to when I first met Serena. The way she kept burying her face into my hoodie and taking deep breaths as if the smell of me offered her comfort. If I can recreate that again for her I will.

We walk through the casino and make our way up to Kenji's office. Declan knocks as he reaches the door.

"Come in..."

We let ourselves in and see Kenji sitting at his desk, across from a woman with another at his back.

"I won't do it, Kenji. It would be bad for business if any of the customers found out," the woman that's sitting says.

"None of them will," the one behind him adds softly.

"I don't think you understand the severity of this Jada," Kenji says coolly. "We just want you to set up check-ins with your girls and to pass out trackers that go on the skin. It kind of looks like a nicotine patch. Do you want your friends to keep disappearing?"

"No..." The seated woman sounds remorseful.

"Then stop fighting me," Kenji tells her.

She looks over her shoulder and eyes Declan and me. "Who are they?"

"They are men who want this to end as much as we do," the other woman tells her.

"Really?" she says in disbelief.

"Really." I nod. "I'm hoping that if you guys do this and one of your girls is taken, we can track them without an issue and it will lead us to the other women that have been taken."

"They took someone important to you," she says after a moment of silence.

I don't open my mouth to confirm or deny. I don't know this woman, and she won't get anything else from me.

"This is bigger than us all, Jada, and our time frame is limited until they come back to town," Declan tells her. "Wouldn't you rather be safe than sorry?"

Jada looks away, biting her lip. "Fine. I'll get a bunch of the girls together and meet you at the motel on Sixth. Does that work for you?" she says, looking at Kenji.

Kenji nods. "We'll be there."

As she leaves, the other woman makes her way over, holding out her hand.

"Miya. Thank you for coming." I shake her hand, noting the possessive look on Kenji's face.

This must be his girl.

"We all want an end to this, but this time it's personal," I admit.

Kenji steps up, wrapping his arm around Miya. "We heard. We will do everything in our power to help get your girl back."

"She's not..." I trail off.

Kenji gives me a knowing look. "Whether she's aware she is yours or not is not important. I can tell by that fire in your eyes that you feel ownership of her which means she is yours by default. We will get her back for you at all costs."

"I appreciate that," I tell him.

"Anything for an ally. Now let's get working on these trackers."

I can only hope one of these girls gets abducted with the tracker on. It's a horrible thought, but it's the only hope I have right now.

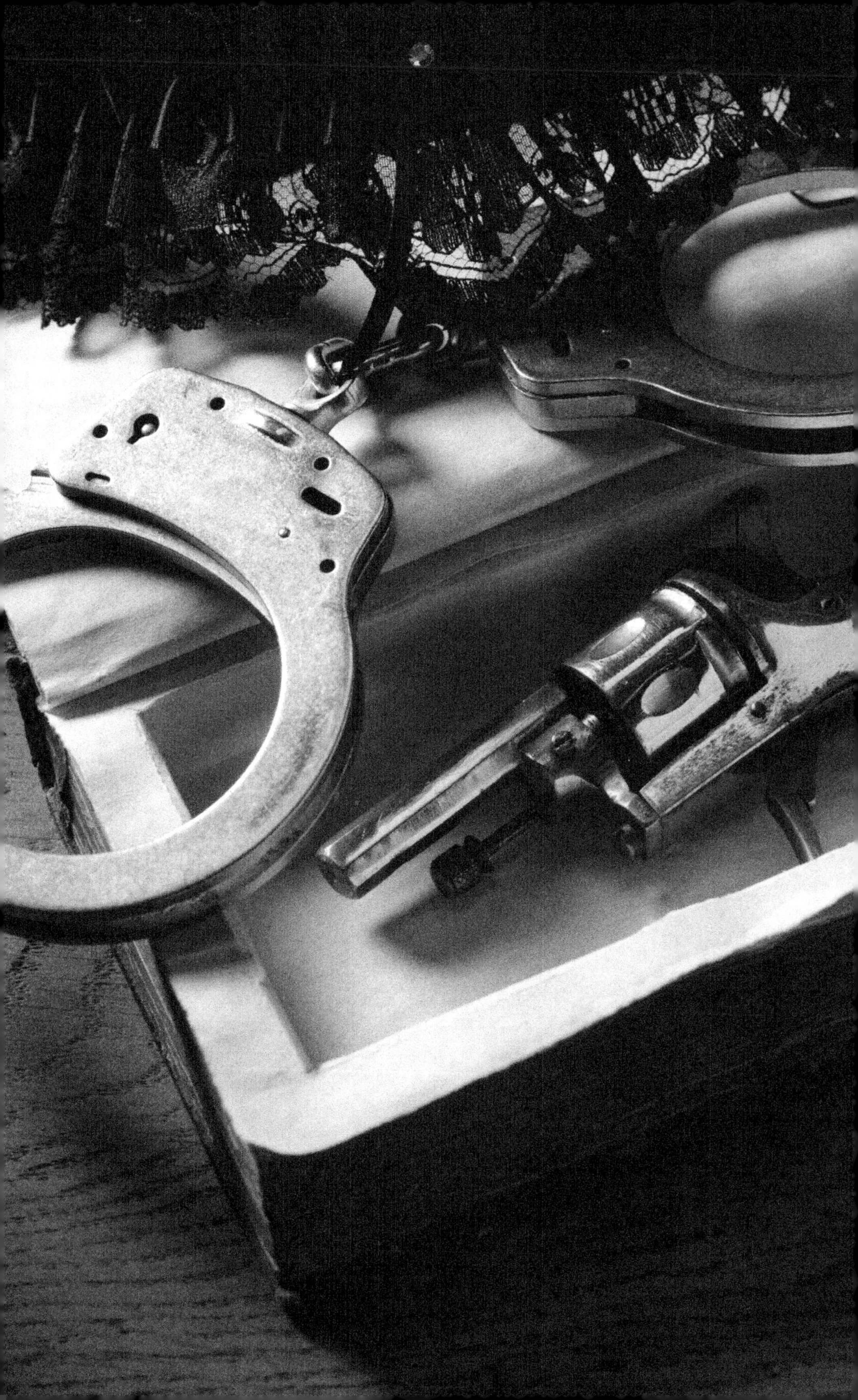

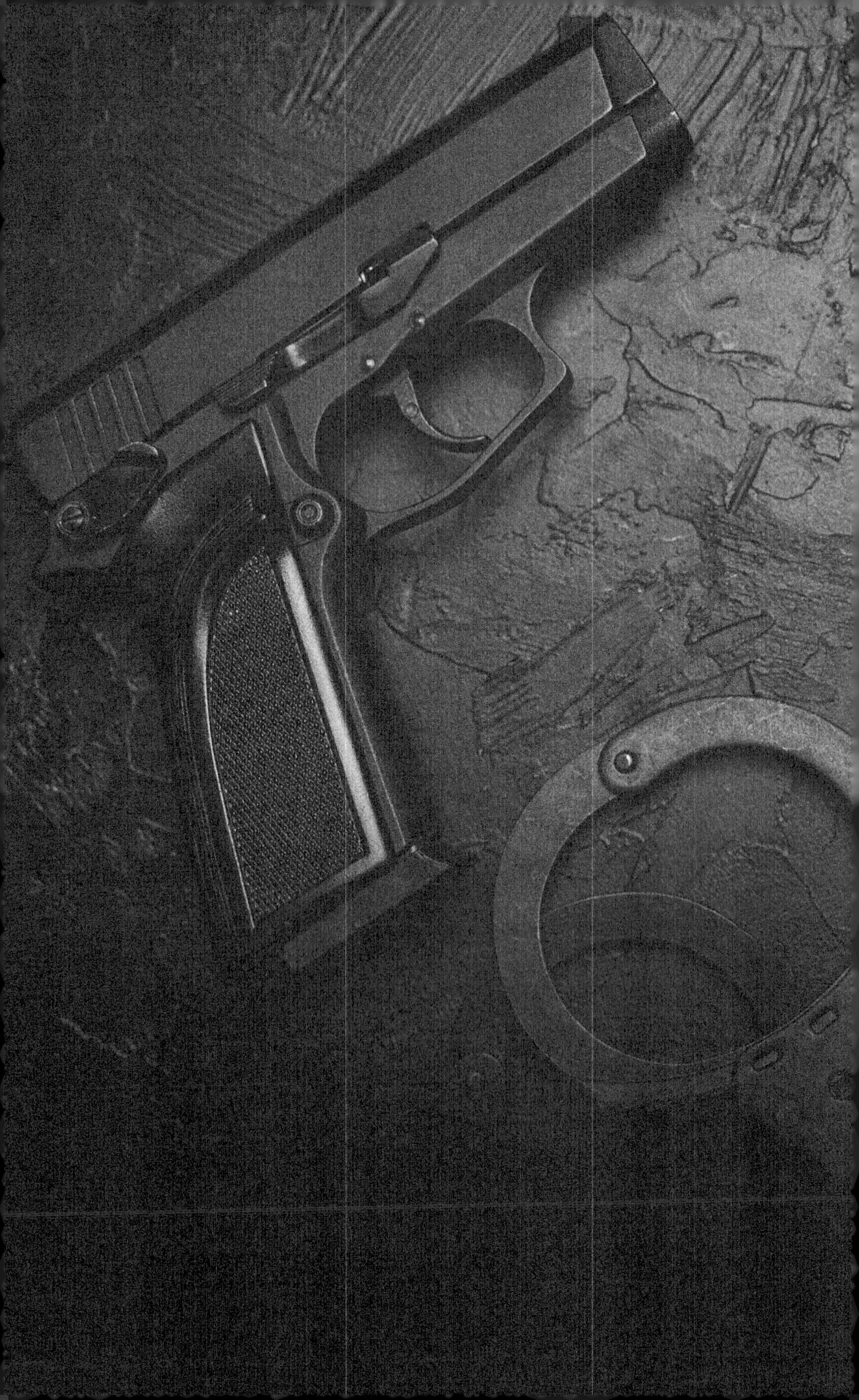

CHAPTER
SIX

Serena

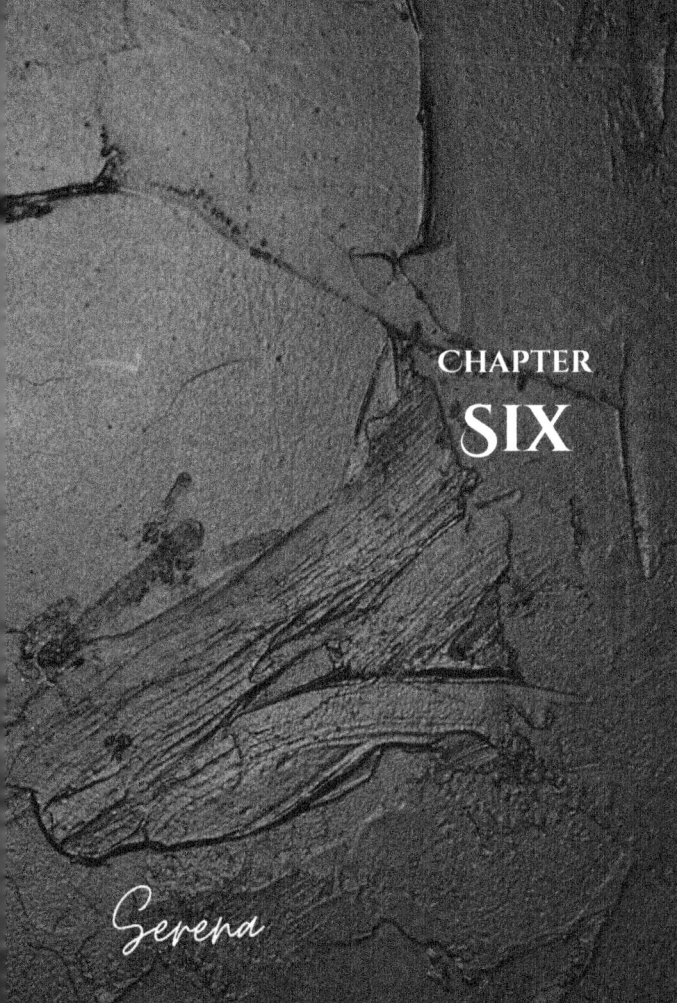

Devastation. Self-loathing. Complete and utter despair.

At first, I was hopeful that I would be found quickly. As time's gone on, I've prayed to every god I could think of.

Now the negativity has seeped into all of us. We all know that no one is coming, not to save us at least.

Earlier, men came in and took us out by twos. They took us into a building and watched us shower. It was the most demoralizing thing I've ever experienced. Standing there naked in front of strangers with my hands and feet chained together, trying to wash my body all while fifteen-year-old Olivia bawled next to me. She was the first of the two new girls to be added to our group. The entire time I stood there, I fought off waves of dizziness.

When we were done showering, they unchained us and held a gun to our heads as they took photos of our emaciated bodies before they gave us a clean hospital gown to put on. Once the clothes were on, they chained us back up.

For one moment I contemplated pushing my luck and fighting them, but I knew I would end up dead. With how starved I've been, I don't have the energy to move at the speed I would need to overtake these men. Add in the fact Olivia was with me, and it wasn't worth the risk.

While I was brushing my teeth, I studied myself in the mirror. It was like looking at a stranger. My hair was wet and limp around my shoulders. I was paler than normal. My full cheeks caved in, but the most startling thing though was my eyes. They held no life.

"A clean container too? What did we do to deserve this five-star treatment?" Mandy says as soon as the door shuts behind her.

"Right? We're living the high life now," I say sarcastically.

"You two are fucked up," a girl sneers from her spot. "Would you two shut up already?"

This particular girl was one of the last taken from Jersey City. She doesn't like that Mandy and I discuss ways to escape. It makes me wonder if she's a plant put in here by the men who took us.

"I'm cold," Olivia says as she burrows into my side.

"Me too," I tell her even though I've gone completely numb.

The coldness stopped affecting me days ago. My body is shutting down. I know it won't be long now. Maybe another week or two?

"You know, I used to sell dirty pics and my used underwear for money to creeps on the internet. I bet they would love to see me now," Nadia, a twenty-three-year-old girl scoffs.

She is the other new girl. They brought the two together.

"You sold used underwear?" I roll my head against the wall and look at her.

"Gross right? I couldn't believe it, but it afforded me to pay for my last year of school in cash." She shakes her head. "I should have used that money to go on vacation. I'll never use that shiny degree now."

I open my mouth to tell her she's wrong but I can't. I refuse to lie to her.

"What did you go to school for?" Mandy asks.

"Architecture. I wanted to run circles around the men." Her tone is wistful.

Almost like it's a dream she had but now realizes it's one she will never reach.

"Male-dominated field." Mandy nods. "I like it. I went to school for cosmetology. I love playing with a good head of hair," she says wistfully.

Nadia tips her chin toward me. "What about you? What did you go to school for?"

"I didn't go to school," I rasp. "I thought college was a waste of my time, so instead I joined the workforce. I learned two languages in high school and taught myself three others on my own time."

I still haven't told them my real name, but everything else we've talked about has been me. If I die here, I don't want to die having lied about everything in my life. It's the little comfort I'll allow myself.

"That's..." Nadia shakes her head, eyes wide.

"Impressive, and you're so young," Melody finishes.

"I look younger than I am. I also graduated high school early, so there's that." I shrug.

"What were you even doing with all of those languages?" Nadia asks.

I tilt my head from side to side. "This and that."

Even when you've lost all hope, you don't break. A little voice in my head chuckles. *Uncle Ben would be so proud.*

"What languages do you speak?" Olivia asks softly.

I look down at her, and my heart hurts. No child should ever go through anything like this, I should know. Worst of all, she won't have a Tristano to save her. Not that I do anymore.

I think that's what hurts the most. I truly believed he would ride in like the dark knight he always promised to be. So far, he hasn't shown. The disappointment is killing me. Knowing I will never hear his voice again.

Shaking my head, I push away the depressing thoughts. "English, American Sign Language, Italian, and Spanish." I pause. "Before I was taken, I was teaching myself Arabic. I also know a few words in Russian and Japanese."

Before they can say anything, the door opens again, instantly sucking the air out of the room. We all tense and hold our breaths. The men have their faces and bodies completely covered, giving nothing away. I watch as they pull another girl across the room before dropping her.

"So thin," the man sneers with a thick Eastern European accent.

The other man chuckles as he locks the door.

"Hey." Mandy nudges the new girl. "Do you know what day of the week it is?"

"Why?" the girl asks as she pushes herself up.

"Because I'm curious," Mandy deadpans.

"I think I was taken last night, but I can't be sure. They knocked me out. If it was yesterday, then it's Tuesday."

"Were you taken in Chicago?" I ask.

"Yeah," she says as she looks around.

She isn't acting like the other girls that have been taken. She's not scared or freaking out. She's calm. Something isn't right about her.

"What is it?" I ask as I study her.

"Can you keep a secret?" she asks quietly as she moves closer to me.

The girls and I, even Olivia, lean forward.

"Yesterday one of the girls I sometimes work with brought three guys around." She licks her dry lips. "Scary guys, but they were nice."

"And..." Nadia waves her hand at the girl, urging her along.

"They gave us these." The girl pulls up her hospital gown, and on her inner thigh is a clear patch.

"What is that?" Melody asks as she leans farther forward.

"I don't know exactly. They just told us all that we needed to wear them because some bad guys were taking women, and if we were grabbed they would be able to find us." She smiles. "I was supposed to check in at noon today and didn't. That means they will be on their way, right?"

I push down the bubbling sense of hope. She has a motherfucking tracker on her.

"What do you remember about these guys that gave it to you?" I ask lightly.

She seems to think this is a good thing, and it might be, but what if the guys rescue us only to force us into something worse? I want to hope for the best but prepare for the worst.

"Besides the fact they were handsome?" She tilts her head. "I think the one was Yakuza." Her eyes widen. "You know, like the Mafia. Jada knew him well, which I know she used to have a cushy job at The Currency at one point. The other two though, I'm not sure. One had a slight accent. Almost sounded Irish or British. The hottest one wasn't from here. He had more of a New York accent." She shakes her head. "None of them looked twice at any of us though. They know they are way above our league. A pity, really. I'd quit the trade for a man like that."

Shutting my eyes, I choke back a sob as she continues to drone on about the men.

It can't be, can it? It's not. My mind is playing games on me. There is no way that he's found me, not now and after all this time. It's some other guy with a New York accent. It has to be.

I can't let myself hope that he found his way to Chicago for me. I'll break when it eventually comes to light that it's not him.

"Are you okay?" Olivia whispers.

"I'm fine." I smile weakly.

"Maybe the men will find us," she says under her breath so the others don't hear her.

She looks so hopeful that I can't bear to crush it, so I force a smile. "I guess we will find out, huh?"

Tristano

"How long have you lived here?" I ask as I look around Declan's place.

"Eh, right after I moved back here from my time with you guys."

"It's...homey." I fight back my laughter.

The place is bare. Nothing on the walls. A futon couch is pushed up against the wall without even a TV in the living room. The kitchen is open-concept but has nothing on the counters, not even a toaster. It looks like he just moved in. If what he is saying is true, he's been here at least two years.

"Yeah, yeah..." he groans. "In my defense, I'm only here to sleep."

I raise my hands. "I'm not judging."

Declan raises his brow as he walks toward me. "I've seen your place. I know you're judging."

Declan stayed with me when he shadowed Greer in New York. They wanted to keep an eye on him since he was coming from a faction that wasn't too happy with Killian's rule. Turned out, the kid was loyal to his true leader, which is why he's now second in command.

"There is nothing wrong with my place," I argue.

"Got it," he says as he grabs his phone from his nightstand before turning to me. "You have enough pillows and blankets to bed a third-world country. What man has throw pillows when he doesn't even have a woman living with him?"

A man who hopes one day he will have a woman living with him maybe? Or maybe I just like nice things. I never had that growing up. I don't admit any of that to him though.

"We need to make another stop before we head to work," I demand.

"Why? What do you need now?" He sighs as if I'm exhausting.

In his defense, most of the people in my life act that way around me. Like I'm a puppy that never stops. I can't help it though. It's just who I am. I blame my mom for abandoning me at my nonna's at such a young age. I didn't get the right attachments.

I point to his bed. "Dude, you have a pillow and a sheet. That's it. I can't in good conscience go back to New York until I know you have proper bedding."

Declan rolls his eyes. "You're ridiculous."

"But you love me," I say as we walk out of the door. "This is a nice building."

"Yeah, it's not bad. Owned by the family."

The door across the hall opens and a woman walks out, but pauses when she sees us.

"Declan," she says coolly, with a slight accent.

I watch as my friend tenses before releasing a breath and turning around. "Nikita."

The two of them stand still, glaring each other down.

"The sexual tension between you two..."

The bombshell finally turns toward me and eyes me up and down. "And you are?"

"His best friend. I like your hair and your style." I point. Her hair is a dark-brown, but the ends are colored a vibrant blue. She's wearing all black. What I have to guess is a bodysuit with skin-tight jeans, a leather jacket, and biker boots. Totally not my type, but gorgeous nonetheless.

"Thanks. I change it often." She smiles. "I should warn you, this one would make for a shit roommate."

Declan scoffs. "As lovely as always, Trouble. I'm sure I'll see you later."

Declan turns and storms down the hall. I wave at the pretty woman and follow behind. Once back in the car, I turn toward him, smirking. "So what's the story there?"

"There is no story."

"Psh, I might have been born at night, but not last night. Tell me."

"Are you going to tell me about your girl?" He shoots me a look.

"You mean what you haven't already figured out?" I smirk. "She's beautiful, inside and out. Even though she's a cop, she doesn't ask questions and lets me do my thing with zero judgment." I pause, shrugging my shoulder. "Then again, it probably helps that we killed someone together once. Seriously though, she's the best."

He does a double take.

"Wait, what? You killed someone together?" he asks as we get into his car.

I grimace. "I'm invoking the best friend pact on that one. I wasn't supposed to tell anyone."

"That's not a thing," he informs me.

"It better be or I'll have to kill you. Two can keep a secret if one of them is dead," I deadpan.

He shakes his head. "She's a cop? You've never worried about being tied to her?"

I shake my head before he can even finish the question. "Nah. We're careful. We only talk on burner phones that I send her. I've only seen her once since that first time. We take all the precautions necessary to keep our friendship private. Enough about us, what about your little Trouble?"

Declan glares before looking back at the road. "Don't call her that. Her name is Nikita."

Holding up my hands, I tell him, "No nicknames, got it. Now tell me."

"She's here on refuge. Her father is Russian and worked under Ivan. He didn't want to run back home with his tail between his legs, so he made a deal with Haruaki. He could stay, but his daughter belongs to the Yakuza. Or us by extension since Haruaki didn't trust her enough to keep her at one of his properties."

"So now you have a hot chick across the hall. I'm not seeing the problem."

He snorts. "She's vile. She creates all kinds of noise all the time. I swear she does it to annoy me."

"Sounds like the key elements to a great hate fuck."

"Fuck her? Hell, no. My dick might fall off."

"Or he would have the time of his life." I shrug.

Before he can say anything else, his phone rings.

"Yeah?" he asks as it connects to Bluetooth.

"It's go time. One of the girls we suited up didn't report in. Location is showing her at a warehouse about twenty minutes south of the city." Kenji's voice comes through the speaker.

Declan looks my way. "On our way."

My heart feels like it could beat out of my chest. This could be it. In just a little while I could be holding Serena in my arms.

Turning, I look out the window and brace myself for both the good and bad. This could be it or it could be nothing. One thing is for sure, I won't stop looking until I find her.

Logically, I understand the waiting and watching, but this time it kills me. I feel as if I'm coming out of my skin. It takes everything in me not to pace.

"Alright, the place is empty. We have guys watching the entrances and exits. We go in, and we get out. Follow me. Faraday cages," he says referring to a device that blocks all signals. "Go on in three, two, one. Move out," Sean says.

As a unit, we walk through the vacant property, clearing it as we go. We come to a stop outside of the warehouse door, and I feel as if I could puke.

This is it.

As Sean starts picking the lock, we all scan the area. When the chain falls, everything goes silent. Turning back to the door, I watch as one of Callum's men slides the door open as several of the men point their guns inside.

Women scream in fear, and as fucked up as it is, I smile.

I don't know if I've found her yet, but we've found women who were being trafficked. Either way, it's a win.

Declan walks in quickly, and I follow. Reaching into my pocket, I pull out a flashlight and pan around the room.

Women. Children. All chained up like they are dogs.

"Sabrina," I call out her cover name first, even though it feels wrong.

"Tris?"

I drop my head to my chest and laugh. Nothing about this is funny, but it's better than crying.

"Where are you, *anima gemella*?" I ask, fighting back the emotion.

"Back here. Seriously Tris, if you don't get these chains off of me, I'm going to haunt you," she jokes, her voice cracking.

Raising the flashlight, I pan it over the area it sounds like her voice came from. Sure enough, I find her with a young girl curled up next to her. I choke back the bile as I look at her. I've never been so thankful for the shadows until now. I thought I was prepared to see her in any condition, but I was wrong. She looks like hell, but I'll never tell her that.

"I thought I taught you how to get out of cuffs?" I say as I approach.

Setting the light on the ground, I reach into my pocket for lockpicks and get to work. The entire time I watch her closely, making sure she doesn't flinch away from me.

"Yeah, well, I was taken by guys with half a brain. They didn't leave anything for me to use, and I've never seen ones like this."

The thick cuffs look as if they should be used on animals, not humans.

I don't know what to say, so I hum. As soon as the cuffs fall off of her, she lunges forward, tackling me. Slowly, I wrap my arms around her and hold her close.

I found her.

She's safe.

I'm never letting her go again.

Relief flows through me. I kept telling myself that I would find her, but after a while that optimism started to dim, and I wasn't so sure.

"I knew you'd come," she whispers into my ear.

I feel the tears falling down her cheeks and hitting mine as I fight back my own.

"Always, *anima gemella*," I murmur, squeezing her tight.

"Guys, we're on a tight schedule. We need to go," Declan calls out, bringing me back to the present.

"Sorry," Serena says softly, voice full of shame.

"It's okay. Now introduce me to your friend," I say, looking back at the young girl.

"This is Olivia."

"Hi Olivia, I'm Sabrina's friend, Tris. Is it okay if I get those off of you?" I ask, pointing at the cuffs.

She nods, holding out her hands. I quickly undo her cuffs, only to be knocked back on my ass as she also rushes into my arms, hugging me.

"Thank you. Thank you so much," she repeats over and over as she cries into me.

I look over her shoulder at Serena, seeing her crying as she watches us.

Moving the girl until I can stand, I pick her up in my arms. Then I hold my hand out to Serena.

She interlocks her fingers with mine as I escort them both out of the warehouse.

We might have won today, but at what cost?

These girls will never be the same again.

I look back to Serena.

How much damage can she take until she breaks for good?

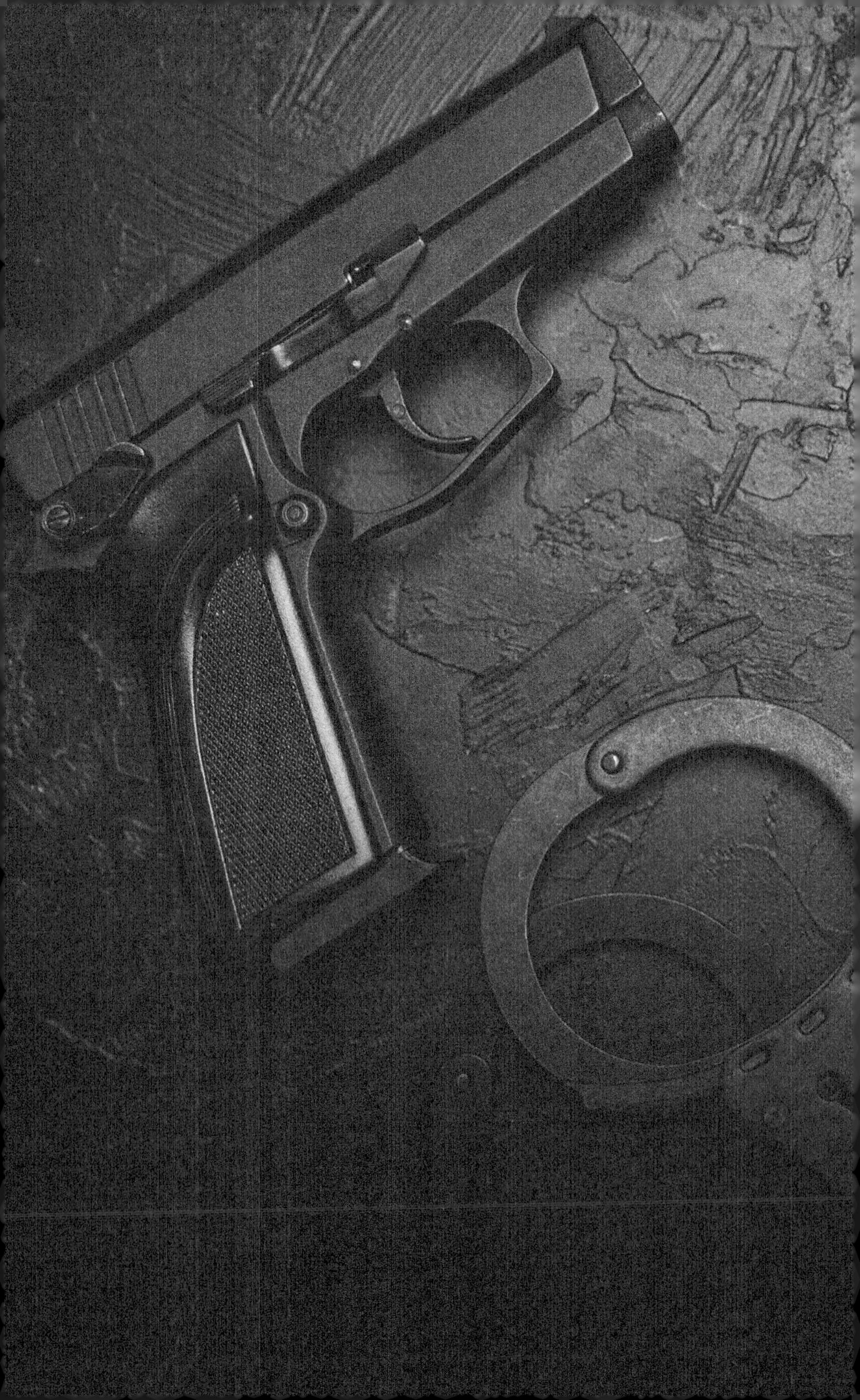

CHAPTER SEVEN

Serena

"Thank you," I say to the nurse as she leaves the room.

My eyes shift toward Tristano. He's sitting in a chair with his legs spread, his arms resting on his knees, and his head bowed. I've never seen him with any facial hair until now, and just like I thought when I was seventeen, it makes him all that more attractive.

"How are you?" he asks, keeping his head down.

"What?" I ask, shaking my head.

Tristano looks up and smirks. "Like what you see?"

I roll my eyes. "You know I do. That sweatshirt looks comfortable."

And smells like you, I don't say.

Tristano stands, and as he takes off the hoodie, it pulls his shirt up, showing off his abs.

I may have just gone through something traumatic, but I'm not dead. Good to know.

"Here," he says, holding the piece of clothing out for me.

"Are you sure?" I ask as I reach for it.

"What's mine is yours. You know that."

I clear my throat. "I'm not wearing anything under this." I point to the hospital gown.

"Do you want me to turn around?" he asks.

"I'm just warning you," I admit softly.

I place his hoodie in my lap. After pulling off the hospital gown, I toss it toward the trash can, not wanting to ever see it again.

Tristano makes a noise. Looking back over at him, I watch him rub the back of his neck as he tries to look everywhere but my chest. Slowly I pick up his hoodie and put it on, and sure enough, I catch him looking one last time.

"So…" I ask.

"So…" He raises a brow. "How are you?"

"Oh, I'm peachy. You?" I say sarcastically.

"Same," he says, playing along. "Anything new going on with you?"

"Oh, you know, got off one case, started looking into something else, got taken, then was saved by a dark knight." I shrug.

I watch as some emotion I can't name goes across his eyes.

"Dark knight, huh? Was he good-looking?" he chokes out.

"Eh." I shrug.

Tristano laughs as he approaches. When he gets within reach, he hesitates, and I hate it.

"You can touch me, Tris. I want you to touch me. Need it even."

"Are you sure?"

I start nodding before he can even finish asking. "I know you would never hurt me."

Holding my arms out, I spread my legs, making room for him to step close. Like always, he doesn't leave me waiting. Tristano steps forward and wraps his arms around me and buries his face in my hair.

Shutting my eyes, I take a deep breath and breathe him in.

I'm safe.

He found me.

It's over.

"I don't know how you do it," I murmur against his chest.

"Do what, *anima gemella*?" he asks as he kisses the top of my head.

"You always know when I need you."

"I made you a promise when we were kids, and I'll never break it. I'd charge through the gates of hell if it meant saving you."

"Don't say that." I shake my head as tears fill my eyes. "The thought of losing you..."

"Hey..." He rubs his hands up and down my back. "Don't worry, you never will."

A knock at the door has us pulling apart.

"Come in," Tristano says.

I watch as one of the men from earlier steps into the room. "Sorry for interrupting."

"It's okay, what's up?" Tristano asks.

The man looks at me. "I'm Declan. A friend of Tristano's."

"Nice to meet you. Thank you for coming when you did."

He flashes me a smile. "You're welcome." He looks at Tristano before looking back at me. "Some of the girls out there are getting restless, wondering where Sabrina is," he says, raising a brow.

I answer without thinking.

"I used my undercover name." I cringe as soon as the words leave my mouth.

This man clearly works with Tristano and now knows I work for the police.

"It's okay," Tristano soothes as he rubs my back. "Declan's safe and already knows."

"No judgment from me on what you do for a job." Declan smirks.

"Same." I smile as I slide off of the doctor's table. "You said some of the girls want me?"

"Yeah. We don't know exactly what all happened to you ladies, so we're keeping our distance for now, but we need to start talking to everyone and making a game plan."

"Sounds good. Could I maybe get some pants first? In fact, all the women will want pants and other clothes."

"I already have Miya working on it. Until she gets here, I can see if the doctor we brought in has any spare scrubs for now."

"Thank you."

He leaves in search of pants as Tris turns me toward him. He lets his forehead fall to mine. We stand like that, soaking in the comfort we each offer one another.

When Declan comes back, he turns around, letting me pull the scrub pants up.

"The other girls are all in our main meeting room. I know it would have been better to take you to a real hospital, but the cops ask too many questions." He winces. "No offense. This was the best we could do. We have everyone hooked up to some IVs and given them something small to eat. The last thing we need is for them to overeat after going without for so long and making themselves sick. We are trying to make this as easy as possible."

"Let's get this done then," I tell him.

"Are you sure you're ready for this?" Tris's brows furrow.

Reaching up, I run my thumb over the spot. "Don't frown or you'll get wrinkles."

"I'm not worried, that's what Botox is for," he says, making me roll my eyes.

"Can you believe this guy?" I stick my thumb out over my shoulder, pointing at Tristano.

"Ridiculous, right? He wanted to stop earlier and pick out a bedding set for me. As if we didn't have other shit to do."

Tristano scoffs from behind me. "And we're still getting you a set. Shit, Serena would agree with me too if she saw the state of your apartment. At this rate, you'll never get laid by Trouble."

Declan glares at Tristano. "Ohhh, who's Trouble?" I ask.

"Her name is Nikita, and right now she's not important," Declan grunts, holding open the door for us.

"She's totally important," Tristano whispers into my ear, making me laugh.

As soon as we clear the door, I see what they meant by the meeting room. I must have been held in an office off of the large room with couches and chairs placed strategically around.

"Sabrina!" Olivia shouts as she rushes toward me.

She hits me so hard she pushes me backward into Tristano.

"How are you doing, sweetheart?" I ask as I run my hand over her head.

"I'm okay. They said I'm only a little dehydrated." She smiles up at me. "Do you think we can go home soon?"

"I'm not sure yet, but I'll figure that out."

"Hey stranger," Mandy says as she approaches.

"Hey." I nod to her.

There's a knowing in her eyes. She was held the longest, so she's been affected the most. We don't have the overwhelming joy like Olivia has. She was only held a couple days. She will bounce back easily. Mandy and I will have a longer road. We will be having nightmares about this for many years to come.

"You didn't tell us you had a boyfriend," Mandy expresses, giving me a small nod back.

We made it. That's what that nod says.

Tristano speaks up before I can. "She didn't," he gasps. "Are you ashamed of me, *anima gemella*?"

"You're ridiculous." I roll my eyes as I fight off a smile.

He's not my boyfriend, but he's always kind of felt like he was. I always wanted him to be.

"It's one of the reasons you love me," he says, squeezing my shoulders.

"You guys are cute together. I'm glad you had someone looking for you," Mandy adds, giving me a sad look.

Mandy wasn't one of the teens taken who have a home to go back to. She was homeless after coming out to her parents. They didn't approve of her lifestyle and told her that she could either go to conversion camp or get out of their house.

She's only seventeen, but she might as well be thirty with everything she's had to live through. I make a mental note to make sure she has somewhere to go after this. She won't be homeless again.

"Ready, Sabrina?" Declan asks using my fake name.

I look at all the girls I was in the warehouse with and take a deep breath. "Listen up," I say, getting their attention. "I know you ladies may be hesitant to be alone with one of these men," I say, looking at the guys lining the wall before turning back to them. "But I can promise you they won't hurt you. They just need to ask you some questions about what we went through, what we saw, and about the night you were taken. They want to stop the people who are doing this, and the only way they are going to be able to do that is if you allow them to do this. Can you do that?"

"Will you stay with me?" Olivia asks, making me look down at her cuddled against my shoulder.

"Of course." I look back up at the women. "If you're under eighteen, I'm going to sit in with you, and if any of you other ladies want me to as well, I will."

I look over at Mandy.

She understands my silent question and steps forward. "Let's get this over with."

Declan steps forward and holds out his arm. "This way."

One by one, the girls break off with different men.

"I'm so fucking proud of you," Tristano whispers before kissing the shell of my ear.

I squeeze my eyes shut and fight off the tears. Would he still be proud if he knew I was barely holding it together?

Tristano

I KNEW before we started interviewing the girls that Serena was barely holding it together. She had this wild look in her eyes that reminded me of when she was seventeen and I found her. The way she wanted to talk about anything other than what she just experienced made me angry, but I held it in. She doesn't deserve my anger. No, the only thing she needs from me is peace, and I'll do whatever I can to give it to her.

When we started interviewing the girls and getting everything down that they remembered, I watched her one by one shut down. At first she kept her face carefully blank. She only allowed emotion to show when the girls weren't looking directly at her. By the end, she had no reaction whatsoever, and it's as if she isn't even here.

I'm afraid she's shut down. Gone numb to it all. She needs to face this, not push it down. I'm worried what it will do to her psyche.

"Are you okay?" I ask as the last girl slips out.

"Have I ever been okay?" she asks quietly as she plays with the cuff of my hoodie.

Pushing off the wall, I walk to her and pull her into my arms without a second thought. At first she was tense in my arms before finally relaxing. Her hands grasp onto my shirt as if it was a lifeline as I press my face into the top of her head.

"I feel broken," she rasps.

"No," I say gruffly. Leaning back, I cup her face and make her eyes meet mine. "You are not broken, Serena, but even if you are, that's okay too."

"What makes you so sure?"

Her eyes look like the deepest of pools with tears falling down her cheeks.

"Because even broken things can be put back together. The pieces might not fit perfectly, but there's beauty in the imperfect at the end of the day, and you, Serena, you are beautiful. I've watched you from afar pick yourself up and put yourself back together, and you'll do it again."

Serena shakes her head. "I-I don't know if I can. I don't know if I have it in me. For fuck's sake, Tris, what were the chances of me getting taken not once but twice in my life?"

"Then I'll do it for you," I say full of conviction. "You have me."

She pulls her face out of my hands and buries it against my stomach to hide her tears.

"You said we couldn't be together. How are you going to put me back together when I can't even be with you?"

"We make changes. Fuck, *anima gemella*, I will tell my Don I'm out right now if that's what you need," I tell her as I run my hands through her hair.

Serena takes a deep breath. "Tris..."

Before she can say anything else, there's a knock on the door.

"Yeah?" I call out as Serena pulls away, wiping away her tears.

The door opens, and Declan pops his head in. "Sorry to interrupt, but Sabrina is the only one left I need to interview."

Instinctively I want to say I can do it, but I don't know if I would be able to separate myself far enough from the situation to be able to do so. There's no way I would make her go through all of that without stopping her to make her feel better.

"Is that alright with you, *anima gemella*?" I ask her.

"If you trust him, then so do I." She smiles at me softly before turning to Declan. "Let's do this."

Declan comes in and shuts the door behind him. He takes a seat and holds out his phone. "Is it okay if I record you?"

"Of course." Serena nods, taking a seat as well.

"Will you stand for a minute, please, *anima gemella*?"

Serena's brows crinkle, but she does as I ask.

"What are you doing?" she asks as I sit down in her chair.

I hold out my hand, and as soon as she places hers in mine, I pull her down so she's sitting in my lap. Wrapping my arms around her middle, I lay my head on her back.

"Are you ready?" Declan asks.

I feel her take a deep breath. "Ready."

As Serena gives him a play-by-play from the moment she left work to the time we found her, I hold on to her. Doing everything in my power to give her every ounce of my strength and to hold her together.

It fills my chest with pride when she says that she knew I would come searching when I didn't hear from her, but it breaks my heart when admits toward the end she started to give up hope.

"The other girls mentioned being drugged and losing pieces of time," Declan says, pulling me out of my head.

"They would give us medicated water and would check under our tongues to make sure we swallowed. I attempted to try and withhold from drinking it as long as possible. I hated losing control like that. I would only sip it, pouring the rest out when I heard them coming."

"I don't blame you," Declan mutters.

I pull my head up and murmur into her ear. "I'm proud of you."

Declan meets my eye, and I can see his silent apology. "I have to ask…"

Serena starts shaking her head before he can even ask. "They never raped me. They wanted to keep the inventory as intact as possible as far as I could tell. I did anger them once and demanded more water. He said something about putting us on the dark web and selling us off. They took photos too."

Closing my eyes, I take a deep breath I hadn't realized I had been holding. Thank God she didn't have to go through that again. If they had raped her, I would have gone crazy knowing I couldn't keep her from that a second time.

"I'm glad. For your sake. We will have to look into this dark web stuff. We have been checking it, but none of you girls have shown up on there yet," Declan tells her.

"What happens now? I mean to the girls."

"Now we start reaching out to the ones with families and getting them home. For the others, we will work on getting them help and to where they want to go. Give them a fresh start at life."

"I like that," she murmurs softly. "Mandy doesn't have a home. I don't want her to ever have to worry again. Can you make that happen?"

"Yes. I promise. I will set her up with a job and give her a paid-for apartment. I will make sure she never has to worry again. I promise."

"Therapy. Make her get therapy too. She's going to need it," Serena murmurs.

"We will. What about you? Are you going to reach out to work?"

"Dec..." I warn, anger seeping into my tone.

Serena squeezes my arm. "It's fine. I expected him to ask." She pauses as she thinks it over. "Did they ever report me as missing or anything?"

"A report was filed by an uncle..." I trail off.

"Uncle Ben. He's a family friend who took me in when my grandfather passed away. He's also the chief of police in Jersey City and my boss," Serena informs us.

"So he knows you're missing," Declan states.

We fall silent as we let her think about that.

"I can't tell him where I was or what I was doing," she finally admits. "He told me to not pursue the missing girls anymore. I went on my own against his wishes. That's how I was taken. I didn't have a team with me. No one watching my back."

I grit my teeth. "Why didn't you tell me? I would have come and watched your back. You can't go off on your own."

She sniffles. "I know. I didn't even think to call you. That's my cop side of life. You're the gray area. I don't mix you two. It never even occurred to me that you might come for something like that."

"Maybe that's the issue. You are leading two lives. You're at the fork in the road now. You're going to need to make a decision," Declan declares.

"Declan, don't pressure her. She can do whatever she wants. It will never affect us." I growl.

"It already is. She didn't come to you for fear that you being a part of that life would either get her in trouble or get you in trouble. She can't keep leading this secret life. She needs to make a choice." He crosses his arms over his chest.

"She has all the time in the world to decide what she wants. Even if she decides to stay a cop forever and even turn me in, I'm still going to have her back. Stop making it seem like she can't have her cake and eat it too."

"She can't."

"STOP!" Serena yells, making us both shut up. "She is sitting right fucking here and can make her own decisions. Tris, I get why you are defending me, but Declan's right. I've always had one foot on each side of the law. I can't live this way forever. I have a lot to think about."

I pause. "Thank you, Declan. I appreciate your advice. I'd like some time to think things over."

He nods. "Of course. I'm not trying to pressure you. Really, I'm not. I just want what's best for you both."

"I get that and appreciate you looking out for Tristano. He needs friends like you."

I can't even say a word as Declan nods once more and slips from the room. I don't like where this is going. She agrees she needs to make a choice.

What if that choice isn't me?

"Can you take me back to your room and lie with me? I don't want to be alone, but I need some sleep."

"Of course. Anything you need, *anima gemella*."

She doesn't even realize that she could ask for the breath in my lungs and I would give it to her.

I'd do anything to ensure she's happy.

Even leave her alone.

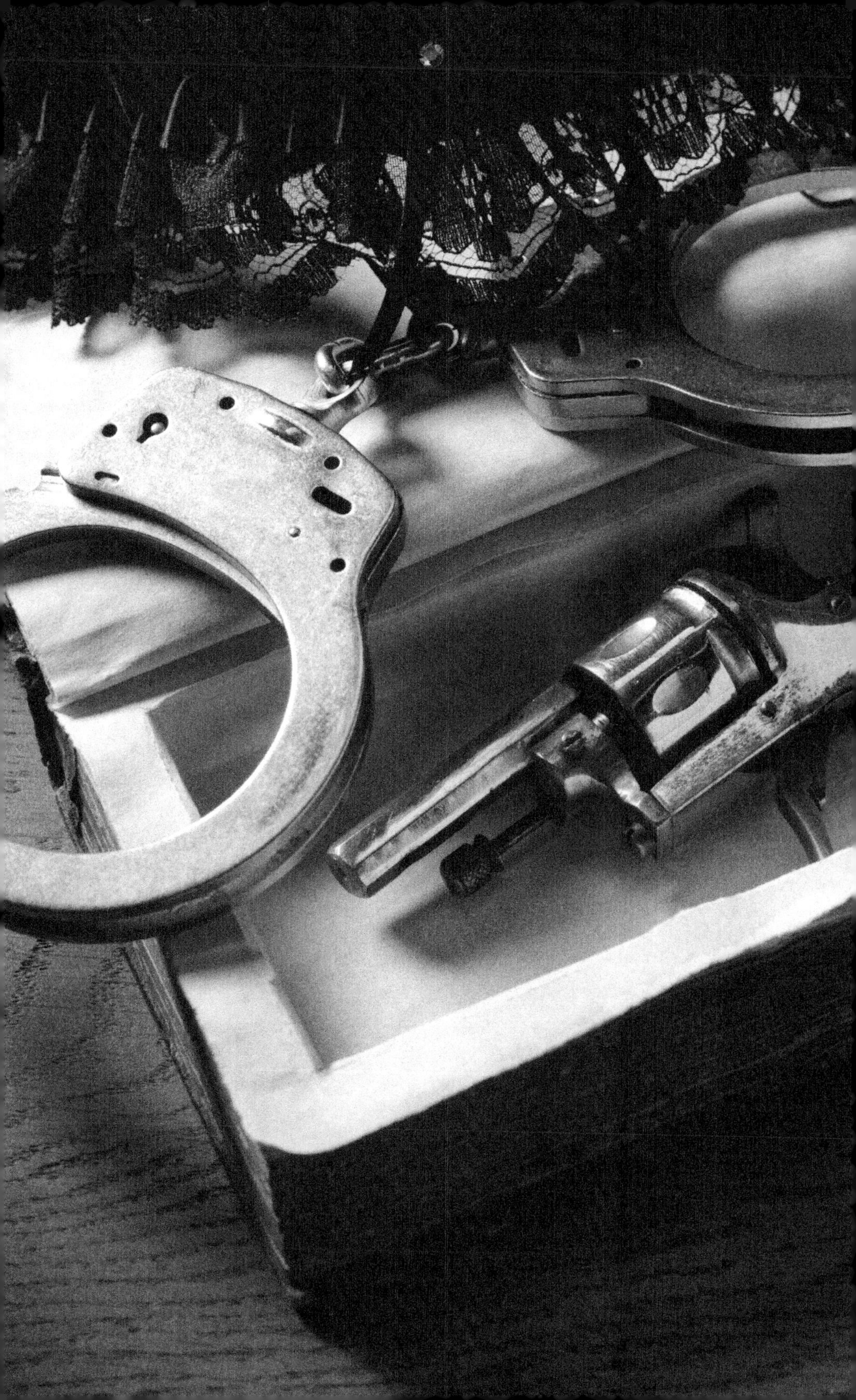

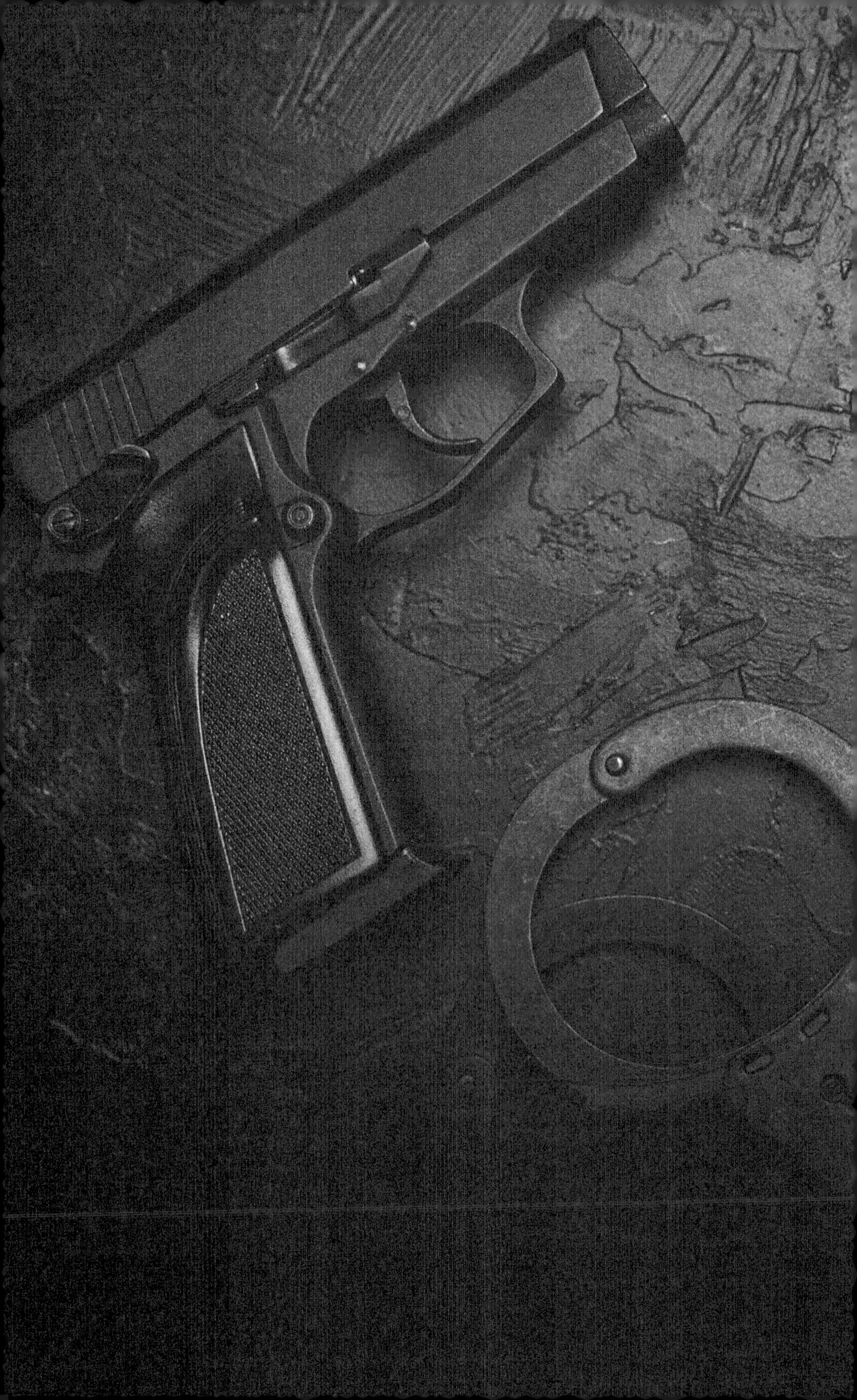

CHAPTER EIGHT

Serena

"Are you hungry?" Tristano asks as we step into the hotel suite.

I shake my head. "This room is insane and totally not necessary."

"Personally, I like it. Now food?" he says as he tosses the key onto the entry table.

"I'm not hungry, but I know I should eat," I tell him as I walk farther into the room. "It's almost like because we haven't eaten in so long that my body is used to it. I think we will need to start light."

This place has windows that span the entire wall, overlooking downtown Chicago. There's a living space in the middle, with a door on each side leading to the two bedrooms. The place is bright white with pops of green. It's probably the nicest place I've ever stayed.

"Serena."

I shake my head and look over my shoulder at Tristano and see him frowning.

"I'm sorry, did you say something?"

He tilts his head to the side, studying me. "Do you have any preferences, or do you just want me to order you whatever?"

"Surprise me," I say as I look away.

It hurts to look at him. Not because he's done something wrong, but because all I want to do is fall into his arms and cry my eyes out. I won't let myself though. It's not his job to pick me up when I fall, even though I know he would do it.

"Does this place have a tub?" I ask as I move toward one of the bedroom doors.

"It does. Why don't you go take a bath, and then I'll call you when the food gets here," he says behind me as I open the bedroom door.

"Sounds good." I walk farther into the room and make my way into the bathroom.

Sure enough, there's a giant soaker tub situated against the wall with a window on the other side, overlooking Chicago. I leave the door open a crack and turn on the tub. As it fills, I strip off my clothes. Once naked, I take a deep breath and look at myself in the mirror.

The girl looking back looks nothing like me. My skin is so pale you can see the purple of my veins popping through. My naturally slim body has only become thinner, my hip bones protruding from my skin. I literally flinch at the sight. All my muscle definition that I worked years for is gone, and I don't even want to think about how long it will take to get it back.

I look sick, hell, I probably am.

Turning away from the mirror, I shut off the tub. I hiss as I get in, the water temperature so hot it instantly turns my skin red. As my body adjusts to the water, the tears start to fall, everything hitting me at once.

After I was taken the first time, I promised myself that I would never put myself in the position to get taken again unintentionally. I knew with going undercover that it could happen, but I was prepared and could breathe easier knowing someone was watching and could save me if I gave them the sign. This time though, I was caught off guard. I let my pride get the best of me and made a stupid decision.

I had been working the streets so long that I was desensitized to the danger of them. It's weird how living a certain way for a period of time can make you forget all about what brought you there in the first place. Even meeting these older men who thought they were getting with an underage girl no longer frightened me. Why would they? Ricky has always been outside, ready to swoop in and rescue me.

Not this time. No, this time I let my complacency get the best of me. I never should have been on those streets. For that one moment, I was one of those girls. Just a working girl getting abducted with no one knowing where they were.

I hate it. I hate being weak. I hate being scared. Holding on to the sides of the tub, I take a deep breath and submerge myself under the water, letting the tears fall faster as my body shakes.

I don't know how long I stay under, but I start to become lightheaded. Before I can come up for air, I feel hands grabbing me, pulling me up. I gasp too soon and suck in a bunch of water.

"What the fuck were you doing?" Tristano hisses as he hits my back as I cough up water.

"What the fuck, Tris?" I say between coughs.

"What the fuck is right, Serena. Were you trying to kill yourself?"

I look over at him and see the fear in his eyes.

Oh shit.

I can see how that might look like I was committing suicide. Especially after what I just went through. Add to that, he knows my past too.

"No." I shake my head as I reach out, grabbing his arm. "No, I promise. I would never."

I mean it too. I have way too much to live for. No matter what life throws at me, I will always fight until the very end. I would never voluntarily give up the ability to breathe.

"You were under there so long you didn't even notice when I came in," he says as he rests back on his haunches as he kneels next to the tub.

"I'm so sorry, Tris." I stumble out of the tub into his lap. "It all became too much. I needed a minute of complete silence, and that was the only way I could get it."

I watch as hurt flashes through his eyes before he shoves it down. "I see."

"It's not you. It's my thoughts. Everything that happened."

His Adam's apple bobs. "I know." He clears his throat. "I came in here to tell you that the food is here."

"Already?"

"Yeah, you've been in here for about forty-five minutes."

"Oh." I hadn't even realized it had been that long.

Tristano pushes me forward until I'm sitting on the floor before he stands. He holds his hand out for me to grab as he helps me stand next to him. Then he turns, grabbing a towel.

As he does that, I turn back to the bath to unplug the drain. I hear a choking sound, making me look back.

Tristano is staring at my ass, a look of surprise on his face.

"Sorry." He coughs, closes his eyes, and holds out the towel. "I'll be in the living room if you need me."

I grab the towel, smiling to myself. I should feel violated having him look at me, but I don't. Seeing the look on his face made me feel desired. Wanted. Like maybe I'm more than the situations that have happened to me.

I'm still a woman.

"I'll be there in a minute."

I can't help but watch him as he walks away. Shaking my head, I dry off and grab one of the robes off the back of the door. Slipping it on, I tie it around my waist. With my hair wet, hanging down around my shoulders, I leave the bathroom.

As soon as I step into the living room, I see Tristano sitting on the couch. He's leaning forward with his head resting in his hands. I honestly don't know if I've ever seen him look so down.

One of the things I love about Tristano Ferrari is that he's so full of life, and right now his spark is missing.

"Hey..." I say hesitantly as I step into the room.

He looks over his shoulder and offers me a small smile. "Hey, come here and eat."

I watch as he places a pillow on the floor between his legs, in front of the table.

"How about you sit here and eat while I deal with your hair," he says with a smile.

Wordlessly, I do as he says. As soon as I sit down, he moves my hair behind me. Picking up the bowl of soup, I bring it to my chest. Then I take a small spoonful of broth.

Slowly I feel Tristano start brushing my hair from the bottom up.

The silence is loud but comforting.

"What's next?" I ask quietly.

"Next we go home," he whispers.

"Where is home?" I scoff.

"That's up to you. You can go back to your place," he pauses. "Or you could come home and stay with me for a while."

We fall silent as I think about it. What do I want to do?

"I-I think I need to take some time off from work. I'm not sure my heart is in it anymore."

He freezes. "What do you mean?"

"I mean, I know I'm doing good right now, but I can only play a seventeen-year-old for so long. Eventually I won't even be able to do that anymore. My uncle never takes me seriously when I think I have found something. I always have to tell Ricky, and then he tells my uncle. That's the only way he will even consider an idea I have. I guess I thought it would be different, instead all I feel like is a pawn."

He hugs my head to him, kissing the top of it. "I'm sorry. I wish it wasn't that way for you."

I shrug. "It's how it's always been. Now I have to go face him and come up with some lie for where I've been. I'm not sure he's going to buy anything I say. It's only going to make him look at me closer."

"Forget your uncle. What do you want?"

"I want to come home with you. Just until I figure out what I want to do next," I admit softly.

"Then that's what we will do. You can stay with me as long as you want, *anima gemella*."

Why does that feel like a promise of forever?

Tristano

THERE'S A RAGE FILLING ME. One that I can barely control.

The only reason I haven't left Serena in this bed to go hunt down those assholes who took her is because of the way she is shaking in her sleep.

After I fed her a meager bowl of chicken soup, she changed into a T-shirt and climbed into bed. I was going to leave her there while I sat in the living room area working through the night, but then she said that one word.

"Stay."

So I curled up in bed next to her, jeans and all. She didn't seem to mind. Instead of keeping her distance, she cuddled right up next to my side until her head was on my chest, prompting me to wrap her in my arms.

In that moment, I knew there was nowhere I'd rather be.

Then the nightmares came. She began to whimper and cry. That's when the red bled into my vision, making me seek death.

My heart is breaking for this girl.

She gasps suddenly, sitting straight up.

"Shhh, Serena. You're safe. I'm here," I soothe her.

"Tris?" Her voice is so broken.

I hate it.

"It's me. Come lie back down. It was a nightmare. Nothing more."

She does as I ask, curling back up in my arms.

"I feel like I can't get warm. I mean, logically I know I am warm, but my mind keeps replaying the cold."

"I'll make sure you're never cold again," I whisper, making her chuckle.

"You can't make a promise like that."

"Sure, I can. I will always try my best to keep it too."

She shakes her head, but she's not crying anymore.

"I still hear the screeching from the train brakes. You think they will be able to find the train line they took us on?"

"Declan is one of the best. He was trained by my boss, Greer. When she's out of the hospital, she will get on it too. We will find them," I promise.

"Why is she in the hospital? Is she okay?" Her voice suddenly seems worried.

I love that about her. She cares so deeply for others, even strangers.

"She's fine. She had a baby. They are both healthy. In fact, they are already at home recovering. I wouldn't be surprised if Greer is trying to type code while breastfeeding the little prince." I chuckle.

"Tell me more about them. More about your life," she pleads.

I've always kept myself so reserved around her. I never wanted to put her in any situation that would require her to betray either me or her profession.

Now it seems silly. I could have lost her.

So I give her what she wants.

"Greer is one tenacious woman. She really knows how to grab a guy by the balls and twist them until they do what she wants. She is a force to be reckoned with. I suppose that's to be expected. She is the little sister of my Don."

"So you work closely with a family member of the head of the Catalini Mafia?" she whispers.

"I do. Are you sure you want to hear this? I don't want you to feel like you have to keep secrets."

"I'm already keeping secrets from my uncle. I want to know you. Tell me more."

"Well, how about I tell you about how I got into the Mafia then?"

"Ooh, is it a good story?"

"I wouldn't say good, but it's not the worst. See, when I was fifteen, I got caught stealing from this bodega. I would go in there every week or so and steal small stuff like candy or bread. Then I was working up to stealing bigger items. Things I could trade for money. What I didn't know was that the bodega paid money to the Catalinis for protection. So the next time I came in, there was a man dressed in a business suit waiting for me. He put his hand on my shoulder and told me I was coming with him. I was shitting my pants too. I thought he was going to kill me. Everyone knew about the Catalinis. They are not to be fucked with."

"He didn't kill you, so what did he do?"

"Well, he took me back to this old warehouse outside the city and tied me to a chair. Then he had another man come in. Together, they questioned me. Who did I work for? Why was I stealing? Where was my family? They threatened me and scared me to the point that I was crying. I know, me, crying. I was pathetic back then. Didn't have the toughness I have nowadays."

"Sure, a real tough guy. You told me you once cried watching a cartoon movie."

"Hey, I was young," I defend myself, knowing what she's going to say next.

"It was three months ago."

"If you don't cry when that little lion's father dies, then you are a psychopath and we cannot be friends."

"Fair enough. Continue with your story, strong one."

My heart is lighter hearing the teasing in her tone. I'm helping her feel better. That's all I want.

So I go into full dramatics for the next part of my story.

"So they have this overhead light they keep shining in my eyes. They finally yell at me asking if I plan to steal again. Being the dumbass I am, I tell them the truth. That I probably would. When they finally pulled the light back and looked into my eyes, they looked astonished. When the lead man asked me why I would admit to that, I told him I knew no other way. My mother abandoned me when I was five. My nonna passed away when I was eleven. Foster families couldn't give a fuck about the kid past the paycheck they provide. All I had were my sticky fingers. They asked why I didn't get a job, and I explained that without identification you can't have a job and I had none. So instead, they took me to a tailor and got me fitted for a suit. Then they initiated me under one of their capos and told me to keep my nose out of trouble and do everything they said. If I did, they would take care of me."

"That sounds like you got lucky."

"Very. Lorenzo is one scary fucker, but he has nothing on Bastiano. I really thought they were going to kill me, so when they dropped me off with Matteo in Queens, I was surprised. I didn't think I would make it past that day and instead they gave me a future. I would do anything for this family."

"When did you realize you liked computers?"

"I always did. I would use the library computers to hack people, especially to change my grades. I don't think the family knew until they were having trouble getting into a phone one day. I jailbroke it, and the rest is history. They assigned me to shadow Greer and made me part of an elite team."

"You love them," she whispers.

"Of course I do. They are my family. I know without a doubt that they would have my back."

"I wish I had that."

"You do. You have me. I will always have your back."

She sniffles. "I'm tired of keeping you at arm's length, Tris. I don't want that anymore. I don't want to go back to only talking to you for five minutes once a month. I need more."

"Shhh. We don't have to talk about this now. We can figure all of this out," I vow.

"The only thing I want to figure out is how to make you a more permanent fixture in my life. I've never felt safer than I do when I'm in your arms," she admits.

"Then this is where you will stay. No one will make you do anything you don't want to do."

"Promise?"

"I promise, *anima gemella.*"

She yawns big. "I'm going to hold you to it."

As she starts to drift off, I whisper against her head, "I hope you do."

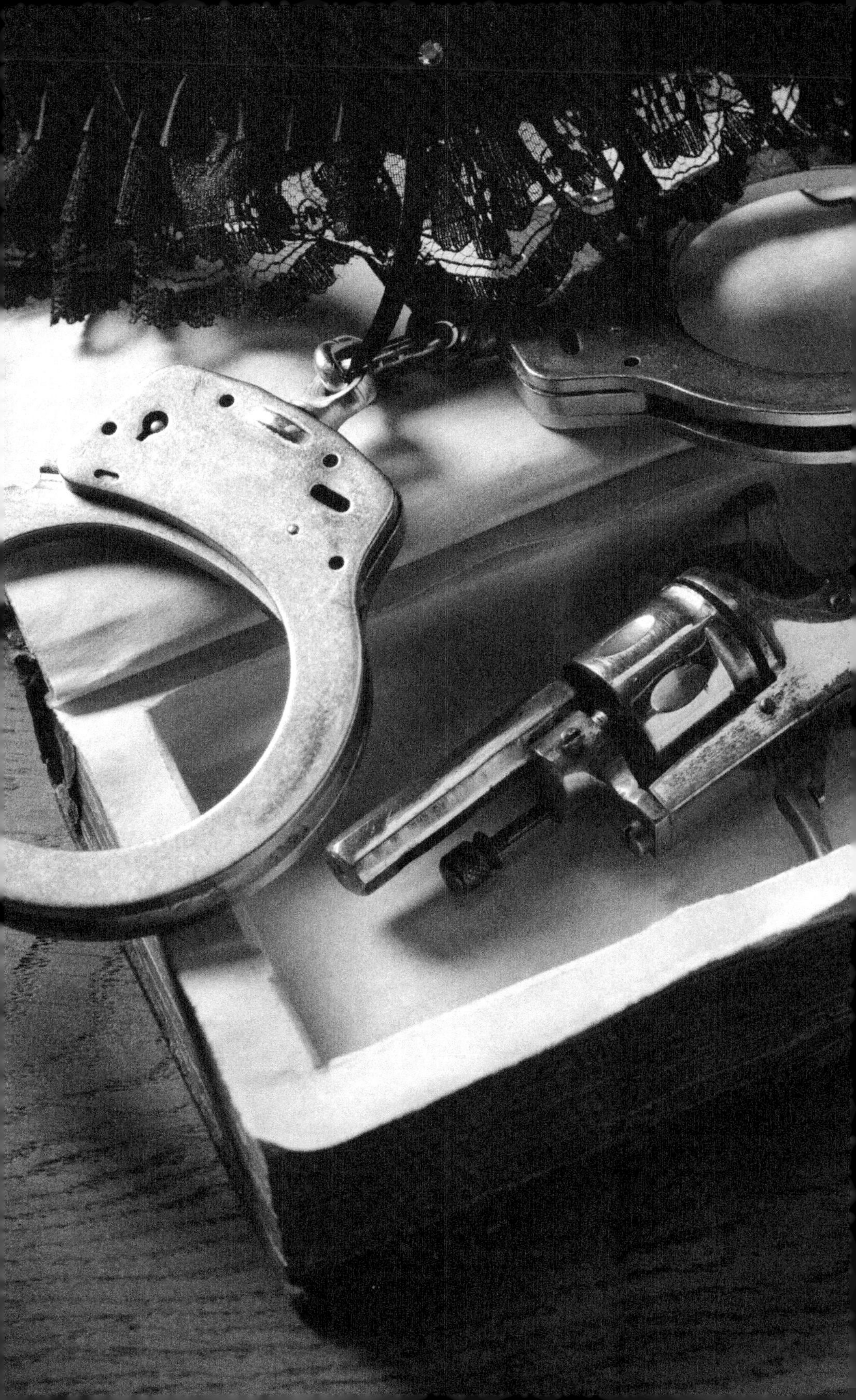

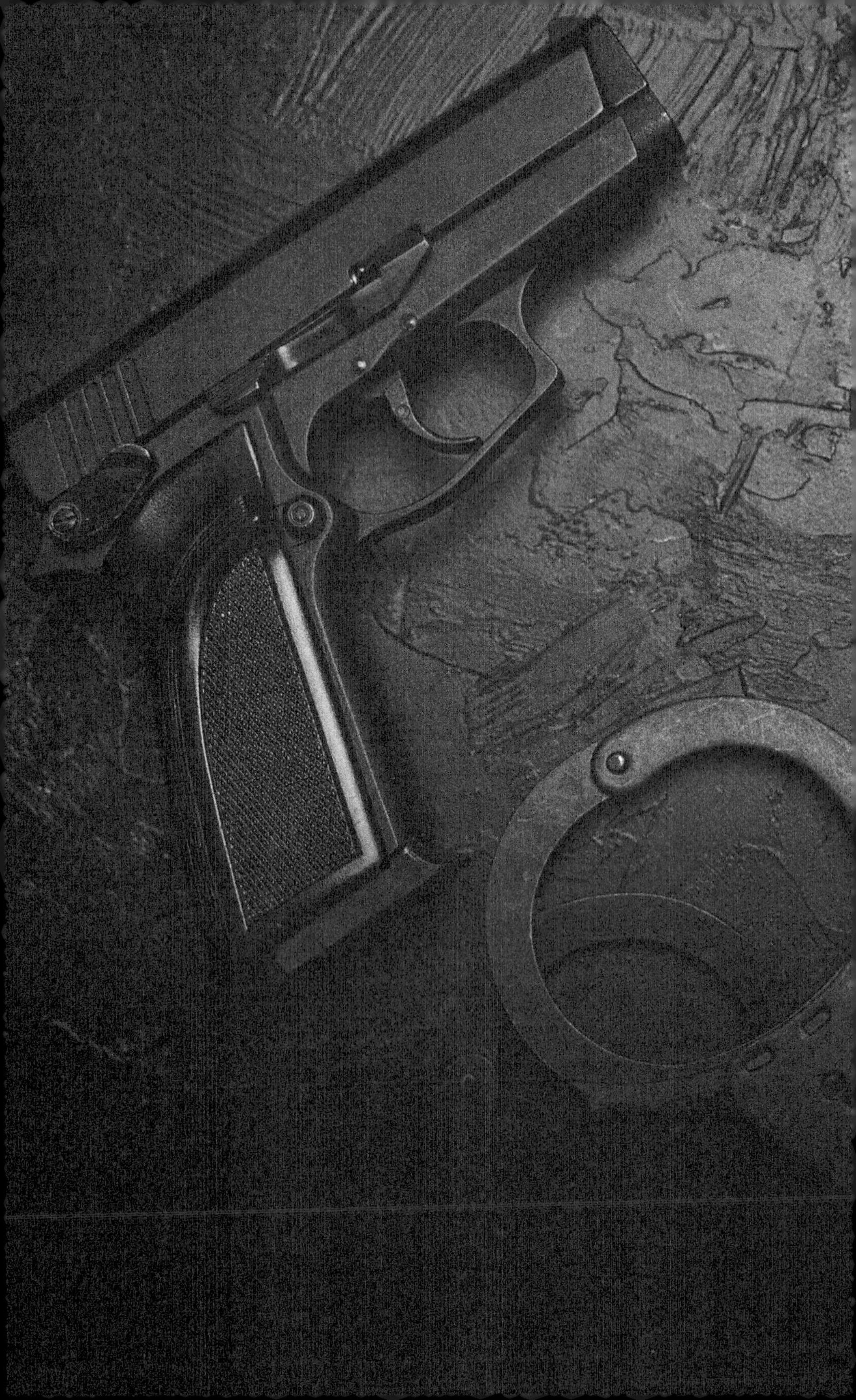

CHAPTER NINE

Serena

I can honestly say that waking up in Tristano's arms is the best thing to ever happen to me. That's not just the trauma talking either.

There's nothing quite like having the scent that calms you surrounding you along with the heat from the male cuddled next to you. Add in the sound of his rhythmic heartbeat under my ear, and I never want to leave.

I want to live here forever.

"I heard your breathing change. I know you're awake, *anima gemella*."

My heart skips a beat at hearing him call me that again. I never thought it would happen. Taking a deep breath, I get myself together. He runs his hands through my hair, letting me have my moment.

"Are we going home today?" I finally ask.

"Tomorrow. I was hoping you would go with Miya to talk to the girls again. They put them all up here in rooms, but now we need to help them transition back into their day-to-day life. Miya believes having you there will help."

"Of course," I agree without hesitation.

"While you do that, will you be okay if I step out with Declan and Kenji? Miya will be with you the entire time, and she has her own guards watching her. They will watch you as well."

My stomach drops. I'm not ready for him to leave my sight. I don't say that though. Instead, I suck in a breath.

"I'll be okay."

"I won't go if you don't want me to," he promises.

Sitting up, I look down at him. He truly is gorgeous with his messy black hair. He could have a million women, but he's here. With me.

"I'll be okay. You'll come back and get me, right?"

"Of course. You'll stay with Miya until I'm done. You won't even leave the hotel."

I nod. "I can do this then."

"I'll leave you with a phone. I'll be only a call away. I promise." He sits up, brushing the hair out of my face.

For a moment, I think he might kiss me.

My heart is in my throat, aching to feel his lips against mine once more. The last time was a long-ago memory that's faded with time.

Instead, he turns, getting out of bed.

"Miya left some clothes for you in the other room. I'll go grab them so you can take a shower. We can grab some breakfast downstairs before I take you to where they are all meeting. You have about an hour."

"Okay," I whisper, disappointed that he hadn't done what I wanted.

"I'll leave your clothes on the bed. Take your time."

I watch as he leaves, letting the sadness overtake me.

Maybe I'm too damaged now.

I thought I made it clear that I wanted this divide gone. If that means I need to leave the force, then fuck that job. What has it ever given me really? The longer I work there, the more I realize that we are all caught up in red tape and political correctness. Day by day, it gets worse, with cameras and the media constantly criticizing us until the government is forced to cut our funds.

That moral compass we are locked into is the reason these women are being taken. We can't even take a step toward taking them down because we need more proof.

Fuck the proof. What we need is to take action and ask questions later.

Renewed with my sense of purpose, I make my way into the bathroom. After taking a quick shower, I find a pair of leggings and a large T-shirt along with Tristano's sweater. I smile when I pick up the T-shirt to find sensible underwear and a bra with them.

Tris must have given her my sizes because they fit me well.

Stepping from the room, I find Tristano dressed in jeans and a T-shirt himself, which is so out of character for him. I've never seen him without his signature suit.

Sure, I might have only seen him face-to-face twice, but I know where he works. I know what he does. I broke down and did some light stalking. It was the only way to sate my need for him over the years. In all those years, I have never seen him wear a pair of jeans.

"This is a new look." I draw his attention to me.

He looks at me from head to toe, making my cheeks blush.

"They don't dress the same here. You look good. How are you feeling?"

My stomach chooses that moment to grumble. "I'm hungry, I guess."

He gives me a small smile. "Let's get you some food then."

I know I was here last night, but I think I was still in shock because the moment we step out of the elevator on the ground level, I am overwhelmed with flashing lights and sounds. It's chaotic.

I hate it.

"Hey, you okay?" Tris whispers to me.

I shake my head, feeling a little dizzy.

He pulls me quickly through the hall from the casino into a lobby area that is much quieter.

"Is this better?"

"Yeah. Sorry, I guess I don't remember that from last night," I tell him.

"We took a service elevator last night. I should have thought about that. I'll do better." He cups my cheek.

He's so sincere that I can't let him feel guilty.

"I'm fine now. Now where's this food you promised me," I tease.

He leads me over to a café in the corner of the lobby. The menu boasts several different types of coffee and pastry items. They even have egg sandwiches and bagels.

"Anything you want. It's on me," he whispers to me.

I smile over at him. It would have to be on him. I don't even have a wallet on me. I don't say that though. Instead, I take the nice gesture for what it is. His way of taking care of me.

When it's our turn, I order a yogurt parfait and a water. Tris doesn't order anything.

He watches me eat, making me feel weird, but I don't say anything. I can see the worry in his eyes.

I don't blame him. I could see my hip bone when I showered this morning. I need to up my calories to gain some weight.

I need to do it gradually though, which is why I ordered something light. My stomach is still not one hundred percent from being starved for two weeks.

So I eat slowly but finish every bite. Then I let Tris lead me down a different hall to another elevator.

"Are you sure you're up for this? Miya wouldn't be upset if you can't help," Tris reassures me.

"No. I need to do this. I know I went through some shit, but they did too. It's not fair of me to hide because I have someone to hide behind. I need to face it. That's what my old therapist would tell me to do."

"Are you going to start seeing her again?" he asks softly.

I hadn't even thought about it. After everything before, Tristano made sure I had access to a therapist he paid for. I could go see her again.

Maybe I should.

"I'm not sure."

He nods. "You let me know, and I'll set it up."

Then the elevator rings, saving me from having to say anything more. I'm not ready for that topic yet.

Stepping out, he leads me down the hall to a conference room. Opening the door, he lets me walk in first.

I smile when I see the girls. All of them except Olivia and the newest girl who had the tracker. I never got her name.

"Thank you for coming," Miya tells me as she comes up.

I smile at her, remembering meeting her the night before when she brought clothes for the other girls. I chose to keep what I had on, not wanting to take from them.

"Of course," I tell her.

Tris leans into my ear, kissing it lightly. "I'm going to go meet Kenji. I'll be back. Don't leave this room. Here's your phone. My number along with Declan's and Kenji's are in there. You call if you need anything at all."

"Okay," I tell him, taking the phone and sliding it into the sweater pocket.

He hesitates a moment like he wants to say more, but instead he presses a kiss to my forehead before leaving.

"He cares about you a lot. You're lucky. Not everyone finds their person," Miya says softly.

Turning to her, I nod. "He's been the blessing I never knew I needed since I met him. Are you still looking for your person?"

"No. I found mine too. Kenji is a great man. Don't tell him I admitted it out loud though. I like to keep him on his toes. Act like a brat now and then, you know."

I chuckle a little. "I've never been a brat a day in my life. I've always given in to what everyone else wanted."

She gives me a sad smile. "Then maybe it's time you learn to say no. Do things for yourself instead of living your life for another. I promise once you start doing that, you will find the happiness you've been craving."

"Maybe I will," I tell her, reaching out to squeeze her arm. "Thanks for that. I think I needed to hear it."

"Of course. Ready to get started?"

"Yeah. Where's Olivia and that other girl?"

"Olivia is a local girl. Since she had only been missing a day or two, we took her back home to her family. We have her set up with a therapist and some group support in the area. I'll keep an eye on her. As for Kat, she's back on the streets. Her choice, not mine. I offered to help her start a new life or even come work here for us, but she said she didn't want all that. She wants to make it on her own. I gave her my card. She knows where to find me if she changes her mind. Since she hadn't even been gone a whole day, she said she didn't want any services and went back to her life."

"That's sad. She can't even trust the help that you want to give."

"I know. You can lead a horse to water, but you can't make them drink. She knows I'm here. That's all I can do."

"The rest of them?" I look over at Mandy talking quietly with another girl.

"Now we help them get back to their lives or start a new one. Are you up for it?"

I take them all in.

"I wouldn't be anywhere else right now."

Tristano

I HATE LEAVING HER BEHIND, but I need to do this. If I don't do something to let some of this rage out, I might do something stupid, and I can't do that right now. Not when I have her to protect.

Kenji is waiting at the end of the hall like he told me he would.

"You ready?" he asks.

"You assigned a guard to her, right? Someone specifically for her?" I ask for the tenth time.

"Kado is the best assassin I have. He has a keen eye and never misses a target. He is quiet, but deadly. When Miya was being stalked, I trusted him with her life. He protected her at all costs. I wouldn't trust anyone more with her other than myself or Kai. She's in good hands."

I let out the breath I was holding. "Thank you. I just needed to hear it again."

He nods in understanding. "We go a little crazy for the women we love."

The elevator dings open. We step inside.

"How long will it take us to get there?" I ask once inside.

"Ten minutes. Declan is already waiting for us. We will make it as quick as we can so you can get back to your girl. I don't like leaving Miya for long anyway."

I don't acknowledge his statement, but I don't need to. He gets it.

The ride to the docks is a quiet one. Kenji doesn't even put music on. He must feel the vibe I'm putting off because the farther away from Serena I get, the more my rage grows.

When we finally greet Declan at the shipping container where the shitstain he caught is being held, I'm ready to blow.

"He hasn't given me much, but I didn't want to push too hard. I figured you would want to get some shots in, brother," he tells me, his hand coming down on my shoulder.

I love this man. We started off as enemies, but after being roommates for so long, we grew on one another. Now knowing the lengths he has gone to for me, I know I've found a friend for life. Not only has he kept this shitstain on ice for me, but he admitted the only reason he didn't have me stay at his place is because he knew I'd want space with my girl. He was that confident that we would find her.

"Thank you," I tell him, moving past him into the dimly lit container.

As soon as the door shuts behind us, I stride to where the man is tied to a chair, naked. Well, man is giving him too much credit. This is more like a kid. He can't be more than twenty. Young and dumb.

"You're not going to like what we plan to do to you, but that's okay," I tell him, a smile filling my face.

"Fuck you. I know nothing. They only had me sit there to watch the place. I had no idea there were girls there." The man has a heavy Russian accent.

I look over to Kenji. "Didn't you have some issues with some Russians here before? Is he one of them?"

Kenji shakes his head. "Nope. This guy has no ties to anyone that we know of. No tattoos. We ran it through our contact in Veles and he has no record of him either. Seems he's just some dumb kid who got caught up in the wrong bullshit."

"He's not from around here either. I already tested him. He doesn't know Chicago at all," Declan adds.

"I bet he knows New York though, right?"

The kid's eyes widen a little, giving away that I was right. He's spent a lot of time over there. I bet he's low man on the totem pole. That was why he was left behind. Low risk for the leaders. He's not much to be missed.

"You know, I believe you. I don't think you know anything," I tell him.

The look of relief on his face is short-lived though.

"Too bad for you, I have a lot of anger because one of those girls? She is mine. Now I know you had no clue what they were doing, but you helped. Seems you were left holding the evidence, and since no one else is here to take the punishment, I'll have to dish it out to you."

Shaking my head, I blow out a breath.

"No. Wait. What?" he screams.

I don't listen to him. The first fist lands on his face. I hear the bones crack as his nose breaks, blood pouring down him. It's not enough though.

I'm not sated.

"Were they crying? Did you listen to them cry as you sat outside that door?" I ask him, throwing two punches against his kidneys.

The kid cries out. He's begging for me to stop, but I'm just getting started.

"I bet you smelled their piss. Their shit. You knew that something was in there and they weren't being taken care of. You saw the food and water that was brought. I know you are smarter than that."

Pulling out a pocket knife, I slam it down into his knee, making him pass out from the pain.

I'm breathing heavily as I give myself a second to collect my thoughts. Then I pat the kid's face until he wakes up.

"Please. I knew the girls were there, but I didn't know why. I was only asked to watch to make sure no one came. I was supposed to text a code if anyone came."

"Did you?" Declan asks from behind me.

"I did. They never responded. Then you grabbed me. That was the only instruction I was given. They said they were going to give me a million dollars to do it."

I snort, shaking my head. "You're a good-looking kid. How old are you?"

He is sobbing now. "Twenty."

"Of course you are. They played you. I bet they were planning to sell you too. Use you for what they need, then get rid of you. I bet that code you texted only made them flee. They didn't give a fuck about you. They can always get another schmuck. Always kidnap more girls. It doesn't matter how involved you were, you still did it. You helped. You could have saved those girls. *My girl.* You didn't, so now you'll pay the consequences."

"Please. I told you everything I know."

"I know you did, but it doesn't matter. You caused her pain and torment that she will never get over. I'll do the same to you."

He all-out wails as he realizes that it doesn't matter. This was never about getting information from him. This was only about one thing.

Getting revenge for my girl.

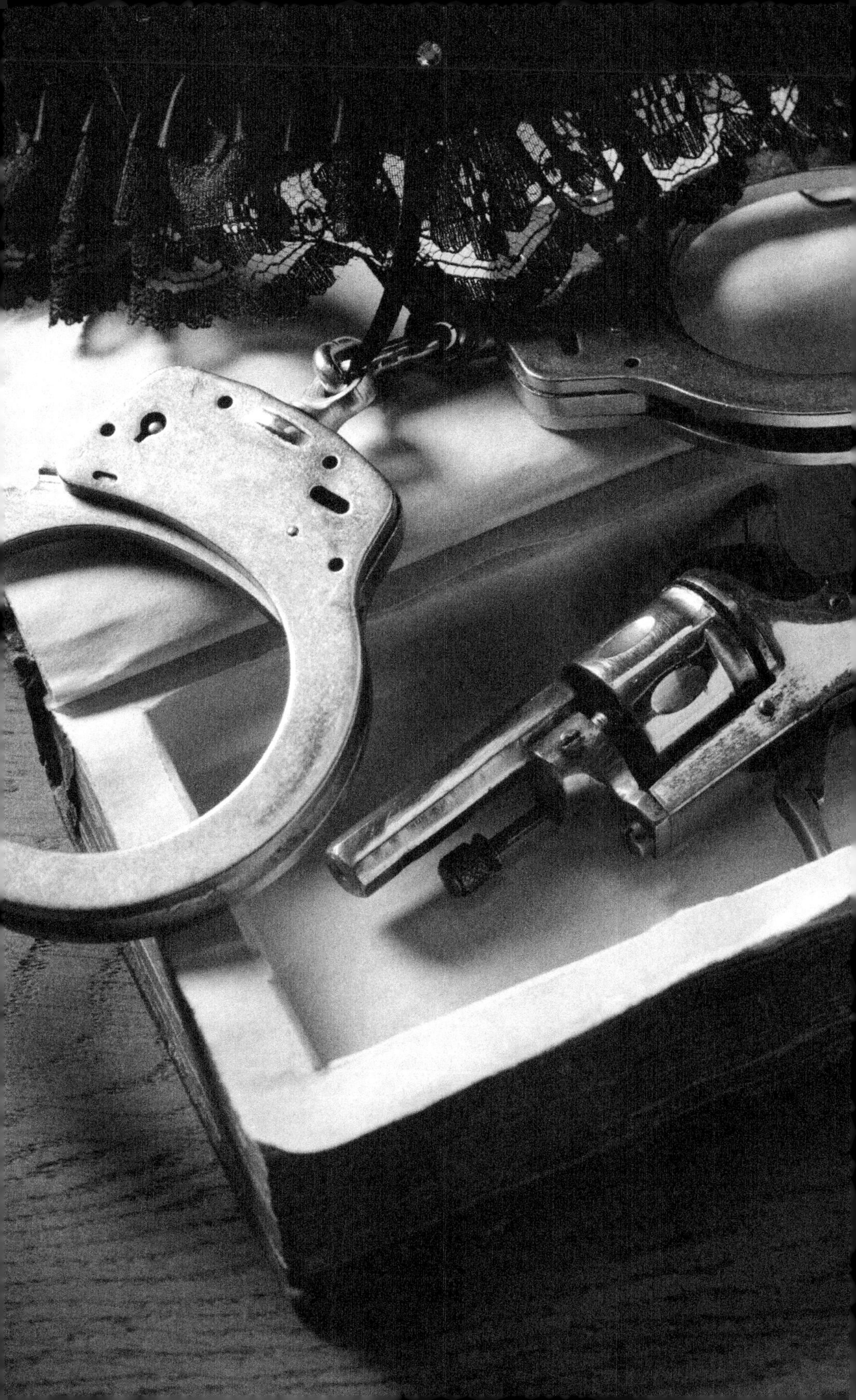

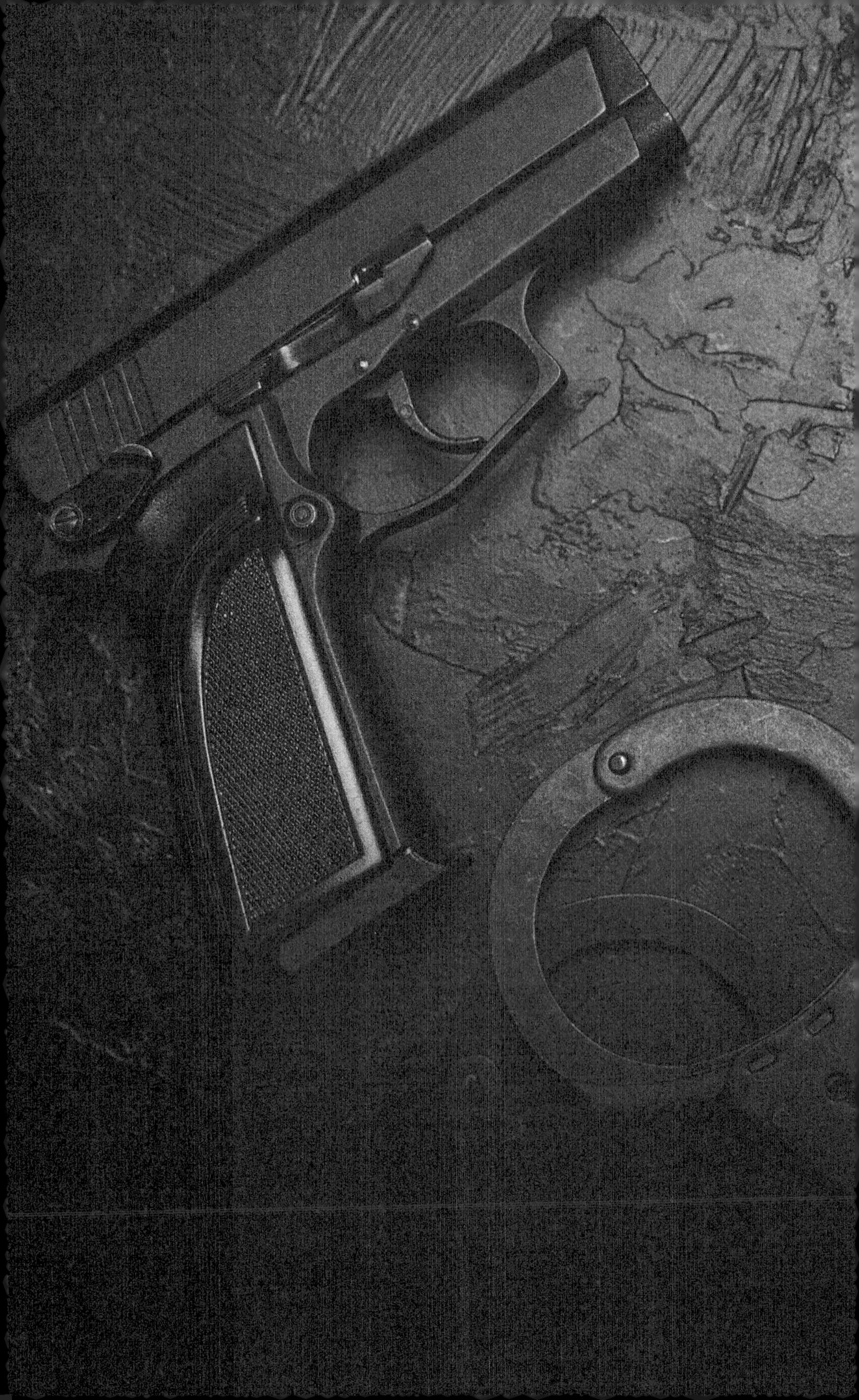

CHAPTER TEN

Serena

"What are you doing out here? I thought you went to bed?" Tristano asks, coming to my spot by the window.

I tried to go to sleep when we got back to the hotel room, but I couldn't. Every time I closed my eyes, all I saw were those girls. They were looking to me like I had all the answers. They wanted my guidance. I didn't know what to tell them. How can I help them heal when I haven't even healed myself?

I did the best I could though. By the time Tristano came back to get me, I didn't even have the energy to ask about the bruises on his knuckles or the fact that he changed clothes and his hair was wet.

Whatever he went to do, I didn't even want to know.

I just wanted to rest.

Only rest wouldn't come.

So while Tris went into the second bedroom to call his bosses back home, I found my way here. Curled up in a beanbag chair with a blanket wrapped around me like a cocoon while I stare at the city skyline.

Sinking down next to me, he pulls me toward him. "What's wrong?"

"They all wanted me to tell them what to do. All I could tell them was that they needed to make the decision for themselves. I feel like I failed them somehow. I feel like I should have had a better answer for them."

"You can't tell anyone else how to live their life. That's not how this works. You did the right thing."

"I guess. Two are staying here and working under Miya. They didn't have anywhere else to go. They chose to sell their bodies at the brothel instead of taking a normal job."

"Are you judging them for that?" he asks.

I shake my head slowly. "No. It hurts my heart. They are so comfortable with that lifestyle that they choose to go back to it when they have other options. Nadia used to sell her underwear online and things of that nature. She did it to get a degree, but instead of using that degree, she chose to willingly give away her body. Why would she do that?"

"Did you ask her?"

I sigh. "I did. She said that it was temporary. She and Miya agreed to it for the time being, but when she's ready, Miya is going to help get her into an architecture firm here in the city. Nadia said that she felt she needed to take her power back somehow, and something was telling her that this was the way to do it."

"Then it sounds like she knows what she's doing. What's bothering you more? That she made that choice or that she was able to make the choice that easily?"

My heart stutters in my chest at his words.

He's right. I'm not upset that she will be selling her body. That's her choice. I'm upset because my decision isn't as clear-cut.

"I don't like that you are being so logical right now."

"I'm sorry. I didn't realize this was just a bitch fest. Let me try again." He sits up, pushing his hair a little. "Oh my god. I can't believe that skank chose to do that. What a hussy."

His attempt at a feminine voice makes me bust out in laughter. He always knows what to say or do to make me smile. I let the lightness fill me until those dark thoughts fade away.

"Thank you," I whisper, leaning against his side. "Mandy chose to take a job with someone named Callum. He had a job in his main office for an assistant. Miya said he will send her to school so that she can get a degree in whatever field she wants, and then he's going to get her a job doing it."

Tris nods. "Callum is a good man. I'm not surprised he stepped up. It's almost unheard of for so many organizations to be connected so closely, but I know without a doubt that the O'Reilly Westies, Takahashi Yakuza, and the Petrov Bratva have our backs. They will always step up when it comes to doing the right thing."

"Unless it means killing someone, you mean," I retort.

"We do kill sometimes, but it's always justified. It's a necessary part of this business."

"Why would it be necessary? Explain it to me," I tell him, needing that thread of reasoning to be okay with this.

"Remember when I took care of your problem at seventeen?" he asks.

I nod.

"I did that so that he would never hurt another person again. That's why we kill. The person we eliminate is someone who did something that hurt someone we care for. We never want that person to do it again, so we end them. Trust me when I say that we do not do it lightly. It's not like in the movies where someone just upsets someone. It's serious offenses only. Lighter offenses are dealt with in other ways."

I swallow hard. That all seems reasonable. When did his life begin to sound reasonable to me?

When the law wouldn't protect you, I think.

"Why isn't my uncle here?" I whisper.

"Red tape, *anima gemella*. Last I checked, he couldn't even trace you past the corner you disappeared on. He attempted to try but got shut down by his superiors. Seems they feel like this is a bit of a habit for you. Running off half-cocked and coming back days later with an excuse as to why you were gone."

I let out a heavy breath. "It's because when you dropped me off that morning, I told them I had gone to a rave in the city. I told them someone had spiked my drink and had raped me and kept raping me for days. I told them they let me go when they were done. I refused to file a report. They let me go to therapy and join the academy, but ever since then, they've treated me like a child with issues. They never take what I say at face value."

"I'm sorry. I wish I was there to make it better," he whispers against my head.

"You were. That first month when I found the package with the phone? I was so happy. I remember when I heard your voice. It made all the bad stuff disappear. It still does. I looked forward to those calls each month."

"I bet you did. Don't think I didn't notice you stalking me too. You know you could have gotten caught."

I gasp. "What? You knew?"

He smirks. "Of course. Did you think I wasn't watching you too? Difference was I did it through cameras. Easier to get away with."

I laugh, moving closer to him. "Why did we even try to stay apart again?"

"You're a cop. I'm a criminal."

"Seems like a stupid reason to me," I say softly.

"It sure does now," he admits just as quietly.

Then a silence takes over as we stare out the window.

I think I know what I need to do when we get home.

Tristano

"Well, this is it." I say as I shut the door to my apartment behind me.

"This place is nice," Serena says as she looks around.

Taking a step back, I try and look at my place through her eyes. The kitchen has white countertops with black cabinets and an island that separates it from the living room. I have a white couch with black end tables and a coffee table. A large TV that I don't use nearly enough for how much I spent on it is mounted to the wall across from it. The place is nice and quite large for being in the city.

"Thanks. Can I get you a drink?" I ask, moving our small bag into the living room.

I was cool with leaving everything in Chicago, but Serena insisted she wanted to take some things with us.

"Water?" she says, looking around some more.

"Sure. Make yourself at home," I say as I head into the kitchen.

Opening the fridge, I pull out two bottles of water. My phone buzzes in my pocket. Setting the water down, I pull it out and look at the screen.

> Declan: What in the hell did you order me?

> Me: White sheets with a dark green comforter. Matching pillows will be there tomorrow.

Slipping my phone into my pocket, I grab the waters and walk to the couch.

"What are you smiling about?" Serena asks as I approach.

"Declan texted."

She nods knowingly. "Let me guess, he saw the bedding."

"Yep," I tell her as I sit down, handing her a bottle of water.

I had Serena help pick out the set while we were waiting at the airport. It was nice seeing her smile so easily. I was worried she would internalize everything like she did the first time. Seems she's bouncing back a bit easier this time.

"Thanks."

"You're welcome. Since I've been gone, I don't have any food here. My cleaning lady will be coming by tomorrow with groceries, so we're stuck ordering takeout tonight if that's okay," I inform her.

"That's fine."

"Do you have any preferences?"

Serena taps her finger against her lip.

I can't help but watch as she contemplates what she wants. Something about it is so innocently attractive. I've had the urge to kiss her many times now, but I've withheld. I can't move on her when she's gone through something so traumatic. She needs time to heal.

Hell if I don't want to though. I have the literal girl who stars in all of my dreams in my home right now. What more could I want?

"Do you have a place where we could get some good ramen? I know it sounds silly, but I'm craving it."

"I know just the place." I kiss her head, pulling her into my side.

Grabbing my phone, I type in the name of the place and hand it to her.

"Check out the menu."

As she scrolls, I turn on the TV, keeping the volume low.

"I put what I want in your cart." She hands the phone back.

I hand her the remote. "Here, find something you want to watch."

I take my phone as I hand her the remote.

Quickly, I place the order and set the phone down on the cushion next to me.

"It will be here in about thirty minutes."

"That fast?"

"That's the power of the city, baby." I smirk as she rolls her eyes.

My phone buzzes again, and I grab it.

> Declan: Matching pillows? Why in the hell do I need those?
>
> Me: So you can get laid… Just say thank you.
>
> Declan: Thanks.
>
> Me: You're welcome.

"It's kind of weird how friendly you guys are," Serena says, reading the text.

"Why do you say that?"

She curls up in a ball, making herself comfortable. "It's just odd. I know you said you are allies with them and the other families, but to see you work together? It's scary. You guys work for different families. I just assumed you would be enemies."

"Nah. I think we would have at one point, but we are all so intertwined now. Greer is a Catalini, but she married a Westie. Then you have the Westies and the Yakuza in Chicago. Callum is the head there, but his sister is married to the Yakuza leader. The only ones who don't really fit in by some connected line are the Petrov Bratva. They are solely in with us because we all have a common enemy. They hate the trafficking as much as we do. I guess Nikolai, the leader over there, had his sister and wife taken by some traffickers a while back. Now they do whatever they can to take them down, which means helping us secretly. Their connection to us isn't as well known as the others."

"That makes sense. When you lay it out like that, I can see it. Does that make you guys bigger targets?"

I shrug. "Maybe, but I think it also makes us stronger. If you mess with one, you mess with us all. It's almost like a dynasty of sorts."

"I guess that will take some getting used to." She smiles as she shakes her head.

"What will?"

"Being able to talk openly with each other without fear of what the other will learn." She tilts her head to the side. "I just hope you know that even then, I wouldn't have betrayed you."

"I know. You warned me more than once," I remind her.

Over the last couple of years, there had been a couple times that Serena had reached out, warning me of whispers about La Cosa Nostra. It was unneeded when we have members inside of the FBI, but it was nice. She didn't know that though. I wanted to keep her clear of all of that, only allowing minimal contact.

Now she's here. I have her with me. Nothing is stopping us from getting closer.

"That I did." She bites her lip as she looks away from me.

"What is it?"

Serena shakes her head. "I don't know how to ask."

"Just do it."

Serena takes a deep breath. "Clearly, you guys and the other families are working together to take down whatever this is. Before I was taken, I wanted to end the trafficking, but now it's personal. I want to help you guys."

Serena looks at me with wide, hopeful eyes.

"I'll do whatever you need me to do. I have skills, use them," she adds after a moment of silence.

"You want to change sides," I say, eyes wide in disbelief.

I never thought Serena would change teams. Yeah, I suspected she would eventually leave law enforcement, but with her law enforcement background, I never saw her going dark.

"I do." She bites her lip. "You guys get results even if you don't go by the book."

"I'm sorry, *anima gemella*, but I can't just let you in. It's not my choice," I say, shaking my head.

"I know, but I'm willing to meet with whoever, pledge whatever I need to. Please, Tris, I need this."

Taking a deep breath, I reach out and run my hand over the back of her head. Serena relaxes into my touch as I think it over.

Would the others be willing to meet with her?

Do I approach Greer first or Bash? I know he's my Don, but she is technically my boss.

"I'll make a call, but I make no promises."

"Thank you," she says softly.

"They aren't going to let you in easily. They won't trust you. Not with the police background. You'll have to show them what I already know. That when you find someone you care about, you are deeply loyal, even against all morals of your own."

"I am. I'll provide it to them. I promise," she vows.

I don't doubt her for a second. There were many times over the years that she could have picked herself. Given me up to earn her stripes on the force. It would have been a fast track to the top, but she didn't. Instead, she used what she heard about our dealings and risked herself to give me the heads up. She might be a cop, but she has always proved that loyalty to me came first.

I guess that's why I find it so easy to reciprocate that loyalty back to her. To make her my number one priority.

"I have faith in you. There will be no going back once I put this into motion. You know that, right?" I warn her.

"I do." She nods. "Make the call, Tris."

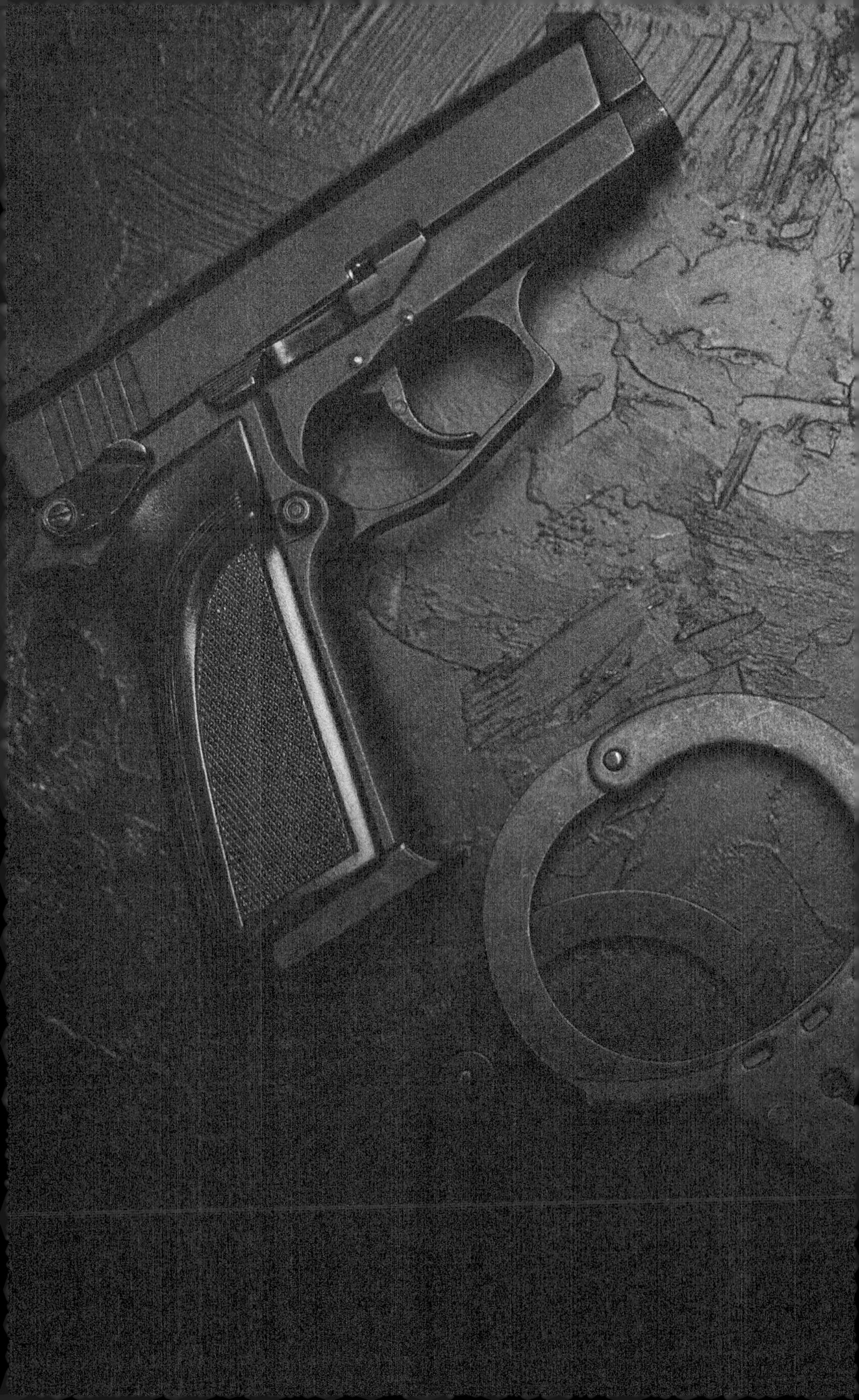

CHAPTER ELEVEN

Serena

As soon as Tristano made the call, things moved fast. Everyone wanted to meet me immediately.

It was making my head spin. Tris is a godsend though. He pushed them off a few days to give me time to prepare. Well, that and I still have to face my uncle.

So instead of meeting the heads of the Catalini family and the Westies, I'm standing outside the Jersey City East District Police Department.

This place has been home for me longer than I've been a police officer. I've spent nearly my entire life here between my grandfather and now my uncle.

Yet standing here now, I feel out of place. Like maybe this isn't where I'm meant to be.

"Excuse me," someone says as they slip by me.

Shaking my head, I step forward and walk into the station.

"Hey, Bert," I say to the lobby security guard as I scan my ID.

"Serena." His eyes light up when he sees me. "I was wondering what happened to you. Everyone is whispering about what you might have been up to."

I frown at him as I scan my ID again, the door still not unlocking.

"Nothing as entertaining as I'm sure is being said. Do you know why my ID isn't working?" I ask.

He pulls out his tablet before wincing. "It looks like your access was revoked. What did you do to piss the boss man off?"

I sigh. "I don't know. Can you call back and get me a visitor's pass?"

"Sure thing."

I watch as he picks up his phone, no doubt calling my uncle. The longer he takes, the more my blood boils. I go missing and what does my uncle do? He files a missing person's report on me under my undercover name, making sure my face isn't out there and possibly fucking up any further stings we have. Then he revokes my access to the station. What a joke.

Walking over to the wall of photos, I find the one I'm looking for. It's Uncle Ben with my grandpa and father. They are all in uniform, my grandpa in the chief's best while my father and uncle wear their rookie uniforms. It was from their graduation day from the academy.

Family. That's what they always said. Even though Uncle Ben was only my father's best friend, he was still family, and family looks out for one another.

From what Tris has said, it doesn't even look like he's made that much of a push to find me. He spent the first two days asking around, but then he just filed the report and dropped it. Hell, he hadn't even been to my apartment. The pot I put in front of the door to tell me if anyone comes through the front door while I'm gone was still in the same spot, dust settled around it.

So if family is so important, why didn't he try harder?

"You can go back now, Serena. He's waiting in his office," Bert tells me.

Guess we are about to find out.

The disappointment sets in with each step back to his office. I became a cop because I wanted to stop other sickos from doing what that man did to me when I was seventeen. Statistically, women are less likely to report their abusers. I wanted to be the voice for those women. I wanted them to see these men on their television screens and know that they might not have come forward, but someone did, and that they can sleep easier knowing the man who abused them was in jail.

I had high hopes, only for them to be dashed each time I brought a new case to Uncle Ben.

He never believed I was good enough. He only appeased me by allowing me to be the bait but never truly allowing me to run a case as the lead.

Have I been blinded all these years? Stuck behind the value of family my grandfather and father hammered into me as a child?

Then I'm there. Standing outside his door. I know as soon as I step through, my life will be irrevocably changed.

I can't tell him the whole truth. He will want to know how I got away. Who saved me. I will have to admit my ties to the mob.

I refuse to do that.

Raising my fist, I knock on the door as my heart races.

"Come in," I hear him call out.

I imagined that when I walked through the door, Uncle Ben would be on his feet rushing to hug me and ensure I'm okay.

That's not what happened though. He didn't even look up from the file in front of him.

Instead, he just barked, "Take a seat."

I try to mask the hurt I'm feeling. It's a stab to the heart. I already knew that this place didn't feel like the safe haven it once was, but he severed that last string of hope I had that he would make this better. That he would reassure me.

"Where have you been? I was forced to put out a BOLO on your alias. You're burned now. We can't send you out on stings. There's too much heat on you." He finally looks up, anger shining through his eyes.

"I was taken captive and held against my will," I say with zero emotion.

"Sure you did. Just like you did when you were seventeen, right? How did you get away this time? Did they also just let you go?"

Tears prick my eyes, but I refuse to let him see them. "No. It doesn't matter though. You obviously don't believe me, so why don't you tell me what you think I've been doing?"

He shakes his head. "I blame myself really. I let you get away with too much after your grandfather died. It's really too bad your father died so young. He would have done a much better job of raising you. Maybe then you wouldn't be acting out."

"Acting out? I was kidnapped. That's not acting out."

He crosses his arms, leaning back in his chair. "Where were you when you were kidnapped?"

"On the corner of Jewett and West Side."

He snorts. "So you were out there looking into shit I told you to drop. Then you got kidnapped? Do you even hear yourself? What? Did you go hide out to make me think you were kidnapped so I would let you pursue this case?"

"What? No. Of course not," I say, completely offended.

"Enough, Serena. I should have never allowed you on the force. I thought you would be a good addition, but I obviously let you live in your delusions too long. You're off the force. I want you to go to your desk and collect your things. You'll find another job outside of the force and you will leave the police work to the actual police. Do you understand me?"

A child. He thinks of me as a child. The condescending way he's speaking to me confirms it. I always thought he was being protective, but that's not it. He truly only sees me as something he can control.

"Go on now. Ricky can drive you home. I expect to see you at Sunday dinner."

I've been dismissed. Just like that, he shoos me off as he looks back to his desk. As if I'm a gnat.

Fuck him.

"No. I won't be at family dinner. I'm starting to feel like this isn't much of a family."

"Fine. If that's what you want, then I want you to move out of the apartment. I've let you live there cheap because we are family, but if we aren't family anymore, move your shit out. I'll give you until the first."

"I'll be out by Monday. Thanks for believing in me, Uncle Ben. I truly feel the love."

Turning, I stride out his door ignoring his protest. Then I slam it. I slam it so hard that I make the officer walking down the hall jump.

I don't say a word to him. Instead, I make my way toward the supply closet and grab a box. I take it back to my desk and start filling it with the few personal items I have here.

I smile as I pick up a picture an elementary student drew for me when I stopped by and talked to the kids about what I did. The department teamed up with the local schools to try and show the kids that not all cops are bad and that we just want to help them.

The kids loved it. They all wanted to try on our hats or hold our badges. We gave them all stickers as honorary little officers. It was a rewarding day.

Looking back on it now though, I think I was only sent because it was grunt work. Something none of the others wanted to do. Just another way my uncle was controlling me.

I keep picking up items, ignoring the stares around me. I don't care about any of these people.

Before I know it, I have everything and place the lid back on the box. I turn, about to leave, when I come to a halt.

Ricky is standing there, a forlorn look on his face.

"I'm going to miss ya, kid," he whispers.

I set the box down, moving into his arms. "Thank you for always having my back. I think you're the only one in this entire department that ever truly believed in me."

"You have good instincts. Keep honing them. This might be a door closing right now, but I know there's a better one waiting for you. If you ever need anything, call me. We might not be on the same team anymore, but I always have your back."

He squeezes me extra hard, making my eyes tear up. I didn't think I'd miss this place, but I will miss him. Ricky is the one bright spot in my life as a police officer.

"Thank you, Ricky. Thank you for everything."

"Take care of yourself, kid." He pats my back before pulling back.

I don't miss the sheen in his eyes as he watches me walk away.

While this might be the end for me, it feels right. Like I outgrew this place in the two weeks I've been gone. Almost as if my experiences made me better than this place.

For so long, I aimed to be a great cop, but I think I was doing it for the wrong reasons. I wanted to live up to my family's legacy and make my uncle proud. I also wanted to do it for all the women out there who are stalked by predators, but if I'm being honest with myself, that wasn't the primary reason.

Letting go of that need to be validated has lifted a weight off of me.

I can't wait to see what life brings me next.

Tristano

Serena's place isn't even dirty, yet I can't help but clean up. The dust is driving me bonkers. Then there's the way she has her books sorted. Who the hell sorts by colors?

It makes no sense.

Then there are the photos that are all haphazardly placed on the walls.

I can't handle it, but I'm trying to.

Or maybe I can't handle her being out of my sight.

I wanted to go with her. Stand outside and stalk her as she went into work. I could tell she was nervous about it, which only made that itch to follow her worse.

She talked me out of it though. It wouldn't be a good look if she was seen with a known member of a criminal organization. I really hate this divide between us. I wish I could eliminate it.

So instead of being with her, I'm here at her apartment wiping down her already clean counters while listening to '90s gangster rap.

"The dunky dunk. Do the dunky dunk," I mutter as I dunk the rag back into the sink full of soapy water.

"Why do you do that?" Her voice coming from behind me has me turning to face her, my fists up.

"Whoa. You can't be doing that to a man. You're going to make me react and do something I don't want to do. I'm just glad I didn't reach for my gun."

She rolls her eyes at me. "Why do you change the song lyrics?"

I shrug. "I always have. I've always naturally changed them to either something related to what I was going through or something that made me laugh. I mean, the songs are masterpieces on their own, but something about changing the lyrics makes them feel more like mine. Then it annoyed Enzo, so now I also feel like it's a game."

She gives me a small smile, moving to sit at the small table she has between the kitchen and living room.

"I like it. It makes me smile. I always wonder what you're going to come up with next."

I set down the rag, washing my hands quickly before I make my way to sit with her at her table.

"What happened?" I ask softly as I pull her hand into mine.

"He fired me," she admits, tears filling her eyes.

"Oh, *anima gemella*. It truly is their loss." I press my lips to her hand, making her smile.

"I'm not even that upset about it really. I'm more hurt. He didn't believe me. He thinks I made the whole thing up to get him to look into the missing girls I've been begging him to look at for months. Then he pretty much said I was no longer useful at work, but he expects me to continue to come to family dinners."

I want to say "fuck him." Pull her into my arms and never let her see that man again. I can't though. He's the only family she has left. I won't take that from her.

"Is that something you want to do?" I ask.

"Fuck no. This has shown me that his view of what family should be like isn't mine. I don't want to be controlled by him any longer. I told him I wouldn't be joining. So he's kicking me out. I have nowhere to go, but I have until Monday to figure it out."

I growl. "He can't kick you out that quick. He has to give you thirty days."

"He did, but I was stubborn and told him I'd be out by Monday." She looks a little sheepish.

Pulling out my phone, I type away. Then I look at my girl.

"Let's go get some boxes. We can start packing today. I've arranged for some of the guys to come get your shit."

"I can't accept that. I don't even know where I'm going to go."

"Stop being stupid, Serena. You know damn well where you are going to go."

"What?" She looks over at me.

"Fine. We are playing this game." I move until I'm kneeling at her feet, her knees on either side of me. Then I take her face in my hands. "You're coming to live with me. If you still want to be a cop, fuck it. We will figure out a way to get you on a force in the city. Hell, Bash could probably get you a spot in the FBI if that's what you want. You're not going to be homeless. I refuse to let this moment bring you down."

"I can't force myself into your life, Tris. That's not fair to you."

"You want to know what's not fair? The fact that I have spent days dreading having to let you go. It's not fair that I had to think about you sitting in this apartment all alone while I'm just across the river missing the fuck out of you. So if we are being honest? I want you to live with me. To be with me even if that's something you can't ever see yourself doing. We will figure out the details later. All I need for you to do is say yes."

She hesitates before nodding. "If we are being honest with one another, I want to live with you too. The moment he said he was kicking me out, all I could think about was that I had a reason to stay with you longer. I've wanted to be with you since I was seventeen years old, Tris. Nothing has ever changed that."

Leaning forward, I press a chaste kiss to her lips. "Then we are in this together. We figure it out as a team. No matter what, we got each other's back."

"How is that different than how it's been since we've met?" She looks dazed from the short kiss.

I'll be doing that again real soon, but first we need to get moving.

"We will be together in real life now." I stand, taking her hand. "Let's go get boxes. We have a lot to do in such a little time."

As I head toward the door with her trailing, she pulls on my hand, getting me to stop.

"Thank you, Tris. I know you joked that you were my dark knight, but I truly feel like you manifested that into reality."

I smirk at her. "If you're not careful, I'm going to manifest a lot of other things into reality. Now get a move on. I want you in my bed sooner rather than later."

I push her ahead of me, smacking her ass.

She giggles, but continues on, leaving me to smile as I watch her swing her hips.

The girl owns me, heart and soul.

I think it's about time I claim her as well.

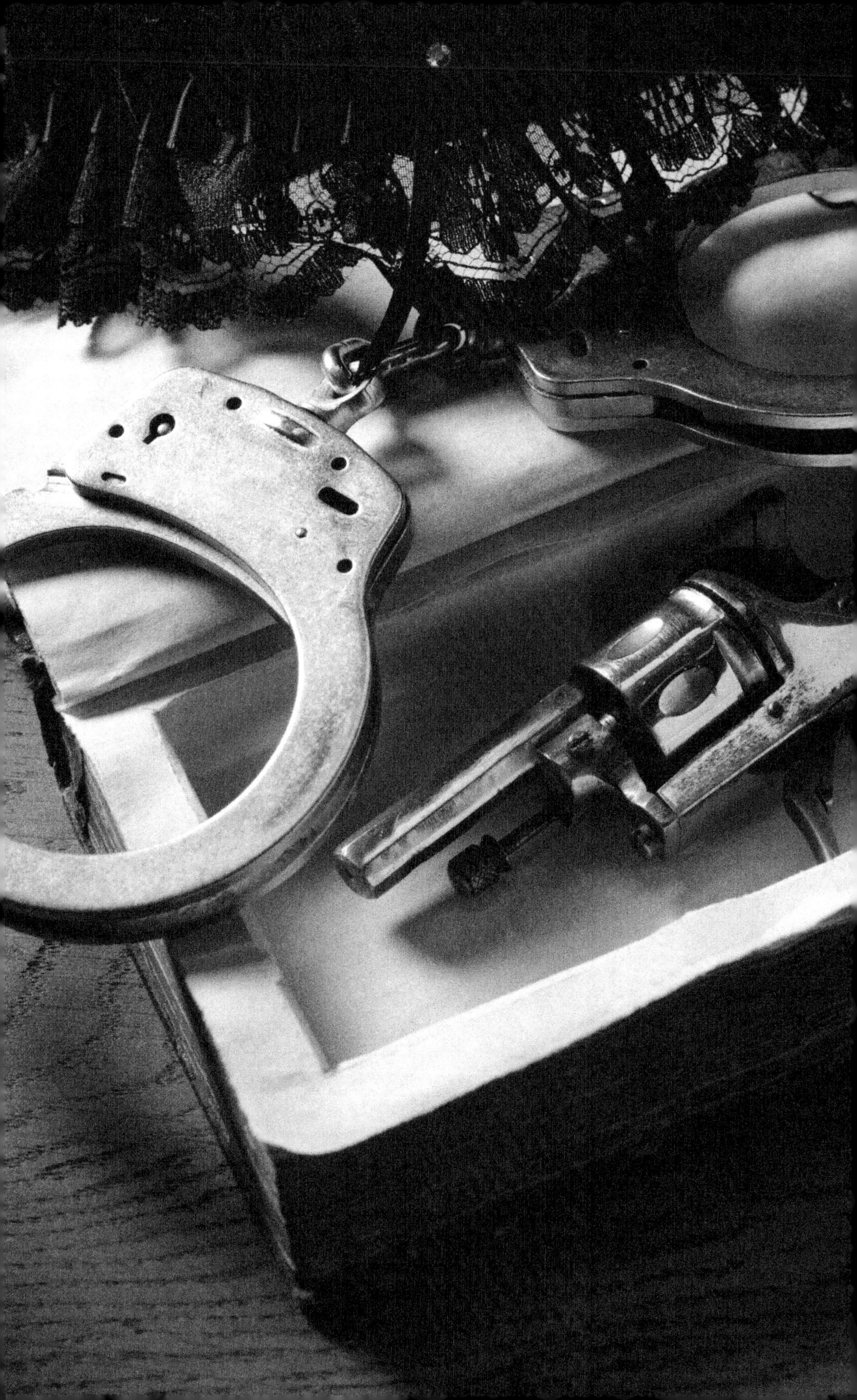

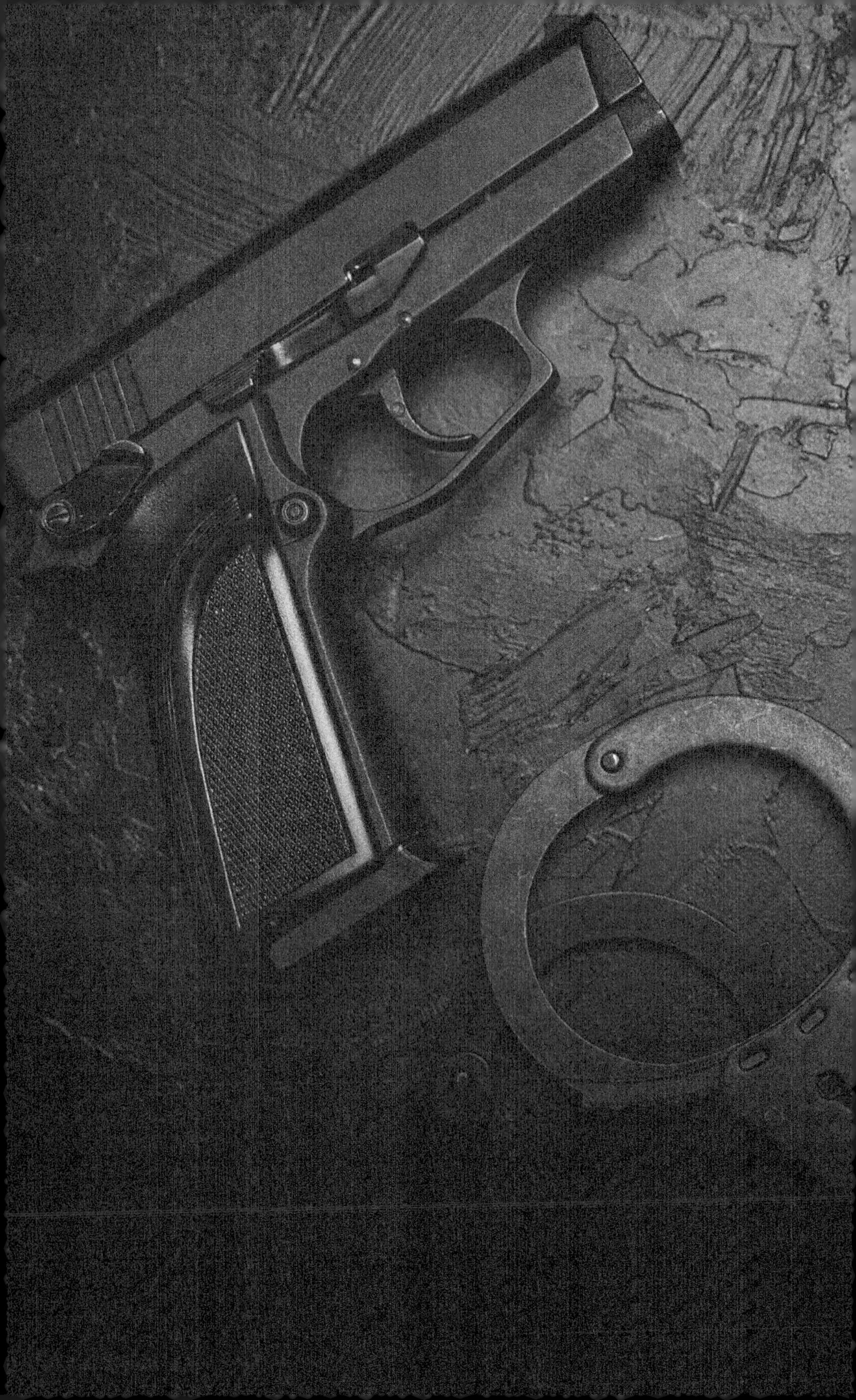

CHAPTER
TWELVE

Serena

"I don't think this is a good idea," Tris tells me for the sixth time.

It might not be, but I can't leave without a word. Most of the girls won't care, but Meredith will. She will worry, and I don't want that.

"I have to go. I know you don't like it, but it's something that's important to me. Ricky will watch my back. I know you want to be there, but I can't be seen with you here. Not until we are out of here. I don't want the drama it will bring."

He knows it's true. Even though I made him put a hoodie on when we went to the store for boxes last night, he still might be recognized. I mean, we passed at least two cops I knew on the short walk to and from the store.

Thankfully, they only nodded and kept on. Seems like word of my banishment has spread. Normally those same guys would have stopped and shot the shit with me.

I'm a pariah now.

"Are you sure you can trust this Ricky guy?"

"Yes. He's the only one I trust. It's not like I'm going in as a sting. I'm not even going to dress as Sabrina. I just want to tell her what's up so she can stay safe and maybe convince the other girls to stay safe too."

He heaves out a sigh. "You keep your phone on you at all times. Ricky gets my burner number and updates me every five minutes. That's my compromise. If I don't hear from him, I will come down there."

Moving closer to him, I rest my hands on his chest. "Have I told you that this possessiveness is kind of working for me?"

"Don't change the subject." He growls.

It's like he doesn't even know how sexy it is that he's gone from aloof friend to possessive boyfriend overnight.

Yesterday he was still walking on eggshells and trying to appease me. Now that I've admitted that I want to be with him too, he's cranked it up ten notches. It's hot as hell. If I didn't have anywhere to be, I might try and convince him that the healing I really need is the kind he can give me between my legs.

I can't get distracted though. We almost have everything packed up already. At least, everything I want to keep.

"Ricky is going to want to know who you are," I admit softly.

"Then tell him. We are a team, remember?" he reminds me gently.

Leaning up, I get right in his face. "Agreed. I'll let him know."

I go to move back, but he grasps me behind the neck, keeping me right in his face.

My heart races. I want him to kiss me again. I thought he might last night, but he kept his hands to himself. At least, until we went to bed. Then he spooned me, but no matter how much I wiggled, he refused to go further.

It was quite annoying, but I get why he did it. Tristano has never been one to rush anything. He takes his time and plots out his course. He has this easygoing personality that makes him seem like he never takes anything seriously, but I see through the facade. He's more than what he wants people to believe.

He's intelligent, kind, caring, and possessive as fuck. He is harder on himself than anyone else could ever be. He wants to make the people around him proud, and I know for a fact that he would give his life for anyone in his family.

So when he only brushes a kiss to the tip of my nose, I don't let the disappointment show. Instead, I smile.

"Be a good girl, *anima gemella*. Do not make any reckless decisions. I'll see you in a little bit."

"I'll be safe and back before you know it."

The knock on the door breaks the tension of the moment. Moving back from him, I go to the door. Opening it, I smile at Ricky.

He's dressed in plain clothes.

"Thank you for doing this," I tell him.

"Of course, kid. It's admirable you wanting to watch out for these girls."

Tris clears his throat, making Ricky stiffen.

"Ricky, I want you to meet Tristano. He's helping me move." I leave out the details of our relationship as I introduce them.

Tris is having none of that though. He steps right into my back, reaching over me to shake the man's hand.

"She's too shy to say it, but I'm her man. Now I am agreeing to this because she needs it, but she refuses to let me go. So here's what you're going to do. I'm going to give you this card," he holds out a card with a phone number on it, "and you are going to text me as soon as she gets out of the car and every five minutes until she is back with you. If anything happens to her, I will hold you personally responsible and come after you."

I swallow hard, not knowing how Ricky is going to take this.

They stare each other down for several moments before Ricky focuses back on me. "You're moving?"

"Uncle Ben kicked me out," I admit.

"Fucker." He looks back over to Tris. "Thanks for helping her out. I'll do as you ask, but for her sake. I don't normally take orders from men like you, but today we will make an exception."

"I don't usually trust your type, so it seems we are both doing something new today."

"Alright. Enough measuring dicks. We have places to be. I'll be back soon."

I step out of Tris's arms, letting him watch us walk away.

The silence all the way to the car is jarring.

I should have known it was the preamble to what was going to happen in the car.

"You know you're boyfriend is part of the Italian mob, right?" Ricky wastes no time jumping into it.

"I do," I admit.

"Glad you know so I didn't have to break your heart. Now why the fuck are you dating a mobster? Is this why Chief is kicking you out and fired you?"

I shake my head. "Uncle Ben has lost his marbles. He doesn't even know about Tristano. I'm hoping to keep it that way."

"Maybe for a while, sure, but you know we are briefed on the criminal organizations quarterly. Before long, you'll be photographed with him and added to the wall."

"Yeah? You think that'll piss Uncle Ben off? I mean, after he pretty much accused me of faking a kidnapping, I think I would like to see him embarrassed a little bit," I bite out, anger filling me.

"What happened to you? You used to love this job. You would do anything to put away the bad guys, and now you're sleeping with one?" he asks, sounding baffled.

He's never seen this side of me until now.

"Who I sleep with is none of your business. Tristano isn't a bad guy. They do a lot of good for the city. Shit no one else ever sees because all they focus on is the shit they do in the morally gray areas."

"You know Tristano alone has over forty unconfirmed kills. He's a murderer."

"I am well aware of who he is and what he does to protect those he cares about. He's done it for me not once, but twice. Why do you think I can look past it?"

Ricky grows silent. "When you were seventeen?"

"I escaped, but not because I was let go. Tris saved me and took care of the man who ruined me."

He swallows hard. "The second time?"

"I didn't disappear on my own, Ricky. You know me better than that. Tristano did everything in his power to find me. He found me, Ricky. How can I focus on the shit he does that I don't like when the man flew across the country to rescue me?"

He lets out a deep sigh. "I'm going to pretend I heard none of that, but I am glad you have him. Just be careful. I don't want to see you fall on the wrong side of the law."

"Don't you ever get tired of walking the straight and narrow? Fighting through all the red tape just to get our guy? I'm not saying Tris always does the right thing, but fuck if he can't make a problem disappear faster. I mean, the man who took me when I was seventeen? He had done it before, and he would have continued to do it. If Tris hadn't stepped in, who knows how long it would have taken the police to find him. That's if they ever did. I thought we were making a difference, but I feel like as each year goes by, the political bullshit just ties our hands more and more. Sooner or later, policing is going to look like being a crossing guard at an elementary school. When is enough going to be enough?"

Ricky slowly pulls the car to the side of the street. I let out a relieved breath when I see Meredith standing on her corner looking our way.

"I get it. I really do. It's frustrating. Are you sure you want to do this though? Throw away your career for him?"

"What career, Ricky? I was only given that spot because of Uncle Ben. I never truly felt seen there. I was only a pawn. I worked so hard to become a cop because I wanted to continue the family legacy, and I hated it. Was I good at it? Sure, but I never felt like I was making a difference, and it ate at me. I just can't do it anymore. I'm going to find my real calling."

"I'll always be here for you."

"I know. Thank you." I pat his hand before slipping out of the car.

Meredith looks at me weird for a moment before recognition hits her.

"Girl, you are a sight for sore eyes. Where have you been? You finally snag you a sugar daddy?" she asks, looking over my shoulder at Ricky.

"Not exactly." I pull out a wad of cash Tris gave me. "I need some of your time."

"I'm not taking money from you," she hisses at me.

"You are because by taking it, you will be agreeing to hear me out. So let's take a seat and talk."

She hesitates, but I see the look in her eye. She needs this money. Reluctantly, she takes it, shoving it in her cleavage before sitting on the curb.

I sit next to her, giving a thumbs-up to Ricky as agreed.

"Who is really in the car?" she asks.

"A friend of mine. Listen, I need you to take what I say very seriously. I'm going to give you all the answers you want, but you need to listen."

She nods but stays silent.

"I was kidnapped by the men who are taking working girls. Only they aren't just taking the at risk. They're taking children from the streets as they walk home from school or when their parents look the other way. It's a ring. They take the girls to a shipping container, then move them to the next city by train. These men are ruthless.

They aren't taking us to rape or kill us. They are selling us. I was rescued before we got that far, but it's serious. I need you to keep an eye on the girls. Report anything that you find."

"I'm not talking to the cops," she interrupts.

I wince, handing her a card. "The top number is to Ricky. He's the man in the car. He is a cop, but he's one you can trust. I promise. The second number is to the Catalini crime family. They will take any information you pass along seriously."

"What the fuck have you gotten yourself into?" she asks, her eyes wide.

"Meredith, I need to be honest with you. My name isn't Sabrina. It's Serena. I've been working as an undercover cop taking down johns who specifically want children."

She gasps, her hand flying to her mouth. I can see she wants to flee, so I reach out, touching her leg.

"You promised to listen. I swear I never meant to deceive you. We were never here for you. All we wanted was the johns. Not even those who are just enjoying a woman. Only those who specifically asked for young girls. I'm talking under eighteen."

She shakes her head as the puzzle pieces start to fall into place. "It all makes so much sense now. How you were so picky about who you saw. I thought you had daddy issues."

"Not quite. I have pedophile issues."

She sighs. "Well, on one hand, I'm pissed that you lied, but the other is so glad that you're not really a seventeen-year-old selling her body. Wait, you're not seventeen, are you?"

"No. I'm twenty-two. I was a cop at Jersey City Police Department, but I've been let go. I'm moving to New York, but I couldn't leave you here without giving you a heads up. I don't want to see anything bad happen to you. I even have a way to give you a tracker if you want one, so if you are ever taken, we can find you."

"No. No way. I get what you are saying, and I'm not even really mad at you, but I can't let you track me. I know it might seem stupid to you, but I can't do it."

"It's okay. If you change your mind, let me know," I try to soothe her.

"The night you were taken..." she starts.

"It was the last night I saw you. You got into that car, and when I went to walk away, I was snatched."

"I knew it." She bites her lip. "The guy I was with. He was good-looking, which is already sketchy, but then he drove around the corner and paid me two hundred dollars to just sit with him. I didn't question it at the time because it was easy money, but I think he was in on it. I remember when I walked up to him, he had his eyes on you. I asked him if he'd prefer something a bit younger, but he said no. He wanted me. Once I got inside, he continued to watch you, even looking in his mirror. I thought it was odd, but you know in this line you can't be picky."

"Do you remember what he looked like?" I ask, my heart now racing.

I hadn't even thought about how they took me or why.

"He was tall and had dirty blonde hair. He had an accent. He got a text at the end and then told me to get out. I did see a tattoo on his wrist. It looked almost like a bracelet with some sort of design on it. I thought it was weird looking for a man to have."

"Thank you, Meredith. That is very helpful. Can you think of anything else?"

"No, but if I do, I will let you know. Which number do I call if I want to reach you?"

"The second one. Tell them you need to talk to me, and I will get the message."

She gives me a sad smile. "I'm going to miss you, but I don't want you coming back here."

"I won't make that promise. Not until I know you're safe."

"I live on the streets and sell my body for money, honey. I'll never be safe."

I sigh. "I don't like your logic."

She stands, so I follow her. Then she pulls me in for a hug.

"Don't worry about me. I chose this life, and I'm happy with it. I wouldn't even know what to do with myself if this was taken away from me. Not you though. You have the chance at a new start. Take it and run with it, girl."

"Thanks. I'll keep in touch," I tell her.

As I walk away, I glance back. My heart hurts for Meredith. She's so lost in this hole she put herself in that she can't see a way out.

Maybe one day, I'll be able to help her find one.

Tristano

STANDING, I drop the tape gun onto the box and look around as I stretch. Boxes are stacked against the wall next to the door. Last night, Serena and I managed to pack up a few boxes before we crashed, but not nearly enough. Thankfully, it gave me something to do while she goes out there to talk to her friend. I hate that she didn't want me there. The caveman in me almost followed anyway.

Then I realized that if I went against her wishes, I was only being controlling like her uncle is. I don't want to be that for her. I want to possess her yes, but I want her to know that she also has her own mind as well. She can do anything she wants with it. I mean, unless she wants to leave me. Then I'll tie her ass to my bed and spank it raw until she changes her mind.

Fuck, that's a dark thought. She's been through enough, yet the idea of tying her up has my dick hard. I'm fucked up.

I shake the thoughts away as I focus back on the task at hand. Ricky texted ten minutes ago, saying they were on their way back. I don't have too much left, but I want to get it done as quickly as possible.

It's weird seeing this side of her. While I've known her for years, we haven't ever spent much time together in each other's space. Other than the one time I showed up for her academy graduation, we agreed to keep our distance, so I've never seen her house. I didn't know that she had a basket full of blankets to curl up on the couch with or a bunch of knickknacks from different places she's traveled.

Having a couple of hours alone in her space has let me see a different side of the woman I've been obsessed with for years.

I can't wait to see her shit mixed with mine.

That thought hits me hard.

Her things will be mixed in with mine because we will be living together. I used to think being tied down to one woman was a death sentence.

When did that change for me?

A flash of brown eyes hits my mind, and I know it's her. Meeting her changed my life irrevocably. I wouldn't change it for the world though.

Walking over to the fridge, I open it looking for something other than tap water to drink. Sighing, I grab the trash can and start emptying the fridge when I find nothing but takeout containers and condiments. For crying out loud, how many different bottles of BBQ sauce does one woman need? Or is the food that bad that she has to smother the taste with this shit?

Lucky for her, she's moving into a house with a fully stocked fridge and into a city with killer food.

I wonder if she will like Bella Italiano. I think to myself.

Fridge emptied, I tie the bag off and take it out to the dumpster.

"Hey you." I hear her voice float toward me.

After tossing the bag into the dumpster, I look over my shoulder.

Ricky waves at me as he pulls off, ensuring she's in my care.

Guy might be a cop, but I respect how he handled today. He

could have refused to keep me updated. Hell, he could have called me out for being a criminal. I know he knows I am one.

He didn't though. He put Serena first, which makes him okay in my books.

"That didn't take as long as I thought."

"I didn't want to hang around too long. Not good for business."

She comes up next to me, and I fall into step with her.

"You okay?" I nudge her shoulder.

She gives me a sad smile. "I will be. Did you get much done while I was gone?"

"Your living room is packed up, and I started in on the kitchen."

"I can't thank you enough," she tells me as we step inside.

"It's nothing." I shrug.

"It's everything." She looks around the place and shakes her head. "It's weird seeing nothing on the walls."

"Let's sit down and take a break. I was about to order some food."

"Food would be good," she agrees, her eyes moving around the empty space.

I order something quick from the Chinese place down the street before moving to find Serena sitting in the middle of the living room on the floor.

I take a seat behind her, pulling her into my arms.

"Tell me about it."

She deflates, her body melting into mine.

"Meredith thinks the john that picked her up that night was in on the abduction. She said he's tall with blonde hair and had some sort of tattoo on his wrist. She said it looked like a bracelet. She has no proof, but I kind of think she's right. I don't remember much about that night, but I remember that he parked away from us. Normally, they pull right up in front of us. Maybe he was trying to lure one of us away."

I run my hands over her hair as she talks, trying to keep her calm. "We will find them. Did she say she would call?"

"She was hesitant, but I think she will call you. I gave her Ricky's number too, but he's a cop. No matter what I say, she's not going to trust him."

"Does she trust you?" I ask.

"I think she wants to, but I don't think she does. It's hard to earn back trust once it's been broken. I'm not sure we will ever get back there again," she says sadly.

"I'm sorry."

She sighs. "I'm not. It needed to happen. Maybe now she will be more vigilant. I don't want anything happening to her."

I don't know what to say to that, so I keep quiet. The last few days have thrown me for a loop. Usually I have something to say about everything, but not now.

After several minutes of silence, she wiggles in my arms until she's looking at me. She has a suspicious gleam in her eye.

"You didn't touch anything in my room, did you?" she finally asks.

"No, I figured I would leave that up to you." I tilt my head, confused.

"Huh." She looks a little disappointed.

"What?" I ask, pulling her into my chest.

I watch as a smile plays on her lips. "And here I thought you would have taken the chance to rifle through my panty drawer in peace."

"On second thought," I say, pushing her from my lap.

Serena busts out laughing, and it's fucking beautiful.

I'll do whatever it takes to make her laugh like that every day.

"Hey, are you okay?"

I shake my head. "Yeah, why?"

"I don't know. You just had this look on your face."

"I think you mean my good looks."

Serena rolls her eyes as she turns and starts walking away. "Whatever you say. Now get to work. We have an apartment to pack up. I'll go finish up my room."

"Yes, ma'am."

For the next hour, we work separately packing up her life, and when the food is delivered, we eat separately while we work. Once I'm done in the kitchen, I head into her bedroom and find her sitting on the floor with piles of clothes on either side of her.

"Aren't you supposed to be packing?" I tease as I fall onto her bed. "For fuck's sake, why is your bed so hard?"

"Because it was that way when I bought it?" She shrugs. "And I decided to go through this shit first. That way we don't move a bunch of clothes I don't want anymore."

"Makes sense. For the record, this bed isn't coming with us. I'll buy you a new one if you want one."

Serena rolls her eyes. "That's not necessary."

"Fine. When you decide to leave, I'll let you take the bed in my guest bedroom."

If I let you leave. I silently tack on.

Serena looks at me with a look I can't quite name.

"What?" I ask, fighting the urge to shift.

"You're something else."

"I'm your something else though."

She rolls her eyes, but I see the smile playing on her lips. She's not ready to admit it, but she wants me to want her. Further proving my point, she stands and turns, stretching in front of me.

My eyes instantly drop down to her ass. Fuck is it a nice one. My mind races with the possibilities of what we could do with her on her hands and knees, just like this, only naked.

"Hey," she says, snapping her fingers toward my face.

I shake my head. "Sorry, what did you say?"

"Like what you see?" she teases.

"*Anima gemella*, you know I do. There's no need to fish for compliments."

I watch as a beautiful blush covers her cheeks. Yeah, I'm definitely going to make her do that every day too.

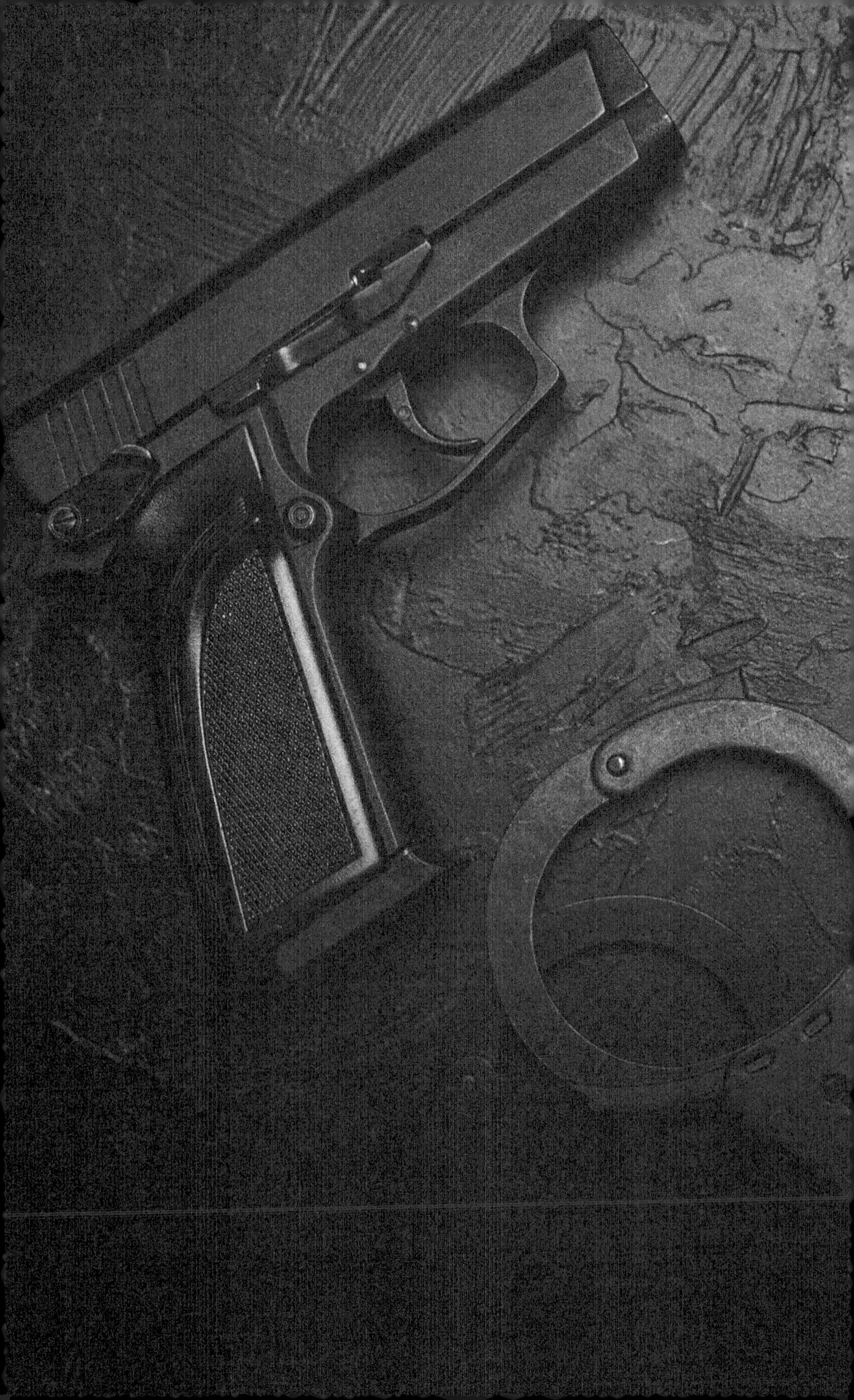

CHAPTER
THIRTEEN

Serena

I look out the window at the street as we pass. This isn't the neighborhood I pictured Tristano living in. I thought it would be all gangs and gun violence. Instead, there's a couple swinging a child between them as they go on a stroll. Across the street, an elderly lady is carrying her groceries. A young kid rushes up to help her as she almost drops it.

This is picturesque. Not at all the life I imagined every time I spoke with him on the phone.

Yet here we are. Riding out to meet not one, but two heads of the family.

I swallow hard, my nerves getting the best of me.

"Fuck," I mutter under my breath as he makes another turn, this one leading to a gated home.

"You good?" Tristano asks as he nods to the guard at the gate.

"Yeah," I manage to breathe out.

You are so far from good it's not even funny.

My chest is tight. These people have the ability to tell me to never see Tristano again. Even worse, they could order my death.

Tristano takes my hand. "It's okay to not be okay, *anima gemella*. I won't let anything happen to you."

I give him a small nod as he parks. Then he gets out of the car, coming around to open my door.

I let him help me out as he escorted me up to the beautiful home. The door opens before we can even get there.

"Tristano. Such a treat to have you actually stop by for once. You know, I was starting to wonder if you had died," the gorgeous dark-haired beauty chastises as she pulls him into a hug.

A twinge of jealousy hits. Who is this woman? She looks familiar, but I can't tell why. Has he slept with her? Does he want to? She sure is pretty.

"Sofia, you know I've had responsibilities." He pulls back, moving to my side. "Please meet my girl, Serena. Serena, this is Bash's wife, Sofia."

"Pleasure to meet you, dear. Maybe you can make sure he checks in a bit more often. Quite rude letting others think you are dead." She glares at him.

He only chuckles.

"Your husband knows what I'm doing at all times," Tris argues.

"*Tesoro,* please let them in past the door. We do have things we need to discuss."

The dark-haired man that walks into the foyer is one that I would recognize anywhere. Bastiano Catalini, head of the Catalini crime family. He's known for being ruthless yet fair. He handles all his business in such a manner that the FBI, CIA, and local government haven't been able to pin a single thing on him. Seems he learned from his father's mistake and built an empire. One where none of his men nor the residents in his city will even speak his name without praising him to the high heavens.

That's intimidating as fuck.

Hell, politicians could learn a thing or two from him.

"Of course. Let's go to the meeting room. Greer will be here momentarily. Seems the little one gave her some issues," Sofia adds, leading us down the hall into a room.

"Please leave all your electronics in the basket," Bastiano asks, placing his own in there.

Tris does the same, holding his hand out for mine. I give him the burner he gave me.

"We really should replace my real cell phone," I murmur to him.

"As soon as we leave here," he promises.

We are all about to take a seat, but commotion from the hall draws us back out there.

"About time you let me in," a woman says as she pushes her way inside past a guard I hadn't even noticed was standing there before.

"Don't mind her, she's a little hangry is all," a tall man with a deep voice and a slight accent says as he walks in behind her.

"I'm used to her moods." Tristano smirks as he calls out.

The woman spots me right away and walks toward me. I summon all the courage I have and step forward, meeting her halfway.

"Hi, I'm Serena," I say as I hold out my hand.

"I'm Greer, and that's my husband Killian. Nice to meet you," she says as she takes my hand.

"You too."

I turn to her husband to shake his hand, only to realize he's holding a car seat.

"Oh," I say, shaking my head, laughing. "I don't know how I missed you carrying that."

Killian smirks as he sets the car seat on the foyer table, pushing the handle back. "It's alright."

"Congratulations on your newest addition," I tell them both before turning toward Greer. "You look fantastic."

"Thank you." She pushes her hair behind her shoulders. "I'm tired as hell, but this little guy is worth it."

"I'll take him so you guys can talk. I need some nephew cuddles." Sofia steps forward, taking the baby from the seat, floating down the hall.

"She has one of her own. I'm sure Izzy is here too helping her. I saw Giovanni when we pulled up," Tris whispers as the others file back into the room.

I trail behind them, taking a deep breath. Once I'm inside the room again, the once-large meeting room seems much smaller.

I swallow hard as everything hits me all at once.

This is fucking real. I'm standing here surrounded by all the faces the police trained me were my enemies.

"Are you okay?" Tristano murmurs, as he catches me off guard, placing his hand on my lower back.

I didn't even hear him approach.

"I'm good." I smile weakly.

"Uh-huh," he mutters before turning toward everyone else.

He leads me to a seat, helping me sit before taking a device and scanning the room. Once he's done, he takes the place next to me, slipping his hand into mine.

"Shall we begin?" Killian asks.

Bastiano tilts his head toward me. "Start from the beginning, Serena, and don't leave anything out."

Taking a deep breath, I squeeze Tristano's hand hoping to stop the shaking. He gives me a reassuring smile, so I start talking. Once I open my mouth, everything comes out. I tell them about how I had been tracking the disappearances and took them to my uncle, only to be told that I didn't have enough, and how that led to me being taken. I relay every single detail that I can remember up until Tristano and everyone saved all of us.

"Jesus," Killian murmurs softly as he shakes his head.

"Those poor children." Greer shakes her head.

"You appear to be holding up well though. Maybe a little too well." Bastiano narrows his eyes.

"Bash," Tris warns, getting a glare in return.

"It's okay," I tell him before turning back to him. "Was I scared out of my mind? Yes, but this wasn't my first time being taken against my will. I think between that and my police training, I've been able to process it better."

"Serena, don't," Tristano says as he grabs my knee.

I turn toward him and shake my head. "It's fine." Taking a deep breath, I turn back toward everyone. "This time was a cakewalk in comparison, considering I wasn't raped."

The men flinch at my words, but I keep going.

"Yeah, my nerves are frayed and I'm having problems sleeping but I'm still breathing. I can pick up the pieces and put myself back together again. So yeah, you might think I'm holding up when really I'm just faking it until I am. I'm going to start seeing a therapist again, but until we stop these people, I can't even think about it. All I know is we need to take care of this and make this city and the surrounding cities safe again."

I watch as respect crosses his face before turning away. "All I want to do is find these bastards and take them down. I don't want anyone else to go through what I or those other women did."

"And who knows how bad it would have gotten had you made it to your final destination," Greer says softly.

I nod. "Exactly."

I try not to shift in my seat as Bastiano stares me down.

"Alright. I'm initiating her into the family," Bastiano says, turning toward me. "For this only. At the end of the day, you're still a cop and I don't trust you. Trust is earned, not given, do you understand?"

"Yes."

He nods. "You can call me Bash. You're going to be part of our inner sanctum, which means we are trusting you. If at the end of this, you've proven yourself to me and are still interested, we can reevaluate. With that being said, Tristano vouches for you and has sworn his life to you. Do you understand what that means?"

I turn and look at Tris, but he's not meeting my gaze. I look back to Bash.

"No, sir."

"It means he is claiming you as his woman. This will afford you protections. Add in my stamp of approval, and no one from our family will touch you. Others might not respect it though. You were still a cop at one point. They won't trust that you aren't still undercover doing an op. You understand?"

"I'm not. I swear. Honestly, I'm not sure I could be a cop with the way things are right now. Knowing that I would have to sit around and let girls be taken? I can't do it. I won't be part of a force like that."

He nods in understanding. "What do you say, Killian? You trust her?"

Killian stares at me a moment before nodding. "I'll vouch for her. You think they will accept it though?"

"I assume Callum will follow your lead. Harukai has always been a loose cannon. The real question is Nikolai. He doesn't trust easily. I don't think he will like her being a cop."

"Former cop," I murmur.

"Let's find out." Greer smiles.

Tristano

SERENA IS FREAKING OUT, but I don't have time to console her. I press the button that pulls the television screen down into the room. Then

I enter the mile-long code, giving it access to the secure channel I set up specifically for this meeting. Only three other people have access.

Their faces pop up one by one.

I hear Serena gasp a little, her hand now digging into my leg. I take it though. I'd take anything for her.

"Thank you, gentlemen, for joining us. We have some updates to provide. First, meet Serena. She's newly inducted into my family. Before we go any further, I need you to know that we have accepted her in and will be having her assist in this endeavor. She is uniquely qualified in two ways. One, she used to be an undercover cop that worked the beat where some of the girls were taken."

I wince as I see Nikolai and Haruaki narrow their eyes. Callum is stoic as always. I assume Declan filled him in though. He knows who Serena is to me.

"She is also one of the women saved, wasn't she?" Haruaki cuts in.

Bash looks angry at the interruption but nods. "That is correct. She was taken while working undercover and recovered with the women in Chicago."

"I'd like to hear from her. Why do you believe we should trust you?" Nikolai asks.

I want to jump in and do this for her. Especially feeling her shake next to me, but I can't. Only she can make these leaders trust her.

"I went into law enforcement because I thought I could make a difference. I thought I would be on the streets getting the men who hurt children and women off of them." I scoff as I shake my head. "I found out what a pipe dream that was. Every time I turned around there would be red tape needing to be cut. Some reason why we couldn't go after this person or that person. I can't be a part of an organization that allows a person to get away with some of the horrific things that I've had done to me. It's not acceptable. I thought I was firmly on the good side, but my moral compass has grown a bit darker in the past couple weeks. I now see that the only way to rid evil from this world is to rip it from its root. In order to do that, you can't be on the right side of the law. I acknowledge and accept that." She lets out a breath, her eyes filling with tears.

I so badly want to pull her into my arms, but I know if I do, it'll make her look weak.

Nikolai is quiet a moment before asking, "What do you think will happen to these men when we find them?"

Serena doesn't look away from the screen, staring right at the man.

"They will be eliminated and will never hurt another woman again."

He gives a slight nod. "You know this is only one ring of many, right?"

"Then I'll keep looking for them until the day I stop breathing," she answers quickly.

"I vote her in," Nikolai responds just as quickly.

"Me too," Callum adds.

"Let's see what the girl's got in her." Haruaki smirks, making me want to shield her from him.

He's not known for being right in the head. He is known as the dark prince for a reason. This is a man who is known to take knives to a gunfight.

"Alright, the next order of business. Do we have any updates?" Bash asks.

Serena raises her hand, making me chuckle.

"What?" she hisses at me.

"This isn't school, *anima gemella*. You don't have to raise your hand."

"Right." She looks back to the room. "The night I was taken, the girl I was with was picked up by a man. She believes he was in on my abduction. Tris and I have been trying to track him down, but we are having issues."

"What do you know?" Killian asks.

I listen as Serena tells them about his description, including the tattoo.

"He's been to a Russian prison. The manacle on the wrist indicates time served," Nikolai helpfully adds.

"That's why I wasn't able to find it. I kept calling it a bracelet," I muse to myself, pulling up photo after photo of the tattoo now that I have the right word. "We will show these to the girl and get confirmation, but it does seem to be Russian."

"I know that at least the ones here were Russian. When we were being held in the container here and on the train, I recognized a few of the words. The ones in Chicago weren't Russian though. They spoke a different language."

"Put together a file with common phrases in each language and have her listen. Maybe she will recognize which one. You mentioned that they spoke of the dark web in your interview with Kenji," Haruaki says.

"Yes. It seemed like they were putting our pictures on there and then selling us. They weren't touching us directly though. Gave us enough food and water to keep us alive. These men, while terrible, weren't even interested in us," Serena adds.

"That is interesting," Callum muses.

"It could be a faction of men not related to any one group. Maybe that's why we are having trouble finding them," Killian adds.

Serena looks down as her body slowly stops shaking.

Ignoring everyone around us, I whisper into her ear, "Are you okay?"

"Hmm?" Serena hums as she blinks slowly.

"Zone out again?" I ask.

"Yeah, sorry." She shakes her head. "This is just a lot. I want to get them, but at the same time I feel like sometimes it all crashes down on me."

"It's okay." I look around the room before looking back at her. "You're doing great. No one is going to blame you if you need to step back."

"No. I need to see this through." She's adamant.

"Then I'll be here for you every step of the way. When it seems heavier than you can handle, lean on me. I can hold it for you until you feel better again."

"That means a lot." She leans her head on my shoulder.

"Alright, we will work on a plan. Let's get these guys," Bash says.

The others agree. After a few other updates, they all disconnect.

"Let's go meet my nephew," I whisper as I escort us from the room while everyone else is still talking.

"Can we just leave?" she asks, looking back at the room.

"Business is done. We can do what we want now. What I want is baby cuddles."

Walking into the living room, I smile when I see Sofia holding Kieran as he fusses.

"Thank goodness you guys are done. He's not happy. I had Izzy take the other kids outside for a while, hoping he would calm."

"Give him here." I hold open my arms.

She chuckles, handing him to me. "He's your problem now. I'm going to go check on the others. Are you guys staying for dinner?"

I look to Serena. She gives me a small smile and nods.

"Yes, we will."

"Great."

As soon as she leaves the room, I move so Serena can see the baby too.

"Serena, meet the little prince, Kieran."

"He's so adorable. You're good with him."

"You should see all the things I bought him. He's going to be spoiled," I singsong to him.

She giggles. "You bought baby things?"

"Of course. What kind of uncle would I be if I didn't?" I scoff.

"You aren't his uncle, I am," Bash says, making his way into the room with the others behind him.

I roll my eyes. "I might not biologically be related to little man, but last I checked, you weren't on food runs when Greer was having cravings the way Enzo and I were."

"Hey, I did my part," Killian says.

"That's your job as my husband," Greer chimes in.

"You should see the baby wrap I got for the office," I tell them, excitement flowing through me at the thought of holding little man on me while I walk.

The only thing that would make it better is if he weren't just my nephew. No, the thought of my own little man in my arms has my heart beating faster as I look at the beauty next to me.

We could have kids together.

Greer laughs as Serena shakes her head with a smile on her face.

"Nothing you say surprises me anymore," Sofia says, walking back into the room.

"I'm the only one with a chair that leans back. I figured I could hold the little guy when Greer needs a break and work at the same time, or take a nap when he does. They say you're supposed to sleep when they do," I tell them, trying not to get lost in the sudden feeling in my chest.

"Who said he's going to work with her? Maybe I'm going to take him." Killian sounds offended.

Greer and I scoff at the same time.

"Please, like momma bear would let you take this little guy out of her sight more than necessary," I tell him.

"How did we go from taking down a sex trafficking ring to who's on baby duty?" Bash jokes.

"Welcome to the family, Serena. We work hard but play harder and apparently get off topic at the drop of a hat," I quip.

I look over at Serena and see a beautiful blush covering her cheeks.

I can't wait to make her flush for other reasons. The best reasons.

"How about dinner? I almost have it ready." Sofia ushers us all into the dining room.

I smile as I trail behind, watching Serena smile as Greer chats with her.

For once, I feel like I'm actually happy and not just faking it.

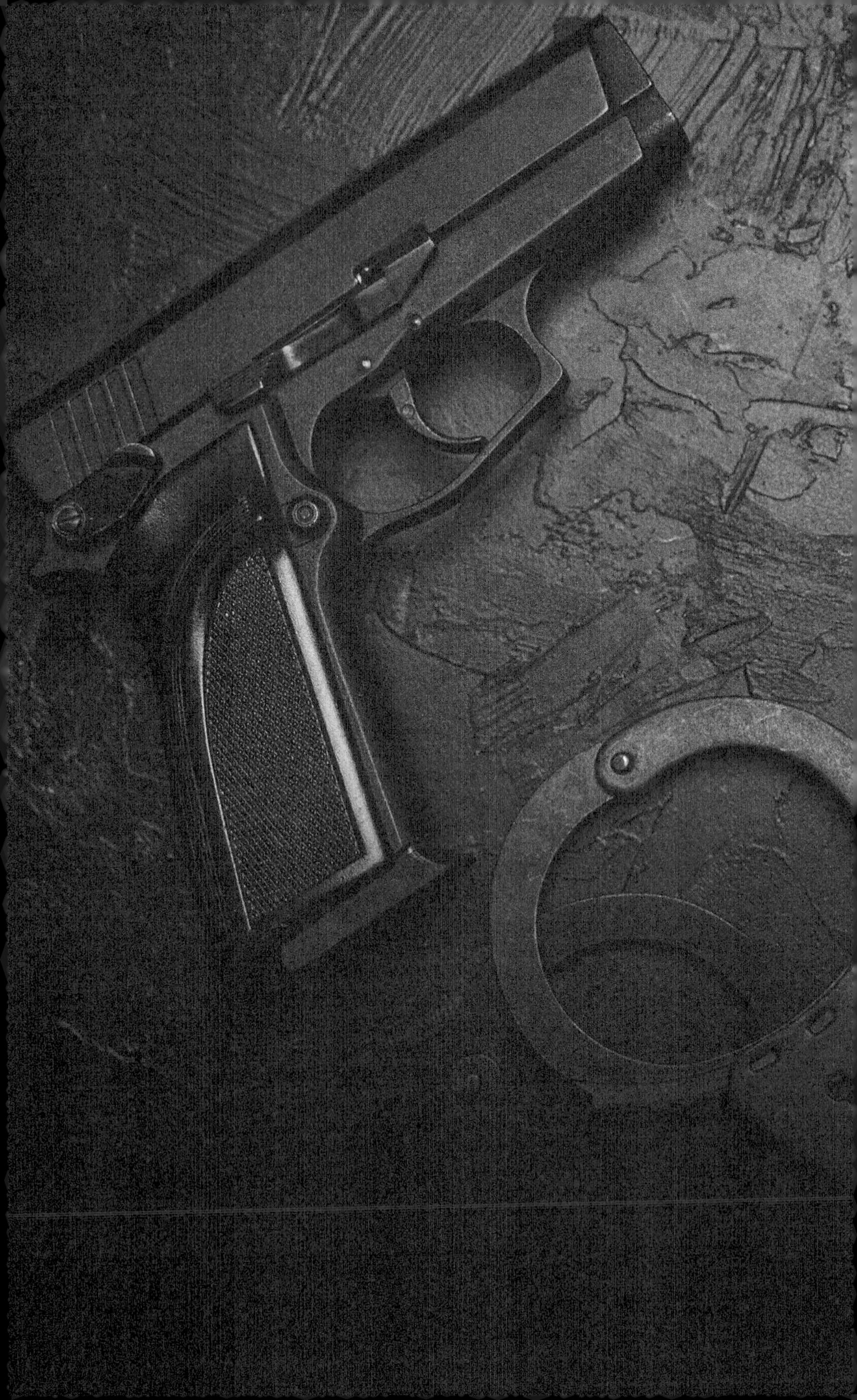

CHAPTER
FOURTEEN

Serena

"Just keep taking deep breaths. Don't get lost," the man says.

I'm not with him right now though. No, I'm back in the shipping container. I can hear Olivia crying next to me.

"*Zamknij ich.*"

"What is that?" I hear the man ask.

"Something I heard them say," I whisper.

My body starts to shake, the coldness seeping back into me.

"I think we are done for now. We have enough. Come back to us slowly. First, tell me what you smell in the room."

"The lavender candle you lit before we started."

"Good. Now when I count to three, I want you to open your eyes. One, two, three."

I open my eyes. The room is dim. It's not exactly hypnotherapy, but Greer thought it might help. I didn't recognize any of the languages they played for me. None of the phrases they played were ever used, so while some sounded familiar, they could be from any European country. This was the second option. Using someone to try and pull some memories from me.

As I sit up, I look over as Greer leads the man to the door.

"Thank you for doing this on such short notice, Dorian." Greer smiles as she shakes the therapist's hand.

"It was my pleasure. I'll have the sketch and my notes to you before dinner," he tells her before turning toward me. "It was a pleasure working with you, Serena, despite the circumstances."

"Thank you. You have a great day," I manage to rasp, my throat feeling dry.

Greer waits until he's left before turning toward me.

"Where is Tristano?" I ask, wondering why he didn't come in as soon as they were done.

He was outside when we started. He wouldn't spend another moment apart from me if he could help it.

She raises a brow. "Afraid to be alone with me?"

"No." I scoff. "I was just expecting him to be here when I got done."

Greer hums. "He had to go handle some business but will be back soon. Would you like to go grab some lunch with me?"

Despite the fact she's phrasing it as a question, I know there's only one answer I can give her.

"Sure."

This feels like a trap. A trap I don't like.

"Fantastic. How do you feel about Italian food?"

"As far as I'm concerned, pasta should be its own food group."

Greer smiles. "I know just the place then."

I eye Enzo as he falls into step with us as we leave the building and get into a waiting town car. As the car begins to move, Enzo turns toward me.

"Have you spent much time in the city?" he asks.

"When I was younger, yes, but not in several years."

"I understand." He nods.

"When Enzo and I moved back from Italy, it took me a month to find what I was looking for. Granted, our neighborhood doesn't have a high turnover rate, but outside of it…" she trails off.

"That's nice though that the neighborhood doesn't change," I tell her.

"It is. Will you miss Jersey City? I know it's right across the river, but I assume you won't be spending much time there." Her question feels weighted.

I tilt my head to the side, thinking about my answer. "I don't think so. I'm sure I'll miss some things but not much. I didn't really have friends thanks to work keeping me busy, and my apartment wasn't anything special. Honestly, I hardly spent enough time there. I was all about work, and when I wasn't at work, I was thinking about it."

"How do you feel now that you aren't working?" she says.

"Honestly? It's a weight off my shoulders. I felt like I had to live up to my family legacy, but I realized that I wasn't living my own life. I feel like this is my second chance."

Enzo looks at Greer before turning toward me. "Well, I know Tristano is excited to have you here with us."

"Yes, and I'll have to make sure you come to girls' night." Greer tips her chin.

The car starts to slow, and I look out the window.

"I would like that," I say quietly.

We stop in front of an Italian restaurant called Bella Italiano.

"Have you ever eaten here?" Greer asks as we walk toward the door.

"No, is it good?"

Greer and Enzo chuckle. "I hope so," she says with laughter in her voice.

The hostess's eyes widen when they see Greer, and she starts to scramble.

"Mrs. O'Reilly, how are you today?" the hostess asks.

"I'm fine, just two for today. Enzo would like a seat at the bar," Greer tells her.

"Of course."

The hostess nods her head so fast she looks like a bobblehead.

Enzo breaks off and heads to the bar as we walk toward a table.

"Is this okay?" the hostess asks hesitantly.

"This is fine. Thank you," Greer tells her as she takes a seat facing the front of the restaurant, even though we are tucked out of view.

I can feel the corner of my eye twitch at the thought of sitting with my back toward the entrance, but I suck it up. I sure as hell won't cause a scene over something like this.

It's not like you carry a gun anymore. A little voice in my head whispers.

I look around the restaurant and spot Enzo easily. He's sitting so he has a direct view of us and the front. Lucky bastard.

"So what's good here?" I ask as I pick up the menu.

"Everything," a server says as she approaches with a smile on her face.

"Izzy, I'm surprised to see you working," Greer says.

Izzy shrugs. "Someone called in and they were short-staffed. It gave me a reason to leave the house and let Gio take care of the kids."

Greer laughs. "Like he wouldn't have if you asked."

Izzy smiles with a love-sick look on her face as she thinks about her husband. "True."

Greer looks at me. "I'm sorry, we get so carried away. You remember Izzy from the other night?"

"Of course. Great to see you again."

Izzy and her husband Giovanni joined us for dinner. It was an impromptu thing, but I still enjoyed it. I could feel the love flowing between them all, even with Killian being there from another family. All I could think was how badly I wanted to belong there.

Maybe this is my shot. I just need to make Greer see that I am serious about Tristano and the family.

She waves her hand toward me. "It's nice to see you as well. Now tell me, what would you two like to drink?"

"Water for me."

"Same." I smile at her.

"Awesome, I'll be back shortly with those and to take your order."

Izzy walks away and Greer turns toward me and just stares. I hold her gaze as I fight the urge to squirm. Slowly a smile spreads across her face.

"I like you."

"Thank you?" My brows furrow. That's not what I was expecting her to say.

"Tristano and you have known each other for years?"

"We have." I smile softly. "He's the best."

"When Tristano told us about you, I was worried. I've known him for a long time, and he has never mentioned you. Which is surprising because the man is an open book. He can't even keep birthday presents a secret."

The dig hurts, but I hide my reaction.

"As soon as your name left his mouth though, I knew that you had the power to destroy him," she admits.

"You're wrong." I shake my head, swallowing hard.

"I'm rarely wrong."

"Why don't you tell me why I'm here then?"

"Tristano is family and once I care for someone, that doesn't stop. If you hurt him." She chuckles darkly. "I'll do whatever necessary to fix it."

"Are you threatening me?"

Greer tsks. "Sweetheart, that's not a threat, it's a fucking promise. So if you are in this for the long haul, then I'll be there the day you get married with the fanciest bottle of champagne, but if you betray him, just know you won't see me or mine coming. Understood?"

I nod as Izzy walks back up to the table. She looks between Greer and me with a raised brow as she sets our waters down.

"Your brother would be jealous if you got first blood on the new floors," Izzy says lightly.

Greer laughs. "Don't worry, the mop doesn't need to be pulled out for us." She looks back at me. "Right, Serena?"

"All good," I say, swallowing hard as I look between the two of them.

After she takes our order and wanders off, I turn to Greer.

"I understand your concern. I'm some girl you've just met and it seems so out of place, but I've been protecting Tris since I was seventeen years old. Not a single day has gone by since the day we met that I haven't thought about him. Yearned for him. He always kept this distance between us. Had he asked me back then, I would have given it all up for him, which knowing him, it's exactly why he never asked. This all seems sudden, but this isn't a whim. The second he expressed the same interest in me that I have always felt for him, I made the necessary moves to make sure I was by his side. You can either accept that and me, or you can back the fuck off because respectfully, my relationship with him is none of your business."

She stares at me for several long moments before she smiles. "Good. I knew you were the one for him. I can't believe I didn't see it sooner. I knew he had the program watching Jersey City, I just never connected that it was to watch you. He is such a flirt and so outgoing that it never even dawned on me that he had a secret girlfriend. Him turning down Natasha makes so much more sense now."

"*Who?*" I grind out between my teeth.

Her eyes widen before she laughs. "Oh yeah. I like you, hellcat. Don't you worry. I have a feeling Tristano has had his eye on you for years. Now that I think about it, I haven't seen him with anyone the entire time he's worked for me."

My heart calms down a little. "Really?"

She nods. "I think he's in love with you, babe."

I can't help the smile that fills my face as she continues.

"I'm guessing you're in love with him too."

I am.

I so am, but I'm not going to let her be the first to hear those words, so I just smile.

Tristano

I walk into Bella Italiano and instantly spot Enzo.

"Hi. Just one today?" the young hostess asks as she bats her eyes and tries to push up her boobs.

Before Serena came back into my life, I would have hung around and flirted with her for a minute and made her feel special. I would have played up the reputation everyone had of me, but now my eyes only seek out one woman. I have no desire to look at another.

"I'm meeting a friend." I nod toward Enzo.

Her cheeks heat with embarrassment at my dismissal. "Head on back."

"Thanks." I don't spare her another glance, heading straight toward him.

"How was it?" He doesn't even turn around to acknowledge me, his eyes moving around the room.

"It was fine," I grumble.

"Good." He nods.

"It could have been done by someone else," I say raising a brow.

Enzo smirks. "Greer didn't want to send just anyone to Natasha's."

I roll my eyes. Natasha is a friend of the girls. She owns a lingerie shop called Seduction. I may have flirted with her on occasion, but

I've never taken her up on her offers of more. She's a gorgeous woman with so many great qualities, but she was never right. She was never Serena.

It doesn't seem to be stopping Greer though. I need to have a talk with her about it. I mean, even Natasha knew something was up. When I showed up, she was dressed to the nines and obviously ready for our flirting routine, but I shut that shit down and quick.

"Okay, who is she?" Natasha asks as she leans against her desk.

"What do you mean?" I ask as I fix her security system. Somehow the touch screen went out.

"You haven't flirted with me," she deadpans. "And I know it's not because I look like shit. So I'll ask again, who is she?"

"Who says I'm not flirting because of a woman?"

Natasha raises a brow as she crosses her arms over her chest. "Don't try and bullshit me. I'd like to think that we have become closer than mere acquaintances. I can see the change in you. You're not wearing the mask anymore."

"Her name is Serena," I confess. "She's..."

"Are you in love, Tristano?" she teases.

"I think I have been for a long time," I admit for the first time out loud.

A smile covers her face. "I'm happy for you, friend. You deserve it. Now hurry up. I have a feeling you need to get back to your girl."

By the time I left the shop, Natasha had filled a bag of lingerie for me to give Serena and told me to bring her in to meet her.

Laughter has me turning and looking at Serena and Greer.

"How are things here?" I murmur, my eyes on my girl.

She looks gorgeous today with her long brown hair falling down her back and that peach dress that makes her skin look like it glows.

I see Enzo nod out of the corner of my eye. "Good. They just got their food."

"And the hypnotherapy?" I ask as I run my hand through my hair.

"He told Greer it went well, and he would have his notes and sketches to us before dinner."

"That's not what I meant and you know it," I hiss.

He's quiet a moment. "She seems okay. A little nervous being with Greer, but she didn't seem overly upset over the visit. You'll have to check in with her as you know her better than I do, but she's strong. She can handle it."

I let out the breath I was holding. I hated leaving Serena alone while I was gone, but it's not like I could exactly say no when Greer asked me to go. She's my boss, and I know Serena would understand that. Besides, I knew she was in safe hands. Greer might be a hard ass sometimes, but she's a good person.

"Should we join them?" I'm itching to be by my girl.

"Sure." Enzo chuckles as he stands.

As we approach, the girls turn and look our way. A smile covers Serena's face, and her shoulders relax as soon as she sees me. My heart skips a beat at the sight.

She fucking missed me.

"Hey you," she says softly as I take a seat next to her.

"Hey, *anima gemella*. How are you?"

"I can't complain. This food is delicious."

"It is. This is one of the places I wanted to take you." I lean into her head, kissing the side of it.

I don't miss the way Greer looks at us, a small smile on her face.

Looking around, I don't see a server near us, making me sigh.

"I ordered you your usual when you texted me that you were on the way," Enzo tells me.

"Thanks, man." I smile. "I knew you loved me."

Enzo rolls his eyes, muttering under his breath something about pain.

"How was Natasha?" Greer asks with a devious smirk on her face.

I feel Serena tense next to me as I shoot a dirty look at Greer.

"Your friend is fine. I don't know what happened though to make the screen of the security system to crash. It was deader than a doornail," I say, shaking my head. I turn to Serena and rest my hand on her thigh under the table. "Natasha is a friend of the girls. She owns a lingerie shop, and we do the security for her."

"That's nice of you guys," she says softly as understanding fills her eyes.

I explained myself to her to reassure her. I needed her to know that Natasha isn't a threat. She never will be now that she knows how I feel for Serena.

I nod before turning back toward Greer. "Natasha told me to have you call her. She thinks she has something that would bring Killian to his knees for you."

"I'm sure she does. I'll have to stop by on my way home." She hums.

"Don't go without little man though, she wants baby cuddles," I tell her.

Greer rolls her eyes. "Never have children, Serena. As soon as you do, everyone forgets about you and only cares about the baby."

"You're one to talk. Remember when we brought Viola home?" Enzo scoffs.

"Who's Viola?" Serena asks.

"My daughter." Enzo jumps into the story about how he didn't know she existed until a local from the village in Italy that they used to live in told Greer while they were visiting. They found her at an orphanage.

Viola is awesome. She's selectively mute so she doesn't talk verbally, but you always know what she's thinking because of her facial expressions.

"That's so crazy. I couldn't imagine," Serena says, shaking her head in awe.

"It was a crazy time, but we got through it," Greer says as she bumps shoulders with Enzo.

"I wouldn't change a single thing about it," Enzo says.

Serena tilts her head to the side. "You wouldn't take away her time at the orphanage?"

"As a parent, of course I would if I could, but logically, I know that if she didn't spend time there then things wouldn't have worked out the way they did. If I would have known about her from the beginning, maybe I would be in a loveless marriage with her mother and still living in Italy? Maybe I wouldn't have met my wife, Danica? No, I think it all worked out the way it was supposed to."

"I like that. I love the way you talk about them," Serena says softly before looking at Greer. "And how did you meet your husband?"

Greer looks at Enzo and laughs while he rolls his eyes.

"Well you see, one night I snuck out and found myself in a bar in Westies territory. This sexy-as-fuck guy sat down next to me. I knew who he was, but he had no idea that I was the sister of his enemy." As she jumps into the story of her and Killian and their crazy history and how he followed her across the Atlantic, I can't help but think about what Enzo said.

I wouldn't redo any of my past with Serena. Of course I would take away her pain if I could, but who could say if things would be how they are now if we never went through all of that shit?

"You okay?" Serena murmurs as she leans into my side.

"Never better."

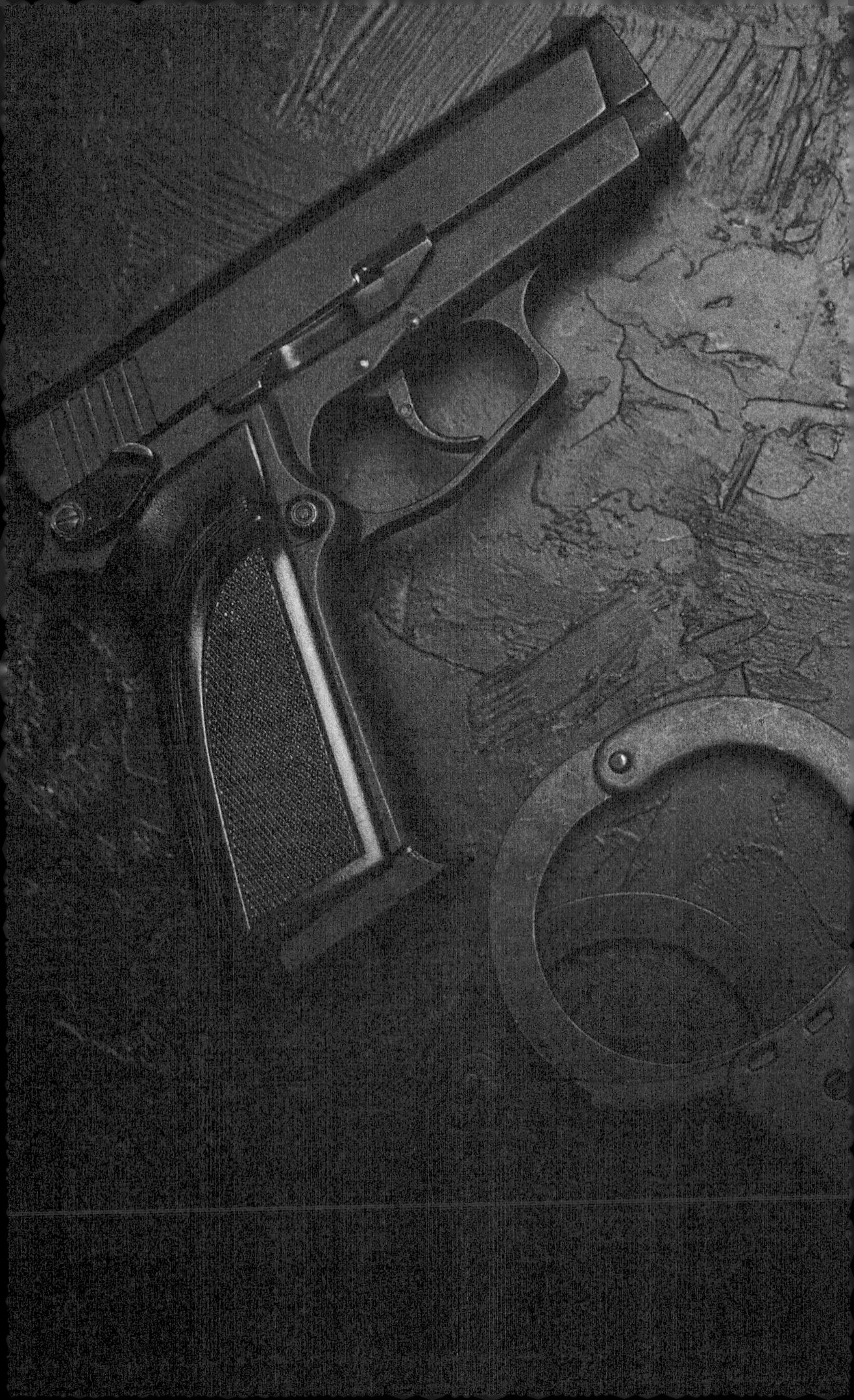

CHAPTER

FIFTEEN

Serena

"What are you up to?" Tristano asks as he comes to a stop right outside of his guest room and leans on the doorjamb.

"I was just going through some of my things." I shrug. "We packed so quickly, I never actually went through any of these boxes. I figured it was time to condense."

"Find anything good in there?" he asks as he pushes off the door frame and walks into the room.

"Eh."

"May I?" he asks, pointing to the keepsake box in front of me.

"Go for it. I was just about to look at it myself. I hadn't realized it, but apparently I keep things I shouldn't," I say as he starts rifling through it.

He picks up a piece of paper and starts reading it. I watch as his eyebrows shoot up, and he fights back a smile.

"Do I want to know?" I ask, full of dread.

"Some boy named Caleb was wondering if you would be willing to go to prom with him. He promises to be nothing but a gentleman. How boring," he huffs.

I groan thinking about Caleb. "He asked me when I was a freshman. Needless to say, he ended up ditching me not even halfway through the dance and hooked up with another senior."

"Asshole," he mumbles as he walks toward the dresser.

"What are you doing?"

I watch as he drops the note in the trashcan. "Putting this in the garbage where it belongs. You don't need any reminders of Caleb or anyone else."

I roll my eyes at his antics and start looking back through the keepsake box.

I find an old photo of me standing between my dad and grandfather. All three of us wear matching grins. It makes my heart ache just looking at it. It hurts to think about the fact that they are no longer alive.

"You look happy," Tristano says.

"I was," I tell him as I set the photo down, refusing to meet his eyes.

"What happened to them?" He settles down next to me.

"My father died in the line of duty when I was six. Suicide by cop turned into a homicide with one stray bullet. My grandfather took over my care after that. He had a heart attack when I was ten. I had no living family members left that we knew of, so Uncle Ben took me in. He was my father's best friend. They came up in the academy together. He took over as chief after my grandfather passed."

"Your mom?" He keeps his tone low.

"Never knew her. She didn't want me, so after she gave birth, she left me in the hospital with my father. I don't think they were in love or anything. He never seemed to miss her."

I can feel the melancholy settling over me. Maybe that's why I always wanted to prove myself. I've felt undeserving from the moment I took my first breath.

"Is this your class ring?" he asks after a few beats of silence.

I look up and nod. "Yeah, I worked all summer in order to be able to pay for it." I shake my head. "A waste of four hundred dollars if you ask me. You wear it for a couple years, and then as soon as you graduate, in a box it goes."

"I never wanted one," Tristano says ruefully. "I wanted the letterman jacket more. They pulled women in like candy."

"You're ridiculous," I say, rolling my eyes.

Tristano pretends to be offended. "Hey, at least I'm not wearing it still. Besides, I don't need to pull women anymore."

"Oh? Is that because they come crawling to you?" I tease.

He stares into my eyes, losing all humor. "I mean, they try, but I only have eyes for one woman now."

I can feel myself blushing. "What am I ever going to do with you?"

"Tie me to the bed? Ride me? Buy me dinner?" He smirks.

"Tris!"

I lean back and grab a pillow. I reach out and slap him on the shoulder with it.

"Abuse!" he cries out. "I didn't know you were so violent, *anima gemella*. I kind of like it. Hit me again, but this time on the ass."

"Of course you would like it," I mumble under my breath as I drop the pillow.

"Any touch of yours I enjoy, even if it brings me pain." He winks at me.

"Oh god. I can't handle anymore of this..." I wave my hand in front of him.

"I get that a lot. I'm a lot to handle. I think you are up for the challenge though."

I push his shoulder, making him fall back.

"Enough. My cheeks are burning."

Not only are my cheeks burning, but my body is tingling. I'm getting turned on simply from this little interaction. It's more than I can handle. I mean, I've dreamed of this for so long that now that I have it, it's overwhelming.

He smiles, brushing some hair back from my face. "I know. I love the color."

Shaking my head, I stand. "I think I need to cool off. How about we go out?"

He gives me a look like he knows why I'm changing the subject. "Get changed into a pretty dress. I'm taking you out on the town."

"Okay," I murmur, watching him edge out of the room.

"I'll be out here waiting." He blows me a kiss.

As soon as he clears the door, I fall back onto the bed and stare at the ceiling. I don't know what I've gotten myself into. Tristano has been the perfect gentleman. Never pushing me too far. I think I want more though. No. Not think. I know I want more, I'm just not sure how to go about it.

I've never actually been with a man. After the trauma from my childhood, I resigned myself to the fact that intimacy wasn't going to happen for me. I never met anyone who made me want to try for anything more.

Except Tris. He's always been the one to get my libido going. Hell, if he knew the amount of times I got off thinking about him, it would inflate his already large ego. Still, am I ready for that?

I think I am,

Pushing myself up, I get off the bed and head toward the closet. Opening it up, I reach toward the back and move a few hangers before I find it. I pull out the black dress and turn toward the mirror, holding it in front of myself.

It's got a deep, square neck that makes my cleavage look awesome for being almost nonexistent. The material clings to me like a glove and hits mid-thigh and has thick straps. It's not overly revealing compared to what most women would wear, but for me, it's out of my comfort zone. I bought it on a whim once when I was out shopping. I don't even know what possessed me to do such a thing. I almost never wear dresses unless it was for undercover work.

Yet here it is, tags still on it and all. It's screaming to be let out. For once, I'm going to listen.

"Fuck it," I mumble as I toss it onto the bed.

Walking over to the dresser, I riffle through my bras and panties looking for something to wear under it. Something emerald green catches my attention, and I pull it out. It's a low-cut lace bra with a matching thong pinned to it, along with a note.

> *I saw this when I was at Seduction, and I thought of you.*
>
> *You are gorgeous no matter what you wear, but if I've learned anything from listening to women talk, it's that a sexy piece of lingerie is a hell of a confidence boost.*
>
> *I would kill to see you in it, but even if I don't, just know you look as amazing in it as you feel.*
>
> *Love,*
> *Tristano*

"Fuck me," I breathe out.

Tears prick my eyes as I reread his words over and over. How is this man so perfect? He always seems to know what to say or do. When I'm sad, he seems to be able to sense it. He will crack jokes until I smile again. When I'm doubting myself, he reassures me so effortlessly.

Why did I waste so much time without him? I refuse to waste another minute. From now on, it's me and him against the world, fuck societal norms.

Setting the note down gently on the dresser, I walk over to the door and shut it, not bothering with the lock. Tris would never enter without permission.

As I walk back over to the lingerie, I take off my sweatshirt and sports bra, tossing them onto the bed. Gently, I undo the safety pin and set the thong off to the side. While staring into the mirror, I watch myself put it on. After adjusting the girls, I stare at myself in awe.

I don't know how he knew I needed this. It's so soft and delicate when I'm anything but. I feel sexy. Like I could invoke desire in a man. Bring him to his knees for me. I feel like a stronger, better version of myself.

Turning my head, I eye the door.

What would he think if I walked out there just like this?

Shaking my head, I finish dressing, marveling at how the dress looks just as sexy on me. I'm a brand new person on the outside, but I feel the same on the inside. It feels right. Like this is where I belong.

The woman at that shop knows what she's doing because if she's selling seduction, then it's working.

I'm going to seduce Tristano one way or another tonight. I have no idea how far it will go, but I know that no matter where we end up, I'll be his and he will be mine.

Always.

Tristano

"My lady." I smirk as I help Serena out of the car.

A pretty blush covers her cheeks. "Charmer."

"Only for you," I tell her as I shut the car door.

Taking her hand in mine, I pull her toward the club doors.

When she stepped out of her bedroom in that black dress that hugged her body so perfectly, just a hint of the emerald lace poking out of the cleavage, I almost dropped to the floor right then and there. She hadn't even done anything other than put the dress on, and it was already overstimulating to my senses. I've been sleeping next to this girl for over a week now, yet she still manages to take my breath away.

Thankfully, I was able to pull it together so I didn't look like a total dork, but I could tell she noticed the pause and she enjoyed it, her cheeks glowing that pretty shade of red.

Tonight, I have something spontaneous planned for us. I haven't been dancing in ages, but as soon as I saw the dress, I knew I needed to see her move in it.

The bouncer nods as he sees me and lifts the rope blocking the entrance.

"Don't we have to go to the back of the line?" She cranes her neck to look at the people waiting in line.

"Nope." I pop the "p" but don't tell her anymore.

As soon as we step inside, the music and bass hits us. Weaving through bodies, I find a spot next to the bar. I pull Serena next to me so her body is flush against mine. Looking down, I bite back a chuckle when I see her eyes are locked on my lips.

Just to fuck with her, I slowly lick my lips, and I watch as her eyes follow my tongue.

She's been wanting me to kiss her. I can tell by the way she leans into me anytime I pull her into my arms, but I don't want to fuck this up. Truth be told, I'm fucking scared to death. If I move too fast, I might damage what we have, and that would kill me.

So I've been playing the long game as I have been since the moment I laid eyes on her when she was nineteen. That was the moment I realize this girl I viewed as a victim in need of my protection had grown up into a beautiful, strong, independent woman who I quickly became obsessed with.

It didn't matter that there was no way that we could possibly work. From that moment on, all others ceased to exist for me. I was out here living my life, but my heart was firmly with her, and she didn't even know it.

"What can I get you?" the bartender yells, pulling me out of my thoughts.

"Can I get a vodka cranberry?" Serena asks.

The bartender nods and turns toward me.

"Vodka Red Bull."

Even though Crimson is owned by Bash, I watch the bartender make our drinks. You can never be too careful.

I feel Serena stand up on her tiptoes, her lips brushing against my ear. "Do you come here often?"

"Sometimes. Bash owns this place along with several other clubs."

"Really? I didn't see him as a club owner," she says as she looks around.

"Here you go," the bartender says as she slides our drinks toward us.

Reaching into my pocket, I pull out a fifty and hand it over. "Thanks."

"Thank you." The bartender smiles when she sees that I tipped her.

Serena and I grab our drinks, and I lead her toward the stairs that lead to the VIP area. The bouncer recognizes me and lets us pass.

"Hey, Tristano," one of the bottle girls says as she passes.

"Friend of yours?" Serena says sarcastically as we stop at an empty booth.

"Not in the way you're implying," I tell her as we sit.

Serena tries to put some space between us, but I won't have any of that shit. I pull her into my side. Hip to hip.

"I've always been honest with you, yeah?"

"Yeah," she says hesitantly as she sets her drink down.

184

I reach out and touch her chin, turning her head toward me, making her meet my eyes.

"I'm not innocent. We both have a past, but it's just that, Serena, the past."

"Is it though?" Her eyes are begging me to confirm that what I'm saying is the truth.

She's afraid that this is all a lie. A dream she made up. I can see it in the way she constantly tenses up as if she's waiting for the other shoe to drop. I can't have that. Not in my girl.

"You don't have to worry about anything in my past. All you need to think about is the present and the future. You know why?"

"Why?"

I lean in close so my lips brush against hers. "Because I laid eyes on you when you were nineteen years old, and I was struck right there, standing at your gate, looking at the beautiful woman you had become. That moment, you became the only woman I see. Not a single woman in this world can compare to you. There's only one of you, and I'm claiming you."

"Tris..."

"I'm playing for keeps." I rest my palm on her chest, over her heart. "This is mine." I watch as her eyes dilate, and I grab her hand with my free one and rest it over my heart. "And this is yours. I'm just waiting for you to accept what's rightfully yours."

She leans in and presses her lips against mine, kissing me. Serena starts off slow and hesitant. Once she realizes I'm not going anywhere, she kisses me harder. I try to let her lead, but I can't manage for long. I bring up my hand and grab onto the back of her head, pulling her into me and kiss her like I've dreamed about.

All concept of time disappear as our tongues duel. She meets me pull for pull until we are basically one. I bite her lip, pulling away slowly. It takes all my self-control to not pull her into my lap as she gasps, her dilated eyes meeting mine.

God, I want this woman something fierce.

"Get a room," someone shouts as they walk by, making us break apart.

I smirk as I brush a piece of hair away from Serena's face. Her eyes are wide and her heart is beating fast. The flush has moved from her cheeks down her chest and it's fucking gorgeous.

"Do you want to get out of here?" she asks as she plays with the collar of my shirt.

I chuckle playfully as I slide out of the booth and stand. Reaching down, I squeeze my cock, which makes her look down. Holding out a hand, I wait until she places hers in mine before pulling her forward.

Leaning down, I whisper into her ear, "I don't know what kind of boys you've been with in the past, but I plan on seducing you tonight. I'm going to take you down onto that dance floor and get you all worked up before I take you home and have my way with you." I pause when her breath catches. "How does that sound?"

"G-good. That sounds good." She swallows hard.

Taking her hand in mine, I lead her back down the stairs and pull her onto the dance floor. Her arms wrap around my neck as she steps into me. My hands grab onto her hips as we start to dance. Song after song, we move as one. Our hands roam one another, her pussy grinding against my thigh as we dance.

I let my hands feel all over her body, staying above the clothes. I file away every little lip bite and gasp that falls from her lips. My eyes stay strictly on her face so I don't miss a single reaction.

The more I touch and feel, the more she looks intoxicated, but it's not the sip of liquor she had upstairs.

No, this girl is drunk on me. It's a heady feeling knowing I can take her to such heights with only the touch of my hands.

Leaning down, I press a kiss to the column of her neck as she throws her head back. Her leg comes up around my hip, almost as if it were instinctive. When she pulls my face back to hers, she's greedily kissing and nipping at me.

Serena sucks on my lip, making me groan. It felt like a straight shot to my cock. I'm all for holding out, making this last as long as possible, but then she reaches down, boldly palming my dick right there in the middle of the dance floor.

"And we're done," I tell her as I pull away, ready to get her home.

"About time," she teases as I pull her through the bar.

I don't even stop to say goodbye to the bouncer. I head straight toward my car, pushing her up against it as I kiss her senseless.

When I finally pull back, her lips are red and puffy. She looks freshly fucked and I haven't even touched her pussy yet. She's going to be responsive as fuck, and I cannot wait.

"In the car. Now," I bark at her.

She startles but does as I ask.

After closing her in and rounding the car, I adjust myself before sliding into the driver's seat.

Glancing over, I see Serena rubbing her legs together. She's probably soaking wet.

I hope she stains my seat.

Unable to help myself, I lean over, pulling her to me so I can kiss her hard and fast. When I let her go, she's even more dazed.

"Hike up that dress, *anima gemella*. Show me what I have to look forward to."

Starting the car, I wait her out. She looks embarrassed. Maybe even a little shy, but eventually she does as I ask. Slowly. Inch by inch.

It's the most pleasant torture I've ever had to endure. When she finally has her thong showing, I reach down, smacking her pussy once.

She gasps but doesn't say anything. Her eyes are on me.

"Keep those legs open and follow my commands."

I put the car in drive, speeding as much as traffic will allow.

"Pull them to the side," I tell her.

My eyes flick to her as she does as I ask. She's glistening.

It's only a fifteen-minute drive to my place, but I'm determined to make it in less. That means less time to play.

"Have you ever played with that pretty pussy?" I ask.

She makes a noise, but it's not an answer.

"Out loud, Serena. Do you play with yourself?"

"Yes." Her tone is husky.

It's enough to cause a shiver in my body. Hearing how turned on she is.

"Did you rub your clit, or would you finger yourself? Show me."

I can audibly hear her wetness as she slides her fingers into it. I glance over quickly, watching her fingers disappear inside her.

"Fuck. I didn't think this through." I rub my hand over my face.

"*Tris,*" she moans.

It almost breaks me. Hearing her moan my name is a fantasy come to life. For years I've imagined this moment while I jacked off, but nothing my brain could come up with could ever compare to having her here in real life.

"Do you think about me?" I ask, taking another corner faster than I should.

"Yes," she breathes.

"Tell me what you think about. How do I touch you in your fantasy?"

I glance over to see her eyes on me. She licks her lips, her fingers still moving at a moderate pace.

I glance back to the street, pressing the gas a little harder.

"I imagine it's your hands touching me. That you're the one making me feel good. I picture your fingers gliding in and out of me, making my body heat. Sometimes I use a sucker so I can imagine I'm sucking you off while you finger me." Her breath catches as she speeds up her pace.

"Let me taste you," I murmur, stopping at the red light.

She drags her fingers out, pressing them to my lips. I inhale deeply, loving the scent of her pussy as I suck her two fingers deep into my mouth. She shivers as my eyes close, my moan vibrating against her fingers.

The horn honking behind me has me smirking at her as I nip at the end of her finger as I take off.

"Delicious." I wink at her before focusing back on the road.

"That was the single most sexy thing I have ever seen," she whispers, making my smile grow.

I like this side of her.

"You have four blocks to make yourself come. I suggest you do it unless you'd prefer a punishment," I say conversationally, but she takes it as the demand it was meant to be.

My eyes volley between her and the road as she circles her clit with one hand while scissoring inside her with the other. She's more vocal now, her moans becoming closer to screams.

Just as I pull into my driveway, I can tell she's about to fall over that edge, but I reach out, pulling her hand free. She is breathing heavily as she looks up at me with glossy eyes. I smirk at her.

"I own your orgasms now." Leaning down, I lick her essence off her fingers before setting them on her thigh. "I'll come help you out."

She doesn't say a word. She lets me get out of the car and to her side before it even registers. When I finally open her door, her dress is covering her center as she glares up at me.

"That wasn't very nice." She holds her hand out for me to help her from the car.

As I do, I inform her, "Good things come to those who wait. You followed my instructions well. Now it's time to get your prize."

"Two more seconds, and I would have had my prize," she snarks.

I slap her ass, making her jolt. "Nah, baby. That was a preview. Trust me. You'll enjoy the real prize."

The way she basically growls at me tells me this is going to be a good night.

I can't wait.

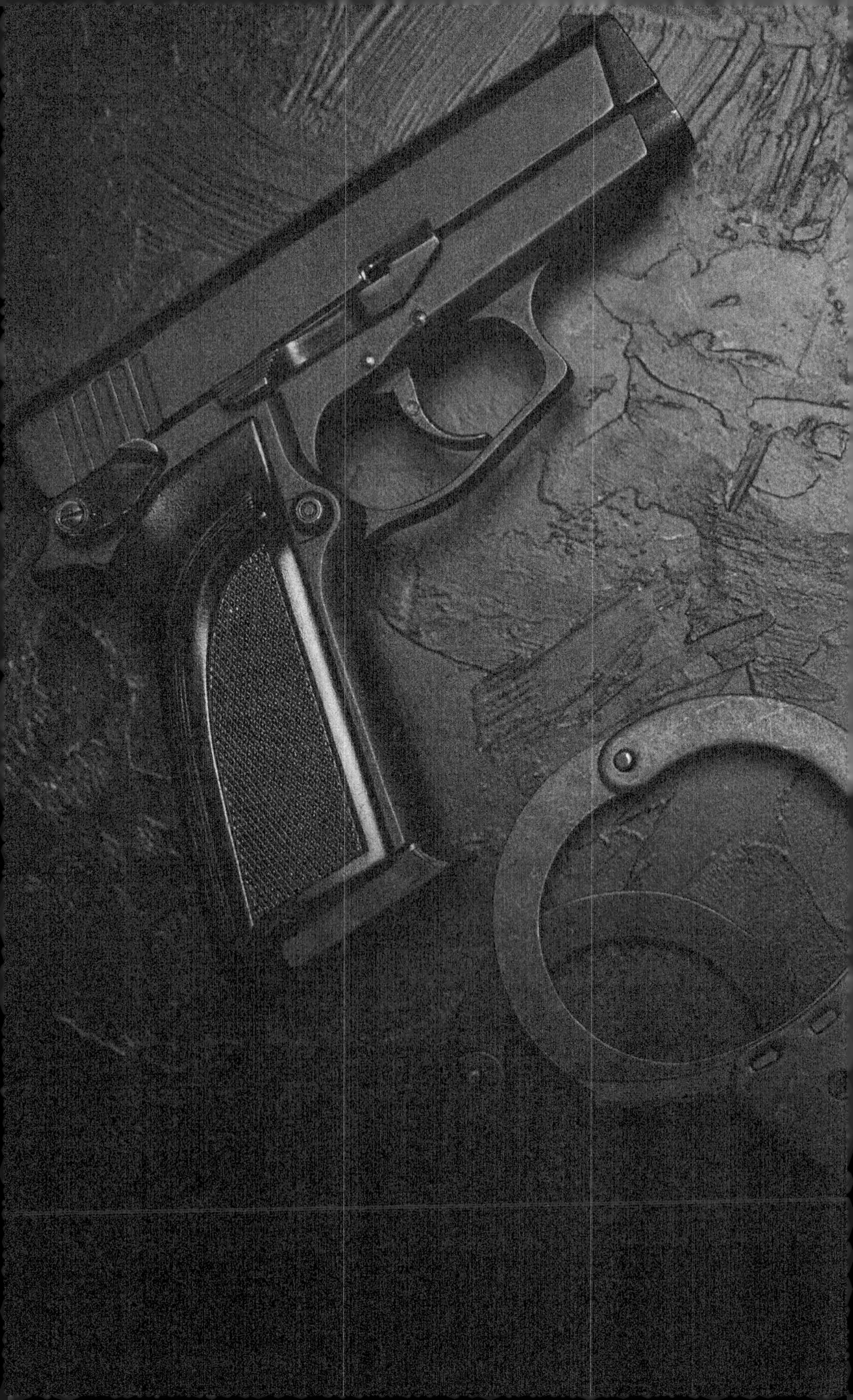

CHAPTER
SIXTEEN

Serena

I want to smack him. Seriously, my body feels like a live wire right now. Even the rubbing of my legs together is only making my body feel more of the pleasure/pain of my denied orgasm.

I think if I had been more in the moment, I would have screamed.

Instead, I sat there like a deer in the headlights as he licked my cum from my fingers.

A shiver makes its way through my body at the memory.

Why was that so hot?

Hell, everything he's been doing is hot. From the way he caressed my body on the dance floor to the way he demanded I play with myself in the car. It's like he's this seduction master and I'm still reading the book for dummies.

I feel so out of my element.

Still, I let him lead me into the house, locking the door behind us as he sets the alarm. Then he turns me, pushing me against the wall.

"You're in your head. What's wrong?" he asks as he gently peppers kisses to my cheeks.

"Nothing. Keep going." I angle my neck for him to move down.

He grabs my chin, forcing me to face him. "Something just now took you out of that high I had you riding. What was it?"

My cheeks heat as I realize that I probably should admit it. He has the right to know.

"You seem so experienced and I've never really, um, done this?" I phrase it as a question.

He looks confused for a moment, but then it clicks. I see the heat in his eyes flare.

"You're saying you've never been with another man," he whispers.

I shake my head no. "I mean, vibrators, sure, but never anything real. I mean, other than…"

"No. That doesn't count. You know that. Are you sure you want to do this now? We can wait," he assures me.

"I don't want to wait. I'm just a little nervous."

"How can I make this better for you?" he asks.

"I want you to do what you would normally do. I don't want you to hold back. I'm not some child or fragile thing. I want to be desired."

He shoves his cock against my stomach. "Trust me, I desire you. I'll make this good for you. I promise. Turn around, hands on the wall with your ass out."

His hands are turning me before I even agree, but it feels good. I like him taking control. It's like my mind goes silent, willing to play along with whatever he has planned.

Planting my hands on the wall, I bend over until my ass is sticking out.

"Tsk tsk, *anima gemella*. You're a cop. You know how to get into the frisking position. Spread your legs." He kicks between my legs until they are spread to his liking.

I hear some clothes ruffling, but as I go to look over my shoulder, his hand lands on my head, forcing me to look forward.

"Eyes forward. Don't move."

My breathing accelerates as I do as he asks. He removes his hand and continues whatever he is doing. Every time a noise sounds, I jump, wondering if he's about to touch me. The anticipation is killing me.

I'm about to beg for him to put his hands on me when I feel my dress being slowly peeled up.

"This green really does look gorgeous against your skin."

I can feel his breath against the skin of my ass. I close my eyes, waiting for the touch of his lips against me, but it doesn't come. Instead, he blows air directly on the center of my wet thong, making my entire body shudder.

"So wet and needy for me. Men have committed murder for much less than the sight before me."

"Tris," I moan, arching back into where I think he is.

He smacks my ass hard, making my clit throb as I pant for more.

"Stay still. I'm worshipping this work of art. You'll stand there and let me look my fill."

"Yes, sir."

The phrase slips out, but damn if I don't like it. I have always imagined him as the older, dark knight. Maybe that fantasy is mixing reality.

"Did you know that you have freckles back here? They are so adorable." His tone is low as his fingers trace invisible lines down my ass to between my thighs.

I don't answer. I couldn't form a complete sentence if he asked me to right now. All I can focus on is the way my body is responding to his. It's as if it's only waiting for his command to jump.

He continues to draw a path up and down my legs until my knees are wobbly from the effort to stay standing.

That's when he strikes.

First, it's a stinging pain in my ass, making me yelp. The pain quickly turns to pleasure as he sucks and licks at the skin. My pussy is clenching as if it has something to cling to, my body primed and ready to go.

Tris doesn't rush things though. No, instead, he takes his time kissing every inch of my ass, leaving bite marks that I know will be there tomorrow.

It feels as if he's marking his territory.

Oddly, I like it.

Once he's done, he moves down between my legs, pausing a moment.

"This is the feast I've been waiting for," he says quietly as he pulls my thong to the side.

Then he dives in. The slow,, languid pace is replaced by this breakneck one that has me struggling to stay upright. He tongues my clit, his fingers finding my entrance, teasing it. When he finally thrusts in, he pushes against me harder, his nose putting pressure against my asshole.

The sudden, overwhelming sensations push me over the edge, making me scream out his name as my legs shake until I fall forward against the wall.

Tris isn't done though. Instead of pulling back, he flips around until he's beneath me, his eyes visible between my legs. Then he pulls me down until I'm seated on his face.

Then he goes to town. My forehead hits the wall, my legs clenching around his head as he continues his assault on my pussy. He pushes me into another orgasm, never letting me fully come down as he picks up his pace.

By the time he pulls back to take a breath, my brain is mush. I feel dizzy, and my throat is raw from screaming.

"God damn, I could live between these thighs," he pants.

I hum at him, but I can't even focus on him. My body feels over-stimulated. As if I'm going to burst at any moment if a single ounce of pleasure hits me.

Tris starts to move forward, but my hand finds his forehead, making him chuckle.

"All done?" he asks.

"I'm stuck. My thighs hurt."

His eyes flash with concern as he pushes on me until he can slide out. Then he helps me stand, pulling me into his arms.

It's now that I realize the man is completely naked. My mouth salivates as his dick stands proudly to greet me. I need a taste of that.

When he finally sets me down in the bedroom, I strip out of my dress. My hands go to undo the bra, but he stops me.

"It looks so great on you." He stares at my chest as his finger caresses my cheek.

Smiling, I leave it on.

He moves for me, but I shake my head as I drop to my knees.

Then I look up at him with a smirk.

Oh yeah.

My turn.

Tristano

How did I get so lucky? Seriously, I am contemplating pinching myself as I stare down at the goddess on her knees before me.

This has to be a prank. There is no way someone as amazing as her would be with me. Right?

Then she reaches forward, her eyes not leaving mine. I hiss when she touches me, my dick jerking in her grip, making her giggle.

She's not giggling long though. No, the girl is aiming to end me.

She doesn't go slow and see if she can handle it. She goes full force like she does everything else in her life.

She takes me from tip to root, gagging against me, on her first try. My hips involuntarily jerk forward, the feel of her throat against me is almost too much. My eyes try to fall closed, but I refuse to miss a single moment of this.

Forcing them to stay open, I watch my girl stare at me as she starts slowly bobbing on my dick. She looks like she's waiting for my permission to go harder. As if she needs something from me.

Reaching down, I pet her head as I start talking to her.

"You're doing so good."

"It feels amazing."

"Look at how pretty you look taking my cock."

Each bit of praise I give her has her confidence building to the point that she's swallowing me with each stroke.

I'm not going to last if she keeps this up. I know I'm not that old, but my stamina isn't what it used to be. All these years out of the game, and I'm about to embarrass myself.

I refuse to let that happen.

So instead, I grip her by the hair, pulling her off of me. Her lips are red and puffy like after I kissed her earlier. It makes me smirk at the memory.

I knew she would look gorgeous like this.

She pouts up at me. "I wasn't done."

"I know. I want to feel your heat around me. The first time I come with you, I want to be inside you."

She licks her lips before biting into her bottom lip.

"I'd like that."

Offering her a hand, I help her off her knees before backing her onto the bed. Once she's on her back, I move toward the nightstand, pulling a condom out.

When I turn back, she's frowning at me.

"I bought these the other day when I went out. I didn't want to make assumptions, but I wanted to be ready. I figured you aren't on any birth control, and I know we aren't ready for kids yet," I explain.

Her worries melt off her face as a look of wonder fills it instead.

"You want to have babies with me?"

Slipping the condom on, I climb on top of her, settling between her legs.

"*Anima gemella*, I plan to marry you as soon as I have you so sex drunk that you can't say no. Then I plan to fill you up until we have a whole baseball team of kids."

Her eyes widen. "I don't want that many kids, Tris. Like three tops."

I kiss her nose. "We can discuss that later. I'd rather get to the practicing part now if you don't mind."

She laughs, and I swear my heart lightens. Most guys would feel insecure in this moment, but it brings me joy. I love making her happy.

Leaning down, I kiss her, her mouth still smiling. Then I kiss her again. I keep pressing kisses to her lips until she opens her mouth against me, chasing me as I try to withdraw.

Once I have her good and distracted, I hike her legs up onto my hips, lining myself up at her entrance. I made sure she was nice and wet, but she's tight. This is still likely to be slightly painful.

Rather than thrust into her in one go, I press against her, slipping in a bit. She gasps against my mouth, but I continue to kiss her. Then I pull out and thrust further. I keep doing this until I'm deep inside of her.

Then I pause.

I have slept with other women, but none have ever made me feel anywhere close to the way I feel right now. I don't know if it's because this is more than a fuck for me or what, but emotions start to swell around inside of me.

I take a moment, my head falling to her chest as I breathe. She strokes my hair, letting me have this moment.

After several moments of silence, she whispers, "I'm not glass. Fuck me, Tris."

Looking up at her, I see the woman who I am going to marry. The one I will spend the rest of my life with. By god, I would do anything for this woman, so if she wants me to fuck her, I'm going to fuck her until she can't see straight.

Nipping her lip, I start to thrust against her. She moves with me, creating her own friction. Moving one leg up onto my shoulder, I angle her hips up until she's making this adorable little squeaking noise every time I hit her deep. Her eyes roll into the back of her head as she moans out.

Reaching between us, I stroke her clit, loving the way her body is shaking against me, her pussy squeezing me like it wants to eat me. I'll gladly let it have me if it lets me feel like this forever.

I feel the moment she orgasms, her body going taut as she lets out this guttural moan. I continue fucking her, my own release close.

Then she goes limp, her eyes falling closed. Two more thrusts, and I spill inside of the condom wishing it was her I was painting white.

Kissing her face, I let myself come down from the intense orgasm. After a moment, I realize Serena isn't with me anymore.

"Serena, baby?" I hiss at her.

She mumbles a little, her eyes opening. She looks dazed.

"What happened? I think I passed out," she whispers.

"Oh fuck. I'm sorry, *anima gemella*. I should have stopped." The guilt hits me hard and fast.

"You finished?" Her pussy clenches around me.

"Yes," I admit, a bit ashamed.

She cups my face, her pussy clenching around me again. "I lied. That's the hottest thing. I don't know why, but that has me ready to go round two. Maybe see if you can make me pass out again."

I laugh, resting my head on her chest. "I'm an old man. I need a break."

She giggles. "I need to get up and take care of girl things."

Moving off of her, I let her up. She hustles toward the bathroom, still in that lingerie set. The thong is stretched way out, but I love the sight. It's proof of a good job.

When she comes back into the bedroom, I pass her, going to take care of my own business.

By the time I make it back to bed, Serena is under the covers. I slide under with her, pulling her to me, smiling when I find her naked.

"No more clothes in bed," she murmurs sleepily.

"Deal."

Then I drift off into a blissful sleep with my girl in my arms.

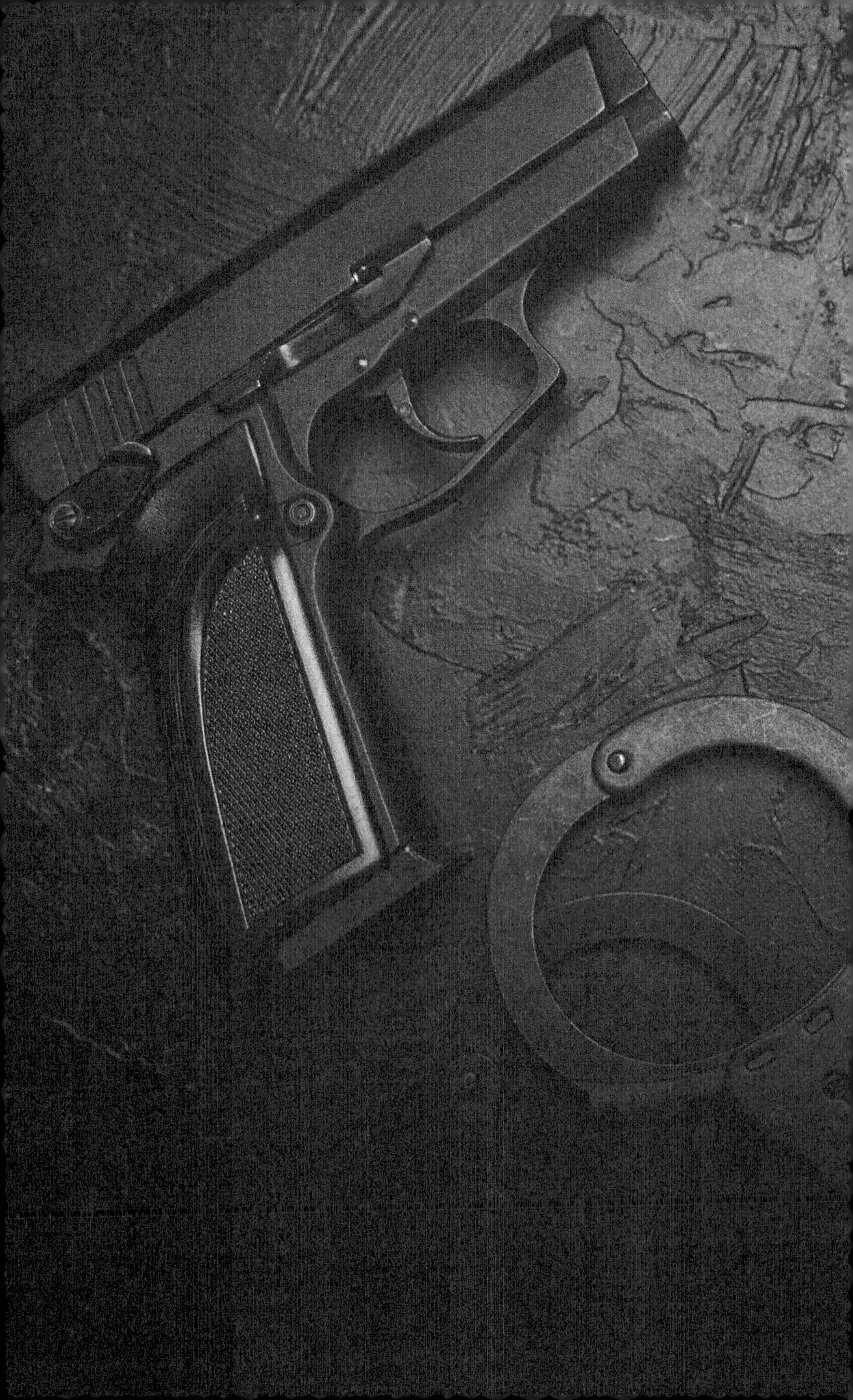

CHAPTER
SEVENTEEN

Serena

I come to a stop in front of a brownstone and check the address on my phone one more time. Sure enough, it's the right place. Putting my phone in my pocket, I stare up at the house. The neighborhood is quiet and peaceful, perfect for raising a family. For some reason, I find it funny that there is a welcome sign leaning next to the door when the owner is a made man. The door opens, and a beautiful woman steps outside. Her long blonde hair is in waves around her shoulders, and she wears a welcoming smile.

"Serena, right?" she asks warmly.

"Hi, Danica?" I say as I finally convince myself to move from where I was standing. Walking up the stairs, I hold my hand out to Enzo's wife. "Thank you for inviting me."

She brushes by my hand and pulls me into a hug.

"Oh," I say as I awkwardly hug her back.

She laughs. "Sorry, I'm a hugger. Come on in. Greer and our friend Rosa are already here, and the others should be too."

"Awesome."

I follow her inside the house, and I'm instantly impressed. The place is far from stuffy. It's clean but you can tell a family lives here.

"Hey, Serena. You found the place okay?" Enzo asks as we step into the kitchen.

"I did. You have a lovely home," I tell him as I squeeze the straps of my purse.

Unfortunately he doesn't miss the action. Enzo's lips twitch and he raises a brow. "Would you like a glass of wine?"

"Sure."

Danica claps. "Enzo is so good at picking out wines, thanks to his time spent in Italy. Do you prefer red or white?"

"I honestly don't know. Surprise me." I shrug.

I know it's ridiculous, but for some reason not knowing whether I prefer red or white makes me feel inadequate.

"I'm not much of a drinker," I blurt out.

Danica reaches out and squeezes my shoulder. "And that's perfectly fine. If you would prefer something nonalcoholic, we have options too. We're just used to everyone drinking when we get together."

"Wine is fine." I nod, smiling awkwardly.

"How about you ladies go sit, and I'll bring you the drinks in a minute," Enzo offers.

Danica waves for me to follow her, and I fall into step behind her.

"Hey, look who I found outside," Danica says brightly.

Greer looks up from her spot on the couch, looking completely at home. "Hey, Serena. Good to see you again."

"Hi, how have you been?" I ask as I take a seat in a chair across from her.

"Aside from lack of sleep, I'm fantastic." She smiles softly.

"You look like you could fall asleep right there?" Danica teases.

She's not wrong. Greer is curled up with her legs tucked under her, a glass of wine in one hand, and her head resting on the arm of the couch.

"Don't tease me with a good time," Greer quips.

Seeing Greer like this is completely different than the other times I've been around her. I've seen her in boss mode, but right now she's just another woman with her walls down.

"Hi, I'm Rosa," a woman says, who's sitting in another chair.

"Serena, nice to meet you." I smile.

Enzo walks into the room carrying a tray with empty wine glasses on it, along with some finger foods. "I'll be right back," he says as he sets it down on the coffee table.

"I should really help him, but I know if I tried, he would just shoo me away." Danica sighs with awe in her voice.

"I trained him well." Greer smirks at her before turning toward me. "I don't know if you picked up on it or not, but Enzo is like a brother to me. For a long time, it was just us against the world."

"The sister I never knew I wanted," he says as he walks into the living room carrying four bottles of wine.

"That's awesome. I always wanted a sibling," I admit.

"It's not all it's cracked up to be." Greer winks.

The doorbell rings, and Danica pops up from the couch. "I'll get it."

Enzo shoots her a pointed look, and she sits back down with a smile on her face. "Or not," she says as he walks out of the room.

As soon as you hear the door open, you can hear women talking a mile a minute. I tense as they make their way into the room. I hate meeting new people because I know I'm awkward. When you know you are, it's like you become hyper aware of it, and you're constantly on edge.

"We meet again," Izzy says as she walks in ahead of Sofia, followed by three other women.

Sofia's eyes light up when she sees me. "Serena, how are you settling in?"

"Fine, thank you," I tell her before turning back to Izzy. "Hi."

Sofia touches the shoulder of a woman with blonde hair who is tiny. "I don't think you two have met yet. This is Mia. She's married to Lorenzo and is the family's doctor."

"Nice to meet you." I wave awkwardly.

Looking at the woman, I would have never pegged her for a doctor.

"Same." She smiles brightly as she takes a seat.

"And this is Natasha," Sofia says, pointing at the last woman. "Natasha, this is Tristano's woman, Serena."

Natasha smiles with a wicked look in her eye. "I've heard all about you. Nice to meet you."

"You too," I say as I shift in my seat.

What the hell does she mean she's heard all about me? From who?

My mind flashes back to the emerald green lingerie set I wore for Tristano last night. This woman picked that out for me. I don't know if I should thank her or slit her throat. Okay, not the second one, but the first doesn't seem right either.

"Last but not least, this is Vanessa. She's married to Matteo, who I don't think you've met yet."

Vanessa doesn't say anything but waves, so I wave back.

"Wine?" Danica asks.

Everyone says yes, and she starts handing out glasses.

The bottles are already open and she holds one up in front of her, silently asking if I would like some. I nod and she fills the glass.

"If you don't like it, we can get you something else," she says quietly.

"Thank you," I tell her honestly.

"Everyone good?" Enzo asks from the edge of the room.

Danica walks over to him and gives him a kiss. "We're fine. Go have fun with the guys and kids."

He smirks down at his wife and whispers something none of us can hear, but if her blush is anything to go by, I'd say it was something dirty.

As soon as he walks away, Sofia claps. "Okay, I'm kid-free for the next two hours, three if I'm lucky. Tell me all the things."

"My husband is sexy as fuck holding a baby. It makes my uterus do something, and I'm not sure how I feel about it yet." Greer frowns, making everyone laugh.

"The struggle is real, right?" Mia says, raising her glass.

"I kind of miss seeing Matteo hold a baby," Vanessa says quietly.

"Do you think you'll have another?" Sofia asks as she leans toward the woman.

Vanessa shifts her seat. "I'm not sure."

"I'm sure if you wanted one, Matteo would make it happen," Sofia tells her.

Izzy chuckles. "He would lock you in the bedroom until it happened."

Everyone laughs as I look around.

"What about you, Danica?" Greer asks as she nudges the other woman with her foot.

"We're not in a rush. We're happy right now giving all of our attention to V, but if it happens, it happens." She smiles softly.

"I love that kid." Rosa sighs.

"How's your son?" Natasha asks.

"Growing like a weed. Cleo has convinced me to bring him for a visit."

"Are you okay with that? I'm sure if you tell her you're not ready to go back, she would understand and come here," Greer tells her.

Danica leans in close and whispers. "Rosa came from the Irish branch in Chicago. Cleo is her son's half sister and Greer's niece."

A pained look crosses Rosa's face for a moment. "I have to face my fears eventually, right?"

"Amen," the women say in unison.

I raise my glass to take a sip when Natasha turns toward me with a devious smirk. "I love hearing about everyone's spawn, but I really need Serena to answer a question for me."

I lower my glass and hesitantly ask. "What?"

"How big is Tristano's cock? Is he all talk, or can he actually give as good as he says he does?"

Everyone laughs as I shrink into my seat. I can feel my cheeks instantly heating up.

"Awe, she blushes," Izzy teases.

"I'm not sure I'm really comfortable answering that," I admit.

Natasha only laughs harder. "Oh goodness. Your face. Girl, you do not have to worry about me. Tristano has only ever been a friend. Trust me."

I cough a bit then give her a small smile. "Thank you for that. You didn't need to reassure me, but it's appreciated."

She gives me a knowing look as she nods. "Society tends to pit women against one another, but we don't have to be that way. Is your man a looker? I don't think anyone here would say no. With that being said, he is a very taken man, and I respect boundaries. You're part of the family now, so he's officially on the brother list. Not eligible for any hooking up."

I laugh a little, then bite my lip. "Well then, your brother gets no complaints from me in that department."

Everyone is silent a moment before the entire room bursts with laughter.

"That's my boy!" Natasha whoops.

"What about you, Natasha? Anyone in your life we need to know about?" Mia smirks.

"Oh, honey, no man will ever tame all this." Natasha tsks. "You know I'm all about hitting it and quitting it."

The others continue to talk as Vanessa comes to sit next to me. I turn to her, smiling while trying to follow the conversation before me.

"It's a bit much sometimes." Her tone is softer than I expected.

"Why do you come then?" I ask.

She smiles as she looks at the girls in front of us. "They are family. They are crazy and should never be allowed to play with weapons, but at the same time, they are weirdly affectionate and wildly protective. I wouldn't trade them for the world."

I look over at them too as they laugh together, each having side conversations with one another.

"That sounds like a wonderful place to be. You're lucky." I turn back to Vanessa, only to find her already looking at me.

"You're lucky too. This is your family now too. No need to feel the way you do. You're not on the outside."

A familiar sting hits my chest. One I hadn't even realized was there until she pointed it out.

"How did you know?"

"I was homeless once. Matteo found me and thrust me into this life. It took a long time to really accept my place here and feel like I was a part of the group. It's okay not to be there yet, but you'll get there one day."

"Damn. That's one hell of a motivational speech."

Her cheeks grow red. "Sorry. I do it a lot for work, so sometimes I forget to shut it off."

My eyes widen. "You give speeches for a living?"

She laughs. "I know I seem so quiet, right? No, I run a non-profit whose aim is to reduce homelessness in the city. It provides resources to help them get jobs and safer shelter conditions. It's my pride and joy, other than my child of course."

"Wow. That actually sounds amazing."

An idea hits me out of nowhere.

"Hey, do you offer counseling for the people you serve?"

"We do. Do you know someone who needs a service like that?" she asks quietly.

"I mean, yes, I know I need to talk to someone, but I already have someone, I just need to be ready for that step. I meant I have an idea I would love to run by you. I mean, if you don't mind."

"I'm all ears." She leans closer.

So I do too.

"I have no clue how this would work, but what if we partnered and maybe offered a center for women who are victims of human trafficking, using similar resources. It could be similar with the offering housing for those who have no home to go back to, or maybe they don't want to for one reason or another. The therapy can be tailored to their experiences. We could even offer legal representation and protection if they want to testify against their abusers."

She smiles. "Wow. I hadn't even thought about that. I mean, we partner with domestic violence shelters, but you're right. There is a whole community of people we are missing out on. Let's get together at the shelter. I can show you what we do, and we can figure out how to incorporate your idea into it."

"That sounds amazing."

"What are you two whispering about over there?" Izzy shouts. "It's time to get drunk."

For the rest of the afternoon, the wine and gossip flows. I lose all sense of time, and I forget why I was nervous to come in here in the first place.

Tristano

"Hey," I say as I walk into Bash's.

"Hi."

"Yo."

"What's up?"

Everyone asks at once. Bash, Lo, Gio, Matteo, and Killian are already here. The only one missing is Enzo, but I'm sure he's on his way.

Lo's kids, Elena and Draco, are on the floor with Bash's daughter, Alessa, and Nico, Matteo's son. Killian is holding Kieran. It looks like a daddy daycare in here.

"Where are Marcello and Francesca?" I ask.

"Kitchen." Gio rolls his eyes. "They convinced Nonna Rosa to make them something sweet." His voice goes high-pitched. "Nonna, Gio, and Izzy don't let us have sweets. They say it's bad for us."

Matteo chuckles. "That's bullshit. Izzy has a massive sweet tooth."

"Sorry we're late," Enzo says as he walks in.

"Right on time," Bash tells him before looking down at Viola. "Hey, V. Marcello and Francesca are in the kitchen if you want to go hang out with them."

She shakes her head with a small smile. We watch as she walks toward the babies and sits down next to them.

"She's so good with them," Matteo says after a beat of silence.

"I think you'll need to make her a big sister sooner rather than later," Lo teases.

Enzo rolls his eyes. "Not all of us like to keep our spouse knocked up."

We all laugh as Lo shrugs with a smile. Poor Mia had both Elena and Draco back-to-back.

"It blows my mind sometimes," Killian says.

"What does?" I ask.

He nods to the floor before looking down at his son. "This is the next generation right here. Everything we do is for them."

"Sometimes it keeps me up at night, wondering what kind of shit they will have to deal with," Bash confesses.

"I don't look at it that way," Enzo says. "The way I see it is, we are paving the way. Will they have their own troubles? Of course, but they will have us all to look toward when they need help. We'll guide them."

We all fall silent as we let what he said sink in. He's not wrong. I know all of us would do whatever we needed to for these kids. Alessa will be the first female head of La Cosa Nostra, and Kieran will be head of the Westies, with the other kids falling in somewhere underneath them.

It hits me that I'm the only guy in the room without a child. Honestly, it's something I'd never really thought about until now. What I wouldn't do to see a little human that's half mine and Serena on the floor with the others.

"You okay over there, buddy?" Gio teases, making me look up.

"What?" I ask, shaking my head.

"You totally zoned out. What were you thinking about?" Enzo smirks.

"I was trying to remember if I changed the laundry before I left," I joke.

"Sure..." Lo teases.

"How are things at home?" Bash asks.

"Good."

He raises a brow. "Serena settling in okay?"

"I think so, yeah."

"Good." He nods with a thoughtful look on his face. "You know, when you first told us about her, I wanted to strangle you."

"Get in line," Killian mumbles.

Bash ignores him and continues. "But after meeting her, I get it. She's your person."

"She is." I nod.

"Knowing she has that law enforcement background makes me wary that she might change her mind one day," Lo admits.

"She won't." I shake my head. "That's the thing about Serena. Once she makes up her mind, that's it. Done deal, no takebacks."

"And she chose you," Matteo says when I trail off.

"Yeah, she's always known about my connection to the family. Hell, I'm pretty sure she went out of her way to make sure she never asked anything that would put her in a bind."

"That's good." Enzo nods. "She willingly walked into this life for you, just like Greer did with Killian. Danica had no idea until she had already started to develop feelings for me and had to make her decision on the fly."

"I tried to push Mia away because I didn't want this life for her, but she pushed back." Lo chuckles, rubbing his hand on his chin.

"Izzy hated this life so much she left me, but eventually came around when she realized Bash's family was different than the rest," Gio adds.

We all look to Matteo.

He gives us a sheepish look. "I mean, I kidnapped Vanessa so I'm not sure she ever really made the choice. I kind of just barged into her life and stayed until she could no longer fathom it without me."

We all laugh at that. He is the most mild-mannered of us, so it's amusing that he's the one who went to the most drastic measures to get his wife.

Bash raises his glass. "To the strong-headed women we call ours."

Everyone grabs their glasses and raises them.

"Enough about our wives. I have news," Bash says, bringing the attention back to him.

"What's up?" Gio asks.

"Lucian is coming home," Bash tells us. "I haven't told Greer yet, but I figured she would take all the help she could get right now."

Lucian is another hacker in the family. When Greer came back to the States, he switched places with her and went to Italy to oversee the day-to-day operations.

Killian nods at his brother-in-law. "She might bitch about it, but she'll be thankful."

"I've talked to him some, but with him being in a different country, it's been hard," Enzo says as he rubs his jaw.

"I've never met him," I say out loud.

Gio snaps his fingers, pointing at me. "That's right, you moved into his spot when he left."

"I think you'll like him," Matteo says.

"He's good people." Bash nods.

"Have you heard anything from your mole?" I ask, referring to Bash's inside man in the FBI.

He shakes his head. "As far as he can tell, these missing girls aren't even on their radar. The detectives assigned to the cases haven't connected any of them."

"I'm not surprised. Did I tell you the Chief is supposed to be like an uncle to her, and as far as I can tell, he never even truly pushed to find her? He put the missing report out with her undercover name, then told everyone else that she was on a case on her own. He fucking fired her." I growl.

"Wait, he fired her? I thought she left." Killian looks over at me.

"No one ever really asked me what happened so I let you believe what you wanted, but no. That fucker fired her when she went back. Literally told her that he believes she went on vacation for two weeks to make him believe she had been kidnapped so he would investigate her case. I swear if she didn't love that man, I would kill him." I slam back my glass of scotch, hating the burn.

"Hey, that's a sipping scotch," Bash chastised me.

"Sorry," I murmur, setting the glass down on the table.

"That's messed up. Maybe we need to dig further into this uncle. He seems like a sketchy guy." Gio rubs his jaw.

I sigh. "I've had tabs on him for years. Nothing ever pops up on him. I think he's just a douchebag. I wish I had some dirt on him so I could get him fired and publicly humiliated. I want him to feel triple of what he made my girl feel."

Enzo moves closer, patting my shoulder. "It's hard caring so much for one person. Don't do anything stupid."

I nod, letting myself mull over his sage advice. The guys remain quiet, all probably thinking about what they would do for their own women. None of them could blame me if I did something irrational.

One of the babies cries, breaking the moment.

"Alessa, did you really have to push Draco over?" Bash sighs as he gets up to grab his daughter. "Why can't you be nicer to your future husband, *Sole*?"

I smile at the nickname he uses. I can totally see why he calls her the sun. She lights up his life.

"Does Sofia know you already have her daughter married off?" Matteo teases.

Bash smirks. "I'm the Don. As soon as Draco was born, we had a contract drawn up."

"Mia wasn't overly happy about it, but she sees the reasoning behind it. Draco will be her protector. He will grow up knowing his priority will always be her."

"I can't wait to watch how this plays out." Killian chuckles.

"Shut it, Westie," Bash says with zero heat.

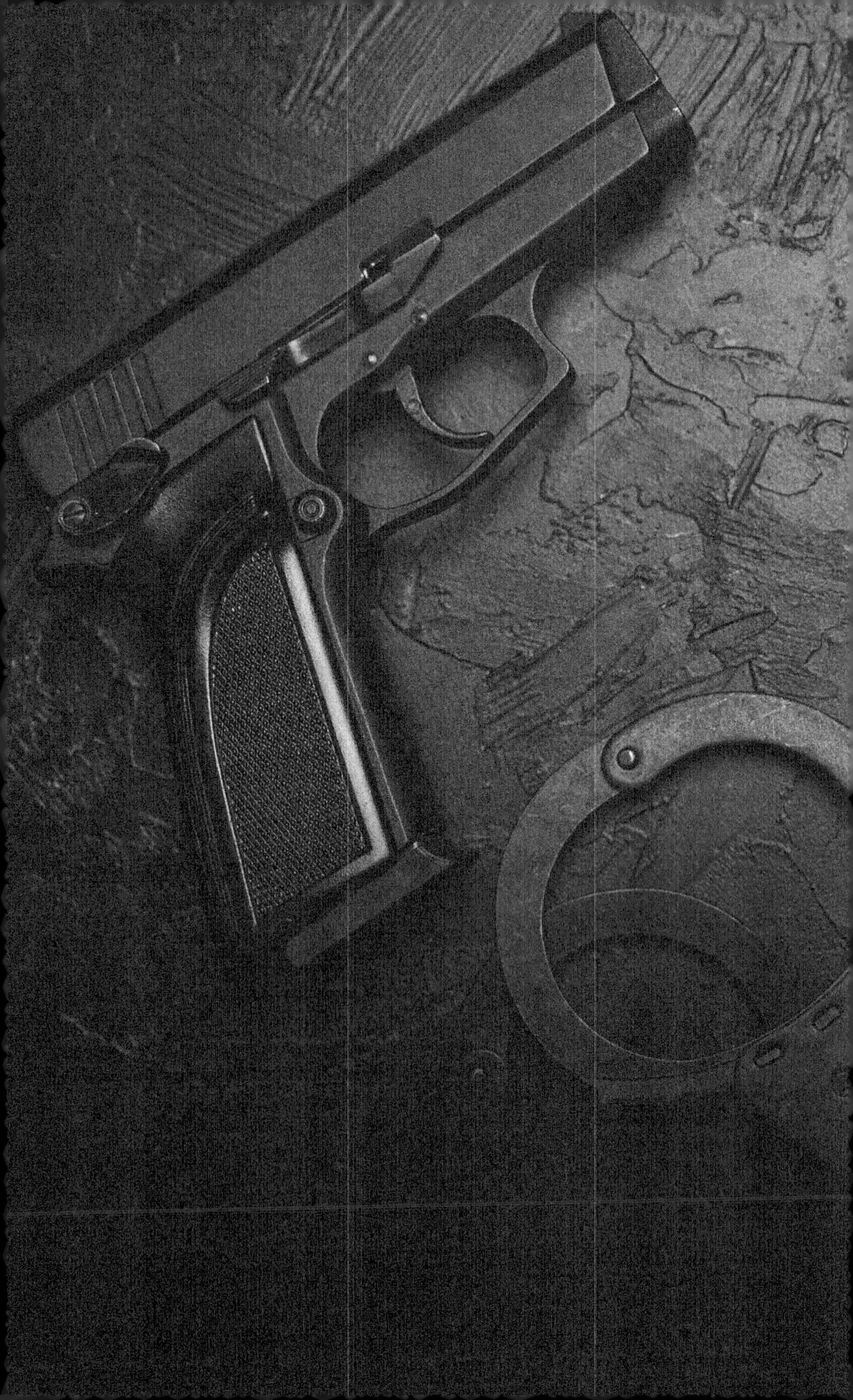

CHAPTER
EIGHTEEN

Serena

Controlling my breathing, my feet pound on the treadmill as I stare at myself in the mirror as I run. I've never done well with sitting idle and not having something to do. When I was little it was extracurriculars, and as an adult, I drowned myself in work.

Now I have no job and no home of my own. Don't get me wrong, Tristano has made me feel more than welcome, but I hate relying on others. I feel useless and like I'm taking advantage of his kindness.

I can feel him before I see him. I don't know what it is about him, but I know when he's around. Through the mirror, I watch him walk into the gym. He rounds the front of the treadmill and braces his hands on the handles, his eyes on my bouncing chest.

Typical male.

I snap my fingers and smirk. "Eyes up here, buddy." I pant.

He raises a brow with a small smile. "Can't blame me for looking when they are right there in front of me."

I roll my eyes as I start to slow down. "What's up?"

"Do you have anything planned for the rest of the day?"

"No, my calendar is jam-packed," I deadpan.

"Would you like me to show you around the neighborhood? Maybe grab some coffee? Ice cream? Something."

I sigh as I come to a stop. "Do I want to? Yes, but I know you're busy with work."

"That's the great thing about what I do, *anima gemella*, I can set up notifications that will alert me as soon as something pops up. I don't have to actually sit at my computer all day." He raises a brow. "I'm sure you've heard that a watched pot never boils. Same thing with computers."

"Are you sure?"

He holds out a hand. "I wouldn't have asked if I wasn't."

I place my hand in his and step off the treadmill. "Do I have time to shower real quick?"

"Sure. Whenever you're ready," he tells me as we walk toward the door.

"You know, it's really nice that you have a gym in your home," I tell him as we make our way up to the bathroom.

"I used to spend a lot of time in here, but lately I haven't been able to get away."

I frown. "Are you sure you should be leaving with me then?"

He smiles. "There is always something that's going to be going on in my work life. Working out was never more important than that. You, *anima gemella*, will always be the most important thing in my life."

My cheeks heat at his admission. It's something I've always hoped he would say, but never dreamed I would hear coming out of his mouth.

It makes this whole situation seem surreal. Almost as if I can't trust it or my feelings.

"Hey." He cups my cheek. "What's with that look? Am I moving too fast for you? I know I can be intense sometimes. The guys tell me to tone it down all the time."

His rambling makes me laugh, which in turn makes him smile. I really like his smile.

"Have you ever had this feeling like your life isn't really your life? Like you are living in some alternate reality?"

"Every single day I wake up and you are still in my arms. I have no idea what I did to deserve an angel like you, but Lord knows I will do everything I can to prove that I will protect you."

My eyes sting at how open and honest he's being. To hear him say all those wonderful things when for the last several years, all I have heard is about how I'm fucking my life up.

Tristano makes me want to be a better person, but not because I'm not a good person now. No, he makes me want to be better because together we are better.

"Me too," I whisper, leaning forward until our foreheads touch.

We stand like that a moment before he pulls back. "Go take your shower."

I raise on my toes to peck his lips before I head down the hall. When I turn around to look at him, he's standing there staring at my ass. I shake my head, loving how his eyes can't seem to leave me.

Maybe for once, I found what I've been looking for.

"THAT WAS FAST," Tristano says as he stands from the couch.

I didn't want to take too long in the shower, so I did the whole wash my body, leaving my hair up in a messy bun before adding deodorant and some nice-smelling spray thing. Then I threw on a T-shirt and a pair of shorts. Slipping my feet into some flip-flops, I was happy with my look.

Seeing him looking at me now as if he could eat me up, yeah, that makes it worth forgoing the makeup and hair.

Taking my hand in his, Tris pulls me out of the door. We make our way down the front steps and onto the sidewalk.

"It's a nice day," I say as I tilt my head back, letting the sun hit my face.

"It is," he murmurs, his eyes on the street around us.

I smile, he's always on alert.

As we walk, Tristano points out different businesses. His favorite pizza place, the dry cleaners he uses, and more. By the time an hour has passed, I feel like I've lived here my whole life instead of only a little bit. He brings this place alive with each story he shares, from the time he puked on Enzo's shoes after one night of too many drinks to the time he gave Declan a piggyback ride.

I feel like I lived those moments with him.

Maybe that's what it is about Tristano. Anytime he talks, he is so enthusiastic about it. He lives each day to the fullest, always finding the positive in every situation. That charisma he oozes bleeds into others and makes them as excited about life as he is.

I realize then that he's my balance.

He helps counteract the thoughts that have long lived inside my head.

"Tell me, ice cream or coffee?" he asks, making me smile.

"Coffee. I could go for a caffeine boost." I press closer to his side, needing to feel more of his skin against mine.

"Let's cross here then." He points across the street. "We're going there."

I look at the sign above the building.

Paradiso.

"That's Italian for paradise, right?"

Tristano nods as he opens the door to the shop. "It is. You learning Italian now?"

As we step inside, I glance up at him. "I maybe already learned it."

He opens his mouth to speak, but then the barista greets us.

"Good afternoon. What can I get you two today?"

After we place our orders, Tristano pulls me into him, wrapping his arms around my waist.

"So why did you learn Italian?"

"I wanted to feel closer to you. I knew you spoke it and that meant it was something of yours. I taught myself it right after we met."

He shakes his head, pulling me into him closer as he kisses the side of my head. "God, I love that."

My heart skips a beat at the word love.

He didn't say he loved me, but it felt close enough. The urge to tell him I love him hits me hard.

Before I can say it, he pulls back, taking my hand. "Do you want to drink your coffee here or while we walk?"

"Walking for sure. I've spent too much time inside lately."

"I'm sorry about that."

I rub his chest. "It's not your fault."

"Here you go. You two have a great day," the barista says as she slides our drinks toward us.

"Thank you," we murmur in unison.

We head out of the shop and I start walking back the way we came.

"What are you doing?" Tristano asks.

I frown and look over my shoulder at him. "Why did you stop?"

Tristano sighs as he walks up to me. Gently, he pushes me to the side so I'm on the inside of the sidewalk and he's closer to the curb.

"My woman doesn't walk on the outside," he says as he takes my hand.

"You're ridiculous," I tell him as we start walking.

"Hey, if some idiot decides to hit pedestrians for points and drives on the sidewalk, I'd rather have them take me out than you."

"That's..." I shake my head. "I don't even know what to say to that."

"How about you tell me what's wrong? I've been hoping you'd

open up on your own, but we only have so long before we have to get back."

I feel my shoulders tense. "I don't know what you mean."

"I've known you for years, Serena. I know when something's wrong with you. Now tell me what it is so I can fix it." He pauses. "Are you regretting all of this?"

Before he even finishes his sentence, I'm already shaking my head. "No, absolutely not."

"Then tell me, please," he pleads as he squeezes my hand.

Suddenly I'm glad I chose to walk instead of sitting at the coffee shop for this conversation.

"I feel lost."

Tristano's quiet as I try to gather my thoughts.

"I've never not worked. I've always been on the go, and suddenly I have nothing of my own. I love being with you, and I don't regret quitting, but..."

"You feel as if you're taking advantage of me." He frowns.

"Yes." I take a breath I didn't realize I was holding. "I know you don't think I am but I can't help how I feel." I shake my head. "I feel like I have nothing to offer you."

Tristano comes to a stop and pulls me in front of him. He drops my hand and cups the back of my neck. "You have everything to offer me," he says as he searches my eyes. "When I realized you weren't going to check in, a piece of me died. I was afraid I wouldn't find you again. I didn't willingly sleep that entire time. Even when I passed out from exhaustion, I only rested a few hours before my mind would wake me back up. I couldn't live without you."

"You found me though," I whisper.

He nods. "I did, and now I have you right where I've always wanted you but have been too afraid to admit." He licks his lips. "I want you in my home, in my bed every night. I want everything with you."

"Tris..."

He shakes his head. "If you don't want me, I need you to tell me.

If you want to find a hobby or a job, I'll go down the rabbit hole with you until you find something you like. I'll do anything to make you happy, you know that, right, *anima gemella*?"

I squeeze my eyes shut. "I want that too."

"Then we'll make it happen. I just need you to be honest with me and tell me when you're struggling. Can you do that?"

I open my eyes and nod. "Yeah."

Tristano leans in and brushes his lips against mine. I lean in to kiss him but he pulls back and takes my hand in his once again.

"Now tell me, how do you feel about painting? Or maybe pottery. There's an art store up ahead we can stop in on our way home."

"I don't know. I've never tried anything like that outside of school."

Tristano smirks down at me. "Then it looks like we will both be trying something new."

Tristano

I'M LAYING on the couch with Serena over me, her legs pinning me down as we make out with a movie playing in the background, when my phone goes off.

Groaning, I break the kiss.

"Ignore it," Serena says between the kisses she's pressing on my neck.

The vibrating stops and we both breathe out a sigh of relief.

"Where were we?" I ask as I pull her head back up, nibbling on her lip.

Serena grinds herself down on me right when my phone vibrates in my pocket again.

"Shit, that felt good," she murmurs, making me laugh.

"Sounds like we should make a stop at Seduction soon then," I tease.

"I wouldn't complain about that."

I raise a brow. "No?"

"I've never tried anything really, and who knows, it might be fun."

"I can promise you one thing, when it comes to our sex life we will always have fun."

She rolls her eyes and leans forward, kissing me one more time before she pushes herself up and slides back further down my legs. Reaching into my pocket, I pull out my phone and see a missed call from Greer and a text from Enzo.

> Enzo: 9-1-1. Get to the office now.

"Shit, I got to go," I mumble as I sit up, texting him back.

> Me: Shit, on my way.

Serena stands up and crosses her arms as she nibbles on her lip. "Is everything okay?"

Standing, I reach out and pull her into me. My thumb goes to her lip. "Only I can bite this."

Serena rolls her eyes.

"I need to go to the office. Do you want to go with me? I don't know when I'll be back."

"Will they be cool with it if I do?"

"I don't see why not." I shrug. "It might be boring though."

"It can't be any worse than sitting here," she says as she walks to the door, slipping on her shoes.

The ride to the office doesn't take long. I chose a house close for this reason. I always wanted to be available.

As soon as we step into the office, it's complete and utter mayhem.

"What in the world..." Serena whispers to herself.

Greer slams her hands down on her desk. "Goddammit!"

Killian leans down and whispers something in her ear.

"Where do you need me?" I ask as I step forward.

Enzo turns toward me, and I watch as his shoulders drop.

"Shit's hitting the fan. We have been keeping everyone on high alert. A girl has been taken inside the city this time. We caught it on one of our cameras. We have a team out there trying to catch up, but I'm afraid we might be too late. It's not only here though. Chicago's been hit as well. One of the working girls beat the guy off her friend with a shoe. She was able to escape," Enzo says.

"We're sending teams out," Killian says as he rubs Greer's back. "We're going to warn the girls. See if anyone will wear a tracker like in Chicago."

"I'm going to call in an anonymous tip to the news stations and hope they will report that women shouldn't be traveling alone at night right now," Greer adds.

Sitting at my computer, I pull up my program. It didn't catch anything, which frustrates me. Then I pull up the video footage of the girl taken here. She was taken in Manhattan.

My blood chills as I watch it happen. She's not some working girl. This is a teen walking home from school, it looks like. The man stops her, seemingly asking for directions. When she goes to walk away after helping him, he stabs her in the neck with something. Within seconds, she's in a car that was waiting.

"That looks like the man Meredith described." Serena moves closer.

"You think so?" I turn my head to the side a little.

The video isn't great, but he does look tall and has blonde hair. I try to enhance the image to see his wrists, but it's too grainy.

"It could be." She hums.

I continue pausing the camera frame by frame to see if there is anything we can use. The car is a modern sedan with no distinguishing features. The tag is conveniently covered. I can feel myself getting worked up. I want to smash something.

Then she touches me, and all the tension melts away. I'm still angry we can't find these guys, but she's with me. It's enough to calm me.

"I-I have an idea..." Serena says hesitantly.

Greer looks over at us. "Go on."

I watch as Serena rolls her shoulders back and takes a deep breath. "The city is too big to have eyes all over, despite having both families come together. When they took us, they moved us by train. What if we staked out the railways? Or maybe the harbors for the shipping containers?"

Everyone pauses and turns toward her, and stares.

She shifts from one foot to the other while I try not to smile.

"That's a really good idea..." Greer says hesitantly.

"It could work." Killian nods. "We could stop all the trains leaving the city and search them if we need to, and we already have access to the harbors."

"Bash is meeting with the other families," Greer says, referring to the other Italian Mafia families in the city. "Trying to round up more bodies."

"I've put in a call with the Rothesteins, to see if they are willing to help out," Killian says, referring to the leader of the Jewish mob in the city.

"What can I do to help?" Serena asks.

"Want to hit the pavement with me?" Killian asks. "It might help having a woman with me while I try and convince these women to take time off to talk to me."

"Are you sure?" Serena asks, eyes wide.

"Better take him up on it before he changes his mind," I say lightly.

"Yes." Serena nods so fast she looks like a bobblehead. "Let's go."

"We'll talk on the way," Killian warns her before turning toward his wife.

While he kisses her goodbye, I walk to Serena and pull her into my arms.

"Be careful." I kiss her. "Don't do anything that makes you uncomfortable."

"You're okay with me going?" she whispers.

I snort. "I'm not your uncle. You make your own decisions. Even if you didn't, I know you are fully capable of handling yourself. Besides, you're not going alone. You're going with family. I know they have your back. You'll be safe."

Leaning up, she kisses me. "You'll never know how much your unwavering support means to me."

I pull away and see a fire in her eyes that's been missing since I found her again.

She's excited.

"I'll watch your girl's six," Killian tells me as he walks by, slapping my shoulder.

"I'd appreciate it," I tell him honestly.

"Here." Enzo holds out two earpieces. "Take these, and we will be able to hear everything. My shipment of mini cameras hasn't come in, so we're flying blind unless we can hack into cameras around you."

"Sounds good." Serena nods as she takes an earpiece. "Thank you."

"I might have some cameras in my office," Killian says as he grabs his earpiece. "I'll have Conor look before he meets us." He turns toward Serena and pushes her toward the door. "Let's go."

I take a deep breath as I watch them walk away. Logically I know she's safe with Killian, but just having her out of my sight right now makes me anxious as fuck.

"It never gets easier."

I turn and look at Greer and see a knowing look on her face.

She feels this too, and if that isn't a kick in the nuts.

"Let's get to work," she demands.

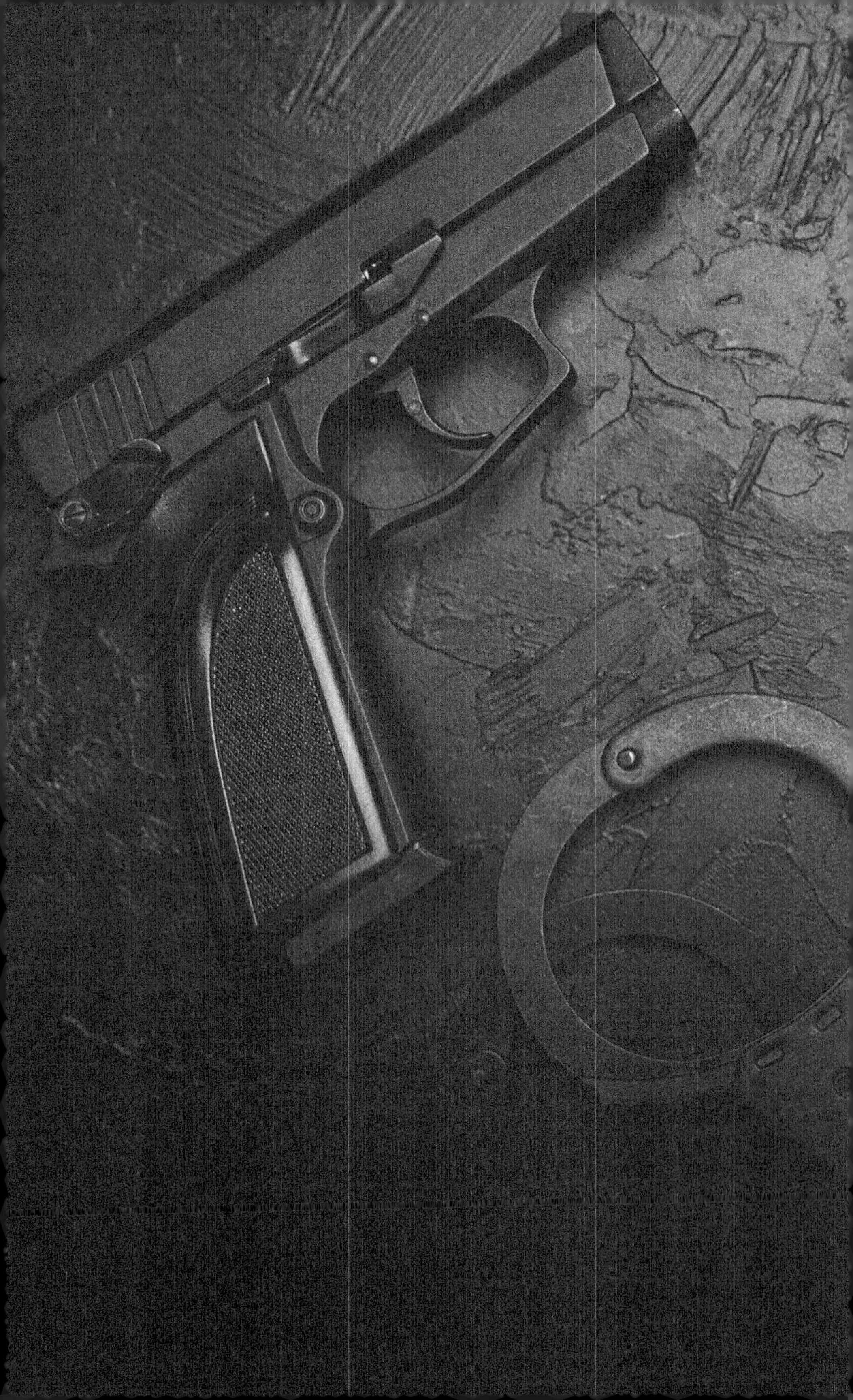

CHAPTER NINETEEN

Serena

The sun is long gone, and a chill has blanketed the streets while the street lights blaze.

"Are you warm enough?" Killian asks.

"I'm good." After a beat of silence, I ask, "Where are we going?"

I watch as a man steps out of a building and turns toward us.

Killian raises his chin. "That's my second in command, Conor. He set up a meeting for us."

Conor stares me down as we approach. I want to squirm under his scrutiny, but I pretend like it doesn't bother me.

"Tristano's girl." Killian nods.

"Serena."

"Conor." He turns toward Killian. "They are waiting."

We head inside with Conor in the lead and head up a dark stairway. Coming to a stop on the second floor, he knocks on a door and it swings open. Walking into the unknown frays on my nerves. It goes against all the training I've ever had, but I follow the guys inside. Putting my trust in them that they won't lead me into a bad situation.

"What's the meaning of this O'Reilly?" a man demands.

"Last I checked, we ain't in your territory so you shouldn't be meddlin' in our business...unless things at home are shit and you're lookin' for a side piece," another says.

"I can promise you, I am more than satisfied with my wife," Killian says.

Both men scoff.

"Get on with it. You're wasting our time," a third says coolly.

I scan the room as they talk and take a mental picture of the five new men in front of me, wishing I could run background checks on them.

"You know about the missing women," Killian says diplomatically.

"Ain't my problem," one man says.

A man leaning against the window grunts. "They got my best girl. Lost me a lot of money that she hadn't paid out when they took her."

"Rumor has it, it's about to ramp up. We're closing in on them. I want you all to talk to your girls and warn them," Killian tells them.

"Sounds like you want us to lose out on money," one on the couch says as he puffs on a cigar.

A man leaning against the wall with his arms crossed lifts his chin toward me. "Who's the girl?"

"One of mine and not for sale," Killian says with heat in his tone.

"I didn't think you dealt in the skin game." The man by the window chuckles.

"I'm not. Look, back on topic. Tell your girls or don't. Some of the women are being grabbed off the street and others we think are getting in the cars willingly. They don't discriminate with size or skin color," Killian says, getting back on track.

"Time to go, boss," Conor says, nodding toward me.

I reach for the door and step out into the hall. Conor and Killian step out, and once again, Conor takes his place in front of Killian.

Pausing, I look back into the room full of pimps. "If you really cared about your girls, or hell, your bottom dollar, you would listen to him," I say before I close the door.

Killian shoots me a look as we start walking down the stairs but doesn't say anything. Once outside, I take a deep breath.

"Fucking cheap cigars. Now we're going to smell like shit for the rest of the night," Conor mutters.

"Have someone to impress, do you?" I quip.

Killian chuckles as Conor shoots me a dirty look.

"Sorry," I say, holding up my hands. "What next?"

"We walk down the street. Warn the girls ourselves and tell them to spread the word. We won't get them all but..."

"But you'd rather try than say you didn't." I nod in understanding.

"Rothestein texted and said he would meet with you and you alone," Conor tells him.

"You two will have to wait outside."

For the next twenty minutes, I watch as women try to pick up Killian and Conor. I don't know how, but they manage to sidestep the offers with ease while issuing the warnings. As for me, some listen while others roll their eyes and ignore me.

"Frustrated yet?" Conor asks as we get back into the car Killian and I came in.

"I don't understand why they weren't taking us seriously," I say, shaking my head as we pull onto the road.

"You can lead a horse to water, but you can't force it to drink," Killian says as he looks down at his phone.

"I don't know why I'm annoyed." I sigh. "It happened when I was undercover too. It's like they all think they're invincible."

"They have a degree of separation right now where most of them don't know someone who's gone missing."

I frown. "I hadn't thought of that."

"Where are we meeting Rothestein?"

"The synagogue," Conor tells him.

"Interesting place to have a meeting," I mutter.

Killian laughs. "I probably shouldn't tell you this, but places of worship are some of the best places to meet."

Conor chuckles. "Or confessionals."

I raise my brow and look at Killian.

He smirks with zero shame and shrugs. "Greer."

"Ah..." I nod even though I don't fully understand.

Did they used to meet up in confessionals before they became public, or is it some kind of kink they have, having sex in a church?

I don't question it. I'd rather not know.

Before too long, Conor parks in front of the synagogue, and Killian slides out.

"I'll be back," he says before he shuts the door.

We watch him walk into the place of worship before Conor gets out of the car. I follow suit and shut the door. We both lean against the car, side by side, staring up at the building.

I watch as everyone walks by, looking at us like we're out of place. "It's like we stepped into a different world," I murmur quietly.

"That's because we did," he says as he nods to a man. "They live a different kind of life than we do. Have beliefs that we don't understand."

"I can't imagine." I shake my head.

"My old neighbor was friends with a girl who was part of this community. She got married when she was sixteen to a much older man. When she would leave, my neighbor would break down, sobbing so loud I could hear her through the wall. I asked her about it one day, annoyed because she kept me up all night with her bawling. Needless to say, I felt like an ass afterward."

"When I was with the PD, I remember a couple people looking

into communities like this. Convinced that they were a religious cult, but they never found anything to stand on and the investigations died."

"I'm not surprised." He nods.

"It's like with everything in life. Where there is good, there is bad that follows. You can't condemn an entire religion just because you don't understand it. And because you don't understand doesn't make it wrong."

"I couldn't have said it better myself."

Killian steps outside, followed by another man. Conor and I push off the car and stand straight.

"That's Rothestein. He's a good man if not a little crazy."

I watch as Killian shakes the other man's hand before walking down the stairs.

"Aren't you all? A little crazy, I mean."

Conor chuckles as he opens the door. "Get in, smart-ass."

I do as he says with a smile on my face.

Tristano

I'M RECLINED in my chair with my feet up on my desk. My eyes are dry as the exhaustion settles in, and I can barely keep them open. I've tried running around the office, doing jumping jacks, and drinking enough caffeine to fuel an entire submarine.

Getting old fucking sucks. I'm only twenty-five, and it feels like pulling an all-nighter is no longer in my wheelhouse of qualifications.

I rest my head on my fist and close my eyes.

Just five minutes.

I don't know how long I've been out when I feel a hand come down on my shoulder, making me jump.

"It's just me," Serena says quietly.

I sit up straight and rub my eyes. "What are you doing here?"

She shrugs when I look at her.

"Didn't you go home?"

"I did." She licks her lips. "But I couldn't sleep without you there."

I groan, feeling guilty as fuck. "I'm sorry, *anima gemella*. I didn't even think of that."

"It's okay." She looks around the room. "Did everyone go home?"

"Yeah. I kicked them out at about midnight. They have kids at home, I can man this while they take care of their families."

"That's sweet of you." Serena's eyes drop from my face to my chest and back. She raises a brow. "What happened to your shirt?"

I look down and chuckle. I completely forgot that I took off my dress shirt earlier and just put my sports jacket back on.

"You don't like this look?" I tease as I run my hand down my chest and over my abs, resting it on my belt.

"You know I do." Serena blushes. "Now are you going to stop teasing me and tell me what happened?"

I pull her into my lap and wrap my arms around her waist. Without prompting, Serena leans down and kisses me.

"I spilled hot coffee on myself earlier, so I took it off," I tell her when I pull away from her lips.

"If you would have texted me, I would have brought you a clean set of clothes."

"That's okay. I texted my dry cleaner down the street. They are just going to drop off my dry cleaning here instead of the house tomorrow."

"That's some kind of service."

I shrug. "They are good people. Now tell me, how was your night? Find anything?"

Serena snuggles into me. "No, it was pretty uneventful. It was interesting to see how the other side works, that's for sure."

"What do you mean?"

Serena starts running her thumb over my chest, and I don't even think she realizes it.

"Nothing bad. Killian just met with some pimps and tried to convince them to warn their girls. They didn't seem too open to the idea, so we did it ourselves for a bit before he met with the Jewish mob."

"Ah, they are an interesting bunch."

"Do I even want to know?"

"Narcotics, mainly pharmaceuticals."

"Huh, I would have thought they were in the gun trade or something."

"Nope." I shake my head. "Crazy group though if you go against them. It went well though?"

"I didn't listen in on that one but I'm assuming so. Killian said they are willing to help."

"Good. Did you have a good time?" I ask as I twirl a piece of her hair.

"Oddly, I did. It reminded me a lot of when I had to gather intel undercover."

I hum as my eyes start to feel heavy once again.

"Hey, Tris."

"Yeah, *anima gemella*?"

"Do you have a couch or something here we can cuddle up on?"

I open my eyes and see that sleep is about to take her too.

"Come on," I say, tapping her hip.

Serena crawls off my lap, and I stand. Taking her hand in mine, I walk down the hall into our bunk room.

"Pick a cot."

Serena moves to the biggest one that can fit two people. Kicking off her shoes, she crawls under the blanket and taps the bed.

"Cuddle with me?"

"Don't have to ask me twice," I mumble as I take off my jacket and shoes.

I get into bed and pull her to my side. Serena places her head and hand on my chest.

I lean down and kiss the top of her head. "Night."

"Night," she mumbles.

Right as I'm on the edge of sleep, I could swear I hear her tell me she loves me.

I have no idea how long I'm out for, but something startles me awake.

With my eyes still shut, I listen and don't hear anything. Even without opening my eyes, I know the sun is starting to rise because of the soft glow filling the room.

Something tickles my nose and I bat it away. Opening my eyes, I'm met with a head full of hair.

Her fucking hair woke me up. I smile to myself.

I run my hand down her back softly as I take in the moment of peace. I know as soon as I get up shit will be crazy. Serena murmurs in her sleep and pushes further into my side.

My breath catches when I realize her fingers are under the waistband of my pants. So close yet so far away. She shifts again, raising her leg over my hips, and I feel her grind into me.

I groan as I squeeze her ass. "Wake up, *anima gemella*."

"I don't want to," she says sleepily. "I was having such a good dream."

"Hmm." I hum. "But if you wake up, I can make that dream a reality."

She turns her head and kisses my chest. "What kind of dream do you think I was having?"

"The kind where I was buried inside of you."

"Are you sure?" I can feel her smile against my chest.

"I think if I were to stick my hand into your panties right now, you would be wet for me."

"Why don't you find out?"

I move so fast, flipping her onto her back, that she laughs.

She fucking laughs when she has me harder than a rock. This woman is going to be the death of me.

"You think this is funny?" I ask as I grind into her.

She spreads her legs further apart and wraps them around my waist.

"I would never." She smiles.

She reaches up and runs her hand over my neck to the back of my head. Serena pulls me down and kisses me nice and slow.

"Can I help you?" I ask between kisses.

"I think so." She sighs.

"Tell me what you want, *anima gemella*."

"You. I just want you. Nice and slow before we have to get back to reality."

I've never done slow before. That's never been what sex was about for me.

Yet, with her, I think I want that. No, I know I want it. Need it even.

Pulling back from her, I pull down her pants and underwear in one go. Tossing it to the side, I slide my own pants down, leaving them on.

Then I position myself at her entrance and look over my shoulder.

"I don't have a condom, but I'll pull out. You gotta be quiet though. I have no idea if anyone is here."

When I look back to her, she's biting her lip. "I'll be quiet. Promise."

I smirk at her, looking all innocent and coy. This is the woman who owns my heart. I wouldn't have her any other way.

Sliding in slowly, I savor the heat surrounding me. She feels like velvet. I swear I can feel her pulse through my dick.

Her breath catches as I pull back to press in again. I look up to find her eyes already on me. She's always watching me, just as I am always watching her.

Who were we to fool ourselves? We were inevitable.

"You're so beautiful," I whisper as I lean down to kiss her.

She meets me halfway, pressing her lips to mine.

My heart is beating faster, but it's not from thrusting. I'm still taking that slow and steady, letting the feeling build up.

No, my heart is beating because as I stare into my girl's eyes, peppering kisses across her face, I realize that I wasn't truly living before her.

"Serena, *anima gemella*," I breathe against her skin.

"Tris," she moans in response.

"I love you, *anima gemella*. I love you so much," I murmur against her skin.

"Tris, I, uh…" she starts, but as she orgasms, she loses all ability to speak.

She's being loud, but I don't have it in me to chastise her for it. I love the sounds she makes. If anything, it drives me higher.

Pulling out of her quickly, I jack myself over her stomach, pushing her shirt up until I can see her breasts encased in another lacy bra.

That does it for me. I spill against her beautiful skin, loving the primal feeling inside knowing she's marked with my essence. It's stupid, but I feel like this only cemented her as mine even more.

The caveman inside me wants to roar so loud the entire city hears as I beat my chest.

Instead, I stare down at my sated woman.

She smiles up at me as she reaches down to play with the cum on her belly.

"I'll get something to clean it up." I go to move, but she locks her legs around me as she spreads it more into her skin.

"It's good for me," she whispers before putting her wet, sticky fingers to her mouth and sucking them.

My spent dick jerks as if it wants to come alive.

"Jesus, you are going to kill me," I murmur.

She's about to respond when the door opens. I flatten myself on her, glaring over my shoulder.

"Time to wake… oh." Greer turns, covering her eyes.

"Listen, I did not need to see a pasty white ass. Tristano, you need to go tan or something. How the hell is your ass so white when the rest of you is so tan? You know what, don't answer that. Get dressed, please, and remind me to have that cot sanitized. We have work to do."

"We will be right there."

"Don't go for round two. As happy as I am about you two, I'm being serious."

My body freezes. "What did you find?"

"Nothing yet, but we are hitting the streets. I need you on the computer. She's going with Killian."

I look down at Serena. She's staring up at me.

Back to reality, it is.

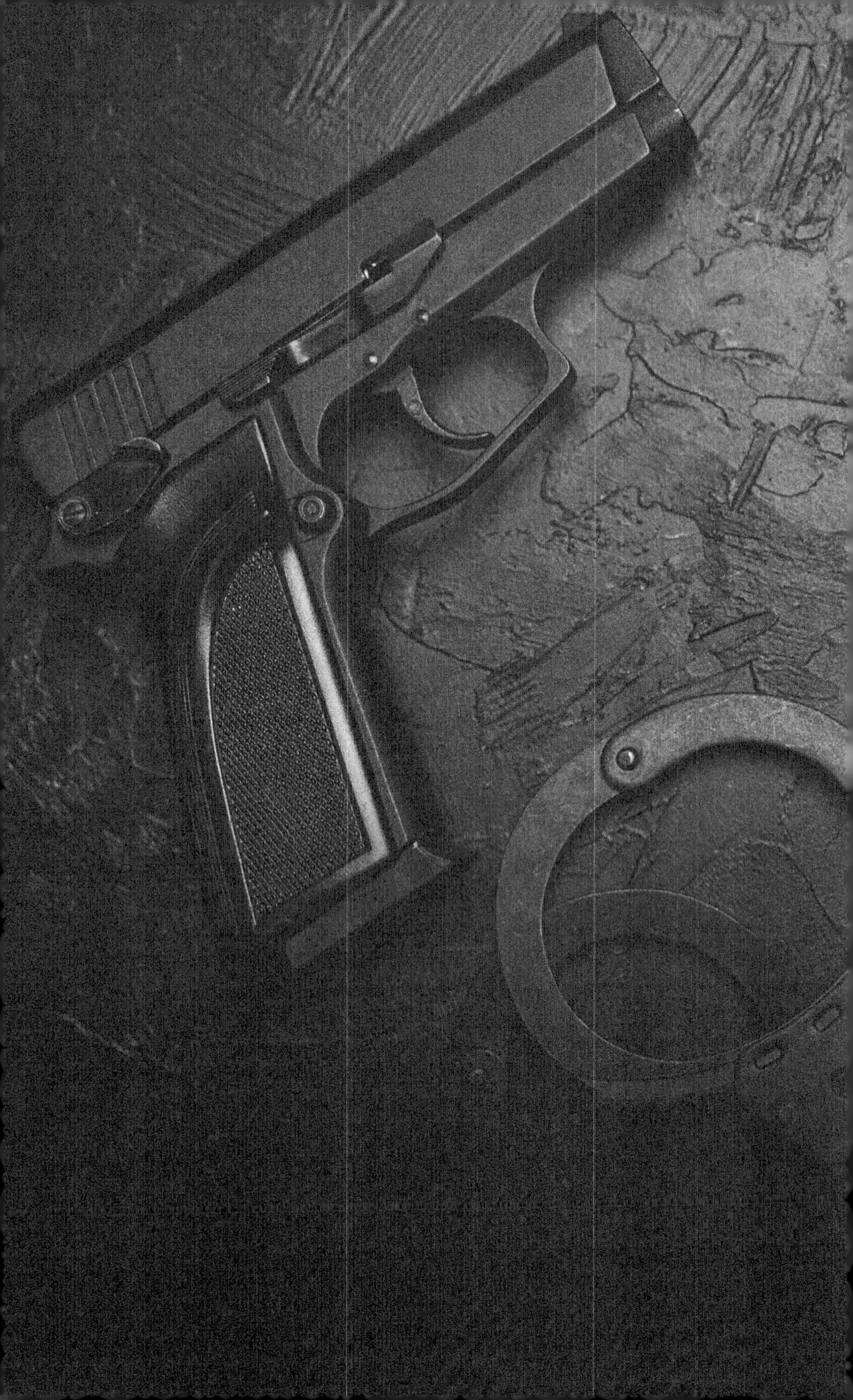

CHAPTER TWENTY

Serena

A sharp whistle pierces the air, rattling off the metal walls of the empty building. Everyone quiets as some of the most dangerous men in the city stand for all to see.

Tristano impresses me more and more each day. After he helped me redress, he led me to the main room where Greer, Killian, and Enzo were preparing for what was to come. Lucian, someone from their Italian family, had arrived to provide added support, but even with him, they needed Tris. Each one assigned to watch a family as they search.

I thought this would mean Tris would urge me to stay with him, but he didn't. Instead, he pulled me into his arms, kissing me senseless before smacking my ass and telling me to be safe.

I've gotten so used to being told what I could and couldn't do that for a moment, I just stared at him as he moved back to his desk and got to work. I couldn't comprehend that he was not only letting me go, but he didn't say one thing about me not being able to do it.

Is this what a healthy relationship with someone looks like?

It only shows me how toxic my uncle was for me. He was supposed to be my biggest supporter, but he only weighed me down. He stifled me when he should have been encouraging me to grow.

I think him firing me is the best thing that ever happened to me.

"Keep your eyes open," Matteo murmurs into the comms, drawing my attention back to the task at hand.

"What should I be looking for?" I ask as I scan the crowd.

"Anything that could be considered a threat to either Bash or Killian."

"Ten-four," I tell him as I start walking around the outskirts of the room.

Before we could go out and search, we had to get everyone together in one place to ensure everyone was on the same page. Today there are no territory disputes. No bad blood.

We come together for a common mission. Save the innocent women of our city.

Bastiano stands tall above everyone, giving out the orders while Killian and some other Mafia leaders stand next to him. There's a clear divide down here in the crowd. Despite the closeness between Bash and Killian, their families stand separately, and the same goes with the other families. I'm sure if I was looking down on them, it would look like large clusters of people all in one room. Or like a clique at a high school dance. I snort at the idea.

What would they think if that's what you told them they looked like?

"We are going to have men hit the Bronx, Brooklyn, and Staten Island freight train stations. I want every rail car inspected. If you find anyone, call it in. Men and women, it doesn't matter. While part of you are doing that, I want the rest of you hitting the streets, warning people not to travel alone. Your bosses and I are in agreement that this is top priority, and you all need to take it seriously." He looks toward the other bosses. "Do any of you have anything to add?"

Killian steps forward. "My men, you know what to do. Make me proud."

Rothestein steps forward and says something in Yiddish, making his men nod.

"Break into your families to get further instructions," Bash says before stepping back.

The crowd starts to rumble, and there's a certain tension in the air that I can't quite place.

"Serena, come meet us over in the northwest corner," Matteo says over the comms.

"On my way."

I weave around the men who don't pay much attention to me.

"Serena, thank you for joining us today." Bash nods when he sees me.

"Anything I can do to help. This is personal for me."

"I can understand that," he tells me.

"Serena," Killian says as he joins us. "Who will you be joining today?"

"Wherever I'm needed." I shrug.

Bash turns and looks at Killian. "Are you sure that's a good idea?"

"The way I look at it, she's been claimed by one of yours who works with mine." Killian raises a brow and turns to me. "She's already gone out with me once. She did good. She might have been a cop at one point, but that only adds to her skill set."

"I know I'm a liability because of what I used to do, but I promise you, I mean you no harm. I only want to help, no matter what that might look like."

Bash stays quiet as he looks at me with a glint in his eyes. Is that respect?

Killian slaps his brother-in-law on the shoulder. "How about she comes with mine today?"

"That works," he says while still staring at me. "When this is all over, we will have a sit down and figure out what it is you want. If you want to stay at home, that's fine, but if you want a job, we will find you one. How does that sound?"

"I can't stay home. I need a job." I nod.

"Alright, then let's get going. We're wasting daylight."

I NOD at one of Killian's men. Grunting, he pulls the train door open. I sigh when I see it empty.

"Fuck," the guy grumbles as we walk toward the next car with a closed door.

We've been going at this all day in the sweltering heat. So far I've heard others over the comms find a few transients and homeless people. Other than that, nothing promising though.

"How's it going?"

I turn and look over my shoulder and see Conor walking toward me with a bottle of water.

"Thanks," I say as I take it from him. Cracking it open, I take a drink before I respond. "So far nothing."

"Both a blessing and a curse."

"Right?"

"I heard that they found a dead body in one of the cars in Staten Island."

I cringe. "That had to have smelled bad with this heat."

"Better them than us."

"Do they think it was related?"

Conor shakes his head. "No, the guy had a needle in his arm."

"Are we going or what?" my assistant snaps.

"He's so welcoming," I mumble.

Conor chuckles. "Yeah, Teddy is a little impatient."

My eyebrows fly upward. "His name is Teddy?"

"No." Conor smirks. "We call him Teddy because when he first joined, he looked like a teddy bear."

"Huh. If he is a teddy bear, he's a grumpy one."

We step forward and get into position. After three more empty cars, we hit the jackpot.

Teddy slides the door open and I see one girl with a gag in her mouth, arms bound above her head. I recognize her immediately as the teen from the video.

"Fuck," Conor grunts.

"Holy shit!" Teddy exclaims.

Holstering my gun, I rush forward and pull myself up into the car.

"Hey, my friends and I are here to help," I tell her as I slowly approach her. "Can I take that out of your mouth?"

She nods.

Bending down, I remove her gag as Conor gets to work on removing her bindings.

"Thank you," the woman rasps.

Her eyes are bloodshot, all cried out.

"You're welcome," I say sincerely.

Her wrists come free, and I help rub feeling back into her arms as Conor calls it in.

"Bash is on his way. I'll wait outside for them," Conor tells me as I wrap the blanket Teddy gave me around the girl.

"What's your name?" I ask her.

"Ellie."

"How old are you?" I hold out my water to her.

She takes it, guzzling it down.

"Slow down. You'll choke," Teddy mutters.

She looks up at him with wide eyes but does as he asks. Once she's finished with the bottle, she answers me.

"Eighteen." She breathes.

"You were taken walking home, right?" I ask.

She nods. "I take some courses at the community college. This guy asked me for some help finding downtown. I gave him directions and then that's the last thing I remember. How long have I been here?"

"A little over twenty-four hours," I tell her.

She lets out a sigh of relief. "Thank God. I haven't seen or heard anyone since I've been here. I was starting to think they left me here to die."

"Not at all. I'm glad we found you."

"Mia is here with Bash," Conor says into the comms so the girl doesn't hear.

"Hey, can I take you to meet my friend, Mia? She's a doctor. She's only going to make sure you're okay."

"Sure. Thank you." She looks to Teddy. "Thank you too. Seriously, you're my hero."

Something soft passes over Teddy's face. "You're welcome."

That's the nicest I've heard his tone all day. All because of this young girl. I shake my head but help Ellie up. Teddy stays close, his eyes taking in our surroundings as I lead her to the SUV with Mia standing outside of it.

"Hello, I'm Mia. Would you mind riding with me back to my office? You will be safe."

Ellie glances over at me then Teddy. I rub my mouth, hiding my smirk.

"Maybe Teddy can go with her? He's the one who found her so she might feel a little better."

She nods her head frantically.

Teddy doesn't say anything. He moves to the SUV, opening the door and helping her inside before climbing in the front passenger side. Mia gets in the back driver's side, and then they are off.

"What now?" I ask Conor and Matteo as we stand around.

"We're placing cameras around the car and stationing men to watch the area," Matteo tells me.

I frown. That's not going to work. By the time we get the alert, they will be long gone, probably with the girl when they realize the other one is missing.

"What is it?" Conor asks when he sees the look on my face.

"I have an idea."

"We are all ears," Matteo asks.

"The guy or guys will come back tonight to drop off another girl, right?"

"Yeah." Conor nods.

"What if one or two of you stay in the car until they show up and take them down?"

"That way they don't come back to an empty car and take off before we can catch them," Conor says, following my lead.

I snap my fingers. "Exactly."

"As soon as they open it and see the girl gone, they will take off," Matteo murmurs. "That, and if they have too many guys, we won't be able to take them."

"That's why you leave me inside. That way you can gauge how many guys they have before you take them down."

"Tristano won't be happy if we use you as bait," Matteo warns.

"Maybe or maybe not. This is my risk to take, not his."

Conor and Matteo share a look before turning back to me.

"It's a solid idea. Let me run it by Bash."

Tristano

SHAKING MY HEAD, I blink slowly. "I'm sorry. Can you repeat that? I could have sworn to God you said they want to use Serena as bait."

Enzo nods. "I did."

I chuckle darkly. "Absolutely fucking not."

"Look, your chick is batshit crazy, and that's on you. With this family though, that's nothing new."

"She's going to turn my hair fucking gray." I stand so fast that the chair flies back, hitting my desk.

"Watch it," Greer snaps. "She's fine. Conor and Matteo are with her in the container with her out of sight."

"They are chaining her up. Again! I promised I wouldn't let that happen to her," I yell.

Greer crosses her arms. "I think you are forgetting the woman you chose to be yours. She made this decision. She has been undercover so many times. If she feels this is something she can handle, then she should be able to do it. She is one hundred percent in control. Even if she wasn't, you and I both know that Conor and Matteo would rush in there to save her before they could hurt one hair on her body. Your girl isn't a delicate little flower, Tristano. She's a badass. She's been trained for this. Let her do it."

I run my hands through my hair. "I know that. I do, but it doesn't fucking mean I like it."

"You knew she became an undercover cop. What the fuck do you think she's been doing on the streets? Acting like an innocent little church girl? Me and her have talked about it a bit. I can guarantee you that was not it," Greer challenges.

"I didn't think about it, okay. She was out of sight, out of mind. I always worried for her, but I didn't watch her close enough to know about her cases. We kept that separate, so no, I didn't know what she did undercover. I pretended like she didn't do it."

"That's your problem. You need to take your head out of the ground and take a look at the woman you are going to marry. This is who she is. Can you handle that?" She crosses her arms, staring me down.

I swallow hard. I can handle that. At least, that's what I've been telling her. I don't like this feeling in my chest though. The one where I feel like she might be in danger and I'm not there to help her.

Enzo raises his hands. "How about we all calm down."

I let out a breath and place my hands on my head as I pace the room.

After several minutes of silence, I stop and look at Greer.

"I know you're right. She's strong and capable. She can handle it, but I don't like knowing that she has to. She's been brushing off therapy until we figure this out. I'm worried she will have an episode and not know how to react."

Greer's hard look softens as she walks over to me. She pulls me in for a hug.

"I hear your concerns. I'm sure she will too, but you have to trust that she knows what's best for her. She won't always make the right decisions, but knowing you will always be there to catch her will boost her confidence and help her heal. Hopefully today we can get a handle on this and get her into therapy. She's family now. We won't let her fall."

I rest my head on her shoulder. "Thank you."

Enzo clears his throat, making us both look over at him.

"You'll be delighted to hear that it worked. She's safe. Matteo just texted. She's on the way over to the basement with Matteo and Conor."

I take a deep breath, letting it calm me.

She's okay.

"Let's head over there." Greer pats my shoulder.

"I'll drive." I grab my keys.

"I don't have a death wish," Greer mutters as she pushes her way in front of me.

Enzo places his hand on my shoulder, stopping me from leaving. "Are you good?"

"How would you feel if Danica put herself in that position?"

"Oh, I'd be fucking furious, but there's a major difference between Danica and Serena. Danica is a former model who would rather pretend the world is perfect with no danger, which I work hard to make happen for her. Serena prefers to look behind the curtain and see the truth. She wants to chase down the bad guys and make the world safer. Like Greer said, she can handle this."

"I know. It's still hard."

"It's that protectiveness in us. Don't stifle her though. If this is what brings her peace, then let her do it."

Greer peeks her head back into the room. "Are we going to watch this interrogation or what?"

Enzo slaps my shoulder and pushes me forward.

"Are you going to lose your shit?" Greer asks.

I scoff. "Who me? Never."

The drive over is a silent one. I don't know if it's because they know I'm holding on by a thread or what, but Greer and Enzo are oddly quiet. It gives me time to lose myself in my thoughts.

Is she really okay? What state am I going to find her in?

The image that keeps popping into my head is seeing her tied up when I found her in Chicago. Why would she put herself in the position to be put back in something like that?

It's riding me hard enough that as soon as Enzo pulls up to the warehouse we use to interrogate our enemies, I hop out before he even stops the car.

Greer curses at me, but I hustle inside and down the stairs.

Walking into Lorenzo's torture room, my eyes instantly find Serena. She's leaning against the wall facing me talking to Conor. She looks okay. My eyes take in every piece of skin that I can see. Other than a little dirt, there are no signs of injury.

As soon as she spots me, she excuses herself and walks toward me.

I watch as she stuffs her hands into her back pockets as she approaches.

"Hey..." she says softly.

My throat feels thick, so I just pull her into my arms, crushing her against me.

I feel Serena sigh in relief as her arms come around me, hugging me back.

"On a scale of one to ten how mad are you?" she murmurs.

"Twenty. I'm so fucking furious with you, *anima gemella*. As soon as we get home, I'm going to paddle your ass red, and not in the fun way," I rasp, and my body slowly relaxes.

She's safe.

Logically I knew that Greer and Enzo were right. Conor and Matteo, along with everyone else who was out there, wouldn't let anything happen to her, but sometimes fear defies logic, and you can't relax until you see the person you love is safe with your own two eyes.

"I would say I'm sorry but I'm not," she murmurs against my chest.

I kiss the side of her head. "I know."

"We apprehended two guys," she adds.

"Good."

"It felt good to slip into that role again. It felt like I was on the force again," she admits softly.

My heart hurts for her. I know I considered how she would feel losing her job, but I didn't realize it would affect her this much. I need to do something about that. I don't want her to feel unfulfilled.

"I'm glad."

Greer and Enzo enter the room from the stairs, just as Bash and Killian walk into the room side by side from the holding chamber.

"Have them separated?" Killian asks.

Matteo nods. "Yeah, we have one sitting on ice while we question this one."

Matteo slaps the man's shoulder, making him flinch.

"Are we ready to get started?" Bash asks.

"I'm ready when you are," Lo tells him.

Bash looks around the room. "If you don't want to stick around, this is your chance to leave."

"Do you want to step out?" I ask quietly.

Serena pulls back slightly and shakes her head. She turns in my arms and faces forward. I pull her into my chest and hold on. I just need to fucking touch her right now.

Bash looks at us and raises a brow. When he realizes we aren't moving, he turns back toward Lorenzo. "Go ahead."

"Let the games begin." Killian rubs his hands together with a wicked smile on his face.

We watch as Lorenzo starts off easy by ripping out the man's nails one by one. The man jerks but doesn't make a peep while he silently cries.

"They never want to go down easy." Lorenzo sighs as he sets his pliers down.

"You like it when they put up a fight," Gio teases.

"True." Lorenzo chuckles. "Help me out here, Matteo."

We watch as both men move the guy across the room and hang him from a hook in the ceiling. The man dangles with his feet just barely brushing the floor.

"Grab a scalpel," Lorenzo tells Matteo while he cuts the man's clothes off.

Serena sucks in a breath and squirms in my arms as they start to cut him all over. Some are deep, while others are shallow.

"Do you want to step out?" I whisper into her ear.

Serena shakes her head but doesn't speak.

Finally the man cries out, breaking.

Lorenzo smirks as he and Matteo step back.

"Are you going to tell us what we want to know?" Bash asks coolly.

"Fuck. You," the man gasps.

"Well, if you wanted to be fucked, why didn't you just say so?" Matteo says lightly as he reaches over, grabbing a baseball bat from against the wall. "Do you want me to warm you up with the handle or should we just go for it with the barrel?"

The man's eyes widen and he shakes his head so fast I'm afraid he's going to give himself whiplash.

"What the fuck is wrong with you?" the man asks.

Bash, Lorenzo, Gio, Matteo, Killian, and Enzo all start laughing.

I try to hold in my chuckle for Serena's sake, but the way she glances up at me tells me I failed.

"What's wrong with us?" Killian asks, touching his chest. "I think the better question is what's wrong with you? Taking women against their will."

"Look, man, it's nothing personal. Those women wanted it."

"They wanted it?" Serena snaps, stepping forward.

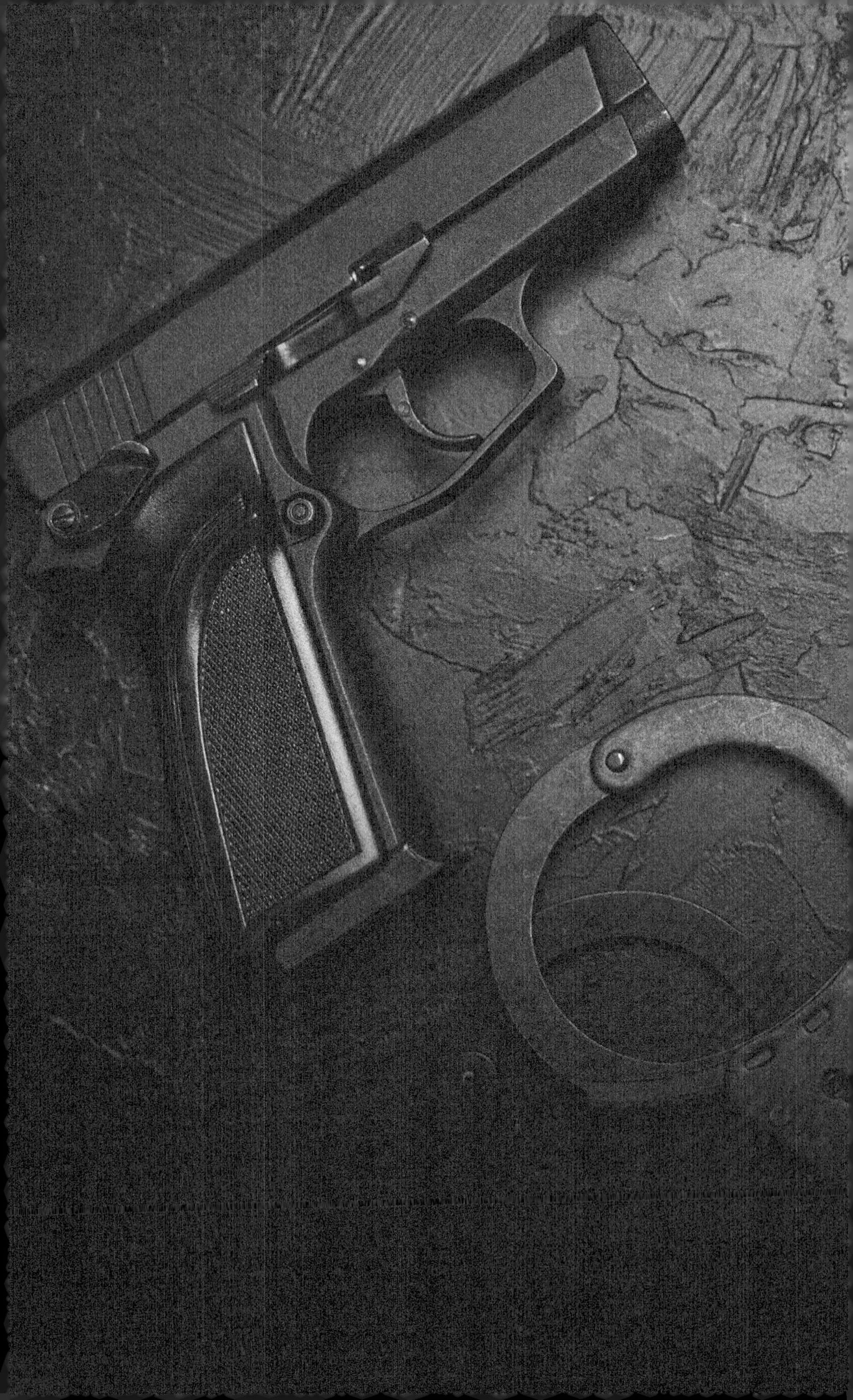

CHAPTER
TWENTY-ONE

Serena

"*Anima gemella*," Tristano warns, trying to stop me.

"No, let her continue," Bash says.

I walk right up to the man and get in his face. "What makes you think they wanted it?" I sneer.

"Look at them. Women today have no self-respect, walkin' down the street half naked."

I scoff. "Really, that's what you're going with? You're trying to justify kidnapping them because of what they were wearing? What about the children?"

Something I can't quite name flashes through the guy's eyes and he shrugs as best as he can. "As far as I'm concerned, we were giving them a better life."

"Tell me about that. Where did you think these women were going?"

"I don't need to tell you shit, lady."

I flinch as his spit lands on my face.

I hear the men behind me move forward but I raise my hand. "I got this," I tell them without turning around.

Anger burns in my gut. How fucking dare this sick bastard.

I spot a half-drunk soda bottle next to an ashtray.

I look over at Lorenzo and point. "May I?"

He smirks. "What's mine is yours right now."

"Thank you."

With shaking hands, I open the bottle. I pick the cigarette butts out of the tray and set them to the side. Very carefully, I pour the ashes into the drink. After placing the lid back on the bottle, I turn back around.

"Are you thirsty?" I ask the guy hanging from a chain.

"Fuck you," he hisses.

Lorenzo steps forward and places a chair off to the side next to the guy. Taking his hand, I stand on the chair and drop the cap.

"Ready?" Lorenzo asks.

I nod and watch as he forces the man's mouth open. I pour as much of the ash-ridden drink into his mouth as possible. As soon as I'm done, Lorenzo grabs his mouth, making him unable to spit it out. Reaching forward, I massage the sick bastard's throat, making him swallow.

"Good boy," I coo as I step back.

As soon as I'm out of harm's way, Lorenzo steps back. We all watch as the man coughs, spitting what he can onto the floor.

"Maybe you'll learn to watch what comes out of your mouth. No woman, no matter how she dresses or what she chooses to do for a profession, should be subjected to being abducted and sold for a man's whims. Children should not have to fear going outside because some degenerates feel the need to take what isn't theirs. If it were up to me, you would spend your life behind bars rotting in your own filth, but that's not the world we live in anymore. Instead, you'll have a very, and I do mean extremely, painful last hours of your life before you are eventually murdered then disappear as if you never existed. Is this what you signed up for?"

The man wavers a little at that. I don't know if it's my anger or the truth in my words, but he shakes his head slowly.

"Good, so then tell me where you were taking these women?"

I cross my arms over my chest.

He attempts to clear his throat before speaking in a raspy tone, "I'm not the mastermind you think I am. I had one job. Collect women when I receive the location and transport them to the secondary location. I only do it for extra cash."

My eyes haze over a little at that. He transports women against their will for cash.

"Are they already drugged when you get them, or do you drug them?" Killian asks, stepping closer to me.

"Already knocked out. It's always the same guy I meet though. I could tell you what he looks like."

Tris moves to my side, his hand lying on my back as he holds up his phone for the man to see.

"Is this him?"

"Yes. That's him. He's the only one I've met, but he's not the one that hired me."

"Who hired you?" Tris asks.

He swallows hard. "I don't know who he is. He came in while I was in lockup a while back. Said he could get me out if I did a job for him. He was a little taller than me with dark hair, but it was graying a little bit. He was a bit pudgy. I don't know how else to describe him."

"Where's your phone now?" Tristano asks.

"I've got it," Conor speaks up.

Tris kisses my head before going to grab it from Conor.

"I have one last question for you," I start. "Were you the one who transported me a couple months ago?"

He takes me in as if he is trying to remember. Eventually, he hangs his head.

"I see so many women. I have no idea. You all begin to look the same after a while."

Stepping forward, I punch him in the kidney before moving to the sink set up at the side of the room and washing my hands.

No one speaks. The only sounds heard are whatever Tris is doing with the cell phone and the moans coming from the prisoner. When I finish, I head back to the group, seeing a mix of worry and awe on their faces.

"Are you done?" Lorenzo asks.

I nod. "Make it painful."

"Yes, ma'am." He dips his chin.

"We'll talk when we're done," Bash says quietly as I walk past him.

Killian and Greer catch my eye next. Killian winks while Greer shoots me a thumbs-up.

I shake my head as I fight back a smile. As soon as I'm close to him, I grab onto Tristano's shirt and pull him toward the door. "Take me home."

He looks away from the phone. "With pleasure."

He holds out his hands for a set of keys. Enzo hands them over easily.

Then he leads me up the stairs and out the door. Once he has me settled into the car, he rounds it, getting into the driver's seat. Then he takes off toward home.

"Are you okay?" he whispers in the silence of the car.

I catalog how I'm feeling. I'm sad. A little disappointed that this man is not the head of this group, but I knew that was unlikely. Am I hurt? My hand hurts a little from punching the guy, but I'm okay.

So I turn to look over at him as he stares out the windshield. "I'm okay."

I watch as he grits his teeth. "No trauma? Flashbacks?"

My heart hurts as I realize why he is so concerned. He thought that by doing this, I would be hurting my mental state.

Reaching over, I pull one hand off the steering wheel and into my lap. He lets me hold it, but he's still tense.

"Not a single one. I didn't make the decision lightly. I knew what I was doing."

He growls, taking his hand back. "We need to stop talking about this. It's making me want to punch something, and I still need to get us home safely."

I sniffle, a sudden burst of sadness filling me at the idea that I hurt this man so much. A man I love with all my heart.

I don't push it though. Instead, I whisper, "Okay."

I keep peeking at him the entire ride home, but he seems to only become more agitated the more time that passes. I go to speak several times, but I don't know how to make this better.

I never wanted to hurt him, but I couldn't stand on the sidelines when I knew my idea would work. I knew I was safe.

When we finally get home, Tris heads straight to the kitchen. I watch as he moves around his kitchen while I sit at the island.

"Okay, let's hear it." I sigh.

Tristano folds a towel and sets it down before leaning against the counter. "Hear what?"

"You're mad at me."

He chuckles darkly. "I'm not mad at you, *anima gemella*. I'm fucking furious."

"I did what I had to do."

"No, you did what you wanted to do. My feelings be damned." He shakes his head. "You took an unnecessary risk."

"If they would have opened that train car and found it empty, they would have known something was wrong before we could have grabbed them. We needed to buy some time for the guys to get there before they slipped away."

"Oh bullshit," he snaps. "That place was surrounded. You just wanted to be in the middle of it."

"Exactly, I wasn't alone! I had backup. I was safe the entire time."

He pushes off the counter, eyes wide. "You think that's reason enough? Come on, Serena! You put yourself in danger. Into a situation you have lived through. Did you even think about how I would feel when I heard about it? Or what about what would have happened if you froze, remembering what you went through?"

All my anger flows out of me. I look at him and frown. Maybe this isn't going to work.

"Tris, this is me. This is what I'm passionate about. If you can't accept that, then maybe we aren't right for each other." I say the words softly, my own heart breaking a little at the admission.

He lets out a breath, rubbing his hand on his face. "No, Serena. No, that's not it. We belong together. You are the other half of my soul. I feel that with every fiber of my being." He sighs. "I know that you are trained to work undercover. I know you can handle yourself out there. That's why I didn't say anything about you going out with Killian to those meetings or going out searching with Killian's men. In my head, I know this, but you didn't even talk to me about it first. I had no idea what was happening until it was already happening. All of a sudden I went from thinking you were safe and sound to knowing you were chained to a fucking train car in the dark all by yourself. Do you know what that did to me?"

He's right. I thought about him being mad, but I didn't consider why it would anger him.

"Would you have let me do it if I had told you about it, or would you have called Killian and Bash to have them order their men to stand down?"

He swallows hard, his eyes red and glassy. "I would have said no..."

"See. That's what I mean."

"*Anima gemella*, let me finish. I would have said no at first. Any man as crazy in love as I am would do the same. I never want to think about you being in danger. If I could, I would put you in a bubble to ensure nothing ever happened to you. I know that's not reality though. So while at first I would have told you no, you would have shown me that tenacious spirit you have which would have convinced me that you had it. You didn't give me the opportunity though. You went behind my back and did it without even a discussion. In a precarious situation, I can see you doing that, but you had time to call."

That's the crux of it. I did have time to call, but I chose not to because I was worried he would be like my uncle and take the decision away from me. He's not my uncle though. He never has been.

"I'm sorry. You're right. I was being selfish. It's going to take time to remember that you aren't like the other men in my life. You support me when they would have smothered me."

He reaches out and pulls me into him, kissing the top of my head. "I'm glad you're safe."

"Did I fuck this up?" I ask as I clench my fists, trying to stop myself from reaching back out to him.

"That's the thing, Serena, no matter what you do, you can't fuck this up." He shakes his head. "You're stuck with me."

Finally, I wrap myself around him. "Everyone I have ever loved ends up leaving me one way or another."

"Not me, *anima gemella*. Even when the Lord takes our souls, I'll still be tethered to you."

I soak in his love as he holds me.

"I love you, Tris."

"I love you more than any man has ever loved a woman, Serena. You are my whole world."

I let one small teardrop fall as I hear his words, as my heart starts to put itself back together.

This feels a lot like healing.

Tristano

"Morning…"

I look over my shoulder and see Serena standing at the edge of the kitchen, looking unsure if she should enter or not.

After last night, we took a shower together then went to bed. I held her to me all night as nightmares of losing her kept sleep at bay.

"Coffee?"

"Yes, please," she says as she steps forward, shoulders relaxing.

"How did you sleep?" I ask as I make her coffee.

"Could have been better. You?"

"Same."

I finish her coffee and slide it toward her.

"Thank you," she says as her hands wrap around the cup. "Tris… we're okay, right?"

I lean back against the counter and really look at her. Her hair is in a haphazard bun on top of her head with hair falling around her face. Serena's eyes are sadder than I've ever seen them before. She's wearing a tiny pair of silky shorts and a tank top, nipples on full display.

She looks like a beautiful disaster, and I can't help but want her.

"Yes, *anima gemella*. Everything between us is fine. I was hurt last night, and that won't disappear right away, but we will work through it. That's what couples do."

Serena shakes her head. "I've never actually dated anyone. I'm not sure I'm good at it."

"You haven't had any examples to follow. I get that. You were constantly put down and gaslit before now. I'm not them though. I know you know that, but I think you need to work through the framework of your brain which tells you that you can't trust me. Until you do that, we are going to be rocky."

She nods solemnly. "I called my old therapist this morning. We had a good conversation. We are going to start sessions backup once a week. My first session is Friday."

Walking around the counter, I pull her into my arms. She wraps her arms around my waist and buries her head into my chest. Leaning down, I kiss the top of her head.

"That's good, baby. Real good. I meant what I said last night. You'll never fuck this up enough for me to walk away."

"You mean everything to me."

"Same, *anima gemella*. We'll figure this out."

My phone starts ringing, sounding like a siren going off.

"Fuck," I say as I pull away, fumbling for it on the counter.

"Could you have picked a more annoying ringer?"

Ignoring her teasing, I unlock the screen. The message fills me with dread.

Bash: 911. Family meeting now at the house.

"Hey, are you okay?" Serena asks as she lays a hand on my arm.

"I gotta go. Something's happened, and a family meeting has been called." I hesitate. "You can come. You're part of the family."

She shakes her head. "I'm still new, and I'll be honest with you. I scared myself a little last night. I think that's what really pushed me to call the therapist. I've never hurt another person on purpose before."

She flexes her hand as she looks down at her fist. Watching her take charge last night turned me on, but seeing the conflict on her face now, I wish she hadn't done it.

"I can stay if you need me. You're priority. Always."

She smiles up at me as she steps into my arms. "No. You go. I'm going to be okay. We have all the time in the world to worry about my problems. They need you now."

Serena moves to step back, but I grab her by the back of her neck and pull her into me. Leaning down, I kiss her hard.

Pulling away, I rest my forehead on hers. "Text me if you leave today. I don't know what's going on or when I'll be home."

"I'll be fine. Just be safe."

"Always." I kiss her one more time before rushing out of the door.

Walking into Bastiano's home, everyone is on edge. I'm ushered into the conference room immediately. Stepping into the room, I see Sofia holding baby Alessa in her arms, looking frightened. Matteo, Giovanni, and Lorenzo all look angry.

Bastiano is hunched over the table, and his head raises when I step inside. "Thank you for joining us."

I nod. "Of course."

"This morning, we received a package." He pushes off the table and points at what he was staring at. "Look at it."

Walking over, I grab a pair of gloves from the box that's resting on the table. Once they are on, I turn the piece of paper toward me.

Alessa is so pretty. Especially when she's sleeping. I wonder, will she look as peaceful when she turns blue? A life for a life. Tick. Tock. Tick. Tock. Her lifeline will be cut short. The question is when. Just know, I'll be watching and waiting.

"What the fuck is this?" I say under my breath.

"Her first death threat." Lo nods.

"Women and children are off limits," I say, shaking my head, trying to wrap my head around this.

When I got the message this morning, this wasn't what I was expecting.

"Did you call Greer?"

"I want this kept in-house," Bash says coolly.

I want to remind him that you can't get much more in-house than his sister, but I bite my tongue. It's clear he doesn't want Killian and the Irish finding out about this. Could he really suspect them?

They have been intertwined with us for so long now that it feels as if we are one entity.

"Yes, sir," I murmur.

"Can you check it for prints or anything?" Matteo asks.

I look over at him and see him standing close to Sofia with his arms crossed. Even when at home, he stays close to her in case she needs him. Forever in bodyguard mode, just like Enzo around Greer.

Looking back down at the table, I pull the envelope closer to me and look it over. "Yeah, I can try, but I don't know." I shake my head. "They actually mailed it and didn't deliver it themselves. So print-wise, if he or she left any, they will get lost with all the postal workers and whoever touched it as well. Our best bet is to try the letter itself."

"Do whatever you need to do." Bash nods.

"I know it's a stupid question, but have you pissed anyone off lately?"

Bash grunts as he starts pacing the room. Getting death threats is nothing new to him, but this is the first time that one has been aimed at his family.

"No, not that I can think of." He looks over at Giovanni.

Giovanni shakes his head. "I can't think of anything either. Honestly, outside of the trafficking, shit's been quiet."

"The other families have remembered their place," Lo says.

"I want them dead," Sofia says, making us look her way. She stands there patting baby Alessa's back as she sways. "I want them dead. Tonight."

I suck in a breath. I understand her desire to have this person's head, but honestly, I don't know if I can deliver in that sort of time frame, and I don't know how to tell her.

"*Tesoro,*" Bash says as he walks toward his wife. "It will be done as soon as possible."

"I don't like this Bash." She shakes her head. "I knew that this would happen eventually, but I didn't expect for her to still be a baby."

"Neither did I." He places his hand on her back and ushers her out of the room.

"You heard her. Let's get to work," Lo says, taking charge.

"You can use the office here," Gio tells me. "By the way, did you get anything off the phone last night? We didn't get anything else from either of the men. His partner seemed to know even less than the main guy did."

"Is this really the time?" Lo growls. "Our princess is being threatened. I know that's important, but this takes priority."

Gio glares at him. "It could be connected for all we know. We need to explore all options."

"Hey, no need to fight," I insist. "Enzo came and got the cell phone from me this morning. I was able to crack the encoder and got in, but I was hitting a wall on the trace for the phone number. Enzo was taking it to Greer so she could work her magic."

"I'll check in with her then." Gio leaves the room.

Following, Lo falls into step by my side. "Sorry. She's like a daughter to me."

I don't say anything. He has nothing to apologize for.

Tensions are high.

All I know is today is about to be a long fucking day.

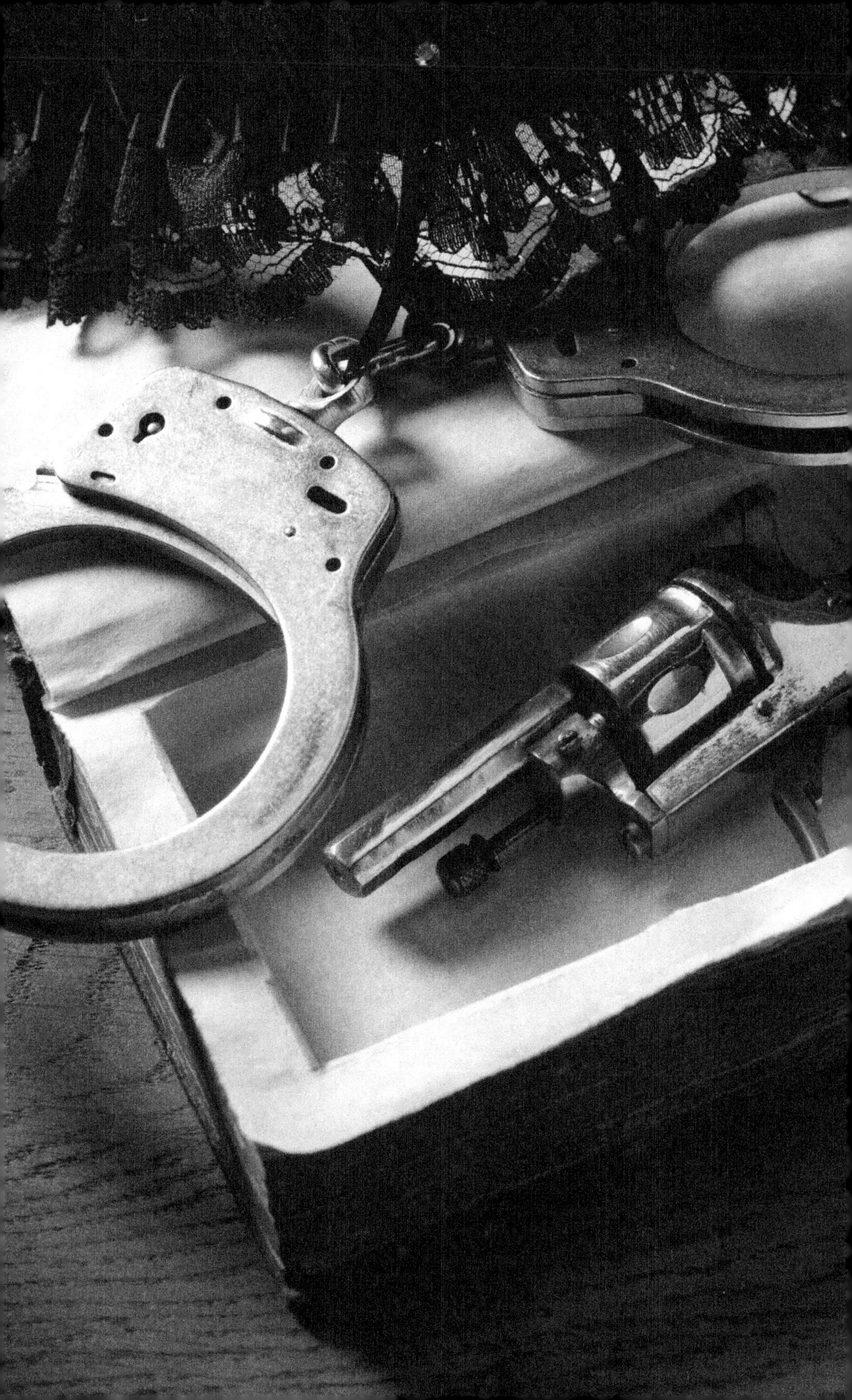

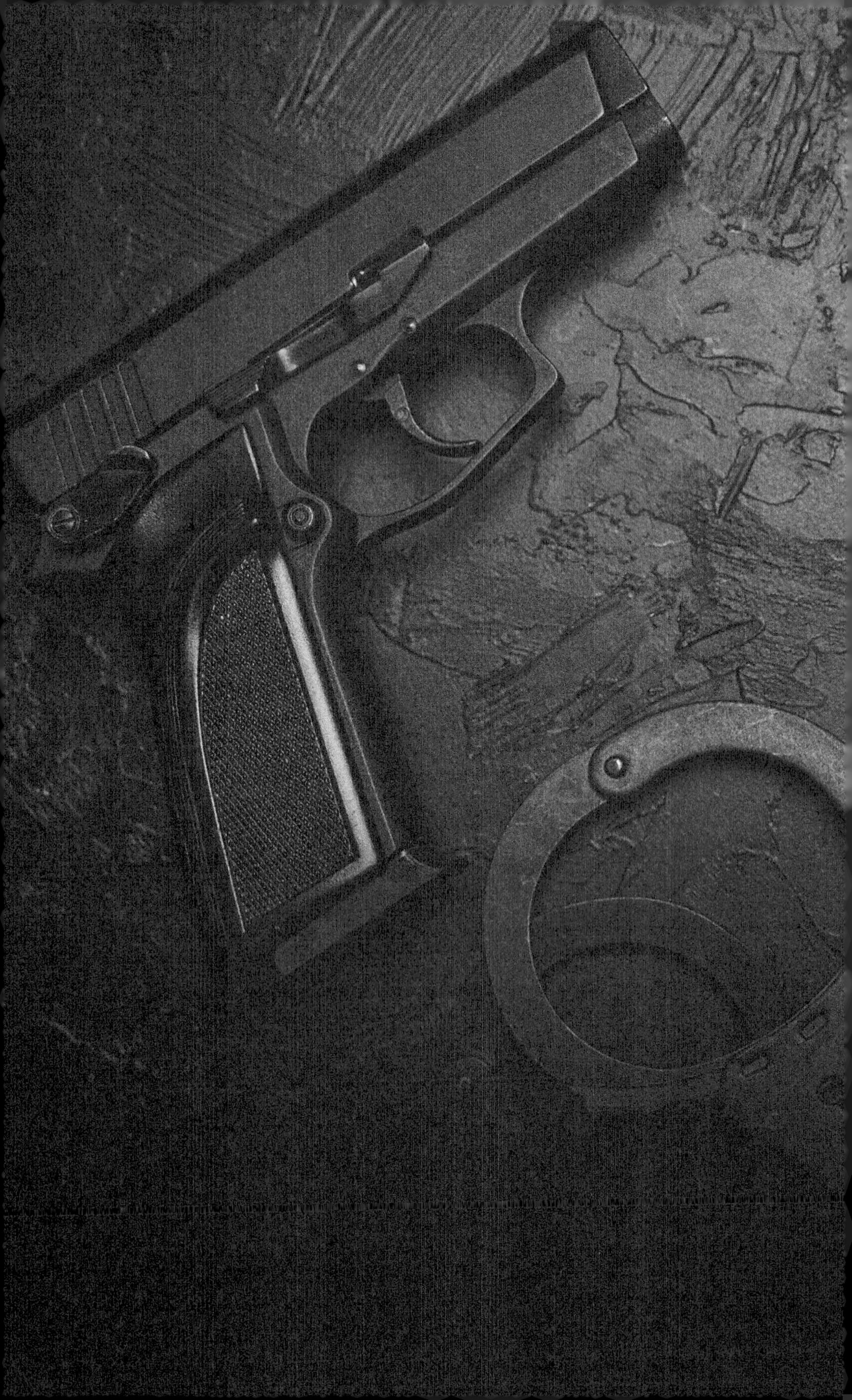

CHAPTER
TWENTY-TWO

Serena

"Thanks!" I wave as the delivery driver walks away. Reaching down, I grab as many bags as I can and carry them inside. When Tristano left for the day, I didn't know what I would do. After poking around in the kitchen, I realized we were running low on food, so I placed a delivery order.

With groceries put away, I'm still jittery, so I start cleaning.

"Alexa, please play music," I call out as I look under the kitchen sink for some cleaning supplies.

"Playing T's happy playlist." Her robotic voice comes over.

The first song that pops on is "No Scrubs" by TLC and I can't help but throw my head back and laugh.

Of course this would be on his happy playlist. Song after song, I sing and dance around the apartment as I dust. It gives me a dose of serotonin I didn't know I needed. My phone vibrates on the kitchen island and I make my way to it.

> Tristano: I like the way you work it…

I frown down at my phone not understanding what in the hell he's talking about. Then I listen to the song that's currently playing.

"No Diggity" by Blackstreet and Dr. Dre.

I laugh, shaking my head as I text him back.

> Me: Of course you do. 😊 How's it going?

I lean against the counter as I wait for his reply. Looking at the time, I'm surprised to see that four hours have gone by since he left.

> Tristano: It's going. Hopefully I'll make it home tonight.

I frown at his text. I kind of wish I had gone with him now. I wasn't thinking about the fact that he might not come home.

> Me: Anything I can do?

> Tristano: Not this time. I got to go. I'll talk to you later.

Sighing, I set down my phone.

Now what?

I think back to the conversation I had with Vanessa. I wonder if she's working today.

Before I can make a real plan, my phone rings. Picking it up, my breath catches when I see the name on the screen.

Uncle Ben.

"Hello?" I answer hesitantly.

"Hey, Serena. How are you doing?"

"I'm okay. Is there a reason you're calling me?" I ask bluntly.

"Seriously? I raised you and you can't even spare a phone call for me?" He sounds dejected.

I sigh. "You're right. I'm sorry. I'm still adjusting."

"It's okay. Listen, I know it's sudden, but I think you are onto something about these missing girls. I was wondering if you would come in and discuss it with me some more."

A sudden smile covers my face. I don't need his approval, but having it means the world to me.

"Yeah, when do you want to meet?"

"How about now? I can be at Goodie's in fifteen," he says, referencing the old diner we used to go to.

"Sure, but it's going to take me a bit longer. I'm in Brooklyn."

"Oh? Is that where you are living now?"

"Yep," I answer cautiously.

"Good for you. I'll wait as long as you need."

Picking up the phone, I dial Tris.

"Hey, *anima gemella*. I'm in the middle of something. Can I call you back?" he answers, sounding distracted.

"Real quick, I'm going to head to Jersey City to meet up with Uncle Ben."

"Serena, I don't think it's a good idea for you to go there alone." He sounds so disapproving.

I can't let him dictate my life though. "He's my uncle. He wants to talk…"

I was going to tell him he wants to talk about the case, but then I realize they might not want me sharing information with him. I get why, but I think it's important we have all the eyes we can out there. So instead of telling him, I let it trail off.

"He doesn't treat you right. I don't want him steamrolling you," Tris admits.

"I know. I'll be okay. It's just lunch. We are meeting at Goodie's. I'll text you when I get there and when I leave."

"Fine, but take my second car. It's in the garage. The keys are already in it."

"Are you sure?" I bite my lip.

"I don't want you going down there on public transport. Take the car."

"Okay. Hey Tris?"

"What?"

"I love you."

I can hear the smile in his voice. "Love you too. Be safe."

After we hang up, I grab my wallet, shoving it into my jeans, before grabbing the house key and locking everything up. I go back to the garage, using the code he gave me when I moved in. The door opens, revealing a pretty red Chevy Camaro.

I've only ever seen him in his black, nondescript SUV, so seeing this makes me smile. It fits his personality much better. I can see why he doesn't use it for work though.

Sliding inside, I inhale, loving that it smells slightly of the cologne that Tris uses. It makes me feel like he's with me.

Setting off to Jersey City, I turn the radio on, smiling when it's set to the Top Forty playlist station. It's an hour drive, but when I finally pull up outside Goodie's, I'm ready. The entire drive, I gave myself a pep talk about how this is going to go. I'll give him some information, but not tell him how I know it. I'll make sure to protect the family at all costs, but also try and get more eyes out there. I won't let Uncle Ben talk down to me either. The second he does, I'm gone.

With this in mind, I get out and head inside. He's already waiting at the back booth with a cup of coffee in his hands. When I approach, he stands, pulling me in for a hug.

"Missed you. Brooklyn life seems to be treating you well," he says as he lets me go.

I give him a small smile. "I like it. It's different."

"What are you doing for work?"

I grit my teeth at that question. Of course he'd ask that. He knows damn well I'm not working as a cop.

"That's not what we are here to talk about. So how can I help you?"

"You're right. It's none of my business. I felt bad after you left, so I started looking into those missing girls like you asked."

I want to tell him I didn't leave. He fired me, but it's not important now. The girls are.

"What did you find?"

"You're right. It seems like there is a pattern. Mostly working girls, but some are middle class as well. Never upper class. They aren't being held for ransom. It's like they are there one day and gone the next."

Is this how slow police work has always been? I've been gone weeks, and he's just now only figured out what I already knew when I left?

Maybe being a cop isn't for me. Seeing how fast the Mafia world moves, I think I'd be better served there.

"That's about what I found out too," I admit.

"I know. I read the notes you left for me."

That irks me even more. So he did read my notes, yet still hasn't progressed? Why am I even here?

Shaking my head, I move to stand. "That's all I know. I really don't know why you called. I don't think I can help you anymore."

"You're just going to leave?"

The indignation in his tone tells me I'm making the right decision. I should have never come out here.

"I can't add anything valuable to this case for you. You've always said that your time is precious," I spit out bitterly. "I'd hate to waste it."

As I'm about to leave, his phone rings. He answers it, looking over at me.

"Yeah? Okay. I'll be right there." He hangs up as he stands.

"You're right. I didn't call about the case itself. I need your help talking to the working girls. They trust you. One of them in particular has some information, but she says she will only talk to you. Meredith?"

My heart pounds in my chest. Why wouldn't she have called

Tris? Maybe she called Ricky, and that's who told Uncle Ben. Uncle Ben most likely told him he was meeting me, so that would make sense. Besides, I don't think Ricky has my new number.

I feel like shit when I realize I haven't even checked on him or Meredith once since I left Jersey City. It's like they ceased to exist for me.

"I'll go see her now." I turn and head for the door.

"We can ride together. I'll bring you back for your car when we are done."

I nod, heading toward his instead.

Settling in the passenger seat, all I can think of is that I hope Meredith is okay.

Tristano

"This doesn't make sense." I stare at the screen as I read the results.

The fingerprints came back, but it's not any criminal we know.

No, it's Nigel Henderson. Chief Benjamin Henderson of Jersey City PD's son.

Why would he be threatening Bash's kid?

"Who is that?" Lo asks from beside me.

"He's a cop down in Jersey City and the son of the chief of police there, who also happens to be the man who raised Serena after her grandfather died."

Lo looks at me suspiciously. "He's related to your girl?"

"Basically, yeah."

"This isn't good," he murmurs. "We need to tell Bash."

I follow him out of the home office toward the meeting room

where Bash took up residence as he barks orders. We step into the room, waiting for him to get off the phone.

"Make it happen. If anything happens to my daughter, it will be your head on a fucking stake."

He mashes the button on his phone before turning to us.

"What did you find?"

"We think it's a police officer in Jersey City."

"Jersey City, like where your girl is from? You think she's involved?" he hisses.

"Absolutely not. She's loyal to us. The cop is someone she knows though. He's the son of the chief of police," I admit.

"Fuck me, Tris. You know how bad this looks for her, right? Get her here now."

I rub the back of my head. I could lie for her, but that would only make her seem guilty. Instead, I opt for the truth knowing my girl is innocent.

"She's in Jersey City meeting with her uncle."

Both Lo and Bash mutter curses in Italian.

Before either of them can continue, the door pushes open as a furious Greer storms in, Killian behind her. Greer unstraps the baby on her chest, handing him off to Killian as she gets right in Bash's face.

"If I ever find out that there is a threat against my niece again, and you didn't tell me, I will slit your fucking throat in your sleep, you overbearing asshole. I know you don't fully trust Killian, but that little girl is my flesh and blood. I would burn this world down for her, and if you doubt that for even a second, then you are a blind fool."

Bash takes her tongue lashing without a word. After she's silent a moment, he nods.

"Understood."

It's the closest she's going to get an apology.

She spins on me. "As for you, the number on that phone finally came back. It's a burner phone, but I was able to link it back to the person who bought it. Benjamin Henderson. Your girlfriend's old boss. We need to talk to her right away."

I swallow hard, looking over to Bash and Lo. They both look pale.

"Shit. I swear she's not in on it."

Bash nods slowly. "I'm willing to give her the benefit of the doubt. That's not why I look worried. Where did you just say she was?"

Oh fuck.

Pulling out my phone, I dial her. She doesn't answer. I press the button again, but she is still not answering.

Everyone is talking around me, bodies moving as if getting ready to mobilize, but I don't focus on them. All I can think about is my girl.

I knew I shouldn't have let her go alone. Why did I listen to her?

Before I can dial again, a call comes through. I don't recognize the number.

"Hello?" I ask.

"Tristano, this is Ricky. You need to get to Jersey City now. I don't know what she's got herself into, but Serena is in trouble."

"What do you mean?" I ask, snapping to get the other's attention.

Putting him on speakerphone, I set the phone on the table.

"I've been keeping an eye on the missing girls case Serena asked me to look into. It goes deep into corruption. I mean real deep. I suspect my chief and his son have something to do with it. I was working with Meredith, a working girl, but she stopped answering today. Then I got an alert from one of our old safe houses that's been decommissioned. I never disconnected my phone from the alarm. Tris, man. They have Serena there. Meredith too, I think. I have no idea what they plan, but it cannot be good."

My body freezes. I know he is still talking, but the words mean nothing.

My girl is in trouble yet again, and I'm still here not able to do a thing to help her. I'm fucking useless.

"Get your shit together," Greer hisses into my ear, snapping me back to the present.

"You stay on that house until we get there. There's no one in your force we can trust. I have a few men in the area that will come surround the house. Do not move in unless you believe there is an imminent danger to her life," Bash tells Ricky.

"Understood." Ricky takes the command well, hanging up the phone.

"Good. The rest of you, get in the car now. Break every speed limit. I've called in favors." Bash claps his hands.

"I'll be tracking you. I'll make sure the lights are all green as you go through," Greer tells him.

He pulls her into him, kissing her head. "Killian, stay here and protect my family with my guards."

It's a small concession to the earlier spat. One Killian doesn't take lightly, his shoulders squaring as he nods.

"Let's head out," Lo calls out.

Then we are on the move.

I swear I'm going to spill blood this time, regardless of her condition.

Her uncle won't live through the night.

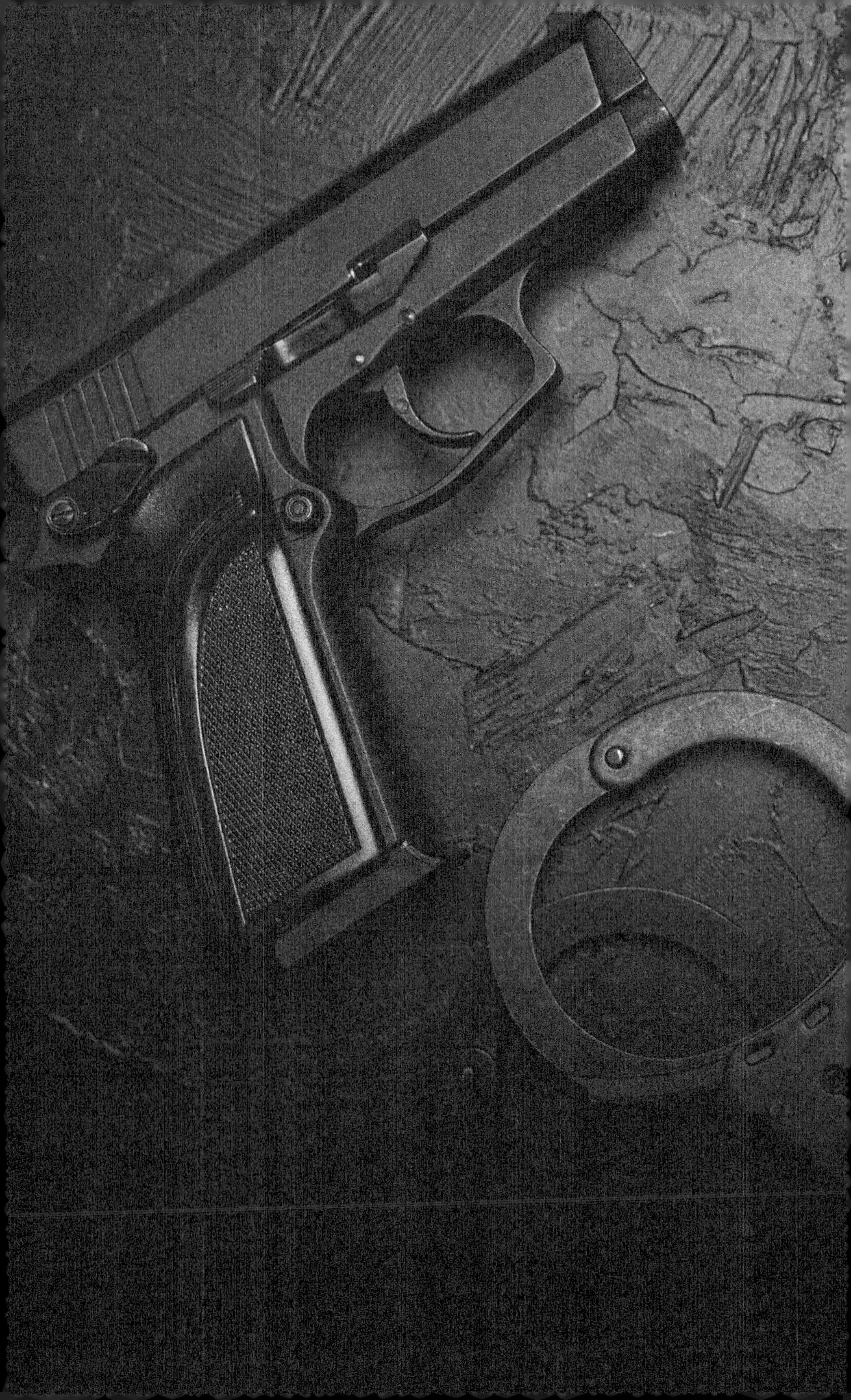

CHAPTER
TWENTY-THREE

Serena

"Where are we going?" I ask as we pass the corner where Meredith should be.

I frown when I don't see her.

"We moved your friend to the safe house. We didn't want her to be out in the open with the information she might have. She could be under surveillance by these criminals."

His words make sense, but they don't sit right with me. We only use the safe house for stings. Why wouldn't he bring her back to the station?

I think back to the last time I saw Meredith. It's likely that she would have refused to go to the station, so maybe this is his way of making her comfortable?

Once we get to the house, I get out, following Uncle Ben up the stairs. He unlocks the door, shutting off the alarm.

Noise from the living room draws me that way, leaving Uncle Ben to trail behind me.

What I find shocks me.

Meredith is here alright, but she's not here willingly. She's hogtied on the couch, mascara running down her face.

"What is going on in here?" I spin to my uncle.

Only Uncle Ben isn't alone. Nigel is with him.

"I told you to mind your own fucking business, but you had to go and start shit, didn't you?" Uncle Ben hisses.

A knot forms in my stomach.

No. Not Uncle Ben.

He was my father's best friend. My grandfather's favorite officer. He took me in after I was left with no one. He wasn't the most loving father figure, but he still gave me a roof over my head and food in my belly.

How could he do this?

"What did I start?" I ask, edging toward the couch.

He waves his hand. "No need to be sneaky. Go sit next to your whore of a friend. Of course you would befriend such a slut. You were always a bit of a slut yourself."

Having his permission, I rush over to her.

"It's okay. It's going to be okay."

I frown when I see her underwear torn off under her skirt, sticky fluid dripping from her. Looking over my shoulder, I glare at the two men.

"Who raped her? Can't get women on your own, so you have to resort to tying them down and taking it without permission? How manly."

Uncle Ben frowns over at Nigel.

"Did you stick your dick in that cesspool?" He smacks him across the back of the head. "You idiot. Now we have to bleach her before we dump her. I should have never knocked up your mother. She didn't have any brain cells."

Turning back to me, he gives me a wicked smile. "Boys will be boys, right?"

"You are disgusting. You knew all along? That's why you wouldn't investigate."

"Knew? Hell, I organized it. Back in my beat days, I got real close with some of the local criminals. After a while, I realized that instead of putting them away, I could use them, so I made them my friends and quickly got them doing my bidding. I would keep the heat off them while they committed the crimes. Then I was approached by this European man. He said if I helped assist him with his trade, he would keep my pockets lined. So my men became his. We've been doing it for years. Since way before I took you in."

My stomach rolls at his admission. The sheer number of girls he's probably helped abduct is disgusting.

"Why let me become a cop?"

He shakes his head. "You're my greatest failure. After your father passed away, your grandfather decided he wanted me to be his right-hand man. It was all fine and well until he caught me giving coordinates to one of my guys one day. He followed them there and found out about my side hustle. My men saw him though and alerted me. He confronted me right there in the office I now hold. I couldn't let him out me, so before he could, I forced him to eat some strychnine. Then I left him for the morning crew to find."

"Serena, darling, your grandfather suffered a heart attack." Uncle Ben kneels before me.

"He's okay though, right?" my little voice asks.

"No, honey. He didn't make it. I'm so sorry."

My wails from that day are so vivid it's as if I'm living it today. Tears fill my eyes as I realize what he's admitting. He killed my grandfather. He's going to kill me too.

God, why didn't I text Tris? It didn't even cross my mind to. He was right about me. I make selfish decisions that are reckless. They put me in situations that could be avoided if I would just trust someone.

I should have trusted him.

If I end up making it out of this, I won't make this mistake again.

"You killed him," I whimper.

"I did. It hurt too. I really did love him like a father. Then I had to take you in. How would it look if I let you go into care when everyone knew how close I was to the family. Thankfully, I had Nigel here."

"You were supposed to be mine," Nigel spits at me. "He promised that if I took care of you that I could have you as soon as you turned eighteen. You were going to marry me and be my wife to do with whatever I pleased. I was good. I didn't touch you. Then you had to go and soil yourself."

"What are you talking about?" I'm genuinely confused.

None of this makes sense. How could I have lived with these men for years and not see them for what they truly are?

"You had to go to that rave and get raped. Chief wouldn't let me have you after that. Said you would rot my dick off." He sneers at me.

Nigel always treated me like a brat. Like he hated me. He's right that he never touched me inappropriately, but he would push me around and make demands of me. Is that the kind of husband he planned to be?

The rave is the made-up lie I gave them when I came back that night. I thought I would hate the man who hurt me forever, but for this one moment, I'm thankful for him. What kind of life would I have had if they had bowled over me until I gave into his request for marriage?

I have no doubt I would have agreed to it. Tris would have never been in my life so I would have never had anything else to hope for.

That terrible night changed my life in more ways than one.

"Why let me become a cop?"

"You wanted to throw yourself into danger, and hell, you were already a whore. I saw a good way to keep an eye on you while solving some other issues I had. Mayor Johnson was the latest. He refused to see things my way, so I took him down using the vice he loved most. Little girls. Do you know how many little girls I delivered him?" Uncle Ben chuckles. "It has to have been hundreds over the years. You were the tool who took him down, but only because I allowed it."

My heart catches. He fed him girls. These men are vile. Unremorseful. Evil.

How did I not see it before?

"Ricky?" I whisper.

The man I trusted to have my back. Who always seemed to care. Was he in on it too?

He shakes his head. "You think I'd let him in on this? Nah, I had to keep things in-house to a small circle."

I let out a relieved sigh. Sitting on the very edge of the couch, I reach back and pat Meredith on the thigh. My other hand curls around the cushion.

That's when I feel it. The knife I'd left there the last time I stayed here. I had shoved it under the cushion as I took a nap. I meant to take it back with me, but Ricky called with an emergency and I forgot.

Thank God.

"Don't sound so relieved. He's not going to save you. No one even knows we are here. I decommissioned this safe house months ago. Now no one knows it even exists. I erased it from the system."

He moves closer as he speaks. I wait until he's within range before I make my move.

It all happens so fast.

One second, I'm on the couch. The next, I've swept Uncle Ben off his feet and somehow ended up on top of him, my hands stabbing him over and over.

I don't know how long I stab him, but when I look up, I expect to see Nigel ready to kill me.

Only I don't. Instead, I realize I'm surrounded by people. Lots of people.

Familiar people.

Lorenzo. Giovanni. Bastiano. Matteo. Conor.

Where is he?

Then I feel him. Turning to look over my shoulder, Tris is crouched behind me. Ready to catch me if I fall.

Always ready to catch me.

"Tris?" I manage to breathe out.

My throat is raw, and my face is wet. When did that happen?

"It's okay, *anima gemella*." He moves closer, taking the knife from my hand. "I've got you."

Looking down, I see all the blood all over me. Then I see the body. The mutilated body of the man I once called my uncle but will never again.

Ben is no more. He's nothing but a fleshy mess beneath my legs.

"I... I..." I stutter.

"Shhh." Tris pulls me into his arms.

I start to sob. "I killed him."

"Don't think about that now. You're safe and okay. Meredith is okay. Everything is going to be okay now."

"How did you find me?"

"Ricky. He found you and called me."

Pulling back, I search the room for the man.

"He's outside figuring out how to play this."

"What do you mean? He's not a crooked cop. He has to report it. I'm going to go to prison. Oh god, I just got you." I reach up, cupping his face. "I just got you, and I'm going to lose you. I had to do it though. You get that, right? He murdered my grandfather. He abducted so many women. He was evil. I swear it." I ramble on and on until he barks out an order to one of the men.

"Matteo, get Ricky in here."

Within a minute, Ricky is pulling me up to my feet and walking me over to a corner.

"Are you okay, kid? He didn't touch you, did he? Hurt you? Do we need to get a doctor for you?" He's looking me over.

282

Tris hovers over his shoulder, but doesn't step in.

Ricky pulls me into his arms then, patting my hair much like a father would.

"I was so worried about you. I thought they were going to hurt you. I wanted to storm in right away, but we didn't want things going sideways. You're okay, right?"

I break down then, crying even harder into his shoulder. I mumble words of regret into his shoulder, but I know they can't understand me.

"She's worried about prison," Tris eventually speaks up.

"Why? There's no way anyone is going to find out about this. I got my men on it," Ricky declares.

Pulling back, I stare at him. "You're not corrupt. You can't cover this up."

"Fuck that. I'm a cop on the right side of shit. I make sure that my people are protected at all costs. If that means working with the Mafia, then fuck yes, I'm in. If that makes me corrupt, then so be it. I made a vow when I took this badge to protect the people of this city. That is my main priority."

"You also vowed to uphold the law."

"Have you ever noticed that we say that second? That's because the safety of the people outweighs the laws that might need to be broken to ensure that. At least in my book. I'm not a dirty cop, but I'm not against using the resources at my disposal. As long as your new Mafia friends don't come at me to get me to murder someone, we're good."

"We will only ever ask you to do things within your morals," Tris confirms.

"When did you two become friends?" I step back from Ricky into Tris's arms.

"When a madman abducted you and decided he was going to kill you," Ricky informs me.

"He's not so bad for being a cop." Tris shrugs.

"You fell in love with a cop," Ricky tells him.

He grunts. "Yeah. She's alright."

I push at his shoulder.

"Take her home," Ricky tells Tris. "I'll handle all of this. Your men can go too. It's best you aren't seen in this city for a few weeks."

"What about Nigel and Meredith?" I whisper.

"Nigel..." Ricky looks at Tris. "Disappeared as far as I'm concerned. Meredith is with a paramedic friend of mine. She's agreed to stay with me for a while so she can heal. I'm going to get her therapy too."

I smile at him. "I'll send you my lady's number. She's great."

"I'd like that. You two get going." Ricky walks away, heading toward Bash.

"Let's get you home and showered," Tris murmurs against my ear.

Home. That sounds amazing.

Tristano

I CAN'T HELP but lie here and watch her sleep. It's like my body cannot accept that she really is here and safe.

When we got home, she showered while I took care of the bloody clothes. I had one of the foot soldiers come get my car to detail it. After tonight, there will be no proof that Serena was ever in that house.

I have no idea what Ricky is planning to do, but Ben was the chief of police. There is no way he is going missing without some flags being raised. I'm interested to see how that plays out.

Dear old Nigel is booked for a month-long stay at Casa de Lorenzo.

On the way home, Serena told me everything she found out. The man is long overdue for a nice long stay with Lo. He will come out the other side looking like a completely different man. Well, if you put the pieces back together, I'm sure he'd look different.

Part of me wants to be there with them. Get my own licks in on the man who helped terrorize my woman. The other part can't imagine not being by her side. I'm not sure I'll be able to leave her sight anytime soon.

"Tris?" Serena mumbles, turning over in my arms to face me.

"Shh. Go back to sleep."

"It's hard when I can feel you staring at me. What's wrong?" I can see her eyes open in the light shining through the window.

"I think I just need to lie here with you and listen to you breathe. I thought I lost you tonight. I couldn't bear the thought."

"I realized I hadn't texted you when he admitted he was behind all of it. I felt so stupid. I swear to you, Tris. I won't forget again. That was scarier than anything else I've ever been through. I trusted him."

"Shhh. You need to rest, not rehash this."

What I'm really afraid of is that she will remember killing him. She admitted to me on the way home that she doesn't remember doing it. She blacked out.

I think her mind is protecting her from the trauma, but one day it will come back to her. I hope for her sake it's in therapy where someone with professional skills can help her. All I can do is hold her and try to reassure her.

I can't even kill the boogeyman in that scenario. It's her own mind that will be the enemy.

"I can't sleep now." Leaning over, she presses her lips to mine.

"What are you doing?" I whisper.

"Show me that you don't view me differently. You've been treating me with kid gloves since you found me. I need to feel like me again. Like you desire me. Prove it to me."

I run my hand over her cheek. "I'm trying to let you heal. What you went through is traumatic."

"It was. I'm not disagreeing with you. I know I have to work through it, but that's not what I need right now. You said that you want me to talk to you more. I'm telling you that I need you right now."

I study her a moment. She's right. I did ask her to communicate with me more. If she's telling me she needs this, then I need to give it to her. I'd give her the world if she'd ask.

"If you freak out at any point, we stop."

She rolls her eyes. "I'm not going to freak out, Tris. I trust you. I feel safe with you. Now fuck me until I pass out."

Shaking my head, I peel her booty shorts off of her. Then I help her sit up as I take her shirt off of her. Once she's lying back on her back, I stand to remove my boxer briefs, grabbing a condom from the drawer.

Once I'm sheathed, I move back to the bed, lying on my back.

"Hop on. I want to see you ride me."

She jumps up, positioning herself over me.

"Are you wet for me?" I murmur, reaching down to feel her wet heat.

"Always."

"Then show me how you take my cock," I demand.

She sinks down in one go, moaning as she does. Once she bottoms out, her eyes flutter open.

"I can feel you even deeper this way."

"Good." I pinch her nipple before leaning up to grab one in my mouth. "Fuck, you have perfect breasts."

She rotates her hips, groaning as I continue to feast on her.

"Tris, you feel so good," she mutters.

"Not as good as you, *anima gemella*."

She continues to grind on me, hiccupping as she hits a spot that must feel extra nice. I thrust up into her as she finds her rhythm. I keep a steady pace as I nibble and suck her breasts until her chest looks like a Dalmatian, spots every few inches claiming her as mine.

Suddenly, her legs lock around my hips, her head thrown back as she makes a noise I have never heard another human make. Her body shakes as she contracts around me, feeling like a goddamn vise. It takes all my willpower not to spill with her, but that orgasm was for her and her alone.

Pulling her to me, I kiss her head, whispering how beautiful she is as she comes down. When she finally seems like she's back with me, I help her off my lap only to force her onto her stomach. She looks back at me as I caress her ass.

"I think you have another one in you," I tell her.

Her eyes gleam with pleasure as I slide into her from behind. She moans long and loud, keeping her legs together so I can feel the friction.

It's the sweetest feeling being inside her. Almost like I found my home. The place I always want to belong. Lord knows I'd be happy if I died right here.

Picking up my pace, I reach down to palm her throat. Then I pull her until her back is against my chest, still pumping into her. I can feel her pulse beat rapidly under my hand.

She clenches around me once, making me tighten my hand as I try to hold on to control. She gasps out a moan, making me loosen my hold.

When she clenches against me again, I tighten my hand even more, leaving her little room to breathe.

As she tries to gulp down air, I feel her pussy milking me.

She likes being choked.

The realization hits me like a freight train, making me tighten even more as I spill inside of her.

I can feel her own orgasm overcome her as she struggles to get any breath in. I grunt as I continue to pump into her, watching her face. Her eyes start to fade and close, so I let go, holding her to me as she gasps for breath.

Pulling out softly, I lay her on the bed. Pulling the condom off, I toss it in the trash can next to my nightstand.

Then I cuddle against Serena. "Are you okay?"

She turns to look at me, pure adoration in her eyes. Her hands find her throat making her shiver.

"That felt amazing. I never thought I'd like that, but with you? You change everything."

I smirk at her. "It's because we were meant to be. Soul mates. *Anima gemella.*"

"*Anima gemella,*" she repeats. "I'm glad you're my soul mate."

"Me too. I love you, Serena."

"I love you, Tristano."

As she fades back to sleep, I cuddle closer to her.

I finally found the one person who is meant to be mine.

I'll do anything to keep her.

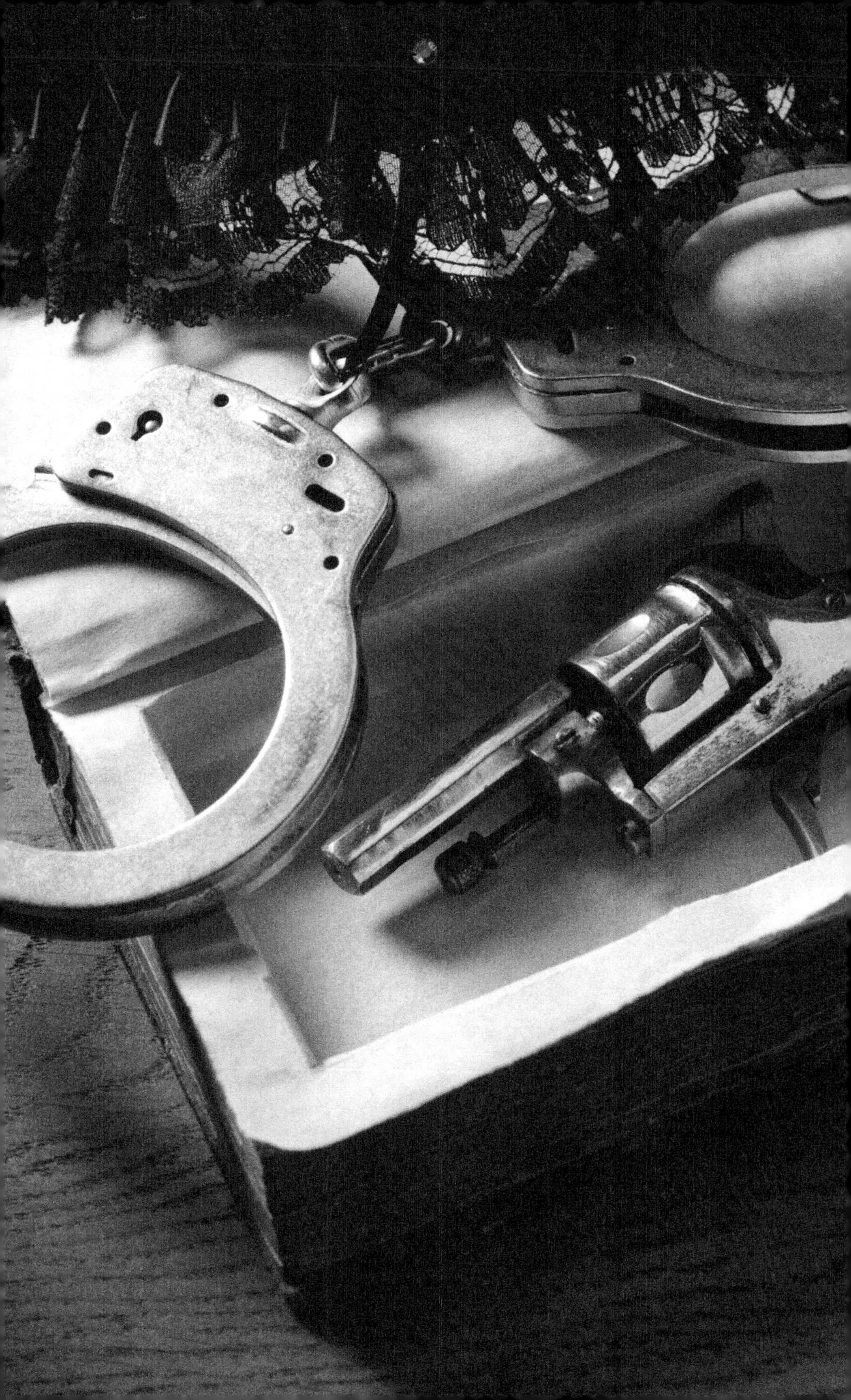

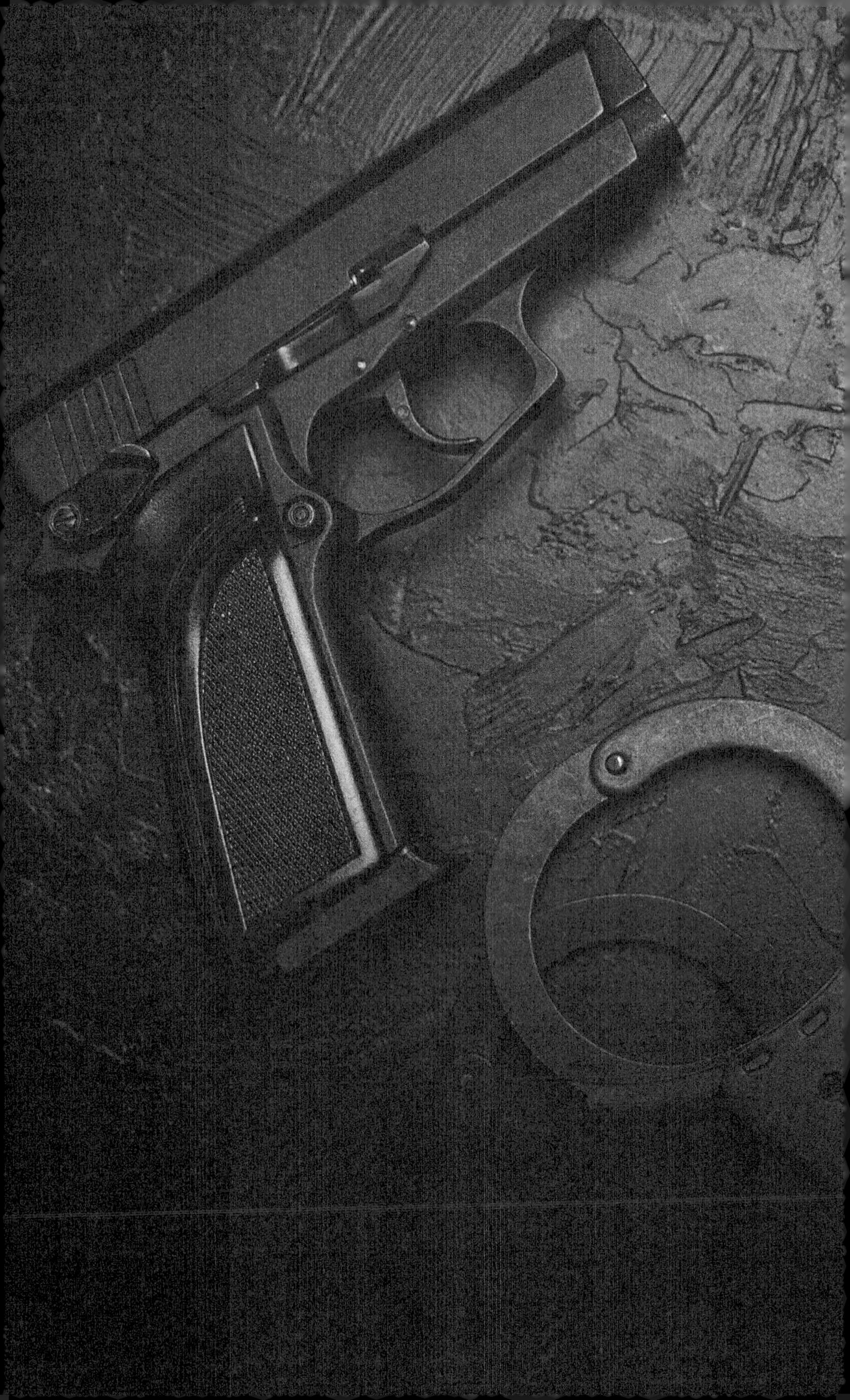

EPILOGUE

FOUR MONTHS LATER

Serena

"This is amazing. I can't believe we were able to pull it off so quickly," I tell Vanessa.

Today we open the first clinic for survivors of sexual abuse, manipulation, or abduction. The clinic has all kinds of resources available for victims. It's not just for women though. Men can be victims too. This center is for anyone who has been harmed, but its focus is on human trafficking.

"It really is," Vanessa agrees. "We couldn't have done it without you. You brought so much to this that we would have never thought of. We are going to make a big difference here."

With my knowledge of undercover work, I'm training new volunteers each and every day to go out into the world and provide assistance to anyone they think is in need.

It all starts with a conversation. Chatting up random strangers around you. Finding out more about them. Then slipping them a business card with information that can help them get out of a situation.

The beauty of it is that if they aren't in that situation, there is no harm done, but if they are, the card looks inconspicuous. It uses terms that would be peppered into conversation so that the business looks legit, but the number leads to a hotline to help those in need.

We also have started handing out the tracking patches that the Yakuza developed. They were kind enough to lend us their prototypes so that we can all work together to make them better.

We are still having more trouble getting them out on the streets here, but we are trying. That's what counts.

If even one person takes one, it's worth it.

If they take it, they are also given a number to text periodically to ensure they are safe. No one is monitoring the data so their privacy is intact, but the tracker is activated as soon as the person misses a check-in.

I love it. I think it works wonderfully. After seeing it in use with the beta testing with the girls at The Currency, I think it's a game changer. The fact that the only people with access to the data are those tied to this family makes it even better. No cops will ever be able to get it to use it against them.

Speaking of cops, I smile as I see Ricky walk in the door of the clinic.

"Now sir, I don't think we need your services yet," I tell him as he walks over to where Vanessa and I are putting together care bags for the women who might come in.

He smirks at me. "Who me? I'm just supporting my community."

Tristano wasn't keen on me setting up the new clinic in Jersey City, but it's my home. I grew up here. My family gave their lives protecting these streets.

So while we still live in Brooklyn, I travel here every day for work. In the red Camaro that has become more my car than his.

Ricky did what he said all those months ago. When we awoke the next morning, tragedy had hit Jersey City. The chief of police was murdered in a home that was not connected to anyone. It is believed he had stumbled upon a drug deal and was simply in the wrong place at the wrong time. His son had gone missing, never to be seen again. Some people speculate that his son was in on the drug bust, and that's why he didn't have backup that night. Either way, Ben was buried with full honors, which sucked, but Ricky got the chief position in his place.

"Are you stalking me?" Meredith asks, coming up beside me.

"How can it be stalking? You live with me," he mutters.

She tries to hide her smile. "You're needed in the back. I'll stay here and help Vanessa finish."

"Thanks, girl."

I squeeze her shoulder.

Meredith is a work in progress. After what happened with Ben, she spent two weeks hiding in Ricky's spare room. It took some time, but we eventually coaxed her into going to see my therapist. The same one I see every week now.

I can see the difference in Meredith now. She's healing, much like I am. She's working through shit from before I even knew her. I guess she had a shitty childhood.

Thankfully Ricky is letting her stay as long as she needs. He's even told her that until she heals her mind, he doesn't want to see her on the streets.

She hates not contributing, but when I told her that it's only because he cares about her, she let it go.

I don't know if she will go back to prostituting when she's done, but we are giving her the resources she needs to do whatever she wants. We will never judge her for her past or her future choices.

Glancing back at my friends one last time, I step into the backroom.

I gasp when someone grabs me, pulling me into a closet.

"Shh. They will hear us." Tris smirks at me.

I shake my head as I look where he pulled me.

"This is the linen closet. What are you doing in here?"

He smirks at me. "You'll see."

His hands slide down until he is cupping my ass. My cheeks burn.

Ever since I admitted that the day that Greer caught us was hot, he has been putting me in situations in which we might get caught. It's made the sex off the charts, but he's killing me. It's embarrassing when I walk out and see the knowing smirks. No matter how hard I try, I can never keep quiet.

Before he can continue caressing me, I pull back. He frowns at me, reaching for me. I giggle.

"Not this time, buddy."

"I miss you though. My dick is cold. Don't you want to warm him up?" He pouts.

I nod slowly at him. "I do."

"Then get back over here."

Instead of doing as he asks, I drop to my knees.

I smile to myself when I hear, "Oh fuck."

Tristano

"Oh fuck," I mutter.

Serena is a fucking goddess on her own, but when she drops to her knees, it gives me this whole other feeling.

The woman could command any man she looks at, but she chooses to drop to her knees for me to command.

There isn't another feeling in the world more powerful than

knowing you have the complete trust and control of a woman of her caliber.

It's enough to make you dizzy.

"Are you going to take my cock like a good girl?" I rasp out.

She gives me an innocent look. "I'm not sure. Is he ready for me?"

He jumps at her talking about him. I swear she knows how to drive me crazy.

Licking my lips, I smirk at her. "Why don't you find out?"

She needs no other instruction. Slowly, she lowers my fly, taking my dick out of my pants. He doesn't need much encouragement.

Ever since I brought Serena into my life full-time, I've learned the joys of going commando. This is one of them. One less barrier to get my dick to her.

She looks up at me as she presses a delicate kiss to the tip. I groan in response. She loves teasing me.

She wants me to lose control. I like to pride myself on having control. It's a game we play.

So instead of taking her head and forcing my dick down her throat, I dig my fingers into the palm of my hand.

She continues to kiss and lick at me, her eyes never leaving mine.

She's a damn temptress.

When she finally sucks the head into her mouth, my head nearly falls back at the pleasure of it.

She strokes me as she takes me little by little, taking her time to work me up.

"Fuck," I murmur. "I need more," I demand.

She gives me that look. The one that says if I need more, I better take it.

I don't know if it's her traumatic past or what, but the woman likes when I get rough with her.

Whatever turns her on, turns me on. Even when she wants to try new things. Like the way she's caressing my balls. Or the way she pulls off my dick to suck her finger. When she moves back to my dick, I shiver.

I know where that finger is going, and I hate to admit it, but I fucking love it.

As she works my cock at a faster pace, I feel her finger circle my hole. Then she slips it in.

I about come right then and there. I hold off, though, thinking about anything but what she's doing to me. I'm not ready for it to be over.

She senses my reserve though. She must because she begins to thrust her finger into my ass, curling it until it hits my prostate.

That breaks my control. My fingers find her hair as I take over, fucking her face.

She lets me hold her as I thrust into her mouth, pausing in the back of her throat. As she struggles to breathe, the tears start falling down her face. She's so beautiful like this. Face full of my cock with tears shining in her eyes.

She takes it like a champ, adding a second finger into my back door, making me clench up.

I pull her off of me with her still fingering my ass, and I come all over her face. Rope after rope hitting her face and hair, some falling on her top.

"Fuck, *anima gemella*. I was supposed to make you scream."

She smirks up at me. "I know. Instead, I made you groan so loud I'm sure everyone heard. You weren't supposed to get cum in my hair though."

Grabbing a towel off the rack, I help her clean up.

"That's for the women."

"I'll buy five more to replace it. Happy?"

She laughs. "Very. I got you for once."

I'm about to pull her to me when my phone rings.

Seeing Declan's name, I frown.

"What's up, brother from another mother?" I ask.

"Tris, I need you in Chicago."

"Why? What's going on?"

"I need a best man," he mumbles.

"A what? You're getting married? To who?"

He groans even louder.

"Nikita."

"What in the ever-loving fuck?" I spit out.

"It's a long story. Just get here, yeah?"

"I'll be there."

Hanging up the phone, I look at Serena.

"That was Declan?"

"Yeah. He's getting married and needs us there."

"Oh? When?"

"Like now."

"Oh shit." She gasps.

Oh shit is right. What the hell did Declan get himself into?

Want a little more Serena and Tristano? We promise you don't want to miss this Bonus Epilogue. Read it HERE!

Thank you for reading Tristano. We hope you love this story as much as we do. Want more of the Syndicates Series? Check out, Declan available now on Amazon and Kindle Unlimited.

Nikita lost everything she knew. Her family's mistake cost her freedom. He was meant to watch her, but now the lines have become tangled and he will make her his. Find out how these enemies become lovers in this arranged marriage mafia romance.

Read Declan HERE!

Author Bio

Author Bio

Cala Riley, better known as Cala and Riley, are a pair of friends with a deep-seated love of books and writing. Both Cala and Riley are happily married and each have children, Cala with the four-legged kind while Riley has a mixture of both two-legged and four. While they live apart, that does not affect their connection. They are the true definition of family. What started as an idea that quickly turned into a full-length book and a bond that will never end.

Acknowledgments

Husbands/Family- Thank you for loving us through the crazy and listening to us ramble.
Jenny Dicks- Thank you for all the swoons & ideas.
Aimee Henry- Thank you for going through everything.
Stefanie Jenkins- Thank you for the motivation & play by plays. Your reactions keep us going.
Nikki Pennington- For always being a cheerleader and listening to us rant.
My Brothers Editor/ Elle- Thank you for being the most laid-back editor and making the entire process painless.
My Brothers Editor/Christine- Thank you for your proofreading skills.
Demi, Kara, and Jennifer- Thank you for lending us your eyes and reading Tristano in advance.
Dark Ink Designs/ Jo- Thank you for the beautiful formatting.
Books and Moods- For always killing it on the design front.
Our ARC/Street Team: Thank you for always cheering us on. We love you.
Bloggers/Readers- Thank you for loving our stories as much as we do and spreading the word.

WHERE TO FIND US

Facebook
Instagram
Bookbub
Amazon
Goodreads
Cala Riley's Boudoir of Sin
Website
Patreon

Printed in Great Britain
by Amazon